PRAISE FOR

UNTIL YOU

"Fans of *Bully* will not be disappointed with *Until You*. Penelope Douglas delivers big-time."
—As the Pages Turn

"This is truly one of the most unique love stories I have read . . . a MUST read! Jared and Tate are true soul mates and their love story is heartbreakingly beautiful."
—Literati Book Reviews

"Absolutely electric."
—Love Between the Sheets

"Oh Lord. This book. THIS. BOOK. I am completely head over heels in LOVE, and it's all because of a boy named Jared. Jared will be the death of me, *I swear. I can't handle his hotness.* Okay, so yeah. I loved this book."
—Booklovers for Life

"A must read. . . . [Douglas] will just completely blow you away again. Her writing is phenomenal and she is most definitely one of my favorite authors."
—Hopeless Book Lovers

continued . . .

PRAISE FOR
THE FALL AWAY SERIES

"I read this book in one sitting . . . as gripping as it was sexy."
—#1 *New York Times* bestselling author Colleen Hoover

"A gritty, racy New Adult tale peppered with raw emotions. This smoking-hot, action-packed story is a powerful addition to the edgy side of the genre, and readers will eagerly anticipate the next installment."
—*Publishers Weekly* (starred review)

"Intensely emotional writing, [an] angst-driven plot, and [an] abundance of steamy sex scenes."
—*Booklist*

"A heated and passionate novel, full of feeling and intensity that will appeal to the reader seeking an emotional rush."
—IndieReader

Until You

A
Fall Away
Novel

PENELOPE DOUGLAS

NEW AMERICAN LIBRARY

NEW AMERICAN LIBRARY
Published by New American Library,
an imprint of Penguin Random House LLC
375 Hudson Street, New York, New York 10014

This book is a publication of New American Library. Previously published in an InterMix edition.

First New American Library Printing, January 2016

For more information about Penguin Random House, visit penguin.com.

LIBRARY OF CONGRESS CATALOGING-IN-PUBLICATION DATA:

Douglas, Penelope, 1977–
Until you / Penelope Douglas.
p. cm
ISBN 978-0-451-47711-8 (paperback)
I. Title.
PS3604.O93236U58 2016
813'.6—dc23   2015030188

Printed in the United States of America

4th Printing

Penguin
Random
House

AUTHOR'S NOTE

This book was never supposed to be written.

After I published *Bully*, I realized that Jared's story was just as important as Tate's, and, to be honest, the readers fought hard for his point of view. They wanted to know his side of the story.

For that, I am eternally grateful. I loved writing this book and watching Jared grow.

Although this novel can be read as a stand-alone, I wouldn't recommend it. Reading Tate's point of view in *Bully* first will increase your enjoyment and craving for Jared's side.

That being said, I want to ease your mind if you have read *Bully*. Point-of-view novels are tricky, and no one wants to be bamboozled into buying the same story twice.

I've worked hard to give you something different.

This is NOT a retelling of *Bully*.

This is Jared's story.

Music helps inspire the development of my characters. Jared is angry and dangerous, and you'll either want him far away from you or all over you. This playlist of songs is Jared's.

"Criticize"	Adelitas Way
"Coming Down"	Five Finger Death Punch
"Adrenalize"	In This Moment
"Cold"	Crossfade
"Love-Hate-Sex-Pain"	Godsmack

"Heaven nor Hell"	Volbeat
"I Don't Care"	Apocalyptica
"Wicked Game"	Chris Isaak
"Tears Don't Fall"	Bullet for My Valentine
"Bottom of a Bottle"	Smile Empty Soul
"Crazy Bitch"	Buckcherry
"Girl from the North Country"	Lions
"Pain"	Three Days Grace
"I Stand Alone"	Godsmack
"(You Gotta) Fight for Your Right (to Party)"	Beastie Boys
"Dearest Helpless"	Silverchair
"Raise the Dead"	Rachel Rabin

This novel is dedicated solely to the readers.
Thank you for believing in Jared and asking for this book.

Until You

PROLOGUE

---

*M*y name is Jared.
My name is Jared.
My name is Jared.

I kept repeating it over and over again, trying to get my heart to stop beating so fast. I wanted to go meet our new neighbors, but I was nervous.

There was a kid living next door now—probably ten years old, like me—and I'd smiled when I saw that she wore baseball caps and Chucks. Other girls in my neighborhood didn't dress like that, and she was pretty, too.

I leaned on my windowsill, checking out the house next door, alive with music and light. No one had lived there for a long time, and even before then it was just old people.

A big tree stood between our houses, but I could still see through the green leaves.

"Hey, sweetie."

I turned my head to see my mom leaning on my bedroom door-frame. She was smiling, but her eyes were teary and her clothes were wrinkly.

She was sick again. She got sick whenever she drank the bottle drinks.

"I saw that we have new neighbors," she continued. "Did you meet them?"

"No." I shook my head, looking back out the window, wishing she'd go away. "They have a girl. No boys."

"And you can't be friends with a girl?" Her voice cracked, and I heard her swallow. I knew what was coming, and my stomach tightened.

"No, I can't."

I didn't like to talk to my mom. Actually, I didn't know how to talk to her. I was alone a lot, and she pissed me off.

"Jared—" she started, but didn't continue. After a moment, I heard her walk away and slam a door down the hall. She probably went to the bathroom to puke.

My mom drinks alcohol a lot, especially on the weekends, and all of a sudden I didn't want to meet the blond-haired girl next door.

So what if she seemed cool and liked to ride bikes?

Or that I could hear Alice in Chains coming from her bedroom? At least I think it was her bedroom. The curtains were closed.

I stood up straight, ready to just forget about it and go make myself something to eat. My mom probably wasn't cooking tonight.

But then I saw the girl's curtains open, and I stopped.

She was there. *That's her room!*

And for some reason, I smiled. I liked that our rooms faced each other.

I narrowed my eyes to see her better as she opened the double doors, but then widened them when I saw what she was doing.

What? Is she crazy?

I yanked up my window and peered out into the night air. "Hey!" I shouted at her. "What are you doing?"

She jerked her head up, and my breath caught when I saw her wobble on the branch she was trying to balance on. Her arms flailed from side to side, and I was immediately out of my window and climbing into the tree after her.

"Be careful!" I yelled as she bent down and grabbed hold of the thick branch with her hands.

I crept into the tree while holding on to a branch at the side of my head for support.

Stupid girl. What is she doing?

Her blue eyes were big as she stayed on all fours, holding on to the tree as it shook beneath her.

"You can't just climb into trees by yourself," I snipped out. "You almost fell. Come here." I leaned down to grab her hand.

My fingers instantly tingled, like when a part of your body falls asleep.

She stood up, her legs shaking, and I held on to a branch above my head as I walked both of us toward the trunk.

"Why did you do that?" she complained behind me. "I know how to climb trees. You scared me, and that's why I almost fell."

I looked over at her as I plopped down on the thick inner part of the tree. "Sure it was." I dusted off my hands on my long khaki cargo shorts.

I stared out at our street, Fall Away Lane, but I couldn't shake the feel of her off my hand. The humming spread up my arm and over my whole body.

She just kept standing there, probably pouting, but after a few seconds she took the seat next to me. Our legs dangled together off the branch.

"So," she spoke up, pointing to my house. "You live over there?"

"Yeah. With my mom," I said, and I looked down at her just in time to see her eyes drop. She started to play with her fingers.

She looked sad for a few seconds, but then her eyebrows came together and she looked like she was trying not to cry.

What did I say?

She was still dressed in the same overalls I'd seen her in earlier, when she was unloading the moving truck with her dad. Her hair hung loose, and other than some dirt on her pants, she looked clean.

We sat there for a minute, staring out at the street, listening to the wind rustle the leaves around us.

She seemed really little next to me, like any minute she'd fall off the branch, unable to hold herself up.

Her lips were turned down at the corners, and I didn't know why she was so sad. All I knew was that I didn't want to go anywhere until she felt better.

"I saw your dad," I started. "Where's your mom?"

Her bottom lip shook, and she looked up at me. "My mom died in the spring." Her eyes had tears in them, but she took long breaths, like she was trying to be tough.

I'd never met a kid that had a dead mom or dad, and I felt bad for not liking my mom.

"I don't have a dad," I told her, trying to make her feel better. "He left when I was a baby, and my mom says he's not a good man. At least your mom didn't want to leave you, right?"

I knew I sounded stupid. I didn't want to make it seem like she had it better than me. I just felt like I should tell her anything to make her feel good.

Even hug her, which is what I really wanted to do right then.

But I didn't. I changed the subject.

"I saw that your dad has an old car."

She didn't look at me, but she rolled her eyes. "It's a Chevy Nova. Not just an old car."

I knew what it was. I wanted to see if she did.

"I like cars." I kicked off my DC Shoes, letting them fall to the ground, and she did the same with her red Chucks. Our bare feet swung back and forth in the air. "I'm going to race at the Loop someday," I told her.

Her eyes perked up, and she turned to me. "The Loop? What's that?"

"It's a racetrack where the big kids go. We can go there when we're in high school, but we have to have a car. You can come and cheer for me."

"Why can't I race?" She looked mad.

Is she serious?

"I don't think they let girls race," I said, trying not to laugh in her face.

She narrowed her eyes and looked back to the street. "You'll make them let me."

The corners of my mouth turned up, but I held back my laugh. "Maybe."

Totally.

She held out her hand for me to shake. "I'm Tatum, but everyone calls me Tate. I don't like Tatum. Got it?"

I nodded, taking her hand in mine and feeling a rush of heat spread up my arm again. "I'm Jared."

CHAPTER 1

Six years later

The blood spills over my bottom lip and onto the floor like a long strip of red paint. I let it pool in my mouth until it dribbles out, since everything hurts too damn much to spit.

"Dad, please," I beg, my voice shaking as my body shivers from the fear.

My mom was right. He's a bad man, and I wish I'd never talked her into letting me spend the summer with him.

I kneel on his kitchen floor, shaking, with my hands tied behind my back. The itchy rope bites into my skin.

"Are you begging, you little pussy?" he snarls, and the strap whips my back again.

I squeeze my eyes shut, wincing, as fire spreads across my shoulder blades. Closing my mouth, I try not to make any noise as I breathe through my nose until the burning fades away. The skin on my lips feels stretched and swollen, and the slippery metallic taste of blood fills my mouth.

Tate.

Her face flashes in my mind, and I crawl back into my head where she is. Where we are together. Her sunshine hair floats on the wind as we climb *the rocks around the fishpond. I always climb behind her in case she stumbles. Her stormy blue eyes smile down at me.*

But my father breaks through. "You don't beg! You don't apologize! That's what I get for letting that cunt raise you all these years. Nothing but a coward now. That's what you are."

My head jerks back and my scalp stings as he yanks me by my hair to meet his eyes. My stomach rolls when I smell the beer and cigarettes on his breath.

"At least Jax listens," he grits out, and my stomach shakes from the nausea. "Isn't that right, Jax?" he yells over his shoulder.

My father releases me and walks over to the deep freezer in the corner of the kitchen and pounds twice on the lid. "You still alive in there?"

Every nerve in my face fires with pain as I try to hold back tears. I don't want to cry or scream, but Jax, my father's other son, has been in the freezer for almost ten minutes. Ten whole minutes and not making a sound!

Why is my father doing this? Why is he punishing Jax when he's mad at me?

But I stay quiet, because that's how he likes his kids. If he gets what he wants, maybe he'll let my brother out. He has to be freezing in there, and I don't know if he has enough air. How long can someone survive in a freezer? Maybe he's already dead.

God, he's just a little kid! I blink back the tears. Please, please, please . . .

"So . . ." My father walks over to his girlfriend, Sherilynn, a crazy-haired crackhead, and his friend Gordon, a fucking creepy-ass lowlife who looks at me weird.

Both sit at the kitchen table, enjoying whatever drug is on the menu today, not paying any attention to what is going on with the two helpless kids in the room.

"What do y'all think?" My father puts a hand on each of their shoulders. "How are we gonna teach my boy to be a man?"

I jerked awake, my pulse pounding in my neck and head. A drop of sweat glided over my shoulder and I blinked, seeing my own room and walls come into view.

It's okay. I breathed hard. *They're not here. It was just a dream.*

I was in my own house. My father wasn't here. Gordon and Sher-ilynn were long gone.

Everything's okay.

But I always had to make sure.

My eyelids were heavy as fuck, but I sat up and hurriedly scanned the room. The morning light blared through my window like an air horn, and I brought my hand up to shield my eyes from the painful rays.

The shit on my dresser had been shoved to the floor, but it wasn't unusual for me to make a mess when I was wasted. Other than some disarray, the room was quiet and safe.

I let out a long breath and inhaled again, trying to slow down my heart as I continued looking left to right. It wasn't until I'd made a full circle that my eyes finally rested on the lump next to me under the covers. Ignoring the ache between my eyes from the alcohol the night before, I peeled back the blanket to see who I was dumb enough—or drunk enough—to let spend the whole night at my house.

Great.

Another fucking blonde.

What the hell was I thinking?

Blondes weren't my thing. They always looked like good girls. Not exotic or even remotely interesting. Too pure.

They looked like the girl-next-door type.

And who really wanted that?

But the past few days—when the nightmares had started again—all I'd wanted were blondes. It was like I had some sick pull to self-destruct over the one blonde I loved to hate.

But . . . I had to admit, the girl was hot. Her skin looked smooth, and she had nice tits. I think she'd said something about being home for the summer from Purdue. I don't think I told her about my being sixteen and still in high school. Maybe I'd spring that on her when she woke up. Just for kicks.

I leaned my head back, in too much pain to even smile at the image of her freak-out.

"Jared?" My mother knocked, and I jerked my head up, cringing.

My head throbbed like someone had stuck a fork in it all night, and I did not want to deal with her right now. But I hopped off the bed anyway and headed for the door before the girl next to me stirred. Opening it just a little, I eyed my mother with as much patience as I could muster.

She was wearing pink sweatpants and a long-sleeved fitted T-shirt— nice for a Sunday, actually—but from the neck up, she was a mess, as usual. She had her hair stuffed into a bun, and her makeup from the day before was smudged under her eyes.

Her hangover probably rivaled mine. The only way she was up and moving around was because her body was a hell of a lot more used to it.

When she cleaned up, though, you could see how young she really was. When most of my friends first got a look at her, they thought she was my sister.

"What do you want?" I asked.

I thought she was waiting for me to let her in, but that wasn't going to happen.

"Tate's leaving." Her voice was soft.

My heart started thumping in my chest.

Is that today?

And suddenly it was like an invisible hand prying open my stomach, and I flinched at the pain. I didn't know if it was the hangover or the reminder of her leaving, but I clenched my teeth to force down the bile.

"So?" I mumbled, overloading on attitude.

She rolled her eyes at me. "So I thought you might get off your ass and say good-bye. She'll be gone for a whole year, Jared. You were friends once."

Yeah, up until two years ago . . . The summer before freshman year, I'd gone to visit my father, and came home to realize that I was on my own. My mother was weak, my father was a monster, and Tate wasn't a friend, after all.

I just shook my head before shutting the door in my mom's face.

Yeah, like I was going to go outside and give Tate a hug goodbye. I didn't care, and I was happy to be rid of her.

But there was a lump in my throat, and I couldn't swallow.

I slumped back against the door, feeling the weight of a thousand bricks fall on my shoulders. I'd forgotten that she was leaving today. I'd been pretty much drunk nonstop since the Beckman party two days ago.

Shit.

I could hear car doors slamming outside, and I told myself to stay where I was. I didn't need to see her.

Let her go study abroad in France. Her leaving was the best damn thing that could happen.

"Jared!" I tensed up when my mother called from downstairs. "The dog got out. You better go get him."

Great.

Wanna bet she let the damn dog out to begin with? And wanna bet she let him out the *front* door? I pinched my eyebrows so close together that it actually hurt.

Throwing on last night's jeans, I jerked open the bedroom door, not caring if Purdue girl woke up, and stomped down the stairs.

My mother was waiting by the open front door, holding up the leash for me and smiling like she was so clever. Snatching it out of her hand, I walked outside and over to Tate's yard.

Madman used to be her dog, too, and he wouldn't have gone anywhere else.

"Did you come to say good-bye to me?" Tate knelt on her front lawn near her dad's Bronco, and I stopped dead in my tracks at the sound of her delighted and uncontrollable giggle. She was smiling like it was Christmas morning, and her eyes were squeezed shut as Madman nuzzled her neck.

Her ivory skin glowed in the morning sun, and her full pink lips were open, showing a beautiful row of white teeth.

The dog was clearly happy, too, wagging his tail with giddiness, and I felt like I was intruding.

They were a pair, loving on each other, and my stomach filled with butterflies.

Damn it. I ground my teeth together.

How did she do that? How did she always manage to make me feel happy to see her happy?

I blinked long and hard.

Tate continued yapping to the dog. "Oh, well, I love you, too!" She sounded like she was speaking to a child, all sweet and shit, as Madman kept nudging and licking her face.

He shouldn't love her this much. What had she done for him in the past two years?

"Madman, come," I barked, not really angry with the dog.

Tate's eyes shifted to me, and she stood up. "You're being a jerk to the dog now, too?" She scowled, and it was then that I noticed what she was wearing.

The Nine Inch Nails T-shirt I'd given her when we were fourteen, and my chest swelled for some stupid, unknown reason.

I'd forgotten she had it.

Okay . . . not really. I guess I didn't realize that she *still* had it.

She probably didn't even remember that I'd given it to her.

Kneeling down to hook Madman's leash onto his collar, I twisted my lips up slightly. "You're talking again, Tatum."

I didn't call her Tate. She hated Tatum, so that's what I called her. I fixed a bored, superior expression on my face.

I'd be happier without her around, I told myself. She was nothing.

And yet I heard the little voice in the back of my head: *She was everything.*

She shook her head, the hurt in her eyes clear as she turned to walk away.

She wasn't fighting back, I guess. Not today. The party on Friday night—when I'd humiliated her and she'd punched my friend Madoc in the face—must have been a onetime deal.

"Is that what you're wearing on the plane?" I asked, sneering.

I should've just walked away, but, hell, I couldn't stop engaging her. It was an addiction.

She turned back to me, her fingers fisting up. "Why do you ask?"

"Just looks a little sloppy, is all." But that was a bald-faced lie.

The black T-shirt was worn-out, but it clung to her fit body like it was made just for her, and her dark jeans hugged her ass, telling me exactly what she would look like naked. With long, shiny hair and flawless skin, she looked like fire and sugar, and I wanted to gorge and burn at the same time.

Tatum was hot, but she didn't know it.

And blonde or not, that was my type.

"But no worries," I continued. "I get it."

She narrowed her eyes. "Get what?"

Leaning in, I taunted her with a smug grin. "You always liked wearing my clothes."

Her eyes widened, and with her flushed skin there was no mistaking that she was pissed. It was raging all over her tough little face.

And I smiled to myself, because I fucking loved it.

She didn't run away, though.

"Hold on." She held up her pointer finger and turned to walk to the truck.

Digging under the front seat, in the emergency pack her dad kept there, she fished out something and slammed the car door shut. By the time she'd huffed back over to me, I saw that she had a lighter in her hand.

Before I could even register what was happening, she'd peeled off her shirt and exposed her perfect chest in a sexy-ass sports bra.

My heart damn near shifted with the fucking pounding in my chest. *Holy shit.*

I watched, not breathing, as she held up the shirt, flicked the lighter, and dipped the hem into the flame, bringing it to ash piece by piece.

Son of a bitch! What the hell was happening with her all of a sudden?

My gaze flashed to hers, and time stood still as we watched each other, forgetting the flaming material between us. Her hair danced around her body, and her storm-filled eyes pierced my skin, my brain, and my ability to move or speak.

Her arms shook a little, and her breaths, although steady, were deep. She was nervous as hell.

Okay, so breaking Madoc's nose the other night wasn't a fluke. She was fighting back.

I'd spent the past two years of high school making her life miserable. Telling a few lies, ruining a few dates, all for my own pleasure. Challenging Tate—making her a high school outcast—made my world go round, but she never fought back. Not until now. Maybe she thought that since she was leaving town, she could throw caution to the wind.

My fists balled up with renewed energy, and I was suddenly paralyzed by how much I would miss this. Not miss hating her or taunting her.

Just. Miss. Her.

And with that realization, I tightened my jaw so hard it ached.
Motherfucker.

She still owned me.

"Tatum Nicole!" her dad yelled from the porch, and we both jumped back to reality. He raced over and grabbed the shirt out of her hand, stomping it out on the ground.

My eyes hadn't left hers, but the trance was broken and I was finally able to let out a breath. "See you in a year, Tatum," I bit out, hoping it sounded like a threat.

She tipped up her chin and only glared at me while her father ordered her inside for a shirt.

I walked back over to my house with Madman at my side and wiped the cool sweat off my forehead.

Goddamn. I sucked in air like it was going out of style.

Why couldn't I get that girl out from under my skin? Her hot little pyrotechnics weren't going to help flush her out, either.

That image would be in my head forever.

Fear took root in my brain as I realized that she was really leaving. I wasn't going to be in control of her anymore. She'd live every day not thinking of me. She'd go on dates with any asshole that showed interest. And, even worse, I wouldn't see her or hear of her. She'd have a life without me in it, and I was scared.

Everything, all of a sudden, felt foreign and uncomfortable. My house, my neighborhood, the idea of going back to school in a week.

"Fuck," I growled under my breath.

This shit had to end.

I needed a distraction. Lots of distractions.

Once inside, I released the dog and climbed the stairs to my bedroom, digging my phone out of my pocket on the way.

If it had been anyone else calling, Madoc wouldn't answer this early. But for his best friend, it took only two rings.

"I'm. Still. Sleeping," he grumbled.

"You still up for throwing a pool party before school starts?" I asked, switching on Buckcherry's "Crazy Bitch" on the iPod dock on my dresser.

"We're talking about this now? School isn't for another week." He sounded like half of his face was buried in a pillow, but it was how he talked these days. After Tate broke his nose the other night, he had trouble breathing out of one of his nostrils.

"Today. This afternoon," I said, walking over to my window.

"Dude!" he blurted out. "I'm still dead from last night."

And, in truth, so was I. My head was still swimming from the liquor I'd tried drowning in the night before, but there was no way I could sit around all day with nothing but my thoughts keeping me company.

Tate going to France for a year.

Standing in the front yard in her bra, lighting fires.

I shook the images from my head.

"Then hit the gym and sweat out the hangover," I ordered. "I need a distraction."

Why did I just say that? Now he would know something was wrong, and I didn't like people knowing my shit.

"Is Tate gone?" he asked, almost timidly.

My shoulders tensed, but I kept my tone even as I watched her come out of her house in a new shirt. "Who's talking about her? You throwing a party or not?"

The line was quiet for a few seconds before he mumbled, "Uh-huh." He sounded like he had more to say but wisely decided to shut his damn mouth. "Fine. I don't want to see the same people we saw last night, though. Who are we inviting?"

Looking over at the Bronco pulling out of the driveway and the fucking blond driver that didn't once turn around to look back, I clenched the phone to my ear. "Blondes. Lots of blondes."

Madoc exhaled a quiet laugh. "You hate blondes."

Not all. Just one.

I sighed. "Right now, I want to drown in them." I didn't care if Madoc connected the dots or not. He wouldn't push, and that's why he was my best friend. "Send out texts and get the drinks. I'll grab some food and head over in a few hours."

I twisted around when I heard the purest little moan coming from the bed. The Purdue girl—I forgot her name—was waking up.

"Why not come over now? We can head to the gym and then gather supplies," Madoc suggested, but my eyes were hot on the bare back of the girl in my bed. Her squirming had nudged the blanket down to the top of her ass, and her face was turned away from me. All I saw was the skin and her sunshine hair.

And I hung up on Madoc, because my bed was the only place I wanted to be at right then.

CHAPTER 2

The next few weeks were like cave diving with a perfectly good parachute that I refused to use. School, my mother, Jax, my friends—they were all around for me to grab onto, but the only thing that got me out of the house every day was the promise of trouble.

I dragged my irritable, pissed-off ass into English III, trying to figure out why the hell I still came to school. It was the last goddamn place I wanted to be anymore. The hallways were always crammed with people but still seemed empty.

My appearance was shit, too. My left eye was purple, and I had a cut across my nose from a fight I didn't remember. Plus, I'd torn the sleeves off my T-shirt this morning, because I couldn't breathe.

Not really sure what I was thinking, but it seemed to make sense at the time.

"Mr. Trent, don't sit down," Mrs. Penley ordered as I strolled into class late. Everyone was already seated, and I stopped to look at her.

I liked Penley about as much as I liked anyone, but I couldn't hide the boredom that I was sure was all over my face.

"Excuse me?" I asked as she scrawled on a pink slip.

I sighed, knowing exactly what that color meant.

She handed me the paper. "You heard me. Go to the dean," she ordered as she stuck her pen into her high bun.

And I perked up, noticing the bite to her bark.

Being tardy or truant had become a habit, and Penley was pissed. It had taken her long enough, too. Most of the other teachers had already sent me out the first week.

I smiled, euphoria washing over my body at any possibility of mayhem. "No 'please' with that request?" I taunted, snatching the paper out of her hands.

Hushed laughter and snorts broke out around the classroom, and Penley narrowed her dark brown eyes on me.

She didn't falter, though. I'd give her that.

Turning around, I tossed the pink slip into the trash and threw open the wooden door, not caring if it closed behind me as I left.

A few gasps and whispers filled the air, but it was nothing new. Most people veered away from me these days, but my defiance was getting old. At least to me. My heart didn't race anymore when I acted like a dick. I was thirsty to up the stakes.

"Mr. Caruthers!" I heard Penley calling, and I turned around to see Madoc walking out of her classroom, too.

"It's that time of the month, Mrs. Penley." He sounded serious. "I'll be right back."

The outright laughter roared from Penley's classroom pretty clearly this time.

Madoc wasn't like me. He was a people person. He could serve you a pile of shit, and you'd ask for ketchup.

"You know"—he ran up beside me and jerked his thumb in the opposite direction—"the dean's that way."

I raised my eyebrows at him.

"All right, all right." He shook his head as if to clear away the brain fart that I'd actually go sweat in the dean's office for who knows how long. "So, where are we going?"

I dug my keys out of my jeans pocket and slipped on my sunglasses. "Does it matter?"

"So, what are you going to do with the money?" Madoc asked as he checked out his new ink.

We'd blown off school and tracked down tattoo artists that didn't ask for ID. We found a place called the Black Debs—"debs" being short for "debutantes"—which hadn't really made sense to me until I'd looked around and noticed that the entire staff was female.

We were under eighteen, so not legally allowed to get tattooed without a parent's consent, but they didn't seem to care.

Some chick named Mary had just finished "Fallen" across Madoc's back, except the "e" was inked to look like flames. Kind of looked like an "o" to me, but I didn't say anything. He wasn't asking questions about what my tattoo meant, so I wasn't going to open a can of worms.

"Only so much I can do with the money right now," I answered, grunting as the needle sliced through my skin over a rib. "My mother put most of it in a college fund. I can have it when I graduate. But I was able to get some of it now. I'm thinking of buying a new car and giving the GT to Jax."

My maternal grandfather had passed away last year, leaving me some land and a cabin near Lake Geneva in Wisconsin. The cabin was falling apart and it didn't have any real sentimental value to the family, so my mother agreed to let some interested developers buy it. She put most of the money into the bank under lock and key.

I actually felt proud of her for insisting. It wasn't normal for her to make such responsible adult decisions.

But I wasn't at all interested in going to college, either.

I didn't want to think about how things were going to change when I finished high school.

My phone rang, and I silenced it.

I closed my eyes while Crossfade's "Cold" played in the background, and reveled in the sting of the needle carving into me. I hadn't tensed up at all, and I hadn't thought about much of anything since walking into the shop. My arms and legs felt weightless, and the ton of shit on my shoulders had faded away.

I could get addicted to this.

I smiled, picturing myself ten years from now, covered in tattoos, simply because I liked the pain.

"You wanna take a look?" Aura, my dreadlocked tattoo artist, asked when she'd finished.

I stood up and walked to the wall mirror, eyeing the words on the side of my torso.

Yesterday Lasts Forever. Tomorrow Comes Never.

The words came out of nowhere in my head, but they felt right. The script was just illegible enough not to be easily read, and that's what I wanted.

The tattoo was for me and no one else.

I squinted at the little droplets of blood spilling off the end of "Never."

"I didn't ask you for that," I pointed out, scowling at Aura through the mirror.

She slipped on some sunglasses and stuck an unlit cigarette in her mouth. "I don't explain my art, kid." And she headed out the back door. To smoke, I would assume.

And for the first time in weeks, I laughed.

Gotta love a woman that can hand you your own ass.

We paid, picked up some food, and took it back to my house. My mother had texted and said she was going out with friends after work, so I knew I'd have the place to myself for a while. When she drank, she didn't come home until she was numb.

And then, to dampen my mood further, there was a care package from France inside my front door.

It was addressed to Tate's dad and must've been sent here accidentally. My mom had unknowingly opened it, thinking it was ours, when she was home for lunch. She left it for me with a note to take it next door when I got home.

But not before my fucking curiosity got the better of me.

After Madoc had gone into the garage, so we could eat while we worked, I peeled back the flaps of the cardboard box and immediately slammed them shut again. A fat, raging fire burned in my blood, and I was hungrier than I'd been in weeks. I didn't know what was in that box, but Tate's smell was all over it, and it was leveling me.

My brief high from the tattoo slowly seeped out and was instantly replaced with piss and vinegar.

I dumped it on her father's front doorstep before charging back over into my garage to drown myself in car work.

"Hold up the flashlight," I ordered Madoc.

He leaned farther under the hood as I tried to unfasten the spark plugs from my car. "Stop struggling with it," he complained. "Those things can snap easily if you're not careful."

I stopped and tightened my grip on the wrench, narrowing my eyes at him. "You don't think I know that?"

He cleared his throat and looked away, and I could feel the judgment all over him.

Why am I barking at him?

Looking down, I shook my head and forced down more pressure on the plug. My hand immediately gave way, and my body lurched forward when I heard the snap.

"Shit." I grunted and threw the wrench under the hood, where it disappeared somewhere in the mess.

Motherfucker.

I gripped the edge of the car. "Get the extractor."

Madoc leaned back to the tool bench behind him. "No 'please' with that request?" He echoed my own words as he grabbed the attachment so I could pry out the spark plug.

It was a bitch to deal with, and he was probably patting himself on the back that he'd called it.

"You know . . ." he started, letting out a sigh. "I've kept my mouth shut, but—"

"Then keep it shut."

Madoc swung the flashlight out from under the hood and I jerked backwards, out of the way, as he flung it across the room, where it shattered against a wall.

Jesus Christ!

His usual relaxed demeanor was replaced with rage. His eyes were sharp and his breaths were fast.

Madoc was mad, and I knew I'd gone too far.

Clenching my teeth, I leaned back down, my hands on the car, and braced myself for his meltdown. They came rarely, which gave them more impact.

"You're sinking, man!" he shouted. "You don't go to class, you're pissing off everyone, we're constantly in fights with random shitheads, and I've got the cuts and bruises to prove it. What the fuck?" Every word crowded the room. There was meaning and truth to everything he was saying, but I didn't want to face it.

Everything felt wrong.

I was hungry, just not for food. I wanted to laugh, but nothing was funny. All of my regular thrills didn't get my heart racing anymore.

Even my own neighborhood, which usually brought me comfort with its familiarity and clean-cut lawns, felt barren and void of life.

I was crammed in a fucking jar, suffocating with everything I wanted but nothing that gave me air.

"She'll be back in eight months." Madoc's quiet voice crawled into my thoughts, and I blinked, taking a moment to realize he was talking about Tate.

I shook my head.

No.

Why would he say that?

This wasn't about her. I. Did. Not. Need. Her.

I tightened my fist around the wrench and straightened my back, wanting to stuff his words back down his throat.

His gaze dropped to my right hand that held the tool and then back up to my face. "What?" he challenged. "What do you think you're going to do?"

I wanted to hit something. Anything. Even my best friend.

My ringer broke the stalemate as it vibrated in my pocket. I dug out my cell, keeping my eyes on my friend.

"What?" I snapped into the phone.

"Hey, man. I've been trying to reach you all day," my brother, Jax, said, a little muffled.

My breathing wasn't slowing down, and my brother didn't need me like this. "I can't talk right now."

"Fine," he barked. "Screw you, then." And he hung up.

Goddamn son of a motherfucking bitch.

I squeezed the phone, wanting it to break.

My eyes snapped up to Madoc, who shook his head, threw the shop cloth onto the workbench, and walked out of the garage.

"Shit," I hissed, dialing Jax's number.

If I needed to be level for anyone, it was my brother. He needed me.

After I'd gotten away from my father two summers ago, I'd reported the abuse. My brother's, not mine. He was taken out of that house and put into foster care, since his mother couldn't be found.

I was all he had.

"I'm sorry," I blurted out, not even waiting for him to say hello when he picked up. "I'm here. What's wrong?"

"Pick me up, will you?"

Yeah, not with the spark plugs yanked out of my car. But Madoc was still here with his car, probably. "Where are you?" I asked.

"The hospital."

CHAPTER 3

"Excuse me, can I help you?" a nurse called behind me as I barged through the double doors. I was sure I was supposed to check in with her, but she could shove her clipboard up her ass. I needed to find my brother.

My palms were sweaty, and I had no idea what had happened. He'd hung up after telling me where to find him.

I'd left him alone—and hurt—once before. Never again.

"Slow down, man," Madoc chimed in behind me. "This will go a lot faster if we just ask someone where he is." I hadn't even noticed that he'd followed me in.

My shoes squeaked on the linoleum as I jetted down the corridors, flinging back curtain after curtain until I finally found my brother.

He sat on a bed, long legs dangling off the side and his hand on his forehead. I reached for his ponytail and yanked his head back to look at his face.

"Ow! Shit!" he grunted.

He squinted up at the fluorescent lighting as I took in the stitches on his eyebrow.

"Mr. Trent!" a woman's voice barked behind me, but I wasn't sure if it was to me or Jax, since we both shared our father's name.

"What the hell happened to him?" I wasn't asking Jax. Others were to blame.

My brother was just a kid, and while he was only a little more than a year younger than me, he was still younger.

And he'd had a life of shit.

His mother was Native American and barely legal when she'd gotten pregnant with him. While he sported our father's azure eyes, the rest of his looks came from her.

His hair was probably black, but it looked a shade lighter and fell halfway down his back. Certain pieces were braided and then everything was brought back to a ponytail midskull. His skin was a couple of shades darker than mine, and everything was overshadowed by his bright smile.

A woman behind me cleared her throat. "We don't know what happened to him," she snapped. "He won't tell us."

I hadn't turned away from Jax to see who I was speaking to. It could've been a doctor or a social worker. Or the police. It didn't matter. They all looked at me the same way. Like I deserved a spanking or something.

"I've been calling you for hours," Jax whispered, and I sucked in a breath when I noticed that his lip was puffy, too. His eyes were pleading. "I thought you'd be here before the doctors called *them*."

And then I knew it was a social worker, and I felt like a dick. He'd needed me today, and I'd screwed it up again.

I stood between him and the woman, or maybe he was hiding from her view. I didn't know.

But I did know that Jax didn't want to go with her. My throat

PENELOPE DOUGLAS

tightened, and the lump inside swelled so damn much that I wanted to hurt someone.

Tate.

She was always my victim of choice, but she was also in every good memory I had.

My brain flashed with the one place that was untouched by hatred and despair.

Our tree. Tate's and mine.

I briefly wondered if Jax had anywhere he felt safe, warm, and innocent.

I doubted it. Had he ever experienced a place like that? Would he ever?

I didn't have the first goddamn clue what life had been like for my brother. Sure, I'd gotten a taste of it during my summer with our father when I was fourteen, but Jax had had a whole lifetime of that shit. Not to mention the foster homes over the years. He looked up to me like I was the fucking world, and I didn't have the answers. I had no power. No way to protect him.

"Did Mr. Donovan do this to you?" the social worker asked Jax about his foster dad, Vince.

He looked at me before he answered. "No," he told her.

He's lying.

Jax wasn't lying to protect Vince. He knew that I could tell when he wasn't being honest. It was the way he'd hesitate and eyeball me before the lie. I always knew.

No, he wasn't deceiving me. He was deceiving her.

Jax and I settled our own scores.

"Okay," clipboard lady, who I'd finally turned around to make eye contact with, snipped. "Let me make this easy for you. We're going to assume that he did this to you and move you to a group home tonight until we find another placement."

No. I closed my eyes.

"You fucking people," I choked out, my stomach hollowing while I tried to keep my emotions in check for Jax.

All of his life, my brother had been sleeping in strange beds and living with people that didn't really want him. Our father had carted him around from shithole to shithole, and left him at sketchy places all of the time growing up.

Enough was enough. Jax and I belonged together. We were stronger together. It was only a matter of time before what little innocence he had left decayed and his heart grew too hard for anything good to grow.

He was going to become like me, and I wanted to fucking scream at these people that I could love him more than anyone else. Kids didn't just need food and a place to sleep. They needed to feel safe and wanted. They needed to feel trust.

Vince hadn't taken that away from my brother tonight, because Jax had never counted on him in the first place. But Vince had made sure Jax would go back into a group home, and again he'd put me in the position to remind my brother that I couldn't help him. I couldn't protect him.

And, goddamn, I hated that feeling.

Grabbing a wad of cash out of my pocket, I yanked my brother in for a hug and stuffed the money into his hand. Without even looking at him, I spun around and walked out of the room as fast as I could.

I didn't deserve to look him in the face.

But I did know one thing. I knew how to push back.

"Are we going where I think we're going?" Madoc strolled up beside me, and I wasn't surprised that he was still here.

He was a good friend, and I didn't treat him as well as he deserved.

"You don't have to come," I warned.

"Would you for me?" he asked, and I looked at him like he was stupid. "Yeah." He nodded. "I thought so, too."

Madoc cruised up to the Donovan house a half hour later, and I hopped out of the car before he'd even stopped. It was late, the house was dark, and the neighborhood seemed lifeless, the deep rumble of Madoc's GTO the only sound.

I turned around to face him and spoke over the roof. "You need to go."

He blinked, probably not sure if he'd heard me right.

The past month had resulted in more hell than I should've put him through. Sure, fighting was fun. Losing ourselves in girl after girl was moderately entertaining, too, but Madoc wouldn't go over the cliff without me leading him there.

Would he walk to the edge?

Sure.

Peek over the side?

Definitely.

But he wouldn't take the step. It was always me who pushed him or let him fall. One of these times, though, he wasn't going to get up, and it would be my fault.

"No," he said resolutely. "I'm not going anywhere."

I gave a half smile, knowing it was next to impossible to get him to leave. "You're a good friend, but I'm not dragging you down with me."

I dug my cell out of my jeans pocket and dialed 911.

"Hello." My eyes were on Madoc as I spoke to the police. "I'm at 1248 Moonstone Lane in Weston. Someone's broken into our house, and we need the police. And an ambulance."

And I hung up and looked at the wide-eyed expression on his face. "They're going to be here in about eight minutes," I told him. "Go wake up my mom. You can do that for me."

Someone, probably a legal guardian, was going to have to bail me out.

Walking down the path leading to the tan-and-red-brick, split-level house, I could hear the TV going from inside. I paused before the steps, aggravated that I hadn't heard Madoc drive off yet but also puzzled as to why my heart was still beating so slowly.

Why aren't I nervous? Or excited?

I may as well have been about to go into a restaurant and order a milk shake.

With Tate, I thrived on that little thrill of anticipating her. It was enough to satisfy me day in and day out. I hated to admit it, but she was always on my mind. I lived for that first glimpse of her in the morning and any interaction with her during the day.

I squinted at the vibrant light from the television screen coming from inside the house and took a deep breath.

The son of a bitch was still awake.

Good.

On the rare occasion Vince Donovan and I interacted, it was with mutual intolerance. He spoke to me like I was a punk, and he treated my brother the same.

As I climbed the porch steps, I heard Madoc drive off behind me. I stepped through the front door and walked into the living room, filling the doorway as I hovered there.

Vince didn't even bat an eyelash as he barked, "What the hell are you doing here?"

Grabbing the long wooden stem of the lamp next to me, I yanked the cord out of the wall.

"You hurt my brother," I spoke calmly. "I'm here to settle up."

CHAPTER 4

"You didn't have to bail me out." I ran my tongue over the sweet sting of the cut at the corner of my mouth.

"I didn't," James, Tate's dad, answered. "Your mother did."

He steered the car through the quiet twists and turns leading into our neighborhood. The sun peeked through the trees, making the red-gold leaves glow like fire.

My mother? She was there?

Madoc and James had been at the police station all night, waiting for me to be released. I'd been arrested and booked, and ended up sleeping in a cell.

Word to the wise about waiting to be bailed out: Nothing happens until morning.

But if my mother had bailed me out, then where was she?

"Is she at home?" I asked.

"No, she's not." He turned a corner, downshifting the Bronco. "She's not in any shape to help you, Jared. I think you know that. Your mother and I talked last night at the station, and she decided it was time to go to the Haywood Center for a while."

James's blue eyes were concentrated out the window, an ocean of things he would never say boiling underneath.

In that respect, he and Tate were one and the same. If James yelled, then you knew it was time to shut up and pay attention. He rarely said anything that wasn't important, and he hated unnecessary chatter.

It was very clear when James and Tate reached the end of their rope.

"Rehab?" I questioned him.

"It's about time, don't you think?" he shot back.

I laid my head back on the headrest and looked out the window. *Yeah, I guess it's time.*

But apprehension crawled its way into my head, anyway.

I was used to how my mother lived. How I lived. James could judge us. Others may feel sorry for me. But it was our normal.

I was never one to feel too sorry for poor kids or people in rough situations. If that was all they'd ever known, then it wasn't suffering the way someone else would look at it. It was *their* life. It was hell for them, of course, but it was also familiar.

"For how long?" I was still a minor. I wasn't sure how this worked with her gone.

"At least a month." He turned the car into his driveway, and the morning light made the tree between Tate's and my windows glimmer like the sun on a lake.

"So where does that leave me?" I asked.

"One thing at a time." He sighed as we got out of the car. "Today, you're with me. You'll shower, eat, and go get a few hours' sleep. I'll wake you for lunch, and then we'll talk."

He handed me a bag from the backseat before we walked up the front steps.

"Your mom packed you a change of clothes. Go to Tate's room, shower up, and I'll get you something to eat."

I halted. *Tate's room? Absolutely not!*

"I'm not sleeping in her room." I scowled, my heart beating so hard and fast that I couldn't catch my breath. "I'll crash on the couch or something."

He paused before unlocking the front door and twisted his head around to fix me with an extreme don't-fuck-with-me expression.

"We have three bedrooms, Jared. Mine, Tate's, and the other one is an office. The only available bed is Tate's." He bared his teeth with every syllable, like he was speaking to a child. "That's where you sleep. It's not difficult. Now go shower."

I stared for a few seconds, lips pursed and not blinking. Too busy trying to think of a comeback.

But I was at a loss.

Finally, I just blew out a huge-ass sigh, because that's all I could do. He'd hung out at the police station all night, and he was trying to help my mother.

I was going to step foot in Tate's room for the first time in more than two years. So what? I could handle it, and, man, would I hear her piss and moan all the way from France if she knew I was in there.

I actually smiled at the thought, and my blood rushed hot like I'd just downed two dozen Pixy Stix.

James veered off into the kitchen, while I headed upstairs to Tate's room, my legs shaking the closer I got.

The door was open. It was always open. Tate never had anything to hide like I did. Stepping inside with soft feet, like I was an explorer on unstable ground, I made a circle of the room and took inventory of what had changed and what hadn't.

One thing I always appreciated about this girl was her abhorrence for the color pink—unless it was paired with black. The walls were halved—the top was black-and-white pinstripe wallpaper and the bottom was painted red, with a white wooden border separating the two parts. Her bedding was a deep gray with a black leaf pattern all over it, and the walls were sparsely covered with candleholders, pictures, and posters.

Very uncluttered and very Tate.

I also noticed that there was nothing of me in here. No pictures or keepsakes from when we were friends. I knew why, but I didn't know why it bugged me.

I dropped my bag and walked over to her CD player that she'd had since forever. She had an iPod dock, but the iPod was gone. Probably in France with her.

Some fucked-up curiosity bit at my insides, so I started hitting switches to start the CD player. I knew she didn't listen to the radio, because she thought that most music that got radio play sucked.

Silverchair's "Dearest Helpless" popped on, and I couldn't help the shake in my chest from the laugh I tried to hold back. Backing up to the bed, I lay down, letting the music hold me tight.

"I don't understand how you can listen to this alternative crap, Tate."

I sit on the bed, scowling at her but still unable to control the smile that wants release. I give her a hard time, but I love nothing more than to see her happy.

And she's so damn cute right now.

"It's not crap!" she argues, widening her eyes at me. "It's the only album I have where I can listen to every song with equal enjoyment."

I lean back on my hands and sigh. "It's whiny," I point out, and she puckers her lips while she plays air guitar.

Watching her—something I could do every minute of every day—I know I'm all bluster. I would sit through a million Silverchair concerts for her.

Things are changing between us. Or maybe just for me—I don't know. I hope for her, too.

What felt friendly and easy before is different now. Every damn time I see her lately, all I want to do is grab her and kiss her. I feel like there is something wrong with me. My blood runs hot whenever she wears the little jean shorts like the ones she's wearing right now. Even her baggy black Nine Inch Nails T-shirt is turning me on.

Because it's mine.

She borrowed it one day and never gave it back. Or I guess I told her she could just have it. One night when I noticed that she was sleeping in it, I didn't want it back anymore. The idea of my shirt on her body while she sleeps makes me feel like she's mine. I like that I'm close to her even when I'm not here.

"Oooh, I love this part!" she squeals as the chorus starts, and she rocks out harder on her invisible instrument.

Even a little sway of her hips or scrunching up of her nose makes my pants tighter. What the hell? We're only fourteen. I shouldn't be having these ideas, but, damn it, I can't stop it.

I mean, shit—yesterday I couldn't even watch her do her math home-work, because the pensive expression on her face was so adorable that I had a strong urge to haul her into my lap. Not touching her downright sucks.

"All right, I can't take it," I blurt out, and get off the bed to turn off the music. Any distraction to kill the hard-on that's growing in my pants.

"No!" she screams, but I can hear the laughter in her voice as she grasps at my arms.

I shoot out and lightly jab her under the arm, because I know how tick-lish she is. She squirms, but now I've touched her and I don't want to stop. We nudge each other back and forth, each of us trying to get to the CD player.

"All right, I'll turn it off!" she yells through a fit of laughter as I move my fingers to her stomach. "Just stop!" She giggles, falling into me, and I close my eyes as my hands linger at her hips and my nose is near her hair.

What I want from her scares me. And I'm afraid it would scare her, too. I know it will definitely scare her father.

But I'll wait, because there is no other choice. For the rest of my life, I won't want anyone else.

It's time to man up and tell her.

"Let's go to the pond tonight," I say, softer than I want. My voice cracks, and I'm not sure if I'm nervous or frightened. Probably both.

Our fish pond is where it needs to happen. It's where I want to tell her that I love her. We go there a lot. Picnics or just for walks. It's not unusual for us to sneak out and ride our bikes up there at night.

She leans back and looks at me with a casual smile. "I can't. Not tonight."

My shoulders slump a little, but I recover. "Why?"

She doesn't look at me but pushes her hair behind her ears and walks to the bed to sit down.

Dread stomps into my brain like a big fat rhinoceros. She's going to tell me something I don't like.

"I'm going to the movies," she offers with a close-lipped smile. "With Will Geary."

I swallow, feeling the thump in my chest damn near break a rib. Will Geary is in our class, and I hate him. He's been sniffing around Tate for a year. His father and Tate's dad play golf together, and that's one part of her life that I'm not involved in.

Will Geary doesn't have anything on me. His family doesn't have more money or a better house. But his family is involved with Tate's, and my parents are . . . well, not involved with anything. Tate's dad had tried taking me golfing once or twice, but it's never stuck. Fixing cars is where we bond.

I narrow my eyes, trying to reel in the anger. "When did that happen?"

She makes eye contact with me for only a second at a time. I can tell she is uncomfortable. "He asked yesterday, when our dads played golf together."

"Oh," I almost whisper, my face rushing with heat. "And you said yes?"

She folds her lips between her teeth and nods.

Of course she said yes. I took my damn time, and another guy swooped in. But it still hurts.

If she wants to be with me, I guess she would've told him no. But she didn't.

I nod. "That's cool. Have fun." *The pitch in my voice probably gives away how hard I'm trying to sound like I don't care.*

I start walking for her bedroom door. "Listen, I have to go. I forgot Madman needs some food, so I'm off to the store."

She's mine. I know she loves me. Why can't I just turn around and tell her? All I have to do is say "Don't go," and the hard part would be over.

"Jared?" *she calls, and I stop, the air in the room almost too thick to breathe.*

"You're my best friend." *She pauses and then continues,* "But is there maybe any reason you may not want me to go with Will tonight?"

Her shaky voice is hesitant, like she's scared to speak, and the moment fills the room like a broken promise. It's the moment when you know that you can have what you want if you're only brave enough to say so. It's a split second when everything can change, but you pussy out because you're too afraid to risk the rejection.

"Of course not." *I turn around and smile at her.* "Go. Have a good time. I'll see you tomorrow."

That night I saw Will kiss her, and the next day my dad called and asked if I wanted to come visit him for the summer.

I said yes.

CHAPTER 5

"Eat." James pushed a plate of meat loaf and potatoes in my face as soon as I sat down on the barstool.

I'd fallen asleep on Tate's bed, listening to Silverchair, and hadn't woken up until two in the afternoon. Her dad pounded on the door to wake me.

After I'd showered and gotten dressed in fresh clothes, I'd come downstairs to an even better smell than Tate's shampoo.

I sat at the center island in the kitchen and stuffed the food into my mouth like I hadn't eaten a home-cooked meal in years. Well, I guess I hadn't. Before the summer with my father, my alcoholic mother wasn't very nurturing. And after that summer, I wouldn't let her be even if she'd tried.

"Don't you have work?" I asked before taking a drink to wash down the food.

It was Friday, and I was missing school as well. I'd skipped yesterday, too, when Madoc and I went to get tattoos.

That seemed like so long ago now.

"I took the day off," he said, crossing his arms over his chest.

To deal with me.

"Sorry." And I honestly was. Mr. Brandt was a good guy, and he didn't deserve drama.

Leaning against the counter opposite the center island, James crossed his arms over his chest, and I knew a talk was coming. Fixing my gaze on my plate of food, I braced myself, because with Mr. Brandt, it was best just to shut up and take it.

"Jared, your mom will be gone for at least four weeks. You're going to stay here while she's away."

"I'll be fine at my house." It was worth a try.

"You're sixteen years old. That's illegal."

"Seventeen," I corrected.

"What?"

"I'm seventeen today." It was October second. I hadn't realized until they'd dated my paperwork this morning at the jail.

That information didn't give James any pause, though. "I spoke to a judge. One that I know well. I worked out a treatment of sorts, in order for that mess from last night to stay off your permanent record."

Mess from last night? That's a strange way to describe it. "I nearly beat a guy to death," I spit out sarcastically. How the hell were they going to keep that off my record?

"If that's true, then why haven't you asked how he is?"

I nearly beat a guy to death.

Yeah, even thinking the words, I still didn't care. Would I care if he were dead?

James continued. "In case you did care, he's fine. Not great, but he'll survive. Some broken ribs, a little internal bleeding that he went into surgery for last night, but he'll recover."

He'd be in the hospital for a while, but I was glad I hadn't hurt him that badly. To be honest, most of last night swirled in my head like water down a drain. The more it moved, the more I lost. I could barely recall most of the attack. I remember hitting him with the lamp and kicking him in the stomach several times. He threw some shit at me, but in the end he was the one on the ground.

Until that asshole cop showed up and stuck his knee in my back, pulled my hair, and called me every name under the sun while he cuffed me.

Why had I called the cops again? I still wasn't sure.

"So the judge would like you to attend counseling." I didn't need to look up to know James was shooting me a warning look. "In exchange, you won't have this latest episode on your record."

"Absolutely not." I shook my head and laughed at his joke.

Counseling? Most people pissed me off. And people up in my shit really pissed me off.

"That's what I told him you'd say," James bowed his head and sighed. "Jared, you're going to have to start taking responsibility for yourself. You did wrong and the world doesn't owe you anything. I'm not going to wipe your nose just because you come from a broken home and you think that gives you a license to behave badly. I call it the 'Fuck up, own up, and get up' policy. Make a mistake, admit it, and move on. We all screw up, but a man solves his problems. He doesn't make them worse."

I should've just eaten and kept my mouth shut.

"Did you fuck up?" he asked, every slow syllable a challenge.

I nodded.

Would I do it again? Yes. But he didn't ask me that.

"Good." He slammed his hand down on the countertop. "Now it's time to get up. Your attendance and grades are in the garbage. You have no real goals beyond high school—that I can tell, anyway—and you suck at making responsible decisions. There's a really good place for people who crave discipline and don't need too much freedom."

"Prison?" I blurted out sarcastically.

And to my surprise, he smiled like he'd just trumped me.

Shit.

"West Point," he answered.

"Yeah, right." I shook my head. "Senators' kids and Eagle Scouts? That's not me."

What was he thinking? West Point was a military college. The best of the best went there, and spent years building up their high school resumes to get accepted. I'd never get into West Point even if I was interested.

"That's not you?" he questioned. "Really? I didn't think you worried about fitting in. Everyone else has to fit you, right?"

Motherf— I sucked in a breath and looked away. This guy knew how to shut me up.

"You need a goal and a plan, Jared." He leaned on the island straight into my space, so I'd have no choice but to pay attention. "If you have no hope for the future or passion for what's to come, then that's not something I can instill in you. The best thing I can do for you is push you in a direction and keep you busy. You're going to clean up your grades, attend every class, get a job, and"—he hesitated— "go visit your father once a week."

"What?" *Where the hell did that come from?*

"Well, I told Judge Keiser that you wouldn't go for the counseling, so this was your only other option. You're required to have one visit a week for a solid year—"

"You've got to be kidding me," I interrupted, the tightness in my muscles so tense that I started sweating. There was no fucking way I could do it!

I opened my mouth. "Absolutely—"

"This is the 'get up' part, Jared!" he yelled, cutting me off. "You don't agree to one of your options, then it's off to juvie . . . or jail. This isn't the first time you've been in trouble. The judge wants to make an impression on you. Go sit in a jail, every Saturday, and see not what got your father in there but what being in there has no doubt done to him." He shook his head at me. "Jail does two things, Jared. It weakens you or kills you, and neither is good."

My eyes stung. "But—"

"You won't do your brother any good if you're sent away." And he walked out of the kitchen and the front door, having made his point.

What the hell just happened?

I gripped the edge of the gray marble countertop, wanting to rip it out of the wall and tear up the whole world in the process.

Fuck.

I struggled to inhale, my ribs aching with every stretch.

I couldn't visit that cocksucker every week! There was no way!

Maybe I should just tell Mr. Brandt about everything. Everything. There had to be another solution.

Pushing off the counter and out of my seat, I ran up to Tate's room, crawled out of the double doors, and through the tree to my own bedroom.

Fuck him. Fuck them all.

I switched on my iPod to Apocalyptica's "I Don't Care" and crashed onto my own bed, breathing in and out until the hole in my gut stopped burning.

God, I missed her.

The reality disgusted me, but it was true. When I hated Tate, my world got small. I didn't see all the other shit: my mom, my dad, or my brother in foster care. If I only just had her here again, I wouldn't be such a jumble of fucking breathing fits and outbursts.

It was stupid as hell, I know. Like she should be around just for me to push whichever way I wanted.

But I needed her. I needed to see her.

I reached out to grab the handle on my bedside drawer, where I kept the pictures of us as kids, but I pulled back. No. I wasn't going to look at them. It was bad enough that I kept them. Throwing them away or destroying them had been impossible. Her hold on me was absolute.

And I was fucking done.

Fine.

Let them think I played their game. My brother was the most important thing, and Mr. Brandt was right. I wasn't any good to him in jail.

But I wasn't going to any fucking counselor.

I exhaled and sat up.

Scumbag father it was, then.

I slapped on some dark-washed jeans and a white T-shirt, and gelled my hair for probably the first time in a week.

Walking down my stairs and out the front door, I found Tate's dad in his garage, removing stuff from his old Chevy Nova. Tate and I used to help him do little jobs on the car years ago, but it was always drivable.

He looked like he was clearing out the trunk and any personal stuff from inside.

"I need to replace the spark plugs on my car," I told him. "And then I'm going to Fairfax's Garage for a job. I'll grab some clothes on my way back and be inside in time for dinner."

"By six," he specified, offering me a half smile.

I slipped on my sunglasses and turned to leave, but stopped and spun back around.

"You won't tell Tate about any of this, right?" I checked. "Getting arrested, my family, me staying here?"

He looked at me like I'd just told him that broccoli was purple. "Why would I do that?"

Good enough.

CHAPTER 6

Not twenty-four hours later, I stood in front of another cop, getting patted down, only this time I wasn't in trouble.

According to Mr. Brandt's judge friend, I didn't have to start the visitations for a few weeks. They wanted my mother's approval first, but I had no interest in waiting. The sooner I started, the sooner I'd be done.

"Through those doors you'll find lockers where you can put your keys and phone. Get rid of that wallet chain, too, kid."

I eyed the neo-Nazi-looking corrections officer like he could take his orders and shove them up his ass. He was bald, white like he'd never seen the sun, and as fat as a dozen Krispy Kremes a day will do to you. I wanted my shit on me, because I fully expected to turn around and walk out of here the moment I laid eyes on the sick bastard that was my father.

My father. My stomach turned at those words.

"How does this work?" I asked reluctantly. "Will he be, like, in a cage, and we talk through some airholes, or are there phones we use?"

Asking questions wasn't my style. I either figured it out for myself or I shut up and fumbled along. But the idea of seeing the twisted fuck made my muscles tense. I wanted to know exactly what I was walking into. Looking like a helpless kid to this cop was nothing if I could walk in there like a man in front of my father.

"Cages with airholes?" the Nazi with a badge teased. "Watching a little *Prison Break* lately?"

Fucker.

He looked like he was trying to hold back a smile as he buzzed me through the double doors. "Thomas Trent isn't here for murder or rape. No additional security needed, kid."

No, of course not. It's not like he was dangerous. Not at all.

Tipping my chin up, I walked calmly though the doors. "The name's Jared," I corrected him in an even voice. "Not kid."

The visitation room—if that was what it was even called—boasted a high school–like common area. Benches, tables, and snack machines filled most of the room, and windows along the south wall brought in enough light, but not too much.

It was Saturday, and the room was packed. Women held children in their arms while the husbands, boyfriends, and significant others smiled and chatted. Mothers hugged sons, and kids shied away from the fathers that they didn't know.

It was all happily horrible.

Scanning the room, I wasn't sure if my father was already in here or if I was supposed to sit down and wait for them to announce him. I wanted to dart my gaze everywhere at once. I didn't like him knowing my position when I didn't know his. My mouth was dry, and my heart pounded in my ears, but I forced myself to slow down and do what I always do.

I surveyed and tried to appear calm and comfortable, like I owned the place.

"Jared," I heard a voice call, and I stilled.

It was the gruff voice in my dreams that I'd never forgotten. It always sounded the same.

Patient.

Like the snake sneaking up on its prey.

Slowly I followed the sound until my eyes landed on a fortyish-looking man with blond hair that curled around his ears and azure eyes.

He sat there, forearms resting on the table and fingers interlocked, dressed in a khaki button-down with a white T-shirt underneath. He probably had on matching pants, too, but I didn't care enough to check.

I couldn't tear my eyes away from his face. Nothing had changed. Other than being clean-shaven now and having a skin tone that was a little healthier—from not being on drugs, I would assume—he looked the same. There was still a little gray in his hair, and his once-average build was now on the lighter side. I doubted inmates got the chance to get fat *in* prison.

But the part that got my palms sweaty was the way he looked at me. Unfortunately, that hadn't changed, either. His eyes were cold and distant, with a hint of something else, too. Amusement, maybe?

It was like he knew something he wasn't supposed to know.

He knows everything, I reminded myself.

And all of a sudden I was back in his kitchen again, my wrists burning from the rope, paralyzed with despair.

I reached into my pocket and pulled out the one thing I knew I would need. Tate's fossil necklace.

I balled it up in my fist, already feeling a little stronger.

It was technically her mother's, but I'd taken it when she left it on her grave one day. At first I told myself that I was keeping it safe. Making sure it survived. Then it turned into another piece of her that I could claim.

Now it was like a talisman. And I was no longer keeping it safe, but it was keeping me from harm.

Narrowing my eyes for good measure, I stalked over to him, not slow enough to look timid and not fast enough to appear obedient. On my own time, because he didn't call the shots anymore.

"So what did you do?" he asked before I even sat down, and I hesitated for a moment before parking my ass in the seat.

Oh, yeah. He's going to talk to me. I'd forgotten about that part.

It didn't mean I had to talk back, though.

I hadn't decided how I was going to handle these visits, but he could go to hell. Fifty-two little get-togethers in the next year, and I may decide to speak to him at some point, but I wasn't starting until I was goddamn good and ready.

"Come on," he taunted. "May as well pass the time."

A little part of me thought that without drugs and alcohol, my father would—oh, I don't know—behave like he had a heart. But he was still a dick.

"Did you steal?" he asked, but then continued as if talking to himself and tapping his fingers on the steel table. "No, you're not greedy. Assault, maybe?" He shook his head at me. "But you never liked to pick battles that you could lose. With someone weaker, perhaps. You were always a little coward that way."

I balled my other hand into a fist and concentrated on breathing.

Sitting there, forced to listen to internal musings that he was so gracious to let me hear, I wondered if he just pulled this shit out of his ass or if he really was that perceptive.

Was I greedy? No, I didn't think so. Did I pick battles with weaker opponents? It took me a minute to consider, but yes, I did.

But that was only because *everyone* was weaker than me.

Everyone.

"So it must be drugs, then." He slapped his hand down on the table, startling me, and I looked down, away from his eyes, out of reflex. "I'd believe that. With your mother and me, it's in the blood."

Everyone. I reminded myself.

"You don't know me," I said, my voice low and even.

"Yeah, keep telling yourself that."

No. He left me—and thank God for that—when I was two. He spent a few weeks with me one summer.

He did not know me.

Clenching Tate's necklace, I stared at him hard. It was time to shut him up.

"How long are you in for? Six more years?" I asked. "What does it feel like to know that you'll have gray hair before you get laid again? Or drive a car? Or get to stay up past eleven on a school night?" I raised my eyebrows, hoping my condescending questions would push him back in place. "You don't know me, and you never did."

He blinked and I held his gaze, daring him to come at me again. It looked like he was studying me, and I felt like I had a sniper scope on me, zoning in.

"What is that?" He gestured to the necklace in my hand.

I looked down, not realizing that I had threaded my fingers through the light green ribbon. It was obvious I had something in my fist, and all of a sudden my heart started thundering away.

I wanted to leave.

Thinking about Tate and my father in the same thought and having my father see something of hers disgusted me.

You know the flowers a magician pulls out of their sleeves? At that moment, I wanted to be the flowers and go back into hiding. I just wanted to sink into the chair and be out from under his dirty eyes, taking the necklace with me, where it would be safe.

"What's her name?" His voice was low, almost a whisper, and I cringed despite myself.

Raising my eyes again, I saw him smile like he knew everything. Like he had me under his thumb again.

"Six years, huh?" He licked his lips. "She'll be in her twenties by then." He nodded, and I saw flames, not missing his meaning by a long shot.

Mother. Fucker.

Slamming my hand down on the table, I heard gasps from those around us as I shoved my chair back and stood up to glare at him.

Whatever I was shooting from my eyes burned like hell.

I wanted him dead. And I wanted it to be painful.

Hot air rushed in and out of my nose, sounding like a distant waterfall.

"What's wrong inside of you?" I growled. "Is it broken, dead, or just numb?"

My father looked up at me, not scared—I wasn't a threat to him, after all—and answered with the most sincerity I had ever seen from him. "Don't you know, Jared?" he asked. "You have it, too. And so will your useless kids. No one wants us. I knew I didn't want you."

My face didn't relax. It just fell, and I didn't know why.

"I have a birthday present for you." Tate's dad appeared in my driveway, hands in his pockets, as I got out of my car.

I shook my head, feeling the fucking weight of the visit with my father crawling all over my skin. I'd just sped all the way home from the prison, and I needed a distraction.

"Not now," I bit out.

"Yes, now," he shot back, turning to walk back to his house, assuming I'd follow.

Which I did. If only to get him to stop busting my balls.

Traipsing behind him into his open two-car garage, I immediately halted because of the disaster in front of me.

"What the hell happened?" I burst out, shocked.

The fully restored Chevy Nova that had sat in this garage for as long as Tate and Mr. Brandt had lived here was completely totaled. Well, not completely. But it was a fucking wreck. It looked like it'd been used in a baseball game between King Kong and Godzilla. Windows were shattered, tires slashed, and that was the easy stuff. Dents the size of basketballs covered the door panels and hood, and the leather seats were cut up.

"Happy birthday."

I jerked my head over at him and pinched my eyebrows together in confusion. "Happy birthday? Are you crazy? This car was in great shape yesterday. Now you've turned it into a piece of junk, and I can have it?"

Not that I needed a car. Jax would get mine as soon as he turned sixteen and got a license, and I'd be buying another car any day now with the money from my grandfather's house.

"No, you can't have it. You can fix it."

Gee, thanks.

"I figured you might need a little automotive therapy after today, so I decided to break out the sledgehammer and invent a project for you."

Were all of the adults in my life on fucking crack?

James walked toward me, to the front of the car. "All that shit you feel, Jared—the frustration, the anger, the loss, whatever it is . . ." He trailed off and then continued. "It's going to find a way out eventually, and you're going to have to deal with it someday. But for now, just keep busy. It won't cure anything, but it will help you calm down."

Slowly walking around the car, taking in the damage and already compiling the materials I would need in my head, I figured it made sense. I still didn't feel any better than I had a month ago, and I had no idea what to think of the things my father had said today. If anything, I felt worse now, but I just didn't want to think about anything anymore.

But Jax needed me, and I couldn't fail him.

Just keep busy.

"This is going to take me months." I peered over at him as I leaned on the hood.

He smiled back and then turned to walk into the house. "I'm counting on it."

So I dove.

Deep.

Day after day. Month after month, I fed off the routine. I buried myself in activity and noise so I wouldn't have time to think about anything. So I wouldn't have time to care.

I stayed in Tate's room. I slept on the floor.

My mom got sober. Then she got a boyfriend.

I got another tattoo. Madoc got a piercing . . . somewhere.

I went to class and my grades improved.

James and I took a tour of West Point. It wasn't for me.

My father continued messing with my head. Sometimes I walked out. Sometimes I didn't. Sometimes we played cards so I wouldn't have to hear that motherfucker speak.

The dreams kept me awake at night, but the pills helped.

I bought a Boss 302. It kept me occupied.

I messed around with some girls. No blondes.

Madoc and I started racing at the Loop. Something else to keep me busy.

Jax got a decent home. I saw him every Sunday.

I had parties at my house. More noise.

Mr. Brandt was sent to Germany to work. Tate wasn't coming home.

They got rid of the Heartland Scramble at Denny's. Fine. Fuck. Whatever.

Everything rolled off of me, because none of it mattered.

Until eleven months later, on a hot August night, when a girl with stormy eyes and sunshine hair breathed air and fire back into me again.

CHAPTER 7

"Piper, come on!" I shouted out to the lake. "Storm's coming. Let's hit the road."

"Don't go," Madoc spoke up from behind me. "Come over to my house. We're taking the party there." He lay on a picnic blanket on the rocky beach, cuddled up to some girl whose name he probably didn't know, while "Love-Hate-Sex-Pain" by Godsmack played from the stereo of my car off in the distance.

We came out to Swansea Lake with about six people this afternoon to swim and hang out, but the party had grown to more than twenty-five before it got dark. I had to work at the garage in the morning, so I was using that as my excuse to leave.

Truth was, I was just bored. I no longer drank in public. Going to parties. Passing out at strange houses. None of it seemed enticing when I wasn't getting wasted, and I no longer thought about what enticed me. I thought only about what passed the time.

"Oh, baby," Madoc groaned to the girl next to him. "Snickers ain't the only thing king-sized."

I smiled to myself, wishing I could live in his skin. Every day was his birthday, and he was five years old, jumping in the ball pit at Chuck E. Cheese. I didn't even need to turn around to know that that line had worked. The girl was giggling, and I was ready for my own action.

"You're not taking me home right away, are you?" My current toy, Piper, trudged out of the lake, flinging water every which way as she wrung out her long dark hair.

Yeah, I'm a dick. She wasn't a toy, I know. None of them were. But my car had more of a relationship with me than they did, so that made them the passing amusement.

Piper was going to be a senior like us and I'd seen her around school for years, but she never caught my interest. She was clingy and way too obvious. She knew she was beautiful and she thought it mattered.

Yep, I had zero tolerance for her. Until . . . I found out on the Fourth of July that her dad was the asswipe who arrested me last year. The douche-bag cop who shoved his knee into my spine and rubbed my face into the floor when he'd handcuffed me.

Yeah, then she became something for me to play with.

"What do you think?" I asked, not really asking. She had an amazing body, and I loved that she was into pretty much anything. As long as she didn't talk too much, we kept hooking up.

"Hey, you know what today is?" Madoc laughed, breaking me out of my thoughts and slurring his words. "One year ago today, that girl Tate broke my nose at that party. Oh, she was fucking pissed, too."

I tensed but continued pulling on my T-shirt, not looking at anyone.

"Jared, isn't she supposed to be back by now?" Madoc asked. "I mean, wasn't she supposed to be gone for only a year?" he pointed out as if I were stupid. "It's been a year."

"Shut up, dickhead." Rolling my eyes, I reached down to pick up my wet clothes. I'd already gone into the nearby woods to change into jeans before calling Piper out of the water.

"What's he talking about?" Piper just stood there, but I didn't spare her a glance.

"Tate. Jared's neighbor," Madoc offered. "She goes to our school, but she left for junior year," Madoc offered, and then turned to me. "So, where is she? I miss that girl."

He sat up, and even though I buried my face in my phone, I knew he was watching me.

Idiot. Dick. Fucking asshole friend.

I shook my head. "Her dad's working in Germany, okay? He got put on an assignment there for seven months and won't be home until December. He said she'll be starting the school year there. All right, dickhead that has to be in everyone's business?"

Mr. Brandt's company had sent him to Germany last spring, so I'd been checking on the house and collecting mail since May.

Madoc looked at me like I just told him he couldn't have ice cream for dessert. "Bummer, dude. But she's probably thrilled," he added. "She hated us."

A twinge of amusement crept into my chest. *Yeah, she sure did.*

When Mr. Brandt had told me about his trip, I'd had another party at my house that night. Instead of getting drunk elsewhere, I had no problem getting wasted at home. And it helped.

I'd expected Tate to be back from France this past June, when the school year ended, but when I found out that she wouldn't be back until December, I wanted to slam someone against a wall.

I loved hating her, and I wanted her fucking home.

But I just swallowed the ache like I'd been doing since last fall. I'd gotten used to going through the motions and pretending that shit didn't matter.

And it was time to dive deep again.

"Let's go." I grabbed Piper's hand and started for my car.

"But I'm still wet. I need to change," she whined.

"Yeah," I said, smiling, "and I'm going to help."

The roads were slick as hell. It hadn't rained much this summer, and all of the oil buildup on the street had me constantly fishtailing.

But it's not like I had the sense to slow down, either.

I sped up onto my driveway and into the garage, even though I knew I shouldn't be in a rush. Nothing waiting for me but quiet at my house, and I didn't like quiet.

Closing the garage, I walked through the door leading to the kitchen, peeled off my black T-shirt, and threw it into the laundry-room basket. Piper was all over it.

"Hey, man," I greeted Madman as he came racing down the stairs. "Come on."

Opening the back door so he could do his business, I left it open and ran upstairs to plug in my dead cell phone.

As soon as I'd turned it on, I saw that I had a voice mail from Tate's dad.

Why is he calling?

We'd just texted a few days ago. He'd checked in on me and his house.

I wasn't sure what he wanted now, but either way, I wasn't calling him back tonight.

I jerked my head, a shrill scratching against the windowpanes causing me to jump.

"Goddamn tree." I tossed my phone on the bed and stalked over to pull up the blinds. This tree between Tate's and my windows was a fucking nuisance. We constantly had to trim it because it was threatening to punch holes into the house. I'd told my mother this spring to just have it cut down, but it was technically on the Brandts' property, and I guess they wanted to keep it.

Mr. Brandt kept it trimmed normally, but he never cut it back very far. I could still reach the branches even after it'd been trimmed.

Pulling up the window and leaning out, I spied the branch sliding against the panes above me. With him gone, I'd have to take care of that tomorrow.

The rain was coming down in sheets and made everything glisten under the bright glow of the streetlights. I let my gaze wander through the maze of branches, shaking off memories of which ones I'd scraped my leg on or which ones I'd sat on with Tate.

I loved the damn tree, and I wanted it cut down.

And then . . . I didn't even see the tree anymore.

My eyes caught sunshine in a midnight sky, and I fucking stilled.

Tate?

"What the hell?" I whispered, breathless and not blinking.

She was standing in her bedroom, leaning on the doorframe of her open French doors. And she was staring at me.

What the hell am I seeing right now?

She was supposed to be in Germany with her dad, at least until Christmas.

Every muscle in my body tightened as I supported myself on the windowsill, but I couldn't tear my eyes from her. It was like I was in an alternate universe, starving, and she was a fucking buffet.

She's home.

I closed my eyes for a moment and swallowed down my heartbeat that was creeping up my throat. I was sick, excited, and grateful all at the same time.

Jesus, she's home.

She wore some little pajama shorts and a white tank top. Not really so different from what I'd noticed she wore to bed a year ago, but for some reason, the sight of her was like a raging fire through my chest. I wanted to rip through the fucking tree and peel all the clothes off her and love her like the past three years had never happened.

Her hair blew around her, and I could feel her eyes, locked in shadow, on me.

My mouth was dry, and the rush of breath and blood through my body felt so damn good.

Until she backed up and closed the doors.

No. I swallowed, not wanting her to go away.

Go on. Go pick a fight, I told myself, but I shook my head.

No. Just leave her alone. She hadn't been thinking about me, and I needed to get over it.

I was crawling the walls inside my head, knowing for fact that I needed to grow up and let her be. Let her go to school without rumors and pranks hovering over her. Let her be happy. We were nearly adults now, and this petty shit had to end.

But . . .

I'd just felt more alive in the past ten seconds than I had in a year.

Seeing that face, knowing I'd wake up to her blaring music and seeing her leave the house to jog in the morning . . .

My phone buzzed with a text, and I walked over to check it.

It was from Tate's dad.

Change of plans. Tate's home. On her own until Christmas. Give her back the house key, and be nice. Or else.

I narrowed my eyes, rereading the text over and over again.

I don't even think I breathed.

She's alone? Until Christmas?

I closed my eyes and let out a laugh.

And all of a sudden I was as thrilled as hell to wake up tomorrow.

CHAPTER 8

"Should I be afraid?" my mother asked as I walked back in from the garage, carrying a small ax.

"Always," I mumbled, passing her at the kitchen counter and heading up the stairs.

I'd decided to take matters into my own hands. Instead of hiring someone, I'd chop off the smaller branches jutting into the house myself. The ax would do the job.

"Just don't hurt yourself!" she shouted after me. "You were hard to make!" And I rolled my eyes at no one as I disappeared up the ladder leading into the attic.

She'd been halfway decent since getting sober. Once in a while she tried making jokes. Sometimes I laughed, but not in front of her. There was still a lot of discomfort between us, a crack I had lost interest in repairing.

But we'd gotten into a routine. She kept herself level, and I did the same.

Crawling through the small window on our dark third floor, I maneuvered myself onto the tree and inched toward the trunk, where the branches were thick enough to support my weight. I figured I'd sit on the inside and chop off the extra growth and then climb down to the ground when I was done. I needed to work top to bottom and eventually get to the branches at my window—the whole reason I'd started this job.

But as I raised the ax to start, I nearly dropped it.

"You think his treatment of me is foreplay?" I heard Tate's aggravated shouting, and I halted.

What? Foreplay?

"Yes," she continued, and I stopped what I was doing to listen. "It was foreplay when he told the whole school I had irritable bowel syndrome, and everyone made farting noises as I walked down the hall freshman year."

My eyes widened and my pulse pounded in my neck. *Is she talking about me?*

"And yes." She kept going, talking to someone I couldn't see. "It was completely erotic the way he had the grocery store deliver a case of yeast-infection cream to math class sophomore year. But what really got me hot and ready to bend over for him was when he plastered brochures for genital-wart treatments on my locker, which is completely outrageous for someone to have an STD without having sex!"

Oh, shit.

She was definitely talking about me.

Grabbing a branch above me, I pushed myself up onto my feet and climbed over to the other side, careful to stay out of the view of Tate's open doors.

Another girl was talking, probably her friend K.C., and I caught something about fighting back.

I slid down another branch, starting to feel like a perv for snooping on their conversation. But, hey, they were talking about me, and that made it my business.

"I've told you a hundred times, we were friends for years," Tate spoke. "He went away for a few weeks the summer before freshman year, and when he came back, he was different. He didn't want to have anything to do with me."

And my fists clenched.

K.C. didn't need to know my shit. Tate had no right airing our business like that.

The familiar swirl of piss and vinegar churned in my gut, and I felt my body warm.

"We're going to have an amazing year." Tate's voice was lower now and stronger than before. "I'm hoping Jared has forgotten all about me. If he has, then we can both peacefully ignore each other until graduation. If he hasn't, then I'll do what I think is best. I've got bigger things on my mind, anyway. He and that asshat Madoc can poke and prod all they want. I'm done giving them my attention. They are not taking my senior year."

I'm hoping Jared has forgotten all about me.

And I'd almost thrown my future away in my need for her?

I'm done giving them my attention.

She hated me. She'd hate me forever, and I was a stupid fucking prick for wanting her when we were fourteen.

No one wants us. I knew I didn't want you. My father's voice crept into my head.

I climbed back over to my window and crawled through, not caring if they saw me. Tossing the ax onto the floor, I walked over and switched on my iPod dock to Five Finger Death Punch's "Coming Down" and grabbed my phone to text Madoc.

Party tonight? Mom's leaving around 4. My mother escaped every Friday night to her boyfriend's in Chicago. I still hadn't met the guy, but she almost always stayed the entire weekend.

Hell, yeah, he texted not a minute later.

Drinks? I asked. Madoc's dad had a liquor store—or close to—in his basement, along with a wine cellar. The guy was hardly ever home, so we took what we wanted, and I supplied the food.

Got it. See you at 7.

I threw my phone on the bed, but it buzzed again.
Grabbing it again, I opened up a text from Jax.

Dad called again.

Son of a bitch.
My father was finding ways to get Jax's number, and he knew he wasn't supposed to be calling him. Abusing him was one of the reasons my father was in jail, after all.
I'll handle it, I texted.
Looking at the clock, I saw it was only ten in the morning.
Just go today, I told myself. *Get it over with for the week, and you won't have to go tomorrow.*
These trips to my father's ate at my insides, and I dreaded them. There was no telling what he'd say to me from one week to the next. Last time he'd told me, in graphic detail, about how he'd dropped my mother off at the abortion clinic one day to get rid of me. And then how he'd let loose on her when she hadn't gone through with it. I didn't know if the story was true, but I tried to just let the insults, stories, and taunts fly past me. Most of the time they did. Sometimes they didn't.
Screw it.
Throwing off a sweaty black T-shirt in exchange for a clean, black V-neck, I snatched my keys off the bedside table and bounded down the stairs.

"I'm heading out for a while," I said as I passed my mother in the kitchen. "See you Monday."

My hands shook, even though I'd been coming here nearly a year already. I hated looking the fucker in the face, especially when he made these visits as awful as possible. I knew he got special privileges for cooperating, but I had no doubt that he enjoyed every sick word that came out of his mouth, too.

"It's Friday. I'm not supposed to have to see you until tomorrow," he grumbled, and sat down at the table in the visiting room.

I forced myself to look him in the eye and even out my tone. "You're calling Jax again. It stops now."

He laughed me off. "That's what you said last time, but you're not in control, Jared."

Yes. I. Am.

"You're not even allowed to make calls." After I reported it to the warden last time, he'd lost the privilege of making unsupervised trips to the phone.

Shrugging with palms up, he answered, "And yet I find a way."

It was only a moment. But in the time it took for my chest to sink and for me to break eye contact, he knew. He knew he was right and that I was powerless. Maybe it was the guards letting him make calls for favors, or maybe he had a fellow prisoner helping him out, but we both knew there wasn't a damn thing I could do to stop him.

I could never stop him.

"Leave him alone." My lips moved, but I barely heard my own voice.

"What bugs you more?" He leaned in and narrowed his blue eyes. "That I call him and not you, or that you can't stop me? I keep telling you, Jared, you have no power. Not really. It may seem like you're the one in control, because you're out there and I'm in here, but I'm the one that haunts you. Not the other way around."

I stood up and stuck my hand in my pocket, gripping the fossil necklace so hard that I thought it would break.

"Fuck you," I growled, and walked out.

CHAPTER 9

"Oh, Jared," Piper gasped my name as I devoured her neck. Gripping her hair and pulling her head back, I tried to get lost in her perfume and her body.

"I told you not to talk," I whispered softly against her skin. "Do as you're told."

"Hats off to the Bull" pounded downstairs, and I could hear voices coming from all sides, both inside and outside the house.

Piper had come to my party uninvited, and I took what was offered. Noise, activity, distraction.

Distraction from the pull next door.

Distraction from my father.

That son of a bitch was right after all. The nightmares that kept me awake? The ones I had to drown out with sleeping pills just so I could get through the night? All of it was me being weak.

"I'm sorry," she giggled. "That just feels so good."

I had one hand buried in her thick dark hair, and my other hand inside her panties, my fingers pushing inside her as she squirmed against the wall of my bedroom.

I grappled at Piper, looking for the magical body part that would get me zoned in. I peeled down the top of her dress, cupping her breasts, kissing her lips, but none of it brought me the peace I wanted.

I'm hoping Jared has forgotten all about me.

I grabbed Piper and hauled her up into my arms and carried her to the bed. The peace would come when I was inside of her. Then I would be happily lost.

"Jared!" I jerked my head toward the pounding on the door.

"Go away!" I shouted as Piper unfastened my belt.

"That girl? Tate?" my friend Sam asked. "She's downstairs, man. You better get down there."

And I halted what I was doing and sat up.

"What the hell?" I mumbled.

Why was she at my house? I looked at the alarm clock that read after midnight.

"Tate?" Piper said, still lying back on the pillows. "I thought you said she was still gone."

I climbed off the bed. "Just get dressed, Piper," I bit out.

"What?" she screamed, and I looked over at her. Her lips and nose were scrunched up, and her chest rose and fell with her hard breathing.

Piper was no attachment and no complications. I appreciated that about her.

But she was pissed, and I didn't stop to explain. I never did. She knew better.

I never let on that I wanted more than a casual thing, and either she'd roll with it or she could leave.

I yanked open the door. Sam waited in the hallway, hands in pockets, looking uncertain.

"Sorry, man." He held up his hands. "Madoc's got his hands all over her. Thought I should get you."

Fucking little shit. I barreled past Sam and down the hallway, ready to stick my best friend's head into the toilet to wake him the fuck up. I was pretty sure he had a thing for Tate, but he was told, years ago, that she was off-limits.

And what the fuck was she doing here, anyway?

Coming down the stairs, I rounded the corner and immediately stopped, my stomach caving in from the loss of breath.

Jesus Christ.

She was so beautiful, it hurt.

She was lost in thought; otherwise she would've seen me, too.

I pressed my hands above my head to both sides of the doorframe. It was my way of trying to look casual, like I didn't care. But, honestly, I just needed the support to keep my legs from caving beneath me.

My heart thundered through my chest, and I wished like hell that I could pause this moment, just look at her until the Earth fell apart.

Her hair was lighter and her skin was darker, probably from being in the sun this summer, and her body had gotten more toned. More grown-up. The shape to the back of her thighs had my mouth going dry. Her nose was still little, her skin still flawless, and her full lips all made her look like the perfect doll. And I never played with dolls, but I damn sure wanted to play with this one.

Right at that moment, I wanted everything from Tate. Everything. Her anger and passion, her hate and lust, her body and soul.

I wanted control of all of it.

I'm the one that haunts you. Not the other way around. My father invaded my head again. He and Tate were always in there.

Neither of them wanted me, and both of them owned me.

But one of them I could control.

"What is she doing here?" I snapped, staring at Madoc but completely aware of Tate snapping her attention my way.

Madoc kept silent, but I could see the corners of his mouth trying to suppress a smile.

"*She* wanted a word with you." Tate's voice was calm but there was a hint of snippiness to it. I smiled to myself, feeling the long-lost adrenaline warming my dry veins.

"Make it quick. I have guests." Dropping my hands, I crossed my arms over my chest and tried to appear bored.

Sam and Madoc veered off into the kitchen, and Tate stood tall with her chin up. Her lips were pursed, and her eyes could light a fire.

I wasn't sure what had happened with Madoc to make her so angry, or maybe she was just mad at me, but I finally felt in my element after a year of walking around dead.

"I. Have. Guests," I repeated, when she didn't speak right away.

"Yes, I can tell." She looked behind me, and I knew Piper was still here. "You can get back to servicing them in just a minute."

I narrowed my gaze, locking her in.

Well, well, well . . . Tate had a low opinion of me. Go figure.

Piper walked over and kissed me on the cheek. Saying good-bye? Reminding me she was here? I have no clue, but she always did little things like that at unexpected times, and it made me uncomfortable. Like she wanted more, and I was obligated to give it to her.

I stood there, willing her to stop waiting for something and just go home. Tate's presence was doing me more good than hers, anyway.

After Piper took the hint and left, Tate spoke up. "I have to be up in about five hours for an appointment in Weston. I'm asking politely that you please turn down the music."

Is she serious? "No."

"Jared, I came here being neighborly. It's after midnight. I'm asking nicely." The begging was cute.

"It's after midnight on a *Friday* night," I explained, trying to sound as condescending as possible.

"You're being unreasonable. If I wanted the music off, I could file a noise complaint or call your mom. I'm coming to you out of respect." She looked around the room. "Where is your mother, by the way? I haven't seen her since I've been back."

Oh, Tate. Don't go there. Don't act like you know me or my family.

"She's not around much anymore." I kept my voice flat and unemotional. "And she won't be dragging her ass down here in the middle of the night to break up my party."

She sighed, looking annoyed. "I'm not saying to break it up. I'm asking that you turn the music down."

"Go sleep over at K.C.'s on the weekends," I suggested, circling the pool table in the family room.

"It's after midnight!" she blurted out. "I'm *not* bothering her this late!"

"You're bothering me this late."

The control was back, and my jaw twitched with a smile.

I felt calm. And very sure about who I was. It was strength, confidence, and trust rushing over me again.

"You are such a dick," she whispered.

I stopped and glared, pretending to be angry. "Careful, Tatum. You've been gone for a while, so I'll cut you a break and remind you that my goodwill doesn't go far with you."

"Oh, please," she sneered. "Don't act like it's such a burden to tolerate my presence. I've put up with more than a little from you over the years. What could you possibly do to me that you haven't done already?"

And I was so elated with the challenge that I almost laughed.

"I like my parties, Tatum. I like to be entertained. If you take my party, then you'll have to entertain me." I surprised myself by how low and unmistakably wanting my voice got. The images of how she could entertain me rushed through my head.

But Tate would never. She was a good girl. Brushed and flossed. Ironed her clothes.

And she didn't do bad things in beds with bad boys.

She tucked her long, wavy hair behind her ear and pinned me with disdain. "And what disgusting task, pray tell, would you like me to do?" She waved her hand in the air dramatically, and my blood rushed with how different she seemed.

She'd gotten smart with me before. And before France, she'd taken some risks.

But every time, she'd seemed nervous and on the verge of tears. Now she looked perfectly comfortable, almost as if this was all a waste of her time.

Good.

Stepping up my game should be fun. And a welcome distraction.

Coming to stand in front of her, I felt heat and a familiar sweet ache in my pants.

Shit. A fucking hard-on right now?

My dick throbbed in my pants, but I tried to ignore it.

Yeah, my body was attracted to hers. So what? I was attracted to most things that wore skirts. Or pajama shorts with black hoodies and Chucks.

My emotions ran wild with Tate, but I knew I couldn't fuck her. It'd be a cold day in hell before I gave her that kind of power over me.

But that didn't mean I couldn't enjoy the view, either.

"Take this off"—I grabbed the hem of her little black sweatshirt— "and give me a lap dance."

Her eyes widened. "Excuse me?"

And I noticed the more nervous break to her voice, and it was like music to my ears.

My gaze firmed up as I challenged her. "I'll put on 'Remedy'—still your favorite song?—you give me a quick lap dance, and the party's over."

Would I really stop the party? No. There would be no situation where I would actually give her what she wanted.

And I would enjoy teaching her that fact. I really hoped, though, that she wouldn't take me up on the offer. Don't get me wrong. Having her body rubbing against mine wouldn't suck, but I wouldn't be able to just fuck her and leave. I walked a thin line with Tate, and I knew I'd want seconds.

She looked at me for a minute, several emotions crossing her sweetly cruel face. Consideration as she actually looked like she was thinking about it. Then anger when she realized she'd only end up being humiliated. Defeat when she accepted that there really was no win here for her. And loss when sadness crossed her glassy eyes. Not sure what that was about. And then something different.

Her brow relaxed, and she tipped her chin down, looking up at me.

Shit.

I knew that look. I wear it all the time.

Defiance.

She twisted around, her hair flying over her shoulder, and my heart skipped a beat as she began shouting throughout my house at the top of her lungs.

"Cops!" she screamed into the living room. "Cops! Everyone get out of here! Cops coming in the back door! Run!"

Motherfucker!

I watched helplessly as all of the drunk and high idiots hanging out at my house dashed to make their escape.

What the hell? They actually believe her!

Heat flared up my neck, and I folded my arms over my chest to keep my heart from jumping out of my body.

People scattered out of the house, fleeing the kitchen and living room and through the front door like there was a fucking fire. Most of them were underage, so they had reason to be on alert, but still. You'd think the stupid shits would at least look around first.

But no, they just fled.

And in no time at all, my house was almost empty. Except for the ones already passed out and whoever was hidden upstairs in the bedrooms.

Blood pumped through my veins like hot sugar, the pain almost unbearable but so mouthwatering that I craved more. Something had changed in her, and now she was challenging me.

Hell, yes.

Approaching my target, I smiled and let out a condescending sigh. "I'll have you in tears in no time," I promised.

She stared at me, almost amused. "You've already made me cry countless times." And she raised her middle finger to me. "Do you know what this is?" she asked as she took it and patted the corner of her eye with it. "It's me, wiping away the last tear you'll ever get."

And she turned around and walked out.

My mouth wouldn't close, and I couldn't tear my eyes away from the empty doorway.

Holy shit.

Tingling started in my throat, and I lost my breath as I started laughing.

Son of a bitch, I'm smiling, too.

I couldn't believe she'd just said that to me. That was definitely a challenge.

Oh, baby. It's on.

"Well, she's different." Madoc was behind me, and I blinked away my smile.

I turned around to face him. "You touched her?" My tone threatened.

"Sorry, man." He looked at me like he hadn't been told ten times already to keep his hands off of her. "I forgot. Won't happen again." He shrugged and walked back to the kitchen.

Yeah, it better not.

I didn't know if he was really coming on to Tate. Sam said he was touching her, but Madoc was a good friend who knew the boundaries.

I wasn't sure what he was up to.

I glanced once more to the front door, remembering how Tate just walked out with her head high, her voice steady, and more confidence than I'd ever seen in her.

Game on.

My shoulders relaxed, and I climbed the stairs and went to bed. This time without a sleeping pill and without any thoughts of my father.

CHAPTER 10

"Ugh, I think my dick is broken," Madoc groaned as he adjusted himself right in the middle of the hallway at school.

I shook my head at him before nodding to a couple of friends passing by.

"Then stick to girls, asshole," I joked. "They're probably softer than the guys you like."

Strolling down the hallway on the first day of senior year, I felt a breeze washing over me that no one else felt. Madoc was bragging about his conquests, I got the classes I wanted, and I was almost done with the visitations to the prison.

In the time that Tate had been back, and a week since her escapade at my party, I'd slept peacefully, too. I almost felt happy.

"So," Madoc spoke up. "Tate's got a little fan club already. I'm assuming you've heard the talk."

I had. As much as I hated the few things I'd heard other guys saying about her, they weren't necessarily bad things. No one had mentioned her tits or ass, so I wouldn't have to pound them into the pavement.

No, they just talked about how beautiful she looked. About how she carried herself now. Confidence she'd gained abroad, I was sure.

And I loved the attention she was getting. After all, the higher she rose, the harder she'd fall.

"Tatum isn't even in her own fan club," I mumbled.

We grabbed some food and sat down at our usual table in the cafeteria. Madoc ate like the athlete in *The Breakfast Club*. He almost needed two trays for the sandwiches, pizza, chips, Gatorades, and brownies he bought, whereas I hated eating big meals during the day. A sandwich or burrito and a couple of drinks were my usual.

The result: Madoc fell asleep during his afternoon classes, and I could make it through work with energy to spare.

"So how are we doing this?" He addressed his question to me as Sam and his friend Gunnar parked it at the table and began digging into their food.

Placing the cap back on my bottle of water and wiping the back of my hand across my lips, I peered up at him, not sure what conversation he'd started that I'd missed. "How are *we* doing what?"

"Tate," he said as if I should've known. "Are we or are we not leaving her alone this year?"

I leaned back in my chair. "I do what I want. I'll let you know if I need your help."

"Shhh," Madoc hissed. "There she is." He jerked his chin toward the doors ahead, my gaze following.

She walked up to the line and got her tray, and I took inventory of everything. For my battle plan, of course.

Her body moved slowly, almost methodically. There was something about how rigid her back looked.

She wasn't relaxed.

I hoped it was me. I hoped she felt me in here, watching her.

I liked watching her move, but I tensed up when I realized that every other guy in here was probably appreciating the same view.

It was a good view, and I couldn't not look.

Her hair used to hang straight, but from the few times I'd seen her in the past week, she seemed to favor a wavier style now. The lights above made the strands sparkle down to their tips. Her long, thin shirt covered her ass on one side but had caught on the waist of her jeans on the other, leaving her ass visible in her tight jeans.

"Well," Madoc piped up, "come up with better stuff this time. The date sabotaging is childish."

What?

And then I realized he was continuing a discussion I didn't remember starting.

"Get yourself paired up on a project with her or something," he continued. "So much you could do with that kind of time together."

Time together?

Oh, yeah. We were talking about the Tate plan of attack. "This isn't foreplay, Madoc." I was setting Madoc straight, just like Tate set K.C. straight. "I'm not looking to hook up with her."

I watched her walk to a far table and sit down . . . with her back to me.

My lips turned up.

She didn't want to risk making eye contact with me, and it was a victory.

Madoc started laughing, almost choking as he tried to swallow his food. "You're right," he coughed out, his eyes watering. "Anyone who sees the way you look at her knows you don't want to hook up with her." He shook his head. "No, right now you're looking at her like you want to tie her up and give her a big, fat spanking."

Stupid ass.

I wasn't into shit like that, or . . . I didn't think I was. Never tried it. Might try it, I guess. You should try everything at least once.

Except crystal meth.

"No?" he challenged, peering over at me when I didn't answer. "Well, I guess this won't make you jealous, then."

And he pushed his chair back, scraping the legs on the floor as he rounded the table and walked toward the other side of the lunchroom. Toward Tate.

Son of a bitch.

I was going to cut off his broken dick and feed it to Madman.

My short black sleeves stretched across my biceps, and I realized I'd tensed damn near every muscle in my body.

I watched, fuming, as Madoc approached Tate and leaned into her ear, speaking. I couldn't hear what he was saying, of course, but I saw Tate's back straighten and knew she was uncomfortable.

Good.

But I didn't feel good. I seemed to get high from pressing her buttons, but I never liked it when others took it upon themselves to follow my example. When Madoc had commented on her chest last year at the party—right before she broke his nose—I'd almost cut his balls off.

Helping me taunt her at times was one thing, but talking shit about her body—and in public—got my fucking temper up. Even I didn't do that. If she hadn't punched him, I would've.

His hand glided down her back, and I balled my hand into a fist.

Goddamn it! Didn't we just have this talk?

Air poured in and out of my nose as I watched, unblinking, his hand fall intimately over her body and descend to her ass.

I shot out of my chair but immediately halted when Tate jerked out of her seat and grabbed Madoc by the shoulders, slamming him in the balls with her knee.

Holy shit!

I sucked in quick, short breaths, trying not to laugh at seeing my best friend fall to his knees, groaning like a wounded animal.

Tate circled him, and I sat down to watch her.

"Don't touch me and don't talk to me," she sneered. "Did you really think I would go out with you?"

He asked her out?

"I hear the girls talk," she continued, "and contrary to popular belief, good things do *not* come in small packages." Her voice was strong, like she was completely comfortable in her skin. Everyone caught the joke as she crooked her pinkie finger to the amused crowd, insinuating that Madoc had a small dick.

"Thanks for the offer, anyway, Madoc," she said in a sweet, singsong voice.

Picking up her tray, she made her way through the crowd, tossed away her lunch, and headed for the doors, as every eye in the room followed her. Even mine.

I leaned back again, remembering how she'd cry or just leave every time Madoc or I did something. Now it was ten-year-old Tate again, rocking my fucking world.

She stopped at the double doors, and I narrowed my eyes on her as she turned around, looking straight at me. Her eyes zoned in, killing the distance between us and bringing me dead in her face, so I could smell her skin.

She is everything. She knew my game, she matched me, and she was going to be a joy to take down. Then, and only then, would I have proven that I didn't need her or anyone else.

Mr. Sweeney, one of the deans, came through the cafeteria, wanting to know what happened, and I stepped in and explained that Madoc had fallen over a chair. Stupid lie, I know, but teachers don't have a lot of power. If one kid claims something and others back it up, it must be true. I didn't want Tate in trouble.

Not with anyone but me.

Before the first afternoon class started, I met Madoc at his locker. Grabbing him by his arm, I hauled him around the corner into an empty classroom.

"Whoa!" he howled, probably surprised by my sudden appearance. "Take it easy!"

As soon as we were away from prying eyes, I twisted around and planted my fist in his gut. The skin on my knuckles stretched, but Madoc caved to the punch, and I knew his pain would be a hell of a lot worse.

Coughing and hunching over, he fell back against the wall as I hovered over him. The strange part was, I wasn't nervous or even angry. I was a little pissed, but otherwise I was in complete command of my actions and emotions.

He knew why he got hit, and now he knew I wasn't bluffing about not touching Tate.

"You heard me this time, right?" I asked.

And he nodded, pinching his eyebrows together and looking nauseous as he held his stomach.

Making my way to my next class, I picked my phone out of my pocket and texted my boss that I wouldn't be at work this afternoon. He was a friend and let me off the hook on the rare occasion I needed a surprise day off.

The job was noise and distraction. Now I had Tate, and she was keeping my head pretty occupied lately.

I passed the rest of the afternoon in a euphoric hunger for what was to come.

CHAPTER 11

M adoc's ego was severely bruised from getting hit twice in one day. We took off after school so he could nurse his wounds with a late lunch, or early dinner, at Sonic. Personally, I think the chicks on roller skates cheered him up more than the food.

At about four thirty, he drove home, and I headed back to school. Tate had cross-country practice this afternoon. I'd checked with Jess Cullen, the captain, earlier today, and Tate was supposed to be trying out for her place back on the cross-country team.

Walking up to the girls' locker-room door, I stood outside and waited. Slipping my hands into my pockets and leaning my head back against the wall, I enjoyed the calm before the storm.

God, I've missed this.

My father crossed my mind briefly, but he almost seemed unimportant now. Like, why the hell had I given him so much of my attention in the first place?

When a girl walked out, hair wet and carrying a gym bag, I knew it was time. The ladies might still be cleaning up, but they should be done with their showers, at least.

Not that they had anything I hadn't seen before, some of them close up, but there was a fine line between a prank and getting myself arrested.

Walking through the door, I turned left and rounded the corner. There were several rows, just like the men's locker room, so I stalked down the aisle, peering in every line of lockers and scanning for the sunshine blonde.

I heard hair dryers going and talking coming from the back, so there weren't too many girls left getting dressed.

But there were definitely some gasps and quick movements to cover themselves.

One girl jerked her shirt up to cover her bra but then lowered it again when she registered who I was. Her lips twisted up as she scanned me up and down. I did a double take, since she looked like she knew me. Like *knew me* knew me, but I couldn't remember at the moment. The past year had been a jumble, and I'd rarely gone back for seconds with anyone. I could've tapped that. She was hot. I probably would have, but I wouldn't be able to say if it was a month or a year ago.

Coming up on the next aisle, I halted, my stomach flip-flopping.

Tate was at her locker, naked except for a towel.

For a second, I thought I couldn't have planned the timing better. And then I remembered that it couldn't have been worse timing. My dick was like a goddamn compass pointing straight to her.

Hardening my eyes and narrowing my brow, I spoke up, ready to put her in her fucking place.

"Get out. Tatum stays," I ordered the room.

Everyone squealed or sucked in a quick breath, and Tate's head snapped up, eyes wide. She clutched her towel like I had the power to rip it off of her with my mind.

If only . . .

Everyone scurried away, and I was grateful that they cleared out without drama. Maybe they went outside or a few rows over to give us some privacy, but all I cared about was that they were gone and Tate didn't have a lifeline.

She was isolated.

"Are you kidding me?" she yelled, her face twisted up in beautiful anger as I approached her slowly.

"Tatum?" My body raged with heat shooting down my arms and legs. "I wanted to make sure I had your attention. Do I have it?"

She licked her lips and breathed through her teeth. Even her mouth, tensed up in frustration, looked full of fight.

"Say what you have to say. I'm naked here, and I'm about to scream. This is going too far, even for you!"

Never too far. There was no limit to how high I could fly from feeding off her.

She'd stopped retreating, and I briefly wondered why. But instead of stopping myself, I couldn't help but get a little closer.

We stood there a moment, neither one of us willing to back off, and the heat rolled off her every time her chest rose and fell.

And then I saw it.

Her eyelids fluttered slightly, her breath caught, and she wouldn't look at me. Not out of fear but out of embarrassment. She was ashamed of something.

Oh, Jesus.

That flash of want on her face. That's what it was.

And, fuck it, I wanted that moment, too.

Roaming her body with my eyes, I took in the caramel tone of her tanned skin and couldn't help but wonder what it would look like covered with sweat. The curve of her neck as it met her shoulder, the water droplets in the dip of her collarbone, her full tits nearly bursting out of the towel—everything got me hard.

Goddamn it. Get a fucking grip.

I brought my gaze back up to meet hers, and forced myself to see her as the enemy she was.

I'm done giving them my attention.

"You sabotaged my party last week." I got in her face, but she stood her ground. "And you assaulted my friend. Twice. Are you actually trying to assert some force in this school, Tatum?"

In my head, she was Tate. Always. But I couldn't call her that now. It was a nickname for family and friends, and we were neither.

Her eyes, the perfect blend of fire and ice, sharpened on me. "I think it's about time, don't you?"

"On the contrary." I leaned my shoulder into the lockers to her side. "I've moved on to more interesting pastimes than punking you, believe it or not. It's been a very peaceful year without your smug, I'm-too-good-for-everyone-else fucking face around these halls."

And that was true. It had been peaceful. Like, death kind of peaceful.

"What? Are you, big bad Jared, feeling threatened?"

What the fuck?

Now that pissed me off.

I bounded off the lockers and caged her in between my arms.

"Don't touch me," she blurted out, and I bit back a grin. She wasn't looking at me again.

I moved my head like a snake, trying to catch her eyes.

Wet strands of hair stuck to her face, and I inhaled her slowly like she was a piece of meat and I was starving. "If I ever lay my hands on you," I threatened in a low voice, "you'll want it."

That fucking scent. It was like some kind of flower and kiwis. "Do you?" I taunted. "Want it, I mean?"

She paused, looking a little surprised, a little confused, and then a whole lot pissed. "I'm bored." Her tone was uncertain but her eyes were resolved. "Are you going to tell me what you want or what?"

"You know, this new attitude you came back with? It surprised me. You used to be a pretty dull target. All you'd do was run away or cry. Now you've got some fight in you. I was prepared to leave you alone this year. But now . . ." I trailed off.

She smirked. "What will you do? Trip me in class? Spill OJ on my shirt? Spread rumors about me so I don't get any dates? Or maybe you'll up your game to cyberbullying. Do you really think any of it bugs me anymore? You can't scare me."

Baby, I've already got you.

At least, I thought I did. She was talking some serious shit. Sure, she'd started branching out before she went to France, but I figured it was all a part of leaving the country. She'd felt she was safe. Hell, she had been safe, I guess. Not much I could do from where I was.

But now she was back.

I braced a hand over her head, against the lockers, and leaned in. "Do you think you're strong enough to take me on?" I asked, part of me hoping she'd rise to the challenge and another part of me hoping she'd stay down.

"It's on." And that promise floated in the air like the words "You've won the lottery."

Hell, yes.

"Tatum Brandt!"

We both jumped out of our own little world and looked to the end of the row, where Coach Syndowski and about half of the cross-country team stared at us.

Oh, shit.

I almost laughed at the sheer luck.

Tate in her towel. Me hovering close. I couldn't have planned it better, and I was a little ashamed that I didn't predict this twist.

This wasn't going to look good on her they're-not-taking-my-senior-year game plan.

"Coach!" Tate gasped, grappling at her towel and making it look like we were guilty of something other than talking.

Smooth, Tate.

But my amusement was short-lived when I saw girls snapping pictures with their cell phones. My stomach hollowed out immediately.

No, no, no. . . . goddamn it.

Tate was mine, to do with what I wanted. And I did not want pictures of her in a towel texted to the whole goddamn school!

"There are other places for you two to do this." The coach's voice sounded like she should be wagging her finger and sending us to bed without dinner. "Mr. Trent?" She scolded me with her eyes. "Leave!"

And I buried my anger about the pictures and walked out just as I'd come in. Like I fucking owned the place.

CHAPTER 12

Days later, I was experiencing more ups and downs than a damn roller coaster. Tate completely aware of my presence and cringing every time she saw me—going up! Douche bags trying to fist-bump me for screwing her, like she was some skanky slut that would throw down anywhere—going down.

Motherfucking cell phone, Internet, technology, and shit!

And, worst of all, I actually felt guilty.

I should've been thrilled. Especially since she had transferred into one of my classes yesterday, and I could fuck with her anytime now.

But things were different this year, and that photo hadn't helped. Guys wanted her. Like, wanted her so badly that no amount of shit I spewed about her eating boogers, having lice, or even dissecting human cadavers in her home would dispel it.

Screw it. There wasn't much I could do on that front anymore, and why would I want to? Why did I care if she dated or not? I didn't.

It simply bugged the shit out me to have a nearly naked picture of her zooming through cyberspace.

Tate would assume I'd planned the whole thing, and she'd know that I would be thrilled about her humiliation. Let her, then. It worked to my advantage.

But that didn't mean that I was happy or okay with it.

"Toni, baby. Come with me." I hooked Toni Vincent, cheer captain, by the elbow and led her outside the double doors of the gym.

"Oh, look who's talking to me after weeks and weeks." Her sarcastic tone was playful but annoyed.

She and I had hooked up a couple of times last year, and while she was confident and fun, I wasn't in it for a relationship. She tried to push that shit.

She was cocky, though, and she knew how to work her tough streak. I admired that about her.

"We're better when we don't talk," I mumbled as I backed her into the wall.

She didn't want to give me an inch, but I saw the small smile peek out before she lowered her green eyes. When she looked back up, her gaze was steady. "So, what do you want?"

"The Cheer blog," I stated. "The picture of Tatum and me? Take it down."

"Why should I?" she sneered. "It's getting a lot of hits."

"Because I'm telling you to," I ordered, not flirting or pretending in the least. "Today."

And I left her there, knowing she'd do it.

Later that day, I made my way to my final class, Themes in Film in Literature. I'd signed up for any courses I could take from Penley this semester. She was sweet, and I felt worse about my behavior toward her than any other teacher last year. It was the teachers who went the extra mile with me that got my respect, and after my dick behavior with her last fall, I'd decided to seize any opportunity I could to show her I was a good student. Or at least a nice guy.

Her classes, while she tried, were my least favorite, though. I hated literature and writing, and definitely hated expressing myself in public when it didn't involve some Patrón or a fast car.

But I looked forward to this class most of all now. Tate sat two seats in front of me, and I could drill a hole into the back of her head the entire class.

"I'm trying to get into Columbia, premed. What about you?" Tate asked Ben Jamison, who sat next to her, and I couldn't help but eavesdrop on the conversation from behind them.

"I'm applying to a few places," Ben answered. "I have no head for math or science, though. It'll be business for me."

And business is what exactly? Greek literature?

"Well, I hope you like some math. Business goes with economics, you know?" Tate echoed my thoughts, and I snorted when Ben looked over at her, eyes wide and clearly confused.

I chewed on my pen to keep from laughing at the dumb-ass.

Tate's back stiffened, and I knew that she knew I was listening.

"So," she continued, ignoring me, "you're on the Homecoming Committee, right?"

"Yeah. You coming?" Ben asked, and I stopped breathing as I waited for her response.

Ben might try to ask her. Maybe he was gauging whether she was interested in someone else. I remembered he was interested in her freshman year, but he was put down pretty easily. Once he heard about the Stevie Stoddard rumor, the one I started about Tate losing her virginity to the grimiest kid in school, he didn't mention her again. He was weak and he was a follower.

But . . . girls loved him. Why? I have no idea. He seemed about as boring as a church movie night. He was nice, though. The guy you brought home to Mom.

"We'll see," Tate answered. "Have you booked a band, or is there a DJ?"

"A band would be nice, but they tend to play one genre of music, so it's hard to please everyone. We'll have a DJ. I think that's what everyone decided. He'll keep the party going with a good mix: pop, country . . ."

Okay, lesson on Tate and music. If fans do anything less than carve the band's name into their skin, then the band isn't worth listening to. Any music that involves more than jumping around and banging your head is about as exciting as Kenny G to her.

Well, to me, too. That's one area we could see eye to eye.

"Oh . . . pop and country? Can't go wrong there." She tried to sound sincere, and for a bubblehead like Ben Jamison it probably worked, but I could smell the cover-up.

Unable to hold back the snicker, I buried my face in my phone when she turned around to glare at me.

But when I didn't look at her, she turned back around.

"So, you like pop and country?" she addressed Ben again, and I found myself tapping my pen in irritation.

Where the hell is Penley?

"Mostly country," I heard Ben answer.

She just nodded at him, hopefully realizing that they didn't have anything in common.

"You know," she continued, "I heard we get to watch *The Sixth Sense* in here this semester. Have you seen it?"

"Oh, yeah. A long time ago, though. I didn't get it. I'm not a big fan of those thriller-mystery-type movies. I like comedies. Maybe she'll let us watch *Borat*."

"Hey, Jamison?" I interrupted, very much done listening to Tate trying to get in this guy's pants. "If you like Bruce Willis, *Unbreakable* is a good one. You should give it a shot. . . . you know, if you're looking to change your mind about thrillers, that is."

There. Now Tate could get back to better things. Like shutting up.

Tate loved Bruce Willis. She liked action movies and thrillers.

And I wanted her to remember that I knew that shit about her.

"All right, class." Mrs. Penley finally walked in. "In addition to the packet I am handing out, Trevor is giving you a template of a compass. Please write your name at the top, but leave the areas surrounding north, east, south, and west blank."

The sound of shuffling papers filled the room, the assembly line of education hard at work. Papers and packets spilled down the rows as each student snatched one up like it was their ticket out of Dodge, and they all had somewhere to go.

"Okay." Mrs. Penley clapped her hands together. "The packets I gave you are lists of films where important monologues occurred. As we've already started discussing monologues and their importance in film and literature . . ."

My mind fogged over, and I heard the noise of Penley's voice but not the words. My eyes were trained on Tate's back, and, before I knew it, I was lost.

She had grabbed all of her hair and swept it up into a long ponytail, the wavy length cascading down her back like a waterfall, or a . . . leash.

I clenched my fists.

Jesus.

I couldn't see my dick, but I swear it swelled up to twice the size it normally did when I was horny.

Her army green Five Finger Death Punch T-shirt wasn't too tight, but it draped slimly over her slender back and complemented her sun-kissed skin. I was nearly bleeding to kiss the patch of skin on her shoulder, at the curve of her neck where the collar rubbed.

That would be a good place for a little tattoo, I thought.

The hair, the outfit—it was the perfect blend of good girl and bad girl, of salvation and danger.

There was no point in lying to myself. As much as I hated her, I wanted a taste of her.

Angry sex is pretty good, from what I hear.

"Go!" the teacher shouted, and I snapped my head up, blinking away the fantasy I'd gotten caught up in.

Oh, shit. Everyone rose from their seats and started walking around the room, carrying their papers and pens.

Was I supposed to get up? Dread gripped my heart as I glanced down at my jeans and then closed my eyes. *Yeah, that's not happening.*

And—fuck!—I couldn't stop the damn images of Tate, in my car, in the janitor's closet, in my bed . . .

There was no way I could stand up right now, so I took some deep breaths and tried thinking about boring shit, like British period pieces and Ferris wheels.

Luckily, Ivy Donner strode up and wrote her name on my paper under east and then my name on her paper. Good thing, because I had no idea what we were supposed to be doing, and my blood was coursing like lava. I was pissed.

Tate was a good distraction from my father, but I didn't need her arousing me so hard and fast that I couldn't even walk out of the room in a fire drill without embarrassing myself.

Concentrating on keeping a scowl on my face and my breathing even, I let two more girls fill in blanks on my paper as I tried to calm myself down. I guess we were supposed to find partners on a compass and switch names for each of the cardinal directions or something. Whatever.

"Mrs. Penley, I'm missing a north. Is it all right if I make a three-some with two others?" I heard Tate ask from the front of the room.

Some people snorted, while others laughed. I didn't do either. I just tried not to look at her or picture her in a threesome, so I could lose this fucking hard-on.

"Hey, Tate," Nate Dietrich called out, his tone husky. "I'll do a threesome with you. My compass always points north."

"Thanks, but I think your right hand will get jealous," she shot back, and the entire class laughed for her and not at her this time.

"Does anyone need a north?" Mrs. Penley shouted out, interrupting the banter.

I looked down at my paper to see I had that space blank, too. But I said nothing. The last thing I wanted to do was help her out.

But then I saw Ben, two seats ahead of me on the left, erasing his north, and I shook my head, determined to be an idiot, I guess.

"She can be my north," I said as calmly as possible.

I had to hand it to Ben. He'd made a dick move, but he wanted Tate, and he was going after her.

Why couldn't I just let it go?

"Well, Tate. Go ahead, then," Mrs. Penley held out her hand, motioning for Tate to sit down.

She didn't look at me, only slammed down in her seat and hovered over her paper, clearly plotting my death. I grinned, basking in her hatred and feeling in control again.

Now I was ready for round two.

CHAPTER 13

"Oh, look. It's the dog . . . and Madman."

I jerked my head up off the grass, spying K.C. walking up Tate's walkway next door. Madman and I had just finished a walk and then collapsed on my front lawn after some man-to-man combat involving his teeth and my gloved hand.

"You know, I can't decide which one of you has the better manners." She carried plastic bags filled with what looked like food but stopped before she reached Tate's front steps. "At least he doesn't shit on people." She jerked her chin at Madman.

K.C. reminded me of that blond chick on *The Vampire Diaries* that runs around acting like every problem in the entire universe has something to do with her.

Yeah, don't judge. Madoc likes the show, not me.

The point is some people think they have a leading role when really they're just supporting cast.

"K.C.?" I leaned back on my elbows and shot her a lazy and confident grin. "You know what's worse than seeing how mean I can be?"

She sighed and jutted her hip out like I was wasting her time. "What?"

"Seeing how nice I can be." My voice floated like silk across the lawn and straight between her legs.

Her sassy expression fell and she looked a little lost. She was probably trying to figure out if I was flirting, or maybe she was just trying to remember her own fucking name.

I laughed to myself.

Yeah, that shut her up.

I didn't have much tolerance for . . . well, most people, but I really hated cattiness. If a girl had to scrunch up her nose and pinch her eyebrows together at the same time just to talk, then she was perfect for the kind of activities that didn't require any talking.

K.C. bolted up the stairs to Tate's house and rang the doorbell like a legion of zombies was after her.

My chest shook with the mental image as I crashed back to the ground and closed my eyes.

The afternoon sun was waning, and the peaceful lull between the nine-to-fivers getting home and eating dinner had commenced. I loved this time of day.

The light to the west created a kaleidoscope of oranges and greens behind my eyelids, and I absorbed the delusion of this neighborhood that I existed around but not in.

Madman licked my hand, and I returned the gesture with a scratch behind his ears. Tate opened her front door; muffled voices. Lawn mower sounded down the street. Cars passed by. Kids called in to dinner.

And I let myself be a part of it for a few moments.

I loved our street and always would. Every little house had its secrets and that's what made it so perfect. I could laugh at Mr. Vanderloo across the street, because he snuck out to his garage every night and smoked pot after his family went to sleep. Mrs. Watson, three houses down, liked her husband to dress up as a UPS man and deliver things to her door. And then he'd deliver her to the bedroom.

Even Tate's dad had a secret.

Over the time we spent together while she was gone, I discovered that he still ate at Mario's every Thursday night by himself. I remembered Tate saying that the Italian restaurant was where her parents had had their first date. I didn't know if she knew he still did that.

My leg vibrated, interrupting my musings, and I reached into my pocket to grab my phone.

Narrowing my eyes in irritation, I touched the screen and answered. "Yes?" No need to be polite. I knew who it was.

"Hello. I have a collect call for you from an inmate at Stateville Prison. Will you accept?"

No.

"Yes."

I waited for the operator to switch over, feeling like I had been pulled out of Neverland and was now surrounded by a dozen soldiers trapping me in at gunpoint.

I knew why my father was calling. He'd called only once before, and it was the same fucking reason this time.

"When you come up tomorrow . . . put money in my account," he told, not asked, me.

I took a deep breath. "And why would I do that?"

"You know why," he growled. "Don't act like you have a choice."

I didn't have the money to give him. I may not have a choice, but I had a problem.

"Then I'll need to earn it, and I can't do that until tomorrow night." It was too late to get in on a race tonight. "I'll be up on Sunday instead."

And he hung up.

I closed my eyes and squeezed the phone, wanting it to be his face, his heart, and his power.

The money I gave him—to stop calling Jax—was supposed to be a onetime thing. But it hadn't been.

He'd give Jax a break, but he always called again.

And I kept paying, just so Jax could have that break.

Don't act like you have a choice. His words pierced my ears as if I could still feel the pain of that day. They were the same words he said to me before he shoved me down the basement stairs.

Right before I'd found Jax with them.

Sitting up, I looked around my street.

Goddamn him.

Trying to bring back the calm, I focused on the neighborhood view again. The square green lawns looked jagged around the edges now, the green less vibrant. All of the houses seemed dead, and my breathing started scaring me.

And then I looked up.

Tate sat angled outside her French doors, her feet propped up on the railing. I focused on her. The rest of her was hidden, but I watched her, anyway. Knowing she was there. Feeling the energy that always rolled off her. Call it hate. Call it lust. It wasn't love, though.

But it was enough, and I needed it.

The breath leaving my body got quieter and quieter. It started pouring in and out like water instead of syrup, and I finally stood up and headed back into the house.

Dialing up Zack Hager, who organized the races at the Loop, I clenched and unclenched my fist, trying to get the needles out.

"Hey, can I race tomorrow night?"

"Well," he paused, "I've got three races going already. But Jones just backed out, so Diaz needs an opponent."

"Put me on the roster, then." I'd need the money. After I bought the car with the money from my grandfather's house, my mother had made good on her promise to tie up the rest of the money in a college account. The only cash I had was what I made from my job, and that wasn't enough to keep Thomas Trent in his cigarettes and extra snacks.

After I hung up with Zack, I texted Madoc to get a party together at my house for that night, and pulled my car out of the garage to double-check the oil.

Since I didn't have anything else to distract me until the party started, I drove out to Weston to get my brother. His new foster parents were pretty cool about letting him spend time overnight at my house, so I brought him up for parties and races sometimes.

"Look at baby Jared!" Madoc shouted as we climbed out of the car. Madoc had arrived at my place early to set up, and from the looks of it, the party had already started.

Laughing, Jax rammed his shoulder into Madoc's chest. "Yeah, I hear you like young boys."

"Only if they're as pretty as you, princess."

And I rolled my eyes as Madoc wrapped his arms around my brother and dry humped him from behind.

I had no idea why Madoc called Jax baby Jared. It had nothing to do with our looks. Our eyes were different, our hairstyles were different, and we both had different personalities. Jax was wild, never afraid to smile and seize the moment.

We were almost the same height, though. He was a little leaner, but he was still only sixteen.

I'd better enjoy the female attention while I could, because in a few years, women weren't going to even notice me in the room next to him.

Not that I cared. I wanted Jax to have everything, because he deserved it.

I scanned the neighborhood as I walked up the driveway and took in the glow of life and noise around me. When my father had called earlier, the pulse of the street had decayed before my eyes. Everything looked sick.

But now, looking up at Tate's window, seeing her light on, the thump in my chest carried me higher.

"Hey, think we'll see some action tonight?" Madoc wrapped his arm around my neck and jerked his chin over to Tate's house.

He was referring to the last time she broke up my party.

I smiled, looking up at her window. "I think she's out of tricks."

And we strode into the loud frenzy of underage disorder known as my house.

"Oh, man, you know how to kiss," she gasped out as I left her mouth and kissed a trail to her neck.

This girl—she'd said her name was Sarah—seemed sweet but completely corruptible. Thankfully, no one had invited Piper, so I was left alone tonight to enjoy everything the party had to offer.

I pressed her up against the back of the bathroom door, and I was feeding like I wouldn't ever be satisfied.

I didn't know her. She went to school two towns over and showed up as a friend of a friend. Her hair was soft, her lips were softer, and she acted like she had a brain.

I'd spent about an hour getting drunk and catching glimpses of her moving to the music in her hot, strapless black dress, when I'd finally decided to make my move. It didn't take long to get her in here, and I wasn't in any hurry to get out, either.

My lips caressed her neck, sweet-smelling and smooth, as my hand glided down her slim body. Her nipple hardened as I lightly brushed it on my way down to her tight stomach.

I ran over her hip bone and reached behind to take a handful of her ass, and pulled her up to meet my cock as I kissed her slow and deep. The taste was good. She wasn't drunk, and she didn't smoke.

"I'm not a slut," she said softly, and I held my head up to look at her.

Yeah, I'm used to this part. Girls usually felt guilty about being too easy, enforcing the double standard that a guy could enjoy sex but not a girl.

And what's worse? Girls were the ones who perpetuated this standard. Guys didn't use the word "slut." We didn't judge. She didn't need to reassure me of anything.

She looked up at me thoughtfully. "I just . . . want to get lost for a while."

And then she dropped her gaze, like some story was going to break through her eyes that she didn't want me to see. I knew how she felt. I didn't want anyone to know mine, either.

"I'm good at getting lost," I offered. "Come here."

Our lips came back together again, and my hand dipped slowly between her legs, losing myself in the moment I wanted. The story behind my eyes that I didn't want anyone else to see.

"Jared?"

I hear her whisper in my ear, and want to crawl up inside her voice.

"Jared?" She takes my hand and guides it up her thighs to her heat. "Do you feel me?"

God, her whisper is desperate. She's raspy and breathless, as if she's lost all control and will spill over the edge. Like the tiniest thread is holding desire and tears at bay, because at any moment she will break and beg for what she wants. The ache is torture.

I open my eyes and see the blue ones I was hoping for, wanting me. Her lip trembles, and a light sheen of sweat makes her face glow. She is fire and need in the most beautiful girl I have ever seen.

"Tate?" My voice cracks, not believing she's letting me touch her like this.

"Do you feel how much I want you? You. Always you, baby," she pleads,

and rests her forehead on my chin, and I close my eyes, my blood boiling violently with the need to live in this moment forever.

My skin feels electrified as her hand rests on my jeans, over my dick that I can't seem to get to stay down around her.

"You want me, too," she moans, the tip of her tongue leaving a wet, hot trail over my jaw. "I can feel it. Don't ruin us, baby. I love you."

My eyes snap open, and I thread my fingers through her hair and hold her head up to face me. "You love me?" I ask wildly.

She doesn't love me. She can't.

"Always you. Always yours. Now take it," she orders.

I can't stand the hunger anymore, and I seize what's mine. I eat up her sweet lips, and we melt in sweat and heat, and want nothing except to dive into this dangerous urgency for each other.

I want it all. All of her.

"Are you okay?" a voice, strong and clear, broke through.

I blinked and found myself still in the bathroom, forehead resting on the shoulder of another girl. My eyelashes felt thick, and there was a blur.

What the fuck?

Was I crying?

Jesus Christ. Motherfucker!

"Are you okay?" she asked again.

Standing up straight, I looked down at the girl I'd been about to have sex with. Brown eyes stared back at me.

Nausea rolled viciously through my stomach, the alcohol shifting my body from a pleasant fog to agony.

"No, I'm not okay," I muttered, and turned to grip the sink ledge. "Just go on out. I feel sick."

"Do you want me to get someone?"

"Just go!" I shouted, and she slipped out the door quickly, while I closed my eyes and hardened every muscle in my body, willing the sickness to disappear.

But after a few seconds, I was fucking done. Here I was, holed up in the bathroom, practically in fucking tears. And why?

Out of control. That's what I was. Always out of control.

Picking my toothbrush out of the holder, I jammed it down my throat and emptied everything I'd eaten today into the toilet. Most of it was the alcohol of the past four hours, and it burned like hell as I gripped the sink to the side and leaned over, retching.

"Jared, you okay?" someone burst in.

"Goddamn it!" I yelled. "Can't people just leave me the fuck alone?" I spit up the rest of what was coming up from my stomach and looked over at whoever was at the door.

Shit.

"Jax," I started but couldn't finish. He was shrinking away.

He didn't speak again. Only looked away and backed out of the bathroom, closing the door.

And in that moment, I was no better than our fucking father.

I knew the look on his face. I'd seen it before. Hell, I'd even worn it myself. Too scared to meet my eyes. Leaving as quietly as you came. Trying to remain off the radar of the drunk lunatic.

I gargled some mouthwash, yanked off my T-shirt, and collapsed against the bathroom wall to rest. I needed to calm down before I apologized to him. He couldn't see me like that again.

I stayed there a minute or two, trying to get my head straight and my stomach to settle.

But as I stood up to leave the room, the entire house went dead. Lights out, music off, and all I heard were the loud barks of pissed-off partyers.

"What the hell?" I felt my way out the bathroom door and to my bedroom.

Stumbling over the shit on my floor, I found a flashlight in the bedside table and switched it on.

It wasn't storming out, and we paid our bills on time. Why the hell was the electricity out?

Walking over to the window, I saw the Brandt's porch light on, so I knew it wasn't the neighborhood.

And then I saw Tate.

No. I zoned in on her like a bullet.

Her silhouette was behind her curtain, and I knew. I fucking knew what she did.

Powering down the stairs and through the drunken assholes falling and laughing around my house and yard, I darted out the back door, hopped on the AC unit, and jumped over the fence.

The key her father left me to watch over the house was still on my key ring, so I dug it out of my pants and charged through the back door, not caring if she heard me.

She'd find out soon enough that I was in the house, anyway.

God! I can't believe she cut the fucking electricity to my house.

My blood swirled like a cyclonic wind inside of me, but, believe it or not, it felt easy. This was where I was strong.

Was I supposed to be in here? No. What would I do or say when I got to her? I had no idea. But I wanted this fight.

Swinging myself around the banister, I barreled up the stairs and caught sight of Tate darting back into her room.

Is that a bat she's holding?

Yeah, that was gonna help. She wasn't safe from me, and now she knew it.

I swung open her door in time to see her try to make her escape through the French doors. "Oh, no, you don't!"

Turning around to face me, she tried to raise the bat, but I was on her before she even got ready to swing. Snatching it out of her hands, I charged into her space, hovering but not touching. Wave after wave of heat washed over me from the inch of air between us.

She was pissed, too, from the look in her eyes. But her breathing wasn't hard and deep. It was fast and shallow. She was scared.

"Get out! Are you crazy?" She tried to dart around me to get out of the room, but I stepped in front of her.

"You cut the electricity to my house." I kept my voice low and even. I didn't want her afraid of me. It's not like I would hurt her. But she had to know that one good turn deserved another.

"Prove it," she snipped.

Oh, baby. My face relaxed, and I orchestrated a very fake and creepy smile. She did not want to play with me like this.

"How'd you get in here?" she snapped. "I'll call the police!"

"I have a key," I responded, enjoying her crestfallen face.

"How do you have a key to *my* house?"

"You and your dad were in Europe all summer," I said, narrowing my eyes. "Who do you think got the mail? Your dad trusts me. He shouldn't have."

James Brandt, I was pretty sure, knew next to nothing about my relationship with his daughter. Tate didn't go whining about the state of affairs between us, because if she did, I was sure I'd be missing a couple of limbs.

"Get out," she ordered, disgust and ire written all over her face, and I clenched my fists.

Advancing on her until she was backed up against her French doors, I hovered down and let her know who was really in control here.

Lesson one, Tate. I don't do what I'm told. "You're a nosy bitch, Tatum. Keep your fucking ass on your own side of the fence."

She met my eyes, not blinking. "Keeping the neighborhood awake makes people irritable."

I almost laughed at her spunk. She was trying to prove what a fighter she could be, and I plastered both of my hands on each side of her head, letting her know that she wasn't even in my weight class.

Why she didn't squirm out from under my arm, I have no idea. I half expected her to. She stood her ground, and, unfortunately, that was hard on the both of us, I think. Eye to eye, nose to nose, tasting her breath, the room crowded with tension or hatred. Maybe both, or maybe it was something else.

Thank God she was the one to look away first. Her eyes dropped, and for a moment I thought I had her.

Until . . . her eyes started roaming over me, and I fucking stiffened. Everywhere.

I watched as her heated gaze blazed a path over the lantern tattoo on my upper arm and down to the script on my torso, over my bare stomach and up my naked chest.

And goddamn, her eyes felt good.

What the hell are you doing, Tate?

Images from my daydream in the bathroom poured in, and my own gaze started to fall down over her uncontrollably.

I enjoyed a great view down her black tank top and over the tops of her perfect breasts. I liked that I could see a sliver of her stomach where the waistband of her little boxer shorts was rolled over. I loved thinking about what she'd sound like moaning my name.

But I hated that looking into her eyes was the best view of all.

She saw me, the real me, and it was the only time I actually felt like I existed.

But she also saw all of the ugliness and confusion.

She saw everything that made me a loser.

And that's when I knew what she was doing. She was playing a game with me. Looking at me, getting me to nearly lose it.

Taking a deep breath, I turned away to walk out. "No one else is complaining, so why don't you shut up and leave it alone?"

"Leave the key," she shot back, and I stopped.

I exhaled a bitter laugh. "You know, I underestimated you. You haven't cried yet, have you?"

"Because of the rumor you started this week? Not a chance."

Yep, she thought those pictures were my idea.

"Please. Like I even have to resort to spreading rumors. Your cross-country pals did that. And their pictures. Everyone drew their own conclusions." And I walked back over to her and got in her face. "But I'm boring you. I guess I have to step up my game."

The threat hung in the air between us.

Her lips pursed, and her eyes must've burned. They were shooting flames.

She was ready to lose it. In 3, 2, 1 . . .

"What did I ever do to you?" she screamed.

I shrugged, not willing to tell her the truth. "I don't know why you ever thought you did something. You were clingy, and I got sick of putting up with it, is all."

She wasn't clingy. She was dishonest and unreliable.

"That's not true. I wasn't clingy." She choked on a breath. "You were over at my house as much as I was at yours. We were friends." She looked at me with such sadness. Her face was tight, and tears pooled in her eyes.

All a fucking lie.

I smiled, but it burned with more anger than amusement. "Yeah, keep livin' the dream."

"I hate you!"

And there it was.

"Good!" I shouted, bearing down on her, my heart beating wildly. "Finally! Because it's been a long time since I could stand the sight of you." And I slammed the palm of my hand against the wall near her head.

She flinched, and my heart did a nosedive straight to my stomach. *Shit.*

I'd scared her.

Why the hell did I just do that?

I backed off an inch.

I'd wanted to hit something, but not her. And I didn't want her to think I'd even come close to doing that. Ever. I'd never hit a girl and would never hit one in my life.

Goddamn it. She wasn't looking at me now.

Things were never this bad between us.

She used to turn tail and run. Before France. Or before she knew she was leaving for France, anyway.

And when she'd bow out, I'd power down.

I could be satisfied.

But now . . . now I wasn't the stronger one. She was going head-to-head with me and taking the challenge.

We both stood there, and she finally looked up to meet my eyes. Something passed in the blue ocean of hers. Despair? Regret?

And, finally, resolution.

My eyes were still trained on her, waiting for her to say something, when she turned around to look out the window.

"Oh, look. It's the police," she said in a light voice. "I wonder why they're here."

I looked over her shoulder to see two black-and-whites, lights flashing and parked in front of my house. A couple of officers climbed up the incline into my yard, looking around at the chaos.

Son of a bitch.

There was no time to call them when I entered her house. She must've filed a complaint earlier.

Right now you're looking at her like you want to tie her up and give her a big, fat spanking.

Madoc's stupid assessment was true. She definitely deserved a huge spanking.

"I promise you will be in tears by next week." I was going to do what I had to do. My tone was calm, decisive, and final, and I left the room, already making my plans.

"Leave the key," she shouted after me.

But I never do what I'm told.

CHAPTER 14

After I cleared everyone out of my house, the cops wrote me a huge-ass ticket and called my mother.

But it all affected me about as much as war in the Middle East.

Trouble with the cops? Old news.

Getting squeezed for cash I didn't have? Child's play.

Jax and Madoc helped me clean up the house before my mom got home, and then I showered and went to bed, letting Jax crash in the spare bedroom.

Tate was the only thing on my mind right now. Any inkling that what I was thinking of doing might be going too far was shoved out of my head. Did she really set out to hurt me? No. Was I setting out to hurt her? Definitely.

But it was all a game.

She didn't care, and anything we shared years ago was nothing to her. Every time I pushed her, it wasn't really about making her feel bad. It was about proving to myself that my head and heart weren't in her control.

And if I could rip her from my head and my heart, kill everything good I felt about her, then I was strong.

"Hey, K.C.," I walked up to the concession counter at Spotlight Cinemas, where Tate's friend worked. "How's it going?"

She looked up from her book and narrowed her eyes. "Don't talk to me, shit-for-brains."

"Ouch." I smiled and gave her a condescending nod. "Good for you."

K.C. was Tate's best friend. Her only friend, really. Winning her over, possibly seducing her, would tear Tate apart, and I was ignoring the voice in my head that kept screaming at me to stop this.

This was going too far.

I was about to use someone to hurt a girl I once loved? Who the hell did I take lessons in pettiness from?

Tate's arrival back home brought ups and downs. My ups were better than I'd felt in a year, but my downs had me clawing at the fucking walls again. K.C. was collateral damage.

I could do this.

"Can I have a large popcorn and a Coke, please?"

K.C. rolled her eyes and walked toward the food.

I strolled down the stand to where she was shoveling popcorn into a bucket.

Here we go.

"So, are you heading to the Loop tonight with Liam?" I asked about her boyfriend.

Without lifting her eyes from her task, she shook her head. "How often do you see me there, Jared?" she asked, annoyed. "A bunch of little boys moaning and groaning about the size of their dicks—oh, excuse me; I mean, the size of their engines—and I'm supposed to find that fun?"

"Take it easy." I held up my hands. "I just thought that since Liam was racing, you'd be there to support him."

Now she looked up. "He's racing?"

"Yeah," I said, trying to keep my tone nonchalant. "He's racing Nate Dietrich. He didn't tell you?"

Lifting her chin, looking none too pleased, she slammed the popcorn on the counter and turned around to get the soda.

Her boyfriend, while a pretty nice guy, was also pretty damn pathetic. He's the type of guy that would give up top-secret information in the first five minutes of torture. I had no respect for him.

And with all of his weaknesses, I also found out one more. Several weeks ago at the Loop one night, I saw that he had a girl on the side.

And that was my ticket in with K.C. Break up her relationship, get her in my corner, and piss off Tate.

"Sorry," I offered. "He probably knows it's not your scene. It gets pretty crazy out there. Some girls love it. Some hate it," I mumbled, trying to sound like the conversation bored me. But on the inside, I was laughing. I couldn't have predicted K.C.'s reaction better.

She handed me my food, refusing to speak, and I gave her a twenty and collected my change.

Grabbing the shit I didn't intend to eat and walking toward a theater I didn't intend to stay in, I turned around and lifted my hopefully innocent-looking eyebrows.

"K.C.?" She looked up when I said her name. "You live on Evans, right?"

"Yeah."

"It's on my way. I'd be happy to give you a lift if you want to surprise him tonight."

My hands were sweaty, or maybe it was the condensation from the drink cup, but I was actually nervous. If she refused—or called Liam to confirm the race—I'd be up shit creek.

"I don't think so."

My stomach sank, but I shrugged my shoulders and offered a tight smile, anyway.

"It's just a ride, K.C. Tate and I have an unusual relationship. I'm not like that with everyone, and you know it." I held her green eyes, seeing the wheels turning. Should she or shouldn't she? She was thinking about it, and that was a good sign. "But okay," I relented. "See you at school."

Walking away, I could almost hear K.C. make up her mind.

"What time are you heading out?" she called after me.

Coming to an abrupt stop like I hadn't expected her to change her mind, I turned around. "Leaving about seven thirty."

"All right." She nodded, her tone a little nicer. "Seven thirty. It's 1128 Evans," she clarified.

"A thank-you would be nice," I teased.

"Yeah, it would." And she returned to her duties.

Once inside the theater, I handed my food to some preteens and headed out the back exit.

"What?"

K.C.'s shriek was probably picked up on Russian sonar, and Madoc and I just stood back to watch the show.

"K.C.!" Her boyfriend—or maybe ex-boyfriend now—squirmed his way out the redhead's arms and rushed up to his girlfriend.

We'd made it to the Loop right on time. I even had Madoc go ahead of me to text and confirm that Liam was at the races tonight and with his side piece.

"Are you kidding me?" K.C. yelled.

"Please—" Liam started, but Madoc cut him off.

"It's not what it looks like?" he finished for Liam, laughing.

"Shut up, goddamn it!" Liam barked at Madoc, while my friend laughed even harder.

Liam reached for K.C., but she pulled away. "Don't touch me. I trusted you!"

"Dude, hands off." I stepped in.

Liam wouldn't look at me but kept his hands to himself now. "Why are you here?" he stammered at K.C.

But K.C. ignored the question. "Who is she?" she looked at the redhead leaned up against Liam's Camaro.

"Please," the redhead, who didn't seem fazed at all, pleaded sarcastically. "We've been seeing each other for two months. Not so bright, are you?"

K.C. was about to lose it, so I took her gently by the crook of her arm and led her backwards, out of the mess.

"Would you take me home, please?" Her breathing was ragged, and she looked embarrassed and heartbroken.

I'm a dick.

"Yeah," I sighed, all of a sudden feeling really shitty. "I have to race first, but Madoc will let you sit in his car while you wait, okay? Give me ten minutes."

I nodded to Madoc, who rolled his eyes, probably wondering what the hell I was up to.

After the race, I drove K.C. home, probably not feeling as bad as her but definitely not feeling good.

Nothing about what I was doing was right, but, fuck me, it was the only plan I had to shatter Tate's world.

"K.C., I'm really sorry."

"Did you know about this?" She used her fingers to wipe away the tears and mascara streaks.

I almost felt like throwing up. "Absolutely not," I lied. "If I did, I wouldn't have told you. Sorry—it's a guy code." And that part was the truth. Unless the girlfriend of a friend is also your friend, then you don't interfere.

"Ugh," she grunted, more angry than sad now.

"Hey, look. Believe it or not, I am really sorry you're hurting," I offered as I pulled up in front of her house. "Go eat chocolate or binge shop online. Whatever girls do to feel better. And I promise to kick his ass in a race next weekend. You can even come along to watch if you feel up to it."

But my joke didn't lighten the mood. "You think you're so much better than him?"

And even though I knew she made a valid point, I did think I was better than Liam. I don't know why. Maybe because I saw Liam as spineless. If I lied, it was for a good reason. Not just because I was too weak to let go of what I no longer wanted.

But I was, wasn't I? I couldn't let Tate go.

"Yes," I finally answered. "I don't cheat on girlfriends, because I don't give the impression that I want a relationship. Look," I started, taking off my seat belt. "I may go through girls faster than gum, but it's not because I feel that they're worthless or disposable, okay? It's all me. I know I'm not good for anything more, so why let people in?"

And for once I wasn't playing a part for K.C. I told her the truth.

I wasn't trying to get into her pants, and I didn't care about her or what she thought about me. For the first time in a long time, I was totally comfortable being honest with someone.

Her gaze was fixed out of the window. "I guess you'll never know," she almost whispered, as if to herself.

No, I do know, I thought to myself. I know very well what happens when you let people in.

"You should try letting go," I suggested, clearing my throat. "There's no reason to cry over someone who wasn't thinking about you when he was with someone else. You deserve better."

She sat there for a moment and finally offered me a tight smile.

"You're still a dick," she conceded as she got out of the car, but

I caught sight of a small grin on her face that told me she was just joking.

Over the next two days, I slowly weaseled my way into K.C.'s life, shooting her concerned texts and trying to appear sincere. I wasn't sure if she was disclosing our communication to Tate, but it was only a matter of time before I made sure Tate found out, anyway.

CHAPTER 15

"Thank you for the ride." K.C. unfastened the helmet and smiled down at me.

It was Monday night, and I'd just picked her up from work after she'd texted, asking for a ride.

When I got there, though, she started acting unnaturally affectionate. Rubbing her fingers through my hair, touching my arm. Familiarity we hadn't gotten to yet.

I looked behind her before she climbed on my motorcycle, and spied her ex with some of his friends inside the theater lobby, watching us.

And that's when I knew what she was doing.

I smiled, pretty proud of her for using me, actually.

And interested.

Tate had been giving me the evil eye today, and if I could continue to get under her skin while helping K.C. make her boyfriend jealous—without actually having to go that far with her—then I was comfortable.

I took the helmet out of her hands and gave her a quick peck on the cheek. "See you tomorrow."

She let out a tiny sigh with her smile.

K.C. was a good girl, and the knots in my stomach settled.

Firing the engine on my bike, I put on my helmet and sped off, not sure to where.

I never wanted to be home anymore.

Or maybe I always wanted to be home.

Tate was alone next door, and I couldn't help where my thoughts traveled. We were both kind of on our own—her dad out of the country, and my mom leaving me by myself most of the time—and my damn dirty mind always entertained ideas of shit I couldn't have with Tate. Every night we'd fall asleep less than fifty feet from each other, and the gnawing sensation in my head had me ready to scream.

All that wasted time.

After spending a couple of hours at the garage where I worked, hanging out with Madoc and doing some maintenance on my bike, I was finally satisfied that Tate was probably asleep. I wouldn't have to look at her bedroom, warmed by the bright light, and wonder what she was doing in there.

Or what she was wearing.

Stopping at a red light, I checked my rearview mirror and did a double take.

Is that . . . ?

A Honda S2K was behind me.

A white 2005 Honda S2K.

Shit.

My heart climbed up my throat.

I knew these guys, and I clenched the handlebars, trying to steady my nerves.

Idiot Vin Diesel wannabes from Weston that didn't know how to lose gracefully. I'd raced the owner of the car at the Loop last week and beat him. He'd made a big show about it being an unfair race, and, from the looks of it, he hadn't gotten over it.

They were the only car behind me, but they'd given me a wide berth.

The light turned to green, and as soon as I laid on the gas, the Honda did, as well.

Damn it. I shook my head. My fears proved true. *Not tonight.*

Slipping my phone out of the front pocket of my hoodie, I dialed Madoc.

"Hey," I said, glancing in my mirror again, "are you home yet?"

"No."

Slowing down for the stop sign, I spoke quickly. "Turn around and head to my house. Got a tail of *The Fast and the Furious* variety. May need some backup."

"I'll be there in five." And he hung up.

Fumbling, I shoved the phone back into my pocket. As I laid off the clutch, I revved the gas and sped off around the corner. A cold rush of wind hit my face, and I strangled the handlebars to keep my body glued to the bike.

Shit.

My heart was damn near pounding through my chest, but I didn't take my eyes off the road, even to look behind me.

I wasn't in a hurry to get there without Madoc backing me up, but I didn't want to risk that they'd start some shit with me still driving my bike, either.

They were in a car. I was the vulnerable one.

Racing up my driveway, I twisted my head around in time to see the Honda speeding to a screeching halt at my front curb.

Ryland Banks, the short, buzz-cut driver and owner of the car, got out right away.

Tate.

I darted my eyes to her house, fear gripping my insides, and I gritted my teeth with the urge to hit myself.

Why had I led them back here?

Tate was alone, and now she was unsafe. Who knew what kind of weapons these guys carried?

Yanking off my helmet, I charged down the lawn, cutting them off before they got any closer.

Everything I wanted to keep safe was behind me, and that's where it would stay.

I advanced. "Not sure what you're looking for, but it ain't here," I growled, bearing down on them.

"We want our money back," Ryland ordered like he had a leg to stand on.

"Get over it," I sneered. "You took the gamble, and you paid the price like everyone else." They tried to push into my space, but I kept my feet planted.

"It wasn't a fair race!" The other, taller and darker one used his pointer finger in my face like a tattletale at recess.

I snorted.

There were two kinds of stupid. Stupid people that got drunk and humped trees, and stupid people that just humped trees. The first one was Madoc. These guys were the latter.

"Yeah, you're right," I laughed. "Your car never stood a chance. Bring the right tires next time. This isn't street racing."

"Fuck you!" Ryland barked. He slammed me in the chest, and I lost my breath as I stumbled backwards.

Coming back up on him, I stared him down. "Get off my property."

Just then, I could make out the rumble of Madoc's GTO, and I immediately relaxed my shoulders a bit when he came into view, speeding down my street.

I didn't even think he turned off the car before he was out and running.

Thank God.

I wasn't afraid of these guys, by any means, but I wasn't stupid, either. Two against one, and all I had in my hand was my helmet for a weapon.

A vicious slam nearly knocked me off my feet, and an ache rocked my head.

Shit. I'd been hit.

No. Sucker punched, actually.

Cowardly motherfuckers.

They both rushed me, throwing fists in my face, and a million goddamn things were going at once.

Arms flying at me . . . crowding me . . . I'm about to fall . . .

My head was still ringing from the hit, and it took me too fucking long to get straight.

I launched my body forward, shoving my shoulder into the stomach of one of them and taking the fight to the ground.

Madoc must've gotten the other one, because I didn't have anyone else coming at me from behind.

My jaw clamped shut and air rushed in and out of my nose as I grabbed the guy—Ryland—by the neck and whipped him onto his back.

Grunts filled the air, and the grass, slippery with dew, made it hard as I tried to climb over him. It was a chilly night, but the sweat glided down my forehead like it was the middle of August.

I threw punch after punch, my knuckles burning with the impact. He brought his hands up, wrapping one of his fists inside the other and hammering down into my stomach.

I lost my breath, and he took the short reprieve to draw a switchblade out of his jeans and slice me across the bicep.

Goddamn it!

I whipped my body back, leaning away.

The hot sting of the cut quickly spread, and my arm turned cold. I realized it was the blood hitting the night air, cooling my skin.

But the rest of me was hot as fuck, my blood pumping so hard. I grappled for my helmet on the ground and slammed him over the top of the forehead with it.

Hard.

His knife fell to the ground, and he covered his bleeding hairline with shaky hands.

Damn coward.

I liked fighting, and I liked trouble, but pulling a fucking knife?

That made me want to damage more than just his window.

Standing up and gripping my arm to stop the blood flow, I carried the helmet over to his Honda and smashed his windshield until it was so splintered that it looked like it was crusted in a winter's worth of frost.

I walked back, tasting the blood in my mouth and hovering over the piece of shit on the ground. "You're not welcome at the Loop anymore." I meant for my voice to come off strong, but my breathing was still ragged.

And the damn blood from the cut was dripping off of my fingertips now. I probably needed stitches.

Madoc had already dumped the first guy, bloodied and unconscious, by the car and was now stepping over to get the other one off my lawn.

"Jared." I heard him say, almost a whisper.

I turned my eyes to him, but then saw he was concentrated on something else. Following his gaze toward the Brandts' yard, I stopped breathing.

Fucking. Hell.

Tate was standing there on the walkway leading up to her porch. Just standing there and staring at us. A little scared, a little confused, and in her goddamn, fucking underwear!

What the hell?

Madoc was here. Two other guys—although unconscious—were here.

My blood boiled and heat immediately rushed to my pants.

I hardened my jaw and breathed hard.

She wore a tight black band T-shirt and cotton boy-shorts underwear. Red. Fucking red.

She was covered, but just barely.

It didn't matter, though. You could still make out everything, and she was perfect. My heart was jackhammering so hard and fast at her skimpy attire that I just wanted to peel everything off her and sink my hands into her body here and now.

Was she trying to kill me?

Get in the fucking house, Tate! Jesus.

Then my eyes fell to the gun in her right hand.

A gun?

No.

I narrowed my eyes, forgetting her legs and her beautiful hair spilling around her.

She wasn't helping us. She wouldn't do that.

She was waiting for the cops or something.

Tate didn't give a shit, and she was just sticking her nose where it didn't belong. But then I blinked.

If she'd called the cops, I doubted she'd be walking around in her panties, carrying a gun.

Why the hell would she help us?

Maybe she didn't stalk out here in her underwear to taunt me. Maybe she was just in that much of a hurry.

But before I could even sift through my thoughts, she quirked an annoyed eyebrow and stomped back up her front porch and through the door to her house, giving me a great view of her ass.

Madoc laughed, and I shoved him in the shoulder before stalking off toward my house.

I had a hard-on and a bloody arm, and I wasn't sure what I needed first: stitches or a cold shower.

Madoc had threatened to call the cops, so Ryland and his friend sped away—broken windshield and all—while I woke up my mother.

I hated waking her—hated stressing her—but I was still technically a minor on her health insurance, so I needed her at the hospital. Madoc went home to nurse his bloody nose, and it took ten stitches and my mother bitching at me for two hours before I was able to make it to bed, too. By the time I woke up three hours later, I was in more knots than before I slept.

Tate with a fucking gun.

What the hell was her game?

Grabbing my phone off its charger, I shook off the voice in my head that told me to slow down.

Need my help today? I texted K.C.

It took her only a second to respond. **Help?**

Liam, I shot back. **Let's make him jealous.**

I leaned forward, resting my elbows on my knees, waiting for her answer.

I heard Tate's Bronco start up next door, and I checked the clock to see that it was still early.

The lab.

I'd seen Tate coming out of the chemistry lab in the mornings and some afternoons. She was probably competing in the Science Fair in the spring and needed to do research. It would look good on her college applications.

She was probably getting ready to apply to Columbia for next year. New York was always where she always wanted to go.

K.C. didn't text back, so I dropped the phone on the bed and went to the shower.

My arm was wrapped tight, but I still needed to get clean.

After my shower, I wrapped a towel around my waist and stopped short at the bathroom mirror, glimpsing my tattoos. I couldn't help but smile, remembering how my mother had yelled at me the night before.

Fighting! she screamed. *Getting arrested! And tattoos without my permission!* she'd said, as if that was the worst one of all.

I'd only laughed under my breath and laid my head back in the car, trying to sleep as she drove us home from the hospital.

I loved the tats, and I was going to get more. I wanted the scars on my back—the ones my father gave me—covered.

Walking back into my room, I dried my hair and noticed that I had a text.

What's in it for u? K.C. asked.

Well, I couldn't tell her the truth.

Fun.

I don't know, she texted. **Tate's already mad at me.**

Tate won't know, I lied, and threw the phone on the bed to go get dressed.

CHAPTER 16

"Do you want to come over tonight?" I rested my forearm on the wall above K.C.'s head and leaned into her, almost touching.

Her breath caught as I trailed my fingers on the sliver of skin peeking out between her shorts and shirt. "What are we going to do?" she played along, looking absolutely turned-on and helpless.

Her idiot ex-boyfriend was in the cafeteria, and we were outside the double doors, hot in each other's space.

Her back was against the wall, but he could see her, and he could definitely see me.

I just wished Tate could see this, too.

My lips hovered a hair away from hers as I ran my hand around her back, about to dive in for the kill. "We could play Monopoly," I suggested, pressing my body into hers. "Or Wii."

Her eyes got wide and her lips tightened, trying to hold back a laugh. While we looked like we were about to get it on, our conversation didn't deliver.

"I don't know," she moaned. "I'm not very good at Wii."

"It's not that hard." My whisper fanned over her lips. "Watch."

And I pulled her into me, kissing her long and slow.

Her slender frame molded into mine, and she tilted her head to the side as I trailed a line to her ear.

She was easy in my hands. Small, soft, bending when I pulled . . . She knew what to do.

K.C. definitely wasn't innocent. I could feel that.

But she was an easy target right now, and I didn't go for that.

And . . . I definitely felt like I'd lost my heartbeat somewhere in the middle of making out with her.

Jesus.

My lips and hands went through the motions. *Kiss, kiss, bite, squeeze* . . . and nothing fucking happened.

What the hell?

I knew I wasn't interested in her, but damn! I should feel some kind of jolt. Some kind of reaction. She had tits, after all.

But no. Nothing. I was dead. I was doing my literature homework. I was playing golf.

I hate golf.

And that's when I realized that I hadn't pursued any girls in a couple of weeks.

The second bell rang. K.C. jumped, and I leaned back, still held hostage by the fact that the only time I'd gotten a hard-on lately was around Tate.

Christ.

I backed off K.C. and tipped my chin at her. "Text if you want to come over later. Liam will hear about it." *And Tate will see you*, I thought to myself. "You don't want him thinking you were sitting at home alone all night, do you?"

I knew that would push her.

But before she had a chance to answer, I slapped her on the ass, knowing Liam would see.

K.C. just smiled, her eyes wide with shock before she turned and ran to class.

I let out a sigh, watching her disappear down the hall.

I wasn't going to class. I had a meeting with the fucking counselor this morning. College-talk time.

No, actually that was last year. Now, since I hadn't made any plans, it was the make-a-decision-or-make-your-own-bed-and-lie-in-it talk.

"Hey, man." Madoc came through the cafeteria doors before I'd even moved. "Was that K.C. that ran off? You haven't tapped that yet?" He fastened the cap on his Gatorade.

I turned, knowing he'd walk with me. "Who's saying I haven't?"

"Uh, because you've never been seen with a girl after you've fucked her. I doubt you even wait until the condom is off before forgetting their names."

I halted in front of the staircase I needed to take. Was he serious? A judging tone, from *him*? "And you do?" I asked, shoving my hands into the pockets of my jeans.

Madoc had probably scored more tail than I had.

"Yeah, yeah. I know." He shrugged it off. "I'm just saying, *you* never had to work this hard to get a girl into bed."

Madoc looked at me expectantly through his bruised eyelids.

"I'm in no hurry. I might want to play around with this one for a while." I couldn't tell Madoc the truth.

I never told anyone anything.

"Tate's going to be pissed," he pointed out, like I hadn't thought of that.

"The whole point."

Madoc nodded. "Oh, so that's the plan."

Well, what the hell did he think I was doing—actually dating K.C.?

Enough. "Thanks again for backing me up last night." I changed the subject and turned to climb the stairs.

But Madoc spoke up again. "This thing?" he started, and I stopped. "With Tate? Why do we do it? I know I've asked before, but you don't tell me shit. I just don't get it."

Jesus Christ.

I turned back around to face him, done talking about this.

He'd asked lots of times before, and each time I'd targeted that girl it was for a different reason.

I like playing games.

I want control.

I'm protecting her.

I never had an answer that satisfied me, let alone one worth repeating. In my head, it always seemed reasonable, but saying it out loud sounded crazy.

But while Madoc was curious, he was also game. Anytime I wanted help spreading a rumor or messing with Tate over the years, he'd always stepped up. At my request and of his own volition.

The party a year ago where he threw her keys into the pool, and she'd broken his nose.

All his idea.

My first party this year when she screamed, "Cops!" Did I tell him to put his hands on her?

I narrowed my eyes on him. "I think you go above and beyond. You mess with her without me telling you, so why do you care?"

He smiled and let out a nervous laugh, brushing me off. "This isn't about me. I never wanted to make an enemy of that girl. She came outside last night like she was ready to back us up. She's hot, athletic, tough, and she can handle a gun. What's not to like?"

Every muscle in my shoulders and arms flexed. I didn't like that

Madoc was veering away from how I wanted people to see her, and I fucking hated that he drooled over her.

I came back down the stairs, my boots pounding on the tile almost as hard as the blood pumping in my veins, and bore down at my best friend.

"Stay away from her."

He held up his hands and smiled like he was trying to calm me down. "Hey, man, no worries. She broke my nose and kicked me in the balls. I think that ship's sailed." He narrowed his eyes and looked confused. "But if you don't want her, why can't anyone else have a shot?"

Why, indeed?

The shit I'd pulled on Tate over the years could be chalked up to hate, anger, need for control.

But not letting other guys near her? That wasn't a game.

That was about my not being okay with anyone else's mouth or hands on her.

And I needed to let that shit go.

"I'm not standing in her way anymore," I said calmly. "If she wants to date and screw every guy in school, she can have a ball. I'm done."

"Well, good," Madoc said, stretching his fat mouth into a wide grin. "Because word is she went out with Ben Jamison last night."

The walls closed in. Madoc got smaller and smaller.

Ben and Tate? No, no, no . . .

My long-sleeved black thermal was suffocating me, and for the first time since last fall I actually felt inclined to rip off the goddamn sleeves again just to breathe.

"That's fine," I clipped out, barely unscrewing my jaws to speak. "I couldn't care less. They can all have her."

But I never, for a single second, meant it.

Tate and K.C. got into it at lunch again. I could see them eating lunch at the picnic tables outside, and both were talking intensely, Tate looking away and shaking her head, and K.C. looking apologetic.

While I told myself that it would be worth it when it was done, I still felt like shit. K.C. wasn't telling Tate about using me to get back at her boyfriend. If she did, they probably wouldn't be fighting. Not that Tate would be okay with it, but she probably wouldn't be barely eating her lunch and scowling so much.

No, Tate thought K.C. and I were hooking up.

Telling the school she had genital warts or lice had been mean but still funny. Trying to steal her best friend was cruel. It would really hurt her.

Exactly what I wanted, I told myself.

But day after day I caught myself mesmerized by her every move. The methodical way she'd sharpen her precious pencils; the way her hair fell over her shoulder when she'd lean down to grab something from her messenger bag. Watching her body bend as she'd sit down or get up. Every bit of skin, every smile, and every time she licked her lips had a lightning storm shooting downward from my stomach to my dick, and I almost wished she was back in France.

At least I could hate her and not want to fuck her every second.

Madoc called it hate-fucking. He told me once that he'd never loved anyone, but he'd had sex with someone he really hated, and it was the best he'd ever had.

Passion, punishment, anger—it sounded like an attractive but dangerous mix.

I let out a breath and straightened my shoulders as I walked into my last class of the day—the class I shared with Tate.

"Leave."

I heard Tate's voice as soon as I walked in the door, and I snapped my attention to Nate Dietrich leaning on her desk, crowding her space.

"That's your last warning," she continued, looking angry and embarrassed at the same time.

"Jared's right," Nate grumbled, and stood back upright. "You're not worth it."

And I was on his fucking ass. "Sit down, Nate."

He spun around, eyebrows raised and looking surprised as we stood in between the rows of desks that were quickly filling up with students.

"Hey, man, no offense." He held up his hands. "If you're not done with her . . ."

My arms tensed with the need to haul this guy out of here by his balls.

If I'm not done with her?

And just then I felt like crawling inside of myself to hide.

My throat tightened.

What the hell?

I wanted her to hurt. I didn't want her to hurt.

I hated her. I loved her.

I wanted to violate her body in a hundred different ways. I wanted to keep her safe.

There was no limit to how fucking confused I was right now, but one thing was for certain.

She wasn't trash.

Over the years, she'd endured a lot of harassment because of me. People are easily manipulated. They want to be accepted, and gossip is taken as gospel. Tell people that someone has their clit pierced or that they eat dogs, and you just have to sit back and watch the school flood with talk.

However, by junior and senior year, my childish rumors were

about as effective as a broken condom. I'd wanted to keep guys away from Tate, but that wasn't working so much anymore. They saw she was beautiful, and now, after the locker-room incident, they saw her as a slut, too.

And for the first time, I wasn't getting any peace from tormenting this girl. I just wanted to wrap her in my arms and see her smile.

My eyes narrowed, and I wished for a perfect world where I could toss darts at this guy's dick. "Don't talk to her again," I commanded. "Go." And I jerked my chin off to a corner he should go fucking hide in.

Was I better than him?

No. But I'd deal with that shit later.

Tate let out an aggravated sigh as Nate walked off, and I turned my eyes on her in time to see her lips tighten. I saw the scowl, knew it was meant for me, but didn't even have a chance to figure out why when she spoke up.

"Don't do me any favors," she sneered. "You're a miserable piece of shit, Jared. But then, I guess I'd be miserable, too, if my parents hated me. Your dad left you, and your mom avoids you. But who can blame them, right?"

I stopped breathing, and the room shrank in on me.

What the fuck did she just say?

I stared at her, feeling torn apart and dead, knowing that it was completely un-Tate to say something like that but knowing she spoke the truth.

I didn't forget to breathe. I just didn't want to anymore.

It felt like every eye in the room was on me and people were whispering behind their hands, laughing at me. I was exposed, and everyone knew my shit.

But when I glanced around, I realized no one was even paying us any attention.

My eyes sharpened on her, and I remembered exactly why I hated her.

She was packaged up to look like a good girl, but make no mistake: There was a bitch in there.

"Okay, class," Mrs. Penley called out, walking through the door.

I said nothing and continued to my seat.

"Please take out your compasses and look up your east. When I say 'Go,' please take your materials and sit next to that person for today's discussion. Feel free to move desks side by side or face-to-face. Go."

I sat there, and Ivy Donner was on me before I even had a chance to pull out my compass.

But I barely heard her chatter.

Tate was joining Ben Jamison, and they were moving their desks face-to-face.

Strange thing was, I felt nothing looking at her. Like I was numb. The need I felt two minutes ago to hold her and tell her I was sorry was completely gone now.

And what's more, I didn't even feel angry, either.

Tate was lost to me. I didn't care.

I was shit. I didn't care about that, either.

She looked at me every once in a while. I didn't want her. I didn't hate her.

I. Just. Didn't. Care.

CHAPTER 17

"Stop!" K.C. laughed. "You're cheating!"

"I don't cheat." I stood there, smirking and leaning on my pool cue. "I made the shot. I get another one."

K.C. and I squared off across my pool table in the family room, and her frustration actually had me itching to laugh.

K.C. the Pool Shark. Who would've thought?

After school and the episode with Tate, I'd cooled off at work and then headed home.

As I'd pulled into my driveway, I'd noticed a black Lincoln parked next door at the Brandts' and had immediately groaned.

Tate's grandmother.

Normally, I would've been pissed that Tate now had an adult around, interfering.

But that wasn't it.

Her grandmother was in everyone's business and always tried to talk to me when she came to visit. I should've known she'd come to stay, with Tate being on her own right now. I just hoped she didn't stay long.

K.C. had come over around eight, and we were going on our fifth game of pool.

"You called the six," she argued. "Not the six and the ten! You can't put two balls in the pocket at the same time. You have to make the shot you call."

"It's called being awesome," I shot back.

She scowled at me and twisted up her lips in frustration.

Her anger was kind of cute, and she was a beautiful mess tonight. Her long brown hair, a shade lighter than mine, was in a loose ponytail, and she had on no makeup.

If there was ever a clearer sign that a girl wasn't into you, this was it.

"Fine." I shrugged and put my hands up in the air, feigning annoyance. "Take your shot."

Her eyes lit up, as did her bright smile, and she leaned down over the table to take her turn.

Even though it was getting on to ten o'clock, I wasn't in any hurry for her to leave.

She won four out of the five games we played, and I thought I'd have to go to the ER to get my balls reattached. I was interested in knowing how an uptight girl who couldn't touch a single thing in freshman biology without saying "Ew" learned how to be a hard-nosed pool player.

We walked toward the living room, and I put my arm around her neck, gently pulling her in.

"So, I have to ask you something."

She let out a long sigh. "Yeah, me, too."

I looked down at her. "You first."

Plopping down on the couch, she stared at her hands in her lap. "I know you're using me to get to Tate, Jared. To make her angry, or"— she looked up at me—"jealous."

My legs stiffened, and I didn't sit down. Crossing my arms, I walked to the rain-splattered window and, out of habit, looked up to Tate's darkened bedroom windows.

Don't.

"Jared," she continued, "I'm using you, too. I'm not even sure if I want Liam back, but I want him to know I'm not sitting at home waiting for him, either. That's why I took you up on the offer to come here tonight. Tate said she was busy, and I didn't want to stay home."

I turned around and cocked my head to the side, peering at her. "You could've used any guy to make Liam jealous, K.C. Why me? You knew that it would hurt Tate if she thought you were hooking up with me."

I could almost see her melt into the couch. Her face fell, and she slowly brought her knees up to her chest, hugging them.

"My mom is"—she almost whispered—"overbearing." She shook her head, like the word "overbearing" was too simplistic. "She picks out my clothes, checks my phone, picks my classes, and she even . . ." But her breath caught and she choked back a dry sob.

My mouth went dry and I stilled.

Jesus.

What wasn't she saying?

Using her thumb, she caught tears as they fell. "Anyway, after Liam, I'm just sick of being me. Sick of being weak and pushed around. I thought Jared Trent would get under Liam's skin like no other."

The corners of her lips turned up slightly, and I understood what she was saying.

We both wanted control.

"But you knew it would hurt Tate," I restated, still searching for a reason why she would hurt her so-called best friend.

"Yeah," she sighed. "Not part of the plan, but I guess I figured it would turn around this game you two play. Move things along, so to speak."

I pinched my eyebrows together. "Even at the risk of losing your friend?" I asked.

But she shocked me by exhaling a laugh. "You're not that powerful, Jared." She looked down and then continued softly, "Tate and I will be fine. She can't know about this, though. She knows who she is. She's not silly or insecure. I don't want her judging me for playing this game with Liam. I don't want anyone to know."

She put her feet back on the carpet and straightened up, meeting my eyes. "Jared, I have no idea what your problem is with her, but I know you're not a bad guy. I thought when she got back, things would be different. You two would be over this mess."

"We are over it," I asserted as I took a seat next to her.

K.C. narrowed her eyes to slits and tipped her chin up. "You love her," she said, not asked, and my face flushed.

"No," I said firmly.

"Good." She slapped her hands onto her lap, and her tone suddenly lightened up, surprising me. "Ben Jamison will be at the race Friday night. It's likely he'll bring Tate. Can you keep your claws in?"

My arms rested on the back of the couch; otherwise she would've seen my fists ball up.

As much as I was trying not to care, Madoc, K.C., and everyone else, for that matter, kept reminding me that Tate was moving on with her life.

"I don't care who does what, K.C," I stated without any emotion.

She looked at me for a few seconds, while I stared ahead.

"Do me a favor?" she asked, smoothing her hands down her faded jeans. "Play along with this through the race for me? Liam is going up against Madoc, and I just—"

"Yeah," I cut her off, knowing exactly what she needed. "You got it."

If she wanted to make Liam jealous, then I could help. It wasn't a very honorable cause, but it was fun.

"Movie?" I suggested, trying to change the subject.

"Sure. Do you like dance movies?"

And I almost kicked her out of my house right then and there.

Thick rain poured down outside, and the air felt dense with energy. I gave K.C. a sweatshirt to cover her head when she left around midnight, and then I locked up the house and jogged upstairs to my room.

For the first time in years, I wanted in that tree.

Tate and I used to climb and sit in it during storms—or anytime, really. I hadn't seen her in the tree for years, either, though.

Sliding up the window, I poked my head out into the wind, and the rain and immediately froze.

Hell.

Tate was in the tree.

My fingers clenched the windowsill.

The first thing that came to mind was an angel. Her hair flowing and shiny. Her legs dangling, long and smooth. She looked perfect where she was, like a painting.

And then I remembered that Satan was also an angel.

You're a miserable piece of shit, Jared. Her words today had cut me more than I wanted to admit.

"Sitting in a tree during a thunderstorm?" I taunted her. "You're some kind of genius." She popped her head up and twisted around to face me.

The look in her eyes—that I could see, anyway—wasn't angry the way it usually was with me. She wouldn't look at me completely. No, her eyes were guarded and a little sad.

"I like to think so, yes," she said, facing away from me again.

Her demeanor had me puzzled. She wasn't timid, but she wasn't engaging, either. Did she feel bad about what she said to me today?

Well, I didn't need her pity. I wanted her fucking anger.

Don't feel sorry for me.

I wanted her to sit there and own what she did. Don't apologize and don't shy away. *Get mad at me, Tate.*

"Tree? Lightning? Ring any bells?" I continued to antagonize her. I knew there was some danger in sitting in a tree during a lightning storm, but it's nothing we hadn't done a hundred times when we were kids.

"It never mattered to you before," she spoke up, emotion gone from her voice as she looked out to our glistening street.

"What? You sitting in a tree during a storm?"

"No, me getting hurt," she shot back and shut me up.

Damn her.

Every fucking muscle in my body tightened, and I wanted to shake her and yell, *"Yeah, I don't fucking care if anything bad ever happens to you!"*

But I couldn't.

I did care—goddamn it—and I wanted to punch a wall because of it. Why the hell did I care about anything she did? Who she dated? Who she screwed?

But then, I guess I'd be miserable, too, if my parents hated me.

Her words spread like tentacles through my brain, sucking the life out of everything good I'd ever thought about her. Every memory.

I had to cut her out of my heart and my head.

"Tatum?" I almost hesitated, but forced out the rest. "I wouldn't care if you were alive or dead."

And I turned my back on her and finally just walked away.

CHAPTER 18

K.C. came huffing over to my table again for lunch the next day. She wouldn't talk about it, and I wouldn't ask, but I assumed it was about either Tate or Liam.

Liam, I couldn't care less about. Tate, I tried to care less about.

"So I just got a text from Zack." Madoc came up and swung a chair around to straddle it backwards. "Derek Roman will be back in town for the weekend. He wants to race you on Friday night."

I groaned inwardly, not because I thought I would lose, but because Roman was a huge bucket of dick.

Yeah, what I did to Tate the past few years, this guy did times ten to half of the school when he went here. I might win or I might lose, but getting my car to finish without a scratch would be a miracle.

I shrugged. "Fine. It'll be a close race, so the odds will pay off big."

And I needed the money. My father was pinching me for cash every week, and it wasn't pocket change. He was smart, though. He wanted money but never got too greedy. Enough to make it hurt me but not enough that I wouldn't be able to deliver.

"You're racing Liam, right?" K.C. asked Madoc.

He looked at her across the table and smirked. "I don't know if we'd call it racing. More like a castration."

"Just be careful, okay?" She looked concerned.

Really?

Madoc leaned his chest forward into the back of his chair. "K.C.?" His voice was low and husky. "I'm picturing you naked right now."

And I couldn't help it. The snort came out and my chest exploded with laughter as I buried my forehead into my hand.

"Ugh!" K.C. grumbled in disgust. Standing up, she straightened her cut-off jean skirt and stalked off toward the cafeteria doors, but Madoc and I still couldn't control ourselves.

God, he's the best.

"K.C., wait!" I shouted after her, not really trying to bring her back.

Madoc stood up, still chuckling. "K.C., come on. It was a joke."

But she didn't turn around.

And we kept laughing.

Tate and I had made eye contact a few times throughout the day. The storm in her eyes had turned to a drizzle, but I didn't spend time thinking about it.

I couldn't. The shit between us was over. It had been over for her a long time ago, but for me, it needed to end pronto.

Themes class passed peacefully, but Penley had us arrange our desks in circles, so I had a perfect view of Tate sitting across from me. Every once in a while, I would catch her glancing at me, the thoughts behind her eyes unclear.

We'd just moved our desks back into the regular position, and Mrs. Penley was talking about monologues that we were supposed to perform in the next two weeks. I was ready to just get the hell out of here and take Madman to the lake. Poor dog had been ignored lately with my work, school, and being gone on the weekends. Sometimes I took him with me when I spent time with Jax, but sleeping in my bed was usually the only time I got to hang out with him.

It briefly crossed my mind to see if Tate wanted to take him sometimes—give the guy some extra attention—but I pushed that thought out of my head right away.

We weren't friends, and I wasn't asking her for shit.

As if reading my thoughts, I noticed her shift in her seat, and I looked up to see her turned around, staring at me.

She blinked, looked down, and back up again like she was sad, lost, and something else. Something like regret or despair. Why was she sad? I narrowed my eyes and tried to look away. I didn't need to know what was going on with her.

"Now, class," Penley spoke, her attention still focused on the piece of paper she wrote on. "Don't forget that the antibullying assembly is on the twenty-ninth. Instead of going to first period, go to—"

Tate's hand shot up. "Mrs. Penley," she interrupted.

The teacher looked up. "Yes, Tate?"

"We have five minutes left of class." Her voice was polite. "May I perform my monologue now?"

What the hell?

This project wasn't due for a while, and everyone's eyes, including Penley's, bugged out.

What the hell was Tate doing?

"Um, well, I wasn't expecting to grade anything yet. Do you have your essay ready?" Penley asked.

"No, I'll have that by the due date, but I would really love to perform it now. Please."

My teeth ground together.

"Okay." Penley let out a reluctant sigh. "If you're sure you're ready . . ."

Great.

The last thing I wanted to do right now was look at Tate or hear her voice. Mostly because I knew it would be a struggle to not watch her.

Noise. Space. Distraction.

Slouching in my seat, I stretched out my legs and crossed my ankles. Picking up my pen, I pressed it onto my notebook paper and started drawing three-dimensional cubes.

"I like storms," I heard her start, but I kept my eyes trained on the lines I drew. "Thunder, torrential rain, puddles, wet shoes. When the clouds roll in, I get filled with this giddy expectation."

I tried not to listen, but I knew right away that it would be impossible to ignore her.

"Everything is more beautiful in the rain. Don't ask me why." She sounded light and natural, like she was speaking to a friend. "But it's like this whole other realm of opportunity. I used to feel like a superhero, riding my bike over the dangerously slick roads, or maybe an Olympic athlete enduring rough trials to make it to the finish line."

She paused, and I lifted my pen, realizing I'd been outlining the same box over and over again.

"On sunny days, as a girl, I could still wake up to that thrilled feeling. You made me giddy with expectation, just like a symphonic rainstorm. You were a tempest in the sun, the thunder in a boring, cloudless sky."

Suspicion inched its way under my skin, and my breathing got shallow.

This wasn't a monologue.

She continued, "I remember I'd shovel in my breakfast as fast as I could, so I could go knock on your door. We'd play all day, only coming home for food and sleep. We played hide-and-seek, you'd push me on the swing, or we'd climb trees."

I couldn't help it. My eyes snapped up to meet hers, and my fucking heart . . . it was like she was reaching out and squeezing it in her hand.

Tate.

Was she speaking to me?

"Being your sidekick gave me a sense of home again." Her eyes were locked with mine. "You see, when I was ten, my mom died. She had cancer, and I lost her before I really knew her. My world felt so insecure, and I was scared. You were the person that turned things right again. With you, I became courageous and free. It was like the part of me that died with my mom came back when I met you, and I didn't hurt anymore. Nothing hurt if I knew I had you."

I couldn't catch my fucking breath. Why was she doing this? I meant nothing to her.

"Then one day, out of the blue, I lost you, too. The hurt returned, and I felt sick when I saw you hating me. My rainstorm was gone, and you became cruel. There was no explanation. You were just gone. And my heart was ripped open. I missed you. I missed my mom."

A tear fell down her cheek as I felt my own throat tighten.

She was looking at me like she used to, like I was everything.

Piles and piles of fucking shit swirled through my mind as I watched her.

All the crap I'd done to prove that I was strong. To prove that I didn't need someone that didn't want me. I swallowed, trying to calm the pounding in my chest.

Had she loved me?

No.

She was lying. She had to be.

"What was worse than losing you was when you started to hurt me. Your words and actions made me hate coming to school. They made me uncomfortable in my own home."

Her eyes pooled with more tears, and I wanted to break shit.

She was hurting. I was fucking miserable. And for what?

"Everything still hurts, but I know none of it is my fault," she continued, and thinned out her lips in a hard line. "There are a lot of words that I could use to describe you, but the only one that includes sad, angry, miserable, and pitiful is 'coward.' In a year, I'll be gone, and you'll be nothing but some washout whose height of existence was in high school." Her eyes zoned in on me again, and her voice grew strong. "You were my tempest, my thundercloud, my tree in the downpour. I loved all of those things, and I loved you. But now . . . you're a fucking drought. I thought that all the assholes drove German cars, but it turns out that pricks in Mustangs can still leave scars."

My hands balled up, and I felt like I was crammed into a tight space, looking for a way out.

I barely registered the class clapping for her—no—cheering for her. Everyone thought her "performance" was great. I didn't know what the hell to make of it.

She acted like she cared about me. Her words told me she remembered everything that used to be good between us. But the ending . . . it was like a good-bye.

She bowed, her hair falling around her with the dip, and she smiled a sad smile. Like she felt good, but guilty that she felt good.

The distant cry of the school bell sounded, and I moved out of my seat, past her desk, where she'd sat back down, and out of the room, feeling like I was in a damn tunnel. People scurried around me, giving Tate congratulations on a job well done, and going about their business as if my world wasn't crumbling.

Everything was white noise around me. The only sound that filled my ears was my own heartbeat as I walked in a daze into the hallway.

I pressed my forehead into the cool, tiled wall across from Penley's classroom and closed my eyes.

What the hell had she just done to me in there?

I could barely breathe. I tried forcing air into my lungs.

No, no . . .

Fuck this.

She was lying. It was all an act.

All I'd wanted when I was fourteen was her. And she hadn't been thinking about me when I was screaming for her. She didn't miss me while I was at my father's that summer. She didn't want me then, and she didn't want me now.

The day I got back, I'd needed her so goddamn much, and she hadn't given me one fucking thought.

Goddamn it, Tate. Don't do this. Don't fuck with my head.

Jesus, I didn't know what I wanted to do anymore. I wanted to leave her alone. I wanted to forget her. But then I didn't.

Maybe I just wanted to hold her and breathe her in until I could remember who I was.

But I couldn't. I needed to hate Tate. I needed to hate her, because if I didn't have a place to sink all of my energy, then I'd spin out again. My father would have me, and I wouldn't have her to zone in on.

"See ya, Jared."

I twisted around and blinked. Ben had called out to me, and she was with him.

She was looking at me like I was nothing. Like I wasn't the focus of her life when she was the focus of everything in mine.

I stuck my fists into the pocket of my hoodie so they wouldn't see me clenching them. It was kind of a natural thing for me to do now when I was in public. To keep my temper in check so that no one would notice what was boiling underneath.

My teeth ground together. *She can't hurt me.*

But the air coming out of my nose was heating up as I watched them fade away down the hall.

She was leaving with him.

She'd just handed me my ass in that classroom.

She was surviving me.

And I clenched my fists tighter until the bones in my fingers ached.

"Give me a ride?"

My jaw instantly hardened as frustration threatened to boil over into rage.

I didn't even have to turn around to know it was Piper.

She was the last thing on my mind these days, and I wished she'd take the hint and back off.

But then I remembered that she was good for one thing.

"Don't talk." I spun around and grabbed her hand without even looking at her and dragged her to the nearest bathroom. I needed to burn off frustration, and Piper knew the score. She was like water. She assumed the shape of whatever container held her. She didn't challenge me or make demands. She was just there for the taking.

It was after school. The place was empty as I barged into a stall, sat down on a seat, and brought her down on top of me. She giggled, I think, but to be honest, I didn't fucking care who she was, where I was, or that anyone could walk in on us. I needed to dive deep. So deep into a cave that I couldn't even hear my own thoughts. That I couldn't even see *her* blond hair and blue eyes in my head.

Tate.

I ripped off Piper's little pink cardigan and attacked her mouth. It didn't feel good. It wasn't meant to. This wasn't about me getting off. It was about me getting even.

I grabbed the straps of her tank top and pulled them down her arms, her bra coming with it, until everything sat at her waist. Her chest was free for me, and I dived in as she moaned.

Nothing hurt if I knew I had you.

I was trying to run from Tate, but she was catching up with me.

I pulled Piper harder against me and inhaled her skin, wanting her to be someone else.

I felt sick when I saw you hating me.

My heart still thumped like it no longer wanted a home in my body, and I couldn't calm down. *What the fuck?*

Piper leaned back and started grinding on me, and my hands were everywhere, trying to find the escape. Trying to find my control.

And my heart was ripped open. I missed you.

I gripped Piper's ass and attacked her neck. She moaned again and said some shit, but I couldn't hear it. There was only one voice in my head that no amount of Piper or any other girl was going to drown out.

I loved all of those things, and I loved you.

And then I stopped.

All the air had left me.

Tate had loved me.

I didn't know if it was the look in her tear-filled eyes or the tone of her voice, or maybe the fact that I knew her almost as well as anyone. But I knew she'd told the truth.

She had loved me.

"What's the matter, baby?" Piper had her arms around my neck, but I couldn't look at her. I just sat there, fucking breathing into her chest, trying to delude myself for even a few seconds that it was Tate I was holding.

"Jared. What's with you? You've been acting weird ever since the school year started." Her whiny-ass fucking voice. Why didn't people ever know when to shut up?

I ran my hands over my face. "Just get up. I'll take you home," I bit out.

"I don't want to go home. You've been ignoring me for a month.

Over a month, actually!" She pulled her shirt and sweater back on, but she still wasn't moving.

I took a deep breath and tried to swallow down the nerves exploding in my stomach.

"You want a ride or not?" I said, pinning her with a look that said "Take it or leave it." Piper knew better than to ask questions. I didn't tell Madoc shit, and I wasn't going to start with this girl.

By the time I got home, my mood had gone from bad to worse. After dropping Piper off, I just drove. I needed to listen to some music, clear my head, and try to get rid of this ache in my chest.

I wanted to blame Tate. Turn a blind eye like I always did when she was hurting.

But I couldn't. Not this time.

There wasn't going to be any running from the truth. No diving into a party or a girl to distract myself.

The truth was, I wish I could go back to that day in the park. Back to the fishpond when I'd first decided that she needed to hurt. I would've done it differently.

Instead of pushing her away, I would've buried my face in her hair and let her bring me back from wherever I'd gone. She wouldn't have had to say or do anything. Just fill my world.

But my anger ran deeper than my love for her that day, and right now I couldn't face what I'd done. I couldn't face that she hated me, that my mother barely wanted anything to do with me, and that my father spent every Saturday reminding me of what a loser I was.

Fuck it. Fuck them all.

I walked into my house, slammed the door, and threw my keys across the room. The place was as quiet as a church, except for Madman's paws scurrying across the floor.

He started clawing at my jeans and whimpering for attention.

"Not now, buddy," I snipped, and walked into the kitchen. Madman couldn't calm me down, and I wanted to hit something. As I yanked open the refrigerator, I noticed that my mother had left a note stuck to the door.

Off for the night. Order a pizza. Love you!

And I slammed the door closed again. *Always fucking gone.*

I gripped both sides of the refrigerator and pressed my head into the stainless steel. *It didn't matter*, I told myself. Everything was okay. I had shitty parents, but who didn't? I'd pushed Tate away, but there were other girls out there. I had no idea what the fuck I was going to do with my life, but I was only eighteen—or almost eighteen.

Everything. Was. Fine.

I gripped the sides harder, willing myself to believe the lie.

And then I saw myself, alone in a kitchen and holding a refrigerator. Telling myself that my life was good.

Fuck.

I started pounding the steel doors. Every muscle in my body felt choked as I slammed my palm against the appliance again and again. Madman yelped and scurried away.

All the shit my mom had sitting up on top turned over or shattered to the ground, and I just kept going. Using both hands to slam it time and again against the wall.

Nothing hurt if I knew I had you.

She was fucking with my head. Why couldn't I just forget her?

I stopped, my shoulders slumped, forcing air in and out of my lungs, but it was never enough. I turned around to head up the stairs. If my mom was gone for the night, then there was no harm in bringing out the Jack. Since she was an alcoholic, I kept that shit hidden. But tonight I needed a way out. I couldn't stomach the hurt. I couldn't deal, and I needed to be numb.

On my way up the stairs, I noticed that the front door was open.

Shit.

It must not have latched when I'd slammed it before. And Madman got out, no doubt.

I kicked the door shut. Hard.

Fucking awesome. Even the dog had left.

Once in my room, I went to the stash Madoc and I skimmed from his father and pulled out a bottle.

Flinging off my hoodie and shirt, I kicked off my boots and unscrewed the bottle, swallowing massive gulps to drown out her voice in my head.

But walking over to my window, I instantly stilled.

There she was.

Dancing.

Closing her eyes and jumping around.

An image of her in a purple nightgown came to mind, but I couldn't place it.

She looked ridiculous and couldn't dance any better than me. I almost laughed when she threw devil horns up in the air and screamed along to the music. My chest swelled with the urge to hold her.

And right then and there, I wanted her back.

But what the hell was I going to say to her? I couldn't tell her everything.

Not everything.

I brought the bottle back up to my lips, closed my eyes, and forced the bile back down my throat.

There was nothing to say. The guy she knew when we were fourteen was gone. My parents had left me. She'd left me.

I was on my own, just like that cocksucker said I'd be.

The stinging nip of hatred and hell crawled its way up my neck and into my head until my nerves burned so badly that I wanted to rip off my skin just to breathe.

I launched the bottle across the room, where it slammed against the wall before spilling to the floor.

Goddamn it!

Leaving the room and charging down the stairs, I went fucking crazy. I kicked over chairs, smashed pictures, and went to bat with some pottery and crystal. I shattered everything, swinging the fire poker at everything and anything. Every picture that my mother had of me smiling and every fucking figurine that gave the impression that we were a happy household was destroyed. In two hours, the house was ripped apart from top to bottom as I got lost and grew exhausted.

When all was done, the house was a disaster, and I was covered in sweat.

But I was as high as a kite. Nobody could hurt me if I could hurt them.

Blissfully numb and calm, I parked myself outside on the back porch with another bottle of Jack from my supply and let the rain cool me down. I didn't know how long I was out there, but I was finally breathing and that felt good. There's something to be said for acting like a five-year-old and breaking some shit. Control had finally settled over me again, and I just sat there and drank, soaking up the quiet in my head.

"Jared?"

I twisted my head and immediately lost my breath. *Tate? Aw, Jesus Christ. No, no, no . . .*

She was here? And in fucking shorts and a tank top?

I turned back around, hoping she'd go away. I didn't want to lose my shit with her. Or do anything stupid. I'd finally calmed down, but my head was nowhere near straight enough to deal with her right now.

"Jared, the dog was barking outside. I rang the doorbell. Didn't you hear it?"

Damn, she was so close. I could feel the pull. I wanted to get closer. To sink into her arms until I couldn't even remember yesterday.

She walked around in front of me, into the rain, and my fingers tingled. They wanted her.

I glanced up, only for a moment, unable to resist the pull.

Jesus Fucking Christ. She was drenched. And I looked down again, knowing what I would do if I kept looking. Her wet shirt stuck to her body, but she tried to hide it by crossing her arms. Her legs glistened with the water dripping down, and her shorts clung to her toned, wet thighs.

"Jared? Would you answer me?" she yelled. "The house is trashed."

I tried looking at her again. Why? Who the fuck knows? Every time I saw her, I wanted to bury my heart and body inside of her.

"The dog ran away," I choked out. *What the hell?*

"So you threw a temper tantrum? Does your mom know you did that to the house?"

And that's when the wall went back up. My mother. Tate looking at me like I couldn't control myself. Like I was weak.

I didn't want to hurt her anymore, but I wasn't letting her in, either.

"What do you care? I'm nothing, right? A loser? My parents hate me. Weren't those your words?" *Yes, this is easier. Just push back.*

She closed her eyes, looking embarrassed. "Jared, I should never have said those things. No matter what you've—"

"Don't apologize," I interrupted, swaying as I stood up to hover over her. "Groveling makes you look pathetic."

She yelled something at me, but I was too light-headed and aggravated to register what she was saying as I walked back into the house.

She followed me inside, and I tuned her out as I dried off the dog.

But then she took the control out of my hands again when she rushed to empty my bottle down the drain.

What?

"Son of a bitch!" I ran up to her and tried prying the Jack out of her hands. "This is none of your business. Just leave." I didn't want her here to see me like this. She shouldn't care about me. I'd done nothing to earn it. And I didn't need it or her!

I jerked the bottle, and her body came flush with mine.

She was the most beautiful thing I'd ever seen. And angry, she was even hotter. A fire was in her eyes, and her full bottom lip glistened from the rain. I didn't want to stop this for anything. I wanted to lose all of my energy on her.

In more ways than one.

I saw her raise her hand, and my head jerked to the side with the sting of it, and I stood there for a moment, stunned.

She hit me!

I dropped the bottle. I didn't give a damn about it, anyway, and I hauled her up onto the counter. I didn't know what I was doing, but it was out of my control. And for once I had no problem with that.

She met my eyes, not looking away for a second, as her body squirmed against mine. I shouldn't be holding her like this. I shouldn't be crossing this line with her. But I had Tate in my arms for the first time in more than three years, and I wasn't letting go. The more I looked at her, and the more she let me touch her, I was completely hers.

And I hated and loved that at the same time.

"You fucked me up today."

"Good," she challenged, and my hold on her tightened.

I jerked her into me again. "You wanted to hurt me? Did you get off on it? It felt good, didn't it?"

"No, I didn't get off on it," she answered way too calmly. "I feel nothing. You are nothing to me."

No. "Don't say that." I hadn't pushed her away completely. I still had her, didn't I?

I could smell her sweet breath as she leaned in, her lips moist with heat and sex. "Nothing," she repeated, taunting me, and I was instantly as hard as a fucking rock. "Now, get off—"

I took her mouth, eating up her sweet little whimper. She was fucking mine, and that was it. Her smell, her skin—everything invaded my world, and I couldn't see straight. My head felt dazed, like I was underwater, weightless and quiet. God, she tasted good.

I sucked on her bottom lip, tasting what I'd been fucking dying to get at for years. And I wanted to taste her everywhere. I went too fast, but I couldn't control myself. It was like I needed to fit in all the lost time right now.

Her chest was pressed into mine, and I was between her legs. I tried to catch my breath between kisses. This was where I wanted to be, and why the fuck hadn't I seen that sooner? She wasn't fighting me, and I smiled as she stretched her neck back for me, inviting me in. I released my hold and dug my hands into her body, pulling her into my hips, so she could feel how much I wanted her.

She'd wrapped her legs around me, and I ran my hands up her thighs, in complete awe of her soft, hot skin. We weren't going to fucking move until my hands or mouth had been on every part of her.

As I kissed her neck, she brought my face back up to her lips, and I reveled in how she responded. She wanted this as much as I did.

Hell, yes.

I knew I didn't deserve it. I knew she deserved more. But I was going to bury myself in this girl or spend my life trying. I couldn't get her close enough or kiss her fast enough. I wanted more.

I dove for the little spot under her ear, smelling and aching for her. I felt freer with her body wrapped around mine than I had in years.

"Jared, stop." She pulled her head away from me, but I just kept going. *Nope. You. Me. And a fucking bed. Now.*

I was about to carry her off when she yelled, "Jared! I said stop!" And she pushed me away.

I stumbled back, shocked out of my trance. Blood raced through my dick like water through Niagara Falls, my body screaming for her so hard. I stood there, trying to fucking figure out what to say to her to bring her back to me, but she didn't give me a chance. She just leaped off the counter and ran out of the house.

Goddamn.

I had no idea what the hell I was going to do now, but one thing was for damn certain.

We weren't done.

CHAPTER 19

"Are you serious?" I leaned down to Madoc's car window, where he sat in the driver's seat, listening to Pink.

"My music is none of your business." He ended the conversation right there and continued staring out onto the track ahead.

It was Friday night, a long two days after my kiss with Tate, and we were at the Loop, getting set for Madoc's race against Liam. He was listening to chick music, and I was trying not to laugh.

Not that Pink wasn't hot as hell, but, personally, I need something louder when I got zoned in.

K.C. rode with me tonight. I glanced over to the side, where I knew she was standing, and I tensed up when I saw her talking to Tate.

My chest swelled with a rush of heat.

"Dude, why are you smiling?" I heard Madoc's voice.

I blinked and darted my eyes back down to him. He sat there, holding the steering wheel and narrowing his eyes at me.

"Was I smiling?" My face fell back into position.

"Yeah, and it's weird. The only time you smile is when you're pulling the wings off of butterflies," he mumbled, but then pinched his eyebrows together and twisted to look over his shoulder out the back window. "Is she here?"

"Who?"

"The butterfly you like to torment," he teased.

"Fuck off," I grumbled, and headed back to my car.

My game plan with Tate had changed, and I had no clue how to explain myself to him.

So I didn't.

But my lips curled up as flashes of how my idea of tormenting Tate had become different.

God, I wanted her.

That was it. Plain and simple.

That kiss—our first—was fucking torture, and I wanted more of it.

She had punished me with that kiss. Showing me what she could do to me. What we could do together. And that was just a taste.

K.C. sauntered over to me as I leaned back on the hood of my car. "Hi, ya."

Tate followed behind with . . . fucking Ben Jamison. I let out a low sigh and averted my eyes to K.C.

"Hi, yourself." I wrapped my arm around her shoulder, but I had no idea why.

K.C. and I were still keeping up the pretense of a relationship, and while she wanted to piss off Liam, I didn't know what I was getting out of it.

"Hey, man." Ben nodded at me.

I wanted to make him bleed from his eyes.

"Hey. How's it going?" I asked, and turned my attention back to the track before he had a chance to answer.

A thick silence filled the air, and my jaw twitched with a pent-up smile.

You could feel the tension like a blister ready to pop, and I was enjoying the hell out of it.

I didn't care if K.C. was comfortable, and I didn't want Ben or Tate at ease, either.

In no universe would I be okay with her seeing him.

Or anyone, probably.

But K.C. decided to push.

"And, Jared, this is Tatum Brandt," she introduced us sarcastically. "Say hi."

Yeah, we've met.

I slid my arm down around K.C.'s waist—because I'm a dick—and I let my eyes slide over to Tate slowly, as if I couldn't care less.

The air coming out of my nose heated up, and I couldn't do anything but tip my chin at her and look away.

She was probably relieved that I could be that civil, but it was all an act. My insides were hot, and I wanted to kiss something and hit everything at the same time.

Ben thinking that he actually had a shot with her pissed me off.

And her outfit really pissed me off.

She was wearing a short black schoolgirl skirt with a thin white shirt—probably a tank top—and a gray jacket over it.

"And we're ready!" Zack called out from the track, and I looked over to him as everyone started clearing the dirt road where Liam and Madoc would race.

Tate took a few steps toward the track, and I immediately took my arm off K.C. and reached in my pocket for the fossil necklace. It wasn't something I carried on me regularly, only on Sundays and for races.

"Ready?" some girl called out from the track.

The crowd cheered wildly as engines revved. Most of them probably had no idea that this was a shit race.

Madoc's GTO against Liam's Camaro?

Not even close.

Camaros could get the job done, but Liam was clueless when it came to modifying his ride. Madoc had this.

"Set?" The girl yelled, but my eyes were glued to Tate, who had turned to watch the takeoff.

"Go!"

Cheers erupted, and everyone's bodies blocked my view of the track as I stayed back against my car. It didn't matter. I knew who was going to win, and there was only one person I wanted to watch right now.

Tate stood with her back to me, and for once I didn't have to pry my eyes away. I wasn't guilty about wanting her anymore, and I was going to look.

She stood on her toes, trying to peer over the other spectators' heads. The muscles in her legs flexed, and I wanted my hands on her.

The smooth contours of her skin and the memory of how, just two nights ago, those legs were wrapped around me made me want to get her into the same position on the hood of my car.

I realized a long time ago that Tate wasn't fourteen anymore. I mean, even at that age, she was beautiful, but we'd both just been kids.

The little desires and urges that used to sneak into my head had turned into full-blown fantasies.

And now we were old enough to entertain them.

"Shit!" K.C. cursed a few feet in front of me. "I spilled beer."

Tate twisted around to see what happened, and the whole world stopped when she found my eyes instead.

That's how she was different from other girls.

I liked it when she looked at me.

Taking off her jacket, she tossed it to K.C., whom I still hadn't looked at. I guess she messed up her shirt and needed something to cover it.

And holy fuck.

I swallowed hard.

Tate's white tank top was thin and tight, and I could see her nipples hardening against the night air.

I looked to Ben, who had done a double take. He was trying not to look at her, but he was failing miserably.

Goddamn it. I clenched my teeth.

The idea of ripping over there and hauling her all of the way home was tempting.

And if he kept fucking staring at her like that, I was going to dig out his teeth with a spoon.

They both turned back to the race, and K.C. put on Tate's jacket.

Madoc and Liam finally rounded the fourth corner, but Madoc had a heavy gain. As he crossed the finish line, the crowd clapped and waved their hands in the air, clearly pleased with their bet and the show.

Ben smiled down at Tate, who laughed at the rush of air brought on by the cars. She hated Madoc, so I assumed she was just fascinated with the scene rather than his winning.

They laughed and talked, looking completely comfortable with each other.

Really?

Tate didn't want comfortable. She wanted to get pushed. She wanted someone's hands and mouth on her, driving her insane. She wanted to be made love to in the rain.

And right now she was trying to be someone she wasn't.

Grabbing K.C. at the waist, I pulled her into me, and her eyes widened in surprise.

"For Liam, remember?" I whispered, not doing this for her in the least.

Trying to make Tate jealous was idiotic, but I wanted to see if she'd react. She'd certainly gotten good at that during the past month.

K.C. looked nervously to Tate, and I was afraid she was over-thinking. Playing around in front of Liam was fine, but she probably had a huge problem doing anything in plain sight of Tate.

After a few moments, though, she gave in and wrapped her arms around my neck. I took the invite and dipped down to kiss under her jaw.

I buried my face in her neck, trailing soft, slow kisses up to her ear, my brain telling my body what to do.

Honestly, I'd rather be kissing Madman, but I could feel Tate's eyes on me.

Stop, I told myself. *If Tate sees you pawing her friend, she won't let you touch her.*

"Everyone clear the road!" I heard Zack shout, and I snapped my head up too eagerly. "Trent and Roman, get your asses on the starting line."

I ran my hand down my face.

Fuckin' finally.

I walked around, climbed into my car, and started the engine, feeling the thunder under my body. I lived for two things: tormenting Tate and tearing up the track.

Even though everything I made at the Loop went to my father, I still loved racing. My foot twitched at the feel of the pedal, and my hands had mastered the maneuvers of my car perfectly. I could work the wheel and get the machine to steer, slide, and turn the exact way I needed it to.

It was two minutes, once a week, when I loved my life.

"Still Swingin'" by Papa Roach screamed from my speakers as I pulled my Boss 302 onto the track. My black Mustang was charged, fast, and completely me. It was the only thing my mother let me buy with the money from my grandfather's house. It was paid for, and my only outlet when I needed to get away from people and get lost.

Derek Roman, a freshman in college and former classmate, made it back to town once in a while to race. He pulled his 2002 Trans Am up next to mine, and my fingers tightened on the wheel.

He carried some weight. Some people bet against me tonight in favor of him. Kind of insulting, but it served my needs. The smaller the odds, the bigger the payoff.

"All right!" Zack called out, his voice deep and commanding. "Clear the track for the main event of the evening."

CHAPTER 20

With the college kids back at school, we had fewer races happening now than during the summer. Madoc's and mine were the only ones tonight.

Reaching into the pocket of my jeans, I dug out the fossil necklace and hung it around my rearview mirror. I caught sight of Tate watching me through the mirror, and my throat got thick. I didn't know if she could see, but I definitely didn't want her to. The necklace, her mother's, would be hard to explain.

Devon Peterson, one of the few hot girls I wouldn't touch with a ten-foot pole, sauntered up in front of our cars in her short schoolgirl skirt and spaghetti-strap shirt. She was a year behind me in school and had made it very obvious that she was available if I was interested.

I wasn't.

She was actually down-to-earth and nice, but she was nice to everybody. That was the problem. Sometimes you just had to know when a good time wasn't worth the risk.

"Ready?" she called out, her eyes sparkling at me.

Come on. Come on. My left knee bobbed while holding in the clutch.

No girls, no parents . . . just me, running from all of them.

"Set?"

Roman and I revved our engines.

"Go!"

My legs jerked into action, one easing off of the clutch and the other hitting the gas with full force. The tires spun for a brief second before Roman and I took off down the track. My stomach dropped, and I smiled at the feeling.

I loved this shit.

Gripping the steering wheel, I pounded in the clutch again as I shifted into second and then straight into third. I'd often forget and try to skip gears the way I did when I wasn't racing, but you can't do that on a track. My mother got aggravated last year when she bought a new car—a manual—and I taught her how to drive it.

"What do you mean, I can skip gears? Jared, they wouldn't put them there unless you're supposed to use them."

I just shook my head at her, realizing it wasn't worth the aggravation.

The Boss jerked again when I slammed down into fourth, and I let the music and the car tear me up into a thousand pieces and scatter me to the wind. I couldn't think or worry about anything even if I wanted to.

This is where I lived. The Boss wouldn't fight me. I owned it, inside and out.

Roman and I charged head-to-head, but the first turn was coming up. I had a slight gain, but he wasn't slowing down.

Fucking prick.

Someday I was going to have to give this guy the beating he deserved. We wouldn't be able to make the goddamn turn together, and he knew it. One of us would have to slow down, and it wasn't going to be him.

And he knew that I knew it.

I strangled the steering wheel and slammed on the brakes, pulling behind him and onto the inside lane. Right on his ass, I breathed hard and shook my head, trying to keep my lead foot from ramming his car.

Pulling the wheel to the left, I rounded the first turn, kicking up dust and feeling the car's rear slide as my heart pounded in my throat.

But Roman's car slid more.

Shifting back into second and hitting the gas, I turned up Godsmack's "I Stand Alone" and fucking took off.

Each second, my blood vibrated through my veins stronger, and I didn't care whether I won or lost. Nothing could ruin this for me, and nothing could make it better.

Through each turn, Derek Roman cut me off and made me pull behind, or I spun out more than I wanted. Either way, I wasn't gaining the lead, because the asshole would rather play bumper cars than race.

I was breathing a thousand breaths a minute, not because I was nervous, but because I was fucking pissed.

He'd rather see our cars totaled than see me win.

Laying on the gas, I gripped the wheel as Roman and I charged ahead. The crowd flew past the car, and my stomach fluttered as we finally crossed the finish line.

I let out a breath and gritted my teeth, slowing the car. I wasn't sure if I'd lost, but I wasn't certain I'd won, either.

And at this point, I really didn't care.

I wanted to hit something, and Roman was it.

I bolted out of the car, my arms rigid as steel bars as I rounded the car and met him halfway.

"You're an asshole," I ground out.

Please. Take a swing.

We were almost nose to nose. Roman was about the same height as me, but not quite.

"You were pushing into my lane!" he sneered. "Or maybe you just don't know how to handle your car."

I almost laughed.

"There are no lanes on the track." *Idiot.* "And let's not talk about who can't handle their muscle."

Roman, greasy black hair slicked back, pointed his finger in my face. "I'll tell you what, princess. Come back after you've grown some balls and taken off your training wheels. Then you'll be man enough to race me."

His voice sounded like garbage cans slamming together, and he needed to shut up.

"Man enough?" I asked, making sure my twisted-up face looked like that was the stupidest thing I'd ever heard. Spinning around to address the gathering crowd, I held up my hands. "Man enough?"

Most of them were my classmates, and they knew better.

And, as if on cue, Piper stepped out of the crowd and headed straight for me. The crowd didn't fight to contain their excitement when she glued her body to mine, with her hand on my ass, and kissed me slow and deep.

It was like an invisible pair of arms pulling me back, trying to get me out of her grasp, and I had to remind myself to dive, not swim.

I grabbed her and ran my hands down her sides, feeling the heat of her tongue touching mine.

This was what I needed.

Piper was easy.

But as the crowd roared at our display, my lips tensed and the kiss got rough.

She tasted like ash.

Tate flashed through my head, and so did the memory of her mouth.

The crowd cheered more as I threw myself into putting Roman in his place, but this was all wrong.

"Okay!" Zack cut through the crowd. "Out of the way, out of the way."

Piper smirked at me and stumbled back into the crowd and her waiting friends, who giggled.

"Listen up. We have some good news and bad news." Zack looked around, speaking more to the crowd than to Roman and me. "The bad news is that we're calling a tie."

Everyone groaned and a few cussed.

Jesus Christ. I let out a breath.

"But the good news is," he rushed to add, "we have a way to solve the stalemate."

And then he let out a God-awful grin that made bile rise in my throat. Zack could be devious.

"A rematch?" I hoped.

"Kind of." His smile widened. "If you boys want to settle this, then your cars will race again, but . . . you won't be the drivers."

My eyes burned. I couldn't blink.

What the fuck?

"Excuse me?" Roman blurted out, inching into Zack's space.

"We know you're exceptional drivers," Zack assured. "The race was close enough to prove that. Let's see who has the better machine."

Enough already.

"So who's going to drive the cars?" I shouted.

Zack's lips thinned out. "Your girlfriends."

WHAT?

"Oh, yeah!" some idiot in the crowd laughed, like it would be great entertainment.

No one, and I mean no one, was fucking driving my car!

The spectators gathered closer to hear the fallout, and, yes, there was going to be fallout. Roman and I would agree that this idea sucked, while most of the crowd would gladly lose money to see a couple of girls race.

"Dude! That's not happening!" Roman scowled and looked over at his girlfriend. She was cute as hell, but the petite brunette looked like she had just enough muscle to drive a moped and nothing more.

I smiled to myself, thinking about how Tate would do against her. *Nope. Don't go there.*

"Zack." I sighed. "I don't have a girlfriend. I *never* have a girlfriend."

"What about the pretty little thing you arrived with?"

I twisted my head and gave K.C. an aggravated look. I assumed he was talking about her.

Her eyes about popped out of her head when she saw our attention focused on her.

"He's just my rebound," she joked, and held up her hands. The crowd covered their mouths and laughed, taunting me like I should be hurt.

K.C. couldn't help but smile at her cleverness, and I raised my eyebrows at Zack, hoping he understood.

"No one drives my car," I stated.

"I agree with the princess here," Roman piped up. "This is stupid."

"The crowd's already seen you two race. They want to be entertained. If you two have any interest in settling this score so people can get paid, then you'll play it my way. Be on the starting line in five minutes or leave." He turned to walk away but stopped. "Oh, and you can ride shotgun if you like . . . you know, for moral support." The last words broke up as they left his lips.

The dickhead was laughing at us.

"This is bullshit." I combed my fingers through my hair and walked back toward Madoc and K.C. Roman stalked over to his crowd.

I straightened and fisted my fingers over and over again. If Zack weren't a friend, I might have to cut him.

Even if it weren't for the money I needed, I still couldn't get out of this. A challenge was a challenge. If Roman wasn't bowing out, neither was I.

"Hey, man. I could drive for you," Madoc spoke up. "We'd just have to tell them about our secret relationship."

He was trying to cheer me up, but he'd be more helpful shoving his foot in his mouth.

I knew girls who could drive. I'd met a good crowd at the garage where I worked and had run into a few on the scene here and there, but the only girls I knew here tonight were the ones I'd slept with or had classes with.

And I didn't trust any of them.

"Jared, I can't race for you," K.C. pointed out as if I didn't know. "There's got to be someone else."

There was.

And the idea of asking her made me want to gag. Not only would she say no, but she'd probably spit in my face for asking.

Don't act like you have a choice.

Shit.

This was when I wanted to hop in the car and drive away. Making hard decisions and accepting when others' needs came before my own hurt, but . . . I didn't have a choice.

And then I heard another father—a better father—in my head.

A man knows what needs to be done and just fucking does it.

My brother deserved someone looking out for him, and I had it in my power to make his life better.

I tilted my head back and sighed.

This was going to hurt.

"There's only one other person who I'd even slightly trust driving my car." I turned and locked eyes with Tate.

Her eyes widened. "Me?" she asked, surprised.

"Her?" Madoc, K.C., and fucking Ben followed in short order.

I crossed my arms over my chest and walked toward her. "Yeah, you."

"Me?" Her voice lowered, sounding like I just asked something stupid. She wasn't surprised anymore.

"I'm looking at you, aren't I?" I snarled slightly.

Her face fell flat, and her eyes narrowed in defiance as she looked to her date, ignoring me. "Ben, can we get an early start to that bonfire? I'm bored here."

She didn't wait for an answer before she spun around and headed out of the crowd.

There was no way I was going to pick anyone else, and I wasn't forfeiting to Derek fucking Roman.

I stalked after her and hooked her elbow. "Can I talk to you?"

I could barely even look at her, and I kept my voice to a mumble. This was as close to begging anyone as I'd come in over three years.

"No," she spat out.

Spiteful little . . .

I put my shoulders back, knowing that she had every right not to help me, but her attitude still pissed me off. "You know how hard this is for me," I whispered. "I need you."

I saw her suck in a little breath, and she looked down for a moment. Well, I'd made her pause, at least.

"And tomorrow when you don't need me?" she challenged. "Will I be shit under your boot again?"

My heart thumped, and my chest ached.

You were never shit.

"She'll do it," K.C. spoke up loudly from behind me.

"K.C.!" Tate's teeth were bared. "You don't speak for me. And I'm not doing it!" she yelled directly at me, and heat pumped through me at her anger.

It reminded me of the kitchen counter, and I wanted to shut her up again just like I'd done that night.

"You want to," K.C. argued with Tate.

"Perhaps," she sneered. "But I do have pride. He's not getting a damn thing from me."

Fuck this.

"Thank you," I ground out through my teeth.

"For what?" Tate snarled back.

I got in her face, but she didn't back down. "For reminding me of what a disappointing, self-serving bitch you are."

"That's enough! Both of you!" Madoc cut into our argument as I stared at Tate's wide, angry eyes. He stepped between us, glaring from Tate to me. "Right now, I don't give a fuck what the history is between you two, but we need asses in that car. People will lose a hell of a lot of money.

"Jared?" He looked at me and continued. "You're going to lose a lot of money. And, Tate?" He looked her, but she was still chewing me to pieces with her scowl. "You think everyone treated you badly before? Two-thirds of the people here tonight bet on Jared. When they hear that his first choice turned him down, the rest of your school year will be hell without Jared or me having to lift a finger. Now, the both of you, get in the goddamn car!"

My eyes fell to the ground, feeling a little childish and a whole lot of stunned.

Madoc didn't usually speak in exclamation points. I'd seen him pissed a handful of times, and he brought out his teacher voice very rarely.

I always got the impression that he was hiding something. Something more.

Everyone was quiet. Even a few bystanders that had caught the outburst.

"He has to ask me nicely," Tate commanded.

"What?"

I *was* nice. The first time.

Okay, maybe not.

"He has to say 'please,'" she spoke to everyone else but me.

I shook my head and laughed to myself.

God, she was a handful.

"Tatum." I looked at her like she was my next meal. "Would you ride with me, please?"

Her eyes narrowed again, but there was a glint of excitement this time. She didn't want to jump on the opportunity too fast, but she was going for it, and I knew it.

"Keys?" she asked, holding out her hand.

Dropping them in her palm, I followed her onto the track as she jogged to the driver's side of my car.

Roman had backed his Trans Am into position as the crowd cleared the track. Whistles erupted around us as Tate climbed in behind my wheel.

We both sank in, and aggravation chipped away my calm at how helpless I felt. I'd never sat on the passenger's side before.

I couldn't keep my eyes forward, and they slipped over to Tate, who was running her hands up and down the wheel.

The picture of her sitting in my fucking seat, with her hands on my fucking wheel, was too much.

I shifted, my dick unable to control itself.

As usual, around her.

I had no idea what it was about the idea of her in my car. Maybe it was how hot I knew she would look, or the thought of the two things that made my heart beat coming together, but my jeans got tight.

UNTIL YOU

I inhaled deeply, suddenly wanting my fucking car slammed with rain and her body glowing with sweat as she straddled me in my seat.

She was beautiful, and it was the worst moment of my life to want something so badly and know I wasn't going to get it.

Not yet, anyway.

Turning the key, she shifted into reverse, and I could only watch in admiration as she put her arm on the back of my seat and looked over her shoulder to back the car into position. She worked the wheel easily and maneuvered the pedals smoothly, flexing her legs every time she braked and shifted.

It was like watching porn.

Tate was at ease and happy, and a smile played at the corner of her lips.

Smiling. In my presence.

Again, a weight descended on my shoulders, and I felt bad for everything I'd done to her. To her and to me.

"You're smiling," I said, wishing she'd stop and hoping she never would.

I wanted to make her smile, and I hated being reminded that she never did.

"Don't ruin this for me by talking, please."

Fair enough.

I cleared my throat. "So, your dad taught us both how to drive stick, and the Bronco is a manual, so I'm assuming you don't have any questions about that part, right?"

"None." Her eyes stayed forward. She seemed half-engaged with what I was saying and half-mesmerized by the feel of the car. Her fingers tapped and her eyes fell everywhere around her.

I gave her a rundown of what to do, when to slow down, and how to turn, but she responded only with nods.

Zack came in front of the cars, probably because the female

drivers wouldn't be interested in Devon Peterson shaking her ass at them, and that's when my heart dropped into my stomach.

Shit!

Tate reached out and touched the fossil necklace. Her necklace, meant for her mother, that I had stolen and kept all these years.

Fuck, fuck, fuck.

Blood pumped through my ears, and it took everything to keep my voice steady and calm. I'd forgotten it was still there.

"Good-luck charm," I explained, fastening my seat belt and averting my eyes. "I took it a couple of days after you left it there. I thought it would be stolen or ruined. Kind of had it with me ever since."

But what was worse than her knowing I had kept it all these years was the knowledge that she'd want it back. I had no right to keep it, after all.

Dropping her hand, I saw her stare out the driver's-side window in silence.

What was she thinking? I wanted to know, but I'd never ask.

"Are. We. Ready?" Zack's voice startled me back to reality, and Tate snapped her head back to the front.

I reached out and found "Waking the Demon" by Bullet for My Valentine on my iPod and turned it up.

Noise, activity, distraction.

We both focused out of the windshield, silent.

"Ready?" Zack shouted, and I smiled as Tate revved the engine.

"Set?" I turned up the music again and braced myself.

I hoped for the best, but wouldn't be surprised if Tate decided to purposefully crash my baby as revenge.

"Go!"

She slammed on the gas, breathing hard and breaking into a wild smile with the excitement of the moment. Maybe it was the feeling of a different car, or maybe it was the thrill of competition, but she was zoned in. Her eyes watched the road like it was her prey, and her fingers worked the stick shift hard and fast.

I watched her muscle handle my muscle, and I shook my head.

Porn.

"The first turn comes up fast," I spoke up, getting my head back in the game.

Tate said nothing, but it looked like she'd stopped breathing as she applied the brake and started rounding the first corner.

Adrenaline pooled in my chest and I clenched my teeth, ready to shout at her to slow down more. She was ahead—not much of a surprise there—but the Trans Am could easily catch up if she got off track.

Checking the rearview mirror, I saw Roman's car gaining speed and gripped the dash harder. Fucking Roman. If Tate wasn't gone by the time it made the turn, they'd slam us.

"Hit the gas!" I yelled after she'd straightened out the car. "And don't turn so hard. You're losing time correcting yourself."

"Who's in first place?" she replied haughtily.

"Don't get cocky."

But she didn't listen. She only turned up the music and slammed the stick shift into sixth. We shot forward, and I tensed up but not from nervousness.

I didn't feel helpless right now, which was weird. Normally, I wanted to be in control, and riding shotgun bugged the hell out of me. But now? I liked watching her.

"Next turn is coming. You need to slow down," I ordered.

She folded her lips between her teeth, but the car's engine wasn't slowing down.

What the hell is she doing?

I narrowed my eyes at her and made my voice deeper. "Tatum, you need to slow down."

Yeah, that didn't work.

My heart beat faster the closer we got to the turn, and I grabbed the dash helplessly with both hands as Tate skidded around the corner and spun the wheel left, then right, and then left again to get centered. She was quick, and she and the car were one. It wasn't smooth or clean. It was fast and dangerous.

"Don't do that again." I wanted her safe.

She was going to win, anyway. Roman's car was behind, and I cringed at the tongue-lashing his girlfriend was probably getting.

Tate didn't need to be reckless. Not in a car, anyway.

I spewed a few more orders her way during the next turn, which she fucking ignored, and we advanced on the final turn at a significant gain. Slowing down to about thirty miles an hour, Tate looked over at me and smiled sweetly.

"Is this okay, Miss Daisy?"

Her eyes lit up with a challenge.

She was trying not to laugh, and I couldn't take my eyes off her full, pursed lips.

And I knew right then and there that I was going to wipe that smug little grin off of her face.

I wanted Tate panting and helpless as I buried myself inside of her. No jokes, no sarcasm, no words. Just me in her eyes.

"Tatum?" I challenged her back. "Stop toying with your opponent and win the damn race already."

"Yes'm, Miss Daisy."

I clenched my fists and my teeth.

God, I can't wait to have her in my hands again.

Tate cruised past the finish line so hilariously slowly that the crowd roared more than Madoc's and my races put together. She brought the car to a stop as the swarms of spectators hovered around the car.

Leaving the Boss in neutral and setting the e-brake, she leaned back and relaxed against the seat.

"Thank you, Jared." Her voice was almost a whisper, sweet and sincere. "Thank you for asking me to do this."

My throat tightened.

She reached up and unhooked the necklace from my rearview mirror and slipped it around her slender neck. Her face was thoughtful but comfortable.

The air turned warm, and it was just us.

Tate and Jared.

I combed my hand through my hair, shaking off the déjà vu feeling, and opened my door to the cheering crowd.

I stopped and looked down to the floor. "Waking the demon . . ." I murmured. I don't know why I picked that song to race to, but it just occurred to me how it fit.

"Thank you, Tate," I whispered, looking over at her.

Tatum didn't fit. It never did, really.

She was Tate and always would be.

CHAPTER 21

"So are you two friends yet?" A very drunk Madoc hooked his arm around my neck at the bonfire after the race.

I knew who he was talking about.

"I wouldn't go that far." I took a sip of my warm beer and kept my eyes forward.

Tate and I had exchanged pleasantries when I arrived, but I knew I'd have to talk to her again tonight.

I was bound and determined to get that necklace back. I had to see my father tomorrow.

"I'm sure it'll work out." He sighed nonchalantly. "Now that she's got a boyfriend, I think you'll both move on to more interesting pastimes than hating each other."

The cup cracked in my hand. "She doesn't have a boyfriend."

"She will," he spat back, and I could hear the smile in his voice. "He's going to try to put his hands on her tonight."

No.

Tate and Ben weren't together tonight as friends. I knew that. But Madoc saying it out loud made my stomach burn with rage.

"You see all those guys?" He jerked his chin and waved his hand to the group that Tate and Ben were chatting with. "They all want to put their hands up her skirt. You know that, right?"

Just breathe.

"And sooner or later," Madoc continued, "she's going to let one of them."

I swallowed and relaxed my grip on the red plastic cup.

Madoc walked away, having done the damage he came to do.

I knew he was just trying to mess with my head, but he was right, and my race high drained out of my head in a steady stream.

She will never forgive me.

She has a future, and mine is questionable.

But I looked over at Tate, who immediately glanced up at me across the fire, and it was like trying to walk away from the water that you knew you needed in order to live.

There was no choice but to drink.

Before I could get my head zoned into what the hell I was going to do next, I felt arms circle my neck.

"God, I've missed you." A sweet-smelling body pressed against me and soft, moist lips groaned against my neck.

Piper.

I calmly unwrapped her arms. "I hear you've kept busy with Nate Dietrich," I challenged, but I didn't care.

She came around to face me. "We went out a couple of times. But I'm all about you," she said, leaning in. "I even have a surprise for you."

"And what is that?" I humored her.

"Oh, goody." She clapped her hands together. "You're interested."

"Do you see that girl over there?" She pointed across the bonfire to a redhead in short black shorts and a fitted tank.

"What about her?" I asked, not sure where this was going.

"How about you, me, *and* her go back to your house?"

What? I blinked, not sure if I'd heard her right.

Did she just offer—

"I've already worked it out. She's game. We can all play, or"—she lowered her voice—"you can watch."

I closed my eyes and ran my hand down my face.

Jesus Christ. A fucking threesome. Was she serious?

My heart jumped, and I felt my jaw twitch with a nervous smile I didn't let out.

A threesome was something I hadn't done yet, and what guy wouldn't want that?

An image of myself in bed with two girls flashed in my mind, and my stomach dropped when both girls looked like Tate.

I looked at Piper and then to the girl across the area, who was sexy as hell and giving me her fuck-me eyes, and I wanted to punch something.

I looked to the ground, blinking with the realization that I didn't want what they were offering.

In fact, thinking about it, I kind of felt like taking a bath.

Christ.

I was going to hate myself for this someday.

I pulled Piper's hands off me again. "Stop." And I backed away.

"What?" she blurted out, her tone surprised and her eyes pissed.

I shook my head. "Just get home safely, okay?" And I walked away.

"Fucking enough," I mumbled. And I went off in search of Tate.

I didn't care if she was Ben's date.

She was leaving with me.

I trudged through the dirt and wet leaves, keeping my ears peeled for any sound. After I'd run into a tipsy Ben—who admitted he'd lost his date—I'd darted into the woods, toward the parking lot, looking for Tate.

She wasn't around the bonfire, and it's not like she had many friends there.

Or anywhere, dickhead.

A loud, guttural moan echoed in the woods, and I twisted my head toward the wail.

What? Shit.

I started running, jumping over logs with my heart pounding so hard that it hurt to breathe.

"Why are the guys at our school such dicks?" I heard a voice growl.

Tate.

I turned left and bounded through a mess of fallen branches and wet foliage.

"Shit!" I heard a male voice spout. "You fucking bitch!"

I peeled through the trees and came into a clearing of fallen trees and sawed-off tree trunks. My chest heaved with every hard breath as I took in the scene before me.

Tate stood over the crumpled mess of Nate Dietrich as he lay in visible agony on the ground. He had one hand covering his eyes and one holding his crotch.

Motherfucker.

"Tatum!" I barked, more out of the sting of fear than the heat of anger.

If she'd attacked him, it was because she'd been threatened.

He's dead.

She spun around, and I struggled to keep myself in check. Nate was already subdued, but I caught sight of her ripped tank-top strap, and every muscle tensed.

"Did he hurt you?" I asked through nearly clenched teeth.

She placed a hand over her shoulder and torn shirt. "He tried. I'm fine." She would barely look at me.

I slipped off my shirt and tossed it to her.

"Put this on," I ordered. "Now."

She didn't rush to obey, not that I had expected her to, but my temper was up, and God help her if she didn't do what she was told.

Alone in the woods. In the dark.

I wanted to throttle her for being so careless.

I walked to Nate, who still lay on the ground. "You have a poor fucking memory, Dietrich. What did I tell you?" I bent down and got in his face.

My warning to him that day in class clearly hadn't sunk in.

I grabbed a fistful of his shirt and hauled him up before slamming my fist into his stomach. He caved, hunching over, as all of the air was forced out of his body.

And I didn't stop.

I punched and slammed, hit and gutted Nate Dietrich, pounding on his body and face until he was too done to do anything but take the abuse.

The ache in my hand vibrated through my bones and traveled up my arm as the full force of my temper descended on him.

Low-life piece of shit!

He is bad news, but I'm not, I kept telling myself. There was a difference between Nate and me.

Nate had forced himself on her.

I've never done that.

He'd sexually harassed her.

My locker-room thing was just to mess with her.

She'd told him time after time to stop.

I'd seen her cry, wanting me to stop.

And the more I hit Nate, the more I didn't see his face anymore, but my own.

"Stop." I heard Tate yell behind me. "Jared, stop!"

I didn't want to stop until he was done breathing, but I was getting Tate the hell out of here. Now.

I yanked Nate by the bend of his elbow and threw him to the ground. "This isn't over," I promised, not feeling the slightest bit guilty about his bloodied eye, nose, and mouth. Blood lined the inside of his lips, and he lay crumpled on the ground, panting and groaning.

I looked over to Tate, whose eyes looked scared. Her chest rose and fell in fear.

A fear she didn't have when I first found her here.

"I'm taking you home." It wasn't open for discussion.

"No, thanks. I have a ride," she argued, tipping her chin up.

She has a ride? I wanted to laugh and growl at the same time.

God, I'm going to enjoy shutting her up.

"Your ride"—I turned to look at her—"is drunk. Now, unless you'd like to wake up your poor grandmother to come out into the middle of nowhere to get you after your date got drunk and you almost get raped—which I'm sure will do wonders for your father trusting you to be alone, by the way—then you'll get in the goddamn car, Tate."

I turned to walk toward my car, fully prepared to throw her over my shoulder if I had to.

CHAPTER 22

"What's your problem?" she blurted out as soon as we were racing down the highway, headed back to town.

"*My* problem?" I was pissed, and she could tell. "You come to the bonfire with that idiot Ben Jamison, who can't stay sober enough to drive you home, and then you walk off into the woods, in the dark, and get groped by Dietrich. Maybe you're the one with the problem."

Reel it in, asshole.

When I thought about what Nate could've done to her—would've done to her—I wanted to kill. Tate was too headstrong. Too independent.

She misjudged her own capabilities and put herself in danger.

"If you recall, I had the situation under control," she sneered. "Whatever favor you think you were doing me only satisfied your own anger. Leave me out of it."

I sucked in my cheeks, breathing in the thick air and zoning in on the road.

The car roared under me, propelling us faster as my hands strangled the steering wheel.

"Slow down," she commanded, but I ignored her.

"There are going to be situations you can't handle, Tate." I was trying to reason with her, but even I didn't know where I was going with this. She couldn't exist in the closed box I'd created for the rest of her life, and I couldn't protect her from everything. Sooner or later, she'd leave.

"Nate Dietrich wasn't going to take too kindly to what you did to him tonight," I continued. "Did you think that was going to be the end of it? He would've come after you again. Do you know how badly Madoc wanted to do something after you broke his nose? He didn't want to hurt you, but he wanted to retaliate."

She overestimated herself. Some guys didn't care about victimizing women.

Obviously.

"You need to slow down."

"No, I don't think so, Tate," I laughed out. "You wanted the full high school experience, didn't you? Football-player boyfriend, casual sex, reckless behavior?"

So I switched off my headlights before she got a chance to respond.

The road before us went black, and Tate let out a small gasp as she pressed herself back in the seat.

The adrenaline of fear and excitement shot through my veins. It was the type of feeling I had lived for while she was away. It made me feel alive.

The dull, pathetic light from the moon poured in through the trees, but it illuminated very little.

"Jared, stop it. Turn on the lights!" Her voice cracked, and she was scared. I wasn't looking at her, but I could still see her, and she was bracing for a crash with one hand on the dashboard.

"Jared, stop the car now!" she pleaded, and I hated the sound. "Please!"

"Why? This isn't fun?" I goaded, and already knew the answer. "Do you know how many squealing airheads I've had sitting in that seat? *They* loved it."

And you're different.

"Stop. The. Car!" she screamed.

"You know why you don't like this?" I turned my head to look at her with quick glances back to the invisible road. "Because you're not like them, Tate. You never were. Why do you think I kept everyone away from you?"

I immediately slammed my mouth shut and groaned.

Why the fuck did I just say that?

Her eyes went wide and then narrowed like bullets.

Here we go. In 3, 2, 1 . . .

"Stop the fucking car!" she screamed as she slammed her fists against her thighs and then hit me on the arm.

I flinched and slammed on the brakes, gritting my teeth at the hundreds of dollars' worth of tires I'd just left on the highway.

The Boss came to a screeching halt, swaying slightly from side to side as I worked the wheel to keep us from flying off into the brush.

Goddamn it.

I downshifted, ripped the e-brake, and turned off the car.

Tate opened her door and flew out of her seat, and so did I, ready to go after her if she decided walking home was a smart idea.

But she didn't run.

She looked about ready to hit me. I could feel the heat of the hell-fire and hatred coming from her eyes.

"Get back in the car." I cut her off before she had a chance to speak.

We were in the middle of the road, and another car could come at any time.

"You could've killed us!" she cried.

I would never put you in danger.

My shirt fell off her bare shoulder, and I saw the ripped strap of her shirt peeking out.

I slammed my palm down on the roof of the car, rage and love at battle in my head. "Get back in the goddamn car!" I shouted.

"Why?" she asked, her voice low and cracking.

Is she serious?

"Because you need to go home." *Duh.*

"No." She shook her head, choking back tears and breaking my heart. "Why did you keep everyone away from me?"

"Because you didn't belong with the rest of us. You still don't," I shot back.

She is better.

But apparently, she didn't like that answer.

Before I could stop her, she'd ducked inside of my car and snatched my keys out of the ignition.

I watched in confusion as she rounded her open car door and jogged up the road, near the rocky ditch off to the side.

My keys. What the hell?

My fingers itched to shake her or kiss her.

I approached her slowly, partly annoyed and partly in awe of the fight in her.

She was beautiful. Strands of hair fell across her eyes and small pieces blew around her face from either the wind or her heavy breathing. Seeing the angry passion on her face built me up the same way bullying her had done.

And when I thought of how I could've felt all of this by simply being close to her rather than hurting her, I was planted—no, stuck—to the ground by the weight of wasted time.

It sat like a boulder in my stomach.

"What are you doing?" I tried to appear aggravated.

"One more step, and you're losing one of your keys. Not sure if it's the car key, but eventually I'll get to that one." She cocked her arm behind her head, and I halted.

Fuuuuuck.

"I'm not getting in your car." Her voice was even and strong. "And I'm not letting you leave. We're not moving from this spot until you've told me the truth."

The air around me got dense, and I felt like I was in a cave. Walls everywhere.

I couldn't tell her everything.

I could apologize. I could try to explain.

But I couldn't tell—

Shit! She raised her arm farther, loading it to toss the first key, and my hand shot out, motioning for her to stop.

A replacement key would be at least two hundred dollars.

My heart beat faster, echoing in my ears.

"Tate, don't do this."

"Not the answer I was looking for," she shot back and flung a key into the woods off the side of the road. I watched, completely helpless, as it disappeared into the thick darkness.

"Dammit, Tate!"

She released another key from the ring and loaded it behind her back, too. "Now talk. Why do you hate me?"

Jesus. The key was gone. Maybe the one to my car. Maybe just the house key. And fuck me if it was the one to the school.

I shook my head and almost laughed. "Hate you? I never hated you."

Her eyes narrowed in confusion, and her voice dropped. "Then why? Why did you do all the things you've done?"

Why was I so mean? Why did I isolate you? Why did I ruin our friendship? Which horrible fucking shit did she want explained first?

"Freshman year." I took a deep breath and started. "I overheard Danny Stewart saying he was going to ask you to the Halloween dance. I made sure he never did, because he also told his buddies that he couldn't wait to find out if your tits were more than a handful each."

I also gave him a bloody nose that day. He still doesn't know why.

"I didn't even think twice about my actions," I continued as she remained silent. "I spread that rumor about Stevie Stoddard, because you didn't belong with Danny. He was a dick. They all were."

"So you thought you were protecting me?" she blurted out, unconvinced. "But why would you do that? You already hated me by that point. That was after you'd returned from your dad's for the summer."

"I wasn't protecting you," I stated, raising my eyes to meet hers. "I was jealous."

If I was protecting her, then I wouldn't have turned around and hurt her myself with that rumor. It wasn't about keeping her safe. It was about not wanting anyone else to touch her.

I continued, "We got to high school, and all of a sudden you've got all of these guys liking you. I handled it the only way I knew how."

"By bullying me?" she challenged. "That makes no sense. Why didn't you talk to me?"

"I couldn't. I can't." *I couldn't trust you.*

"You're doing fine so far," she pressed. "I want to know why all of this started in the first place. Why did you want to hurt me? The pranks, the blacklisting from parties? That wasn't about other guys. What was your problem with *me*?"

I inhaled deeply, trying to buy myself some time. I couldn't go there. Not now. Not with her.

I blew out a breath and lied. "Because you were there. Because I couldn't hurt who I wanted to hurt, so I hurt you."

Please just leave it at that.

"I was your best friend." She spoke slowly, making me feel her disgust. "All these years . . ." Her eyes shimmered with unshed tears.

"Tate, I had a shitty summer with my dad that year." I inched closer. "When I came back, I wasn't the same kid. Not even close. I wanted to hate everybody. But with you, I still needed you in a way. I needed you to not forget me."

Part of it was about control, and part of it was about my anger, but most of it was about not being able to let her go. I needed to be in her life. I needed her to see me.

"Jared, I've turned it over and over in my head, wondering what I could've done to make you act the way you did. And now you tell me that it was all for no reason?"

I continued moving in.

"You were never clingy or a nuisance, Tate. The day you moved in next door I thought you were the most beautiful thing I'd ever seen." My voice dropped to a near whisper and my eyes fell to the ground. "I fucking loved you. Your dad was unloading the moving truck, and I looked out my living-room window to see what the noise was. There you were, riding your bike in the street. You were wearing overalls with a red baseball cap. Your hair was spilling down your back."

Even then I knew Tate would be important to me.

Shortly after she'd moved in, I'd found out that her mom had passed away. My father wasn't in my life, and Tate and I connected instantly. We had things like music and movies in common.

And the rest was out of our control. We'd found each other.

"When you recited your monologue this week, I . . ." I let out a breath. "I knew then that I'd really gotten to you, and instead of feeling any satisfaction, I was angry with myself. I wanted to hate you all these years—I wanted to hate someone. But I didn't know how much I was hurting you until the monologue, and I hated it."

Stepping in front of her, I felt the hairs on my arms stand on end.

The heat from her body—so close—radiated toward me, and it took everything I had not to circle my arms around her waist and bring her into my arms. The memory of how she felt the other night only made me think of all the things I wanted.

"You're not telling me everything." She looked like her head was spinning, like she was half in and half out of the moment.

I reached up and cupped her face with one hand, wiping away a single warm tear.

"No, I'm not." My voice was barely audible.

Her eyes were hooded, but she tried to keep going. "The scars on your back," she started. "You said you had a bad summer, and that when you came back you wanted to hate everybody, but you haven't treated anyone else as badly as—"

"Tate?" I cut her off and closed the inch left between us, our breathing in sync as we met chest to chest. All I could see were her lips, full and soft. "I don't want to talk any more tonight."

She stood there, watching me close in, and the moment was a hair from coming together or coming apart.

She wanted my lips on hers, but she might not like that she wanted it.

Please don't stop me.

Her skin was like touching cool silk, was smooth like butter, and I fisted my hand in her hair.

And then she jerked, as if waking up.

"You don't want to talk anymore?" Her strong voice broke the spell, and my legs tensed, waiting for her to hit me again. "Well, I do," she yelled. And I sprang into action when I saw her twist around to launch another key into the forest.

Hell!

Circling my arms around her body, I pulled her, struggling, into my chest.

Damn it! I'd explained! I knew she wouldn't forgive me right away, but why was she still so upset? *What more did she want?*

You don't apologize. You don't beg!

My father's mantra. Repeated over and over again that summer.

I hated almost everything he'd taught me, but that was one lesson I'd committed to practice. Apologizing was a sign of weakness.

But I wanted Tate back.

My heart beat only for her, and I'd rather spend my life hating, loving, fucking, and breathing her than losing her.

You need to apologize, dickhead.

"Shhh, Tate," I whispered into her ear. "I won't hurt you. I'll never hurt you again. I'm sorry," I said, closing my eyes as I swallowed the bitter pill.

She twisted from side to side. "I don't care about you being sorry! I hate you!"

No.

Still securing her with both arms, I used my hands to peel open her fingers and pry out my keys.

I let her go, and she stepped forward and spun around to face me.

"You don't hate me," I challenged with a grin, before she had the chance to speak. "If you did, you wouldn't be this upset."

"Go screw yourself," she spat back, and turned, stomping away.

Um, where did she think she was going?

If she thought I was going to let her walk home in the dark, on a deserted road, she was out of her fucking mind.

Digging my feet into the ground, I took off after her, spun her around, and threw her over my shoulder like I wanted to do earlier. She landed hard, her stomach caving to my shoulder, and I had a huge desire to keep her there and walk home.

Fuck the car.

Well, almost.

"Put me down!" She kicked her feet and punched my back, and I tightened my hold, willing my fingers to stay put.

Her ass was next to my head, and, goddamn, I wanted to take advantage of her position in her short skirt.

But in her current mood, she'd probably cut off my dick.

"Jared! Now!" she ordered, her tone low and commanding.

Reaching the car, I swung her back upright and planted her ass down on the hood of the car. I immediately came down, placing my hands on each side of her thighs and leaning in.

Very slowly.

I knew I should just back off.

Give her time. Win back her trust.

But I'd had a taste of her, and I'd rather give up breathing.

I still made the rules, and we weren't wasting any more time.

"Don't try to get away," I warned. "As you remember, I can keep you here."

It wasn't a threat. I just wanted her to remember. The way she'd devoured me on that kitchen counter, wanting me as much as I wanted her.

She tipped her chin down, looking hesitant. "And I know how to use pepper spray and break noses," she retorted and leaned back, keeping a wary distance, like she didn't trust herself.

I could see her pulse beating in her neck, but she wasn't trying to get away.

She watched me watching her, and the moment stood still as her chest rose and fell with shallow breaths.

She wanted me like I wanted her, but she didn't like that she wanted me.

She was a mess, and I loved it.

I do that to you. No one else.

"I'm not Nate or Madoc . . . or Ben."

Our noses almost touched as I searched her face. A line of sweat fell down my back, and my dick throbbed, making me feel like I was on fire.

"Don't," she whispered as my mouth hovered over hers.

Oh, I won't. You will.

"I promise. Not unless you ask." Having her feeling sorry the next day that she gave in to me would suck. I didn't want that blame. She was going to be a part of this as much as I was, and I wanted her crazed and confused over me. And then I wanted her to surrender.

I guess that's what I'd been after all along.

I moved my lips around her face and neck, breathing her in but never kissing her.

I could still taste her, though.

My lips grazed her soft cheek, and I just about touched her lips right then when she let out a little moan.

Fuck.

Every second my mouth glided over her face, her jaw, her neck, I fought to keep my teeth from sinking into her. I was that hungry.

"Can I kiss you now?" I half asked, half pleaded.

She didn't say yes, but she didn't say no, either.

"I want to touch you," I whispered against her lips. "I want to feel what's mine. What's always been mine."

Please.

Her breath caught, and I could tell she was fighting it. Weakly, she pushed me away and jumped off the car.

"Stay away from me," she said as she headed for the passenger's side.

Yeah, no.

I tried to keep my laugh quiet. "You first," I teased.

CHAPTER 23

"Give me two." My father put down two cards to exchange, and my lips twisted up just a little.

No "How are you?" "What's new with you?" Or "Happy fucking birthday, son."

Nothing.

I was eighteen today, and my father clearly didn't remember.

Or he didn't care.

I flipped two more cards off the top of the deck and tossed them across the table to him.

To hell with it. Ten minutes down, fifty to go.

We'd been silent since I arrived. Speaking, as usual, only when needed.

And my stomach was still rolling.

After the episode with Tate last night, I'd felt great. Relaxed, excited, calm.

But every week, I got sick before I came to the prison, and my high from last night was now gone. The dreadful anticipation of whatever lousy shit my father was going to say to me made me nauseous. I could never eat anything in the mornings. And most of the time my hands shook so badly that driving was hard.

That's why I opted to drive up last night after I'd dropped off Tate. There was no way I was going to get to sleep with my body in knots over her, so I just got the fuck out of there. Drove up to Crest Hill. Stayed in a motel, and came here as soon as visiting hours began. I usually calmed down after I left. I felt safer the closer to home I got.

The only thing that got me through the visits week after week without throwing up was the necklace.

And I hadn't gotten that back last night.

Right now, though, my insides were caked with acid and burning a trail up my throat. It hurt, and I kept swallowing it down, hoping that he couldn't see me thinking of her. I knew it sounded weird. How can someone see what you're thinking? But my father had a knack for reading me, and he was the only person who made me feel weak.

"So, where is it?"

I ignored his question.

Who knew what he was talking about? I was always sorry when I let him get me to talk. I just shut the fuck up and breathed.

"You've been practically keeping one hand in your pants pocket almost the entire time of every fucking visit except today. What do you keep in there like a goddamn security blanket, and why don't you have it all of a sudden?"

I chewed on my lip, tapped my foot, and then tried saying my cards in my head over and over again.

2, 4, 5, 6, 7. Spade, spade, spade, spade, heart.

The room, with its high ceilings and long hallways off to the sides, echoed with conversations I couldn't make out, and the bustle of visitors filled the air. Light poured through the windows, but it didn't make anything feel happier.

"You think I'm an asshole." My father put another card down and spoke quietly. "I am an asshole, Jared. I've made you hard, but I've also made you strong. No one will hurt you again, because you're untouchable. Even to that girl, you're out of reach."

I snapped my eyes up to meet his, and my cards crumpled in my fist. The deep rumble of his raspy laugh ripped Tate from my head.

"You got your money," I gritted out, tight-lipped. "Shut up."

He just shook his head and continued arranging his cards. "Does she know about you? About what a coward you are? About how you abandoned your brother?"

Jax.

"There is no *she*." My lie came out as a mumble.

"You're right," he retorted. "You'll always be alone, because you know that that's better. And she'll find someone to marry her and fill her with babies that aren't yours."

My stomach caved, and I didn't think.

I slammed my cards down on the table, launched out of my chair, and popped my father right across the jaw. The ache in my fist spread up my arm, and I watched as he fell out of his chair onto the floor, still laughing his ass off.

My chest heaved as I breathed through my nose.

"Next week is my last visit," I told him. "I won't miss you, but I know you'll miss me."

"That's enough of that." I heard a voice say before I was grabbed by the arm.

Looking up, I saw a guard, a little taller than me and with dark hair and light eyes, scowling.

I yanked my arm away from him. "No worries. I'm gone." And I turned around, my jaw hard as cement as I walked out.

"Don't worry, Jared," my father yelled behind me. "We won't stray far from each other. I'll always be in your head."

As soon as I got home from the visit, I found my mom in the kitchen with a cake.

"No way. I'm not in the mood." My tone was hard and I didn't mean to cut her, but I backed out of the kitchen and walked toward the stairs.

"Jared, please," she shouted after me.

I stopped, every muscle in my chest so stretched that I was ready to scream, and I spun around and charged back into the kitchen.

My mother stood on the other side of the kitchen table, brown hair in a high bun and arms at her sides. She was dressed nicely in jeans, heels, and a short jacket.

Gripping the back of the chair until the wood creaked beneath my fingers, I stared at her, trying to swallow down the fight I wanted.

"I appreciate the effort," I told her. "I really do. But we've gotten along just fine without having to pretend that we're an actual family. You do your thing. I do mine."

My stomach was in knots, and my words spilled out like mud.

Her eyes dropped, but she recovered and lifted her chin.

"I want Jax to come and live with us," she said matter-of-factly and out of nowhere.

I stopped breathing and narrowed my eyes on her, too shocked to even respond.

Excuse me?

Jax live with us?

She smiled a little and circled the table toward me before I even had a chance to process if she was kidding.

"Jared, I've already spoken to a lawyer. Nothing is for sure, but . . ."

she paused, eyeing me carefully, "but he might be able to help. Do you want your brother with us?"

I wanted my brother safe.

I tightened my grip on the chair's back. "Do *you* want him here?" I asked her.

Her eyes dropped, and her lips turned up with a thoughtful smile. "Yes. I like Jaxon." And then she looked up at me again. "He brings out the best in you. Just like Tate used to."

I couldn't eat cake.

I didn't like attention, and the idea of my mother making me blow out candles had me gagging.

I went to my room and closed the door, enjoying the dark and quiet for however long I could have it.

Jax with us? I thought as I lay on my bed.

I still couldn't believe she'd thought of it. That she wanted to take him in.

It was expensive, but she didn't seem to care.

That was one issue I never pushed, even though it confused me. She worked in an accounting firm, earning enough to support us but not enough for what we had. Our house was paid for, I always had the best cell phones, and she had a nice car. Paid for.

To be honest, I was just afraid to ask. I didn't want to know how we lived so well.

I got a text from K.C. saying she hoped we were friends, and she offered a thank-you for the help with her dipshit boyfriend.

He'll be cheating again in a month. They always do. But I didn't tell her that.

She also let it slip in a not-so-subtle way that Tate was on her own now. Her visiting grandmother had left town.

My lips turned up, and I was about to stalk over there and pick another fight with Tate when I got a text.

Everything good?

Tate's dad.
Fine, I typed back.

You got the house key back to Tate, right?

Yes, I lied. I wasn't ready to give that up yet.

Thanks. Happy 18. Present should be arriving soon.

Thanks, I typed back, not good at being gracious.
Tate's birthday is in a week. Find out what she wants, he ordered.
I let out a sigh.
That might be difficult, I texted.
He shot back not thirty seconds later, **A man . . . ?**
And I punched the bed with my fist.
. . . takes care of business. I reluctantly finished.
Make it happen, and thank you, he shot back.
I threw off my shirt and jumped in the hot shower, lulling me into some fucking peace and quiet for once in the past twenty-four hours.

I still couldn't believe I'd hit my father. I'd never done that before, even to defend myself that summer.

I didn't know why that comment about Tate having another man's babies had gotten me so angry. My father had accomplished what he'd set out to do, and I'd fallen for it again.

I couldn't think of myself as a father, now or anytime in the future.

But one thing was for certain. Whether it was now or ten years from now, I didn't want Tate having anyone else's kids.

But someday she'd want them. Most people did.

And I swallowed the baseball-sized lump that it wasn't going to be me in her future.

CHAPTER 24

_____

t was Monday morning, and I was breaking and entering for the first time in my life. Of my own free will, anyway.

My hands weren't even shaking as I loaded the key into the lock and walked into the Brandts' empty house. Tate had left for school a half hour ago, and I was a little aggravated that I was late for school, too. I'd hoped she'd be off early this morning, doing whatever she did in the chemistry lab, but not today. She'd left late, and now I was behind.

Tate's dad wanted me to find out what she wanted for her birthday, like we were friends or some shit, and he knew better. The only way I was going to find out the answer was to ask her, and our relationship wasn't on good foundations.

So . . . I decided to snoop.

Yep, that's what I thought was a good idea.

Check the history on her laptop, sift through her fucking journal, maybe look through her drawers for open boxes of condoms . . .

My leg tingled, and I took out my vibrating phone.

Where r u?

Madoc.
Late, I typed.

Closing the back door and slipping my keys back into my pocket, I walked through the kitchen and over to the stairs.

She was everywhere. The smell of her shampoo—like warm strawberries—made my mouth water.

I hadn't seen or heard a thing from Tate all weekend. The truck had been in the driveway, but she seemed to be in hiding since Friday night.

I sucked in a long breath before I entered her room. Not sure why.

All I knew was that I felt turned on and perverted all at the same time.

I decided to be quick about it and get out.

I wasn't a pussy. I had the guts to sneak through someone's shit.

Clothes were strewn throughout the otherwise neat room, and she'd added some more pictures and posters to the walls since I'd been in it.

My eyes roamed the space as I slowly walked around, and I saw her laptop but bypassed it and sat down on her bed instead.

My throat was dry.

Fuck.

I picked this moment to develop a conscience?

Her computer history might reveal exactly what I needed, or it might show me shit I didn't need to know. She could be Googling face creams and designer umbrellas. Or she could be e-mailing some jerk she'd met in France or admissions offices for colleges far away.

I decided to start slow and opened her bedside-table drawer instead.

There was some hand lotion, a small bowl full of rubber bands, some candy, and . . . a book.

I picked up the tattered, faded paperback that I hadn't seen in years, but it seemed like just yesterday.

Memories poured in all at once.

Tate stuffing it in her backpack on her first day of junior high.

Tate trying to read some poem about Abraham Lincoln to me after swimming at the lake.

Tate's dad taping the binding when Madman had run off with it.

The book—*Leaves of Grass* by Walt Whitman—was older. Like, twenty years. It had belonged to her mom, and Tate always kept it close. She used to take it with her anytime she left town for a trip.

Flipping through the pages, I searched for the poem—the only poem—that I liked. I couldn't remember the name, but I remember she'd underlined the passage.

No sooner had I started flipping through when some pictures spilled out. I forgot the book and picked up the photos off my lap instead.

My heart pounded in the back of my throat.

Jesus.

It was us.

The pictures were of her and me. There were two, both when we were twelve or thirteen, and a ton of fucking emotions fell on me at once.

Tate kept pictures of me?

They were in her mother's book that she treasured.

And she'd most likely taken these to France with her, along with the book that held them.

I shook my head, my feet feeling like they were stuck in a bucket of cement.

She kept pictures of us like I kept pictures of us, and I smiled, feeling like I'd just won something.

And then the tiptoeing-through-the-fucking-tulips feeling that I was enjoying crashed to the ground as soon as I spied a black lace bra lying on her dresser. The tingling sensation of someone roller skating across my heart moved south, and now I wanted to leave here in search of her.

My jaw moved, and I almost bit my tongue to keep my dick in check.

Well, well, well . . . Tate wears lingerie.

Her sleek body dressed in black lace blanketed my brain, and then I blinked.

Wait.

Realization dawned.

Tate wears lingerie.

Tate. Wears. Fucking. Lingerie!

What the hell for? And for who?

I ran a rough hand through my hair and felt the sweat on my forehead.

Fuck it.

Let her dad give her some money. That's what every other teenager wants for her birthday, isn't it?

I threw the book back into the drawer and stalked out of the room and down the stairs, and out the front door.

I don't even remember driving to school.

The images of Tate wearing lingerie for some needle-dick asswipe were the only things I saw for a while.

My morning classes passed in a fog. I sat there with my arms crossed and my eyes on my desktop, ignoring those around me. By fourth period, I gripped my desk, chair, or anything else to keep my ass from storming into her French class and picking a fight.

Teachers didn't call on me, so I didn't worry about paying attention. My grades stayed up, and I smarted off when they did ask me questions, so they ended up saving themselves the trouble of engaging me.

I took my time getting to lunch.

She would be there, and I didn't want to sit back and watch us both try to ignore each other when I just wanted her next to me.

"Tatum Brandt!"

What the . . . ?

I halted in the lunchroom at the sound of someone calling her name.

I had spied Sam and his friend Gunnar at our usual table, and I'd just gotten done grabbing a drink and sandwich when I'd heard a low voice yelling very loudly.

I zoned in on Madoc, facing away from me, fucking kneeling in the middle of the room!

"Will you please go to the Homecoming dance with me?" he shouted, and when I followed where he was looking, I clenched my fingers, destroying the sandwich in my hand.

Shiiiit.

A very surprised Tate had turned around, her shoulders tensed and eyes avoiding everyone else's like she was more annoyed than embarrassed.

Tate couldn't stand Madoc.

Oh, what the hell is he doing now?

The packed cafeteria hushed to a silence.

Madoc walked on his knees up to Tate and took her hand.

A few giggles sounded around the room, and a push-and-pull force was battling in my limbs.

Move! He's pursuing her. He's always wanted her.

No, stay put. He's your friend. He wouldn't do that.

"Please, please! Don't say no. I need you," he yelled, more to the audience than Tate, and everyone erupted in laughs and cheers, egging him on.

"Please, let's make this work. I'm sorry for everything," he continued, and I could see Tate looking down at him, wide-eyed and flushed, like she was sick.

Sick and pissed.

She mumbled something to him I couldn't hear, and then he shouted, "But the baby needs a father!"

WHAT. THE. FUCK?

My stomach dropped, and everything in the room turned red.

Tate's face fell, and the crowd hollered their enjoyment of Madoc's spectacle.

Her lips moved, but only just barely.

What the hell was she saying to him?

He seemed fucking pleased, because he stood up and enveloped her in his arms, swinging her around to the delight of the audience.

Everyone whistled and applauded, and I threw my lunch in the trash without even looking.

She said yes?

I turned around and stalked out before he'd even put her down.

CHAPTER 25

"Goddamn it!" Madoc howled as his hand shot up to his face, and he crashed backwards into the row of lockers behind him.

We shared PE together, and I hadn't even waited for him to make eye contact before I'd run up and clocked him right in the eye.

The class in the locker room got out of the way, and I stepped over the bench to sit down in front of my best friend, who'd slid to the floor.

I rested my elbows on top of my knees and looked down at him.

"I'm sorry," I breathed out, and it was the truth. "But you do know you're pushing me, right?"

"Yeah," he nodded, squinting with one hand over his eye.

He always pushed me, and it pissed me off, but I knew why he was doing it. He wanted me to act. To grovel at Tate's feet and make her want me.

But she'd said yes.

That pissed me off, too.

Me not even thinking to ask her to the dance myself pissed me off.

I hated dances.

I hated dancing.

But, thanks to me, Tate didn't go to things like that in the past, and she obviously wanted to.

A bitter taste settled in my mouth.

It's the taste you get right before you choke down a mouthful of pride.

"Hey, Dr. Porter." I ran into my sophomore-year chemistry teacher in the hallway after school. "Is Tatum Brandt working in the lab today?" I gestured to the door behind him.

"Yes," he blurted out, wide-eyed and looking oddly relieved to see me. "She is. But it just occurred to me that she's alone. Are you free? Would you mind spotting her? I'm usually there, but I have a meeting."

"Alone?" My jaw twitched with a pent-up smile. "No problem."

He kept walking, and I opened the lab door, my heart already rushing with the promise of the kind of trouble I wanted to drown in.

The room was empty, but I heard shuffling and clattering coming from the supply closet, so I took the seat at the teacher's table and propped up my feet, waiting for her.

The lab was on the larger side of the classrooms at the school. It held about twelve tables with two to three seats per table. The tops were lined with beakers and flasks, burners and sinks.

I liked the tables.

They were a good height.

I half laughed, half sighed at the images floating through my head. *Jesus Christ.*

I'd never fantasized about a girl the way I did with Tate, but I was getting ahead of myself. She might never let me get to second base again, let alone third.

Running my hands through my hair, I hooked my fingers behind my head and tried thinking about the Lifetime Movie Network to keep my dick in check.

The closet door swung open, and Tate stepped out with a crate of supplies in her arms.

Her hair was parted in the middle today, and it flowed around her face and body, partially obscuring her eyes.

But she saw me.

Even through the blond wisps, I could pick out the storm.

Her legs stilled, and she looked surprised, unnerved, and a little pissed.

We had the same effect on each other.

"Not now, Jared. I'm busy," she warned as she carried her crate to a table off to my right. Her tone was steady and curt.

She was putting me in my place.

"I know. I came to help you."

It was a lie, but I guessed I could help her. I knew my shit in chemistry as well as math. It was the touchy-feely subjects like English and psychology that bit my ass.

"Help me?" Her eyes lit up like I'd said the most ridiculous thing. "I don't need help."

"I wasn't asking if you did," I shot back.

"No, you're just assuming," she retorted, not meeting my eyes as she continued to unload her supplies.

"Not at all. I know what you can do." My voice cracked with amusement, but I wanted her to look at me.

"I thought that if we're going to be friends," I continued, "this might be a good place to start."

Getting off my chair, I walked toward her, hoping she would know I wanted anything but friendship.

"I mean . . ." I kept going when she didn't say anything. "It's not like we're going to be able to go back to climbing trees and having sleepovers, is it?"

Her chest filled with a quiet breath, and she stopped unloading for a split second. Her eyes met mine, and for a moment I thought she'd let me plant her ass on the counter and show her how a sleepover between us would work.

But then she narrowed her eyes and talked more with her teeth than her lips. "Like I said, I don't need help."

"Like I said, I wasn't asking," I repeated, not missing a beat. "Did you think that Porter was going to let you conduct experiments with fire by yourself?" I had no idea what her experiment was, but after catching sight of some of her materials and Porter's apprehension about leaving her alone, I gathered that it would involve the burners.

"How do you know about my experiment? And who said we're going to be friends?" she sneered before bending down to get something out of her bag. "You know, maybe too much damage has been done. I know you've apologized, but it's not so easy for me."

This was not the Tate I knew. Tate was tough. Even when I'd made her cry over the years with my pranks, she held her head high and moved on.

Tate didn't need grand gestures. Did she?

"You're not getting girly on me, are you?" I was trying at sarcasm, but I wanted a fucking miracle.

Yes, Jared. Thank you for apologizing, and I forgive you. Let's move on.

That's what I really wanted.

But she buried her face in her binder and ignored me. Or tried to look like she was ignoring me.

My fingers were humming, and I balled up my fists to try to erase the urge to touch her.

She kept staring at her papers, but I knew she wasn't reading anything. She was feeling me like I was feeling her.

Finally she sighed, giving up the pretense, and looked up at me like my mother did when she'd had enough. "Jared, I appreciate the effort you're putting in here, but it's unnecessary. Contrary to what your ego is blowing you up with, I've been surviving just fine without you for the past three years. I work better alone, and I would not appreciate your help today or any other day. We're not friends."

My pulse throbbed in my throat, and I swallowed.

Fine without me?

And I hadn't breathed a single day without her on my mind.

She leveled me with her resigned expression and flat eyes. I wondered if she'd believed what she'd said.

I wondered if it was true.

She turned back around to her worktable, not giving away anything until she knocked her binder to the floor and its contents spilled everywhere.

I stepped behind her, and we bent down together to pick up the papers.

Is she nervous?

Tate wasn't usually clumsy.

Gathering up the papers, I pinched my eyebrows together and studied the Internet printouts of cars for sale that were among the papers. "You're looking at cars?" I asked.

The selection included a Mustang, a Charger, a 300M, and a G8.

"Yeah," she snipped. "I'm getting myself a birthday present."

Birthday. I nearly said it out loud.

I guess now I knew what to tell her dad she wanted.

She'd want the car soon. Her birthday was coming up in less than a week. I wondered if he'd trust me to tag along with her to go buy one instead of making her wait.

Would *she* trust me?

"Jared?" She held out her hand for the papers.

I blinked, coming out of my thoughts. "I forgot your birthday was coming up," I lied. "Does your dad know you're looking to buy a car so soon?" I asked as I came up beside her at the table.

"Does your mom know you provide alcohol to minors and sleep around on the weekends?" she retorted, serving my shit back to me.

"'Does my mom care?' would be a better question." I couldn't hide the disdain in my tone as I started helping her unload her crate.

Even before I'd met Tate, my relationship with my mother was broken. I roamed, left to stick up for myself or my mom on the few occasions one of her asshole drinking buddies got rough. Not that I could throw much weight around at that age, but I tried.

In her monologue, Tate reminded me of how she healed me when she thought I'd healed her. We were both fighting for happiness. Fighting to just be kids when we met.

Those four years we spent together were the best I'd ever felt.

I snapped my head to the side when I heard glass shatter to the floor.

What the . . . ?

Tate had whipped around, probably having tried to catch the flask, and leaned on the counter looking down at her mess.

What the hell is going on with her?

She stared at the damage, almost looking like she was in pain as her chest rose and fell in hard, deep breaths.

Tate wasn't what I would call controlled, but she'd been holding her own with Madoc and me since her return.

Until now.

"I make you nervous," I said regretfully, looking at the shattered glass on the floor.

"Just go." I heard her pained whisper and flinched.

Looking at her, I saw the embarrassment and frustration in her eyes. She didn't want me here. I didn't know if it was because she hated me and needed me gone or because she wasn't sure what she wanted.

I was finally seeing how I had twisted her up. I was playing with her, even though I didn't mean to. I thought I hated her, so I pushed her. Now I wanted her, so I was pulling her back in.

Time and again, it was about me and never her.

"Look at me." I brought my hand up to her cheek and a shock of heat traveled through my arm. "I'm sorry. I should never have treated you the way I did."

Her eyes met mine, and I willed her to believe me.

Her breathing got shallow and she searched for something in my eyes.

Or waited for something.

Placing my other hand on her cheek, I never broke contact. She watched me inch in, not welcoming me but not resisting it, either.

I moved my lips closer, never taking my eyes from hers as I waited for her to push me away. As the seconds ticked by I finally snatched up her mouth before I let her have any more time to reconsider.

Hell, yes.

I held her in my hands, tasting her sweet, full lips like I couldn't get enough.

Tate. My Tate. My best friend and my worst enemy. The girl that turned my world upside down with her overalls and red baseball cap.

The only person in every one of my good memories.

Her hands were hesitant at first, but then they snaked around my neck, and I felt her unfold around me.

Goddamn, her body rubbed against mine, the softest moan coming out of her mouth, and my fists tightened in her hair. I was about to lose it. She had the power. Always had and always would.

She moved her hips up against mine, and I ran my hands down her sides and around to her perfect, rounded ass.

Grabbing it in my hands, I jerked her into me.

Mine.

The fucking wet heat of her mouth and the curve of her breasts against my chest made my cock ache for release. I wanted to push all this shit onto the floor and take her on the table.

I wondered if she was a virgin, and my neck broke out in a sweat at the thought of anyone else kissing her like this.

"I've wanted you for so long," I whispered against her mouth. "All the times I'd see you next door . . . it drove me crazy."

She opened her mouth wider and dove in for more.

Yeah, we weren't leaving here for a while.

wasn't about to make love to Tate for the first time on a lab table—
not that she'd let me—but I wasn't letting go of her yet, either.

Unfortunately, she had other ideas.

"Don't . . ." She ripped away from my lips and pulled back.

What? No.

I opened my eyes, breathing hard and suddenly feeling very empty.

I searched every inch of her face, wondering why the hell she'd
made me stop. Her mouth had been molded to mine, totally kissing
me back.

She'd wanted that.

But not now. Her blue eyes narrowed angrily, and she looked like
she had on invisible armor.

Her body wanted it, but she didn't.

She didn't.

So I backed off. "Then I won't," I replied coldly.

She stared at me, looking a million miles away. "What are you up to?"

"I want us to be friends." I let out a bitter laugh.

"Why now?"

Jesus.

"Why so many questions?" I retorted.

"You didn't think it was going to be this easy, did you?"

"Yes," I lied. "I was hoping we could move forward without looking back." I knew it was too much to expect, but I let myself hope that Tate would see the bigger picture.

That with all of the anger and damage, with all the distance and misunderstanding, we still fit.

"We can't," she shot back. "You go from threatening me one day to kissing me the next. I don't switch gears that fast."

Me?

"Kissing you? You kissed me back . . . both times," I pointed out. "And now you're off to the school dance with Madoc. You might say I'm the one with whiplash here."

She blinked and her face faltered for a moment. "I don't have to explain myself to you," she replied pathetically.

"You shouldn't go."

"I want to. And he asked me." She returned to her work, signaling the end of the discussion.

No fucking way.

My arms burned. I wanted to bring her back into them.

Stepping up behind her, I breathed her in. The top of her head fell just below my chin, and her whole torso—arms included—fit the width of my chest.

She fit.

"Has *he* been on your mind, Tate?" I inhaled the scent of her hair and braced both of my hands on the table on each side of her, caging her in. "Do you want him? Or is it me you dream of?"

Her hands slowed what they were doing, and I took that as a good sign, so I kept going.

"I said that when I put my hands on you, you'd want it. Remember?" I asked smoothly, trying to touch her with my words.

She paused for a moment and then turned around to look at me. "I don't think it's any secret that I like it when you touch me. When you're ready to tell me everything you're holding back, then maybe I'll trust you again. Until then . . ." And she turned back around, cutting the connection.

I stared at her back, trying to figure out another way in.

She wanted to know shit. I got it.

But that wasn't going to happen. I didn't broadcast my problems. And I wasn't bringing my father into our world.

Backing away, the truth settled in my gut like a rock.

Tate was not going to let this go.

No way, no how.

"Jared? There you are."

I blinked and shifted my eyes to the doorway, where Piper stood in her black-and-orange cheerleading uniform.

Shit.

"Weren't you giving me a ride home today?" She put on a show, adjusting her long dark hair and skirt.

I couldn't see Tate's face, but I knew she was annoyed. She concentrated a little too hard on her materials and papers, trying to look busy.

"I've got my bike today, Piper." Which was the truth. Piper had never asked for a ride.

"I can handle it," she shot back. "Let's go. It doesn't look like you're busy here anyway."

Tate wasn't looking at either of us, and my stomach hollowed like the night I saw some other guy giving her her first kiss.

But I still didn't want to leave. I'd rather have Tate feeding me her thorns than Piper feeding me her sweets.

But Tate was done. She wouldn't let me off the hook. At least not today.

Fine, then. I let out a breath and stood up straight.

"Yeah, I'm not busy." I walked toward the door, feeling colder and colder the farther away from Tate I got.

"So, Terrance?" Piper piped up.

Oh, Jesus. She was talking to Tate.

"You didn't go and give your Homecoming date a black eye, did you? He can barely see. You should really stop beating up on guys, or people will start thinking you're a dyke."

Fucking catty girls.

"She didn't give Madoc a black eye," I cut in. "I did."

I didn't care if Tate knew I was jealous. She definitely knew I wanted her by now.

"Why?" Piper asked.

I ignored the question as we walked out.

I never explained myself.

CHAPTER 27

hanks for the gift. I texted Tate's dad.

The huge toolbox he'd given me was used, but it easily would've cost fifteen thousand dollars new. Without it being in mint condition, it still would've cost a pretty penny. When it arrived today, I almost had the guy take it back.

But Mr. Brandt knew me. He knew how much I wanted a professional, heavy-duty set like that, and so I took it. It was the first time in a long time that I'd smiled at a gift.

You're welcome. Sorry it's late. Anything on Tate? he asked.

The first thing I thought about was the black lingerie I'd seen in her room, and my dick instantly sprang into action when I imagined what she'd look like wearing that for me.

Hurriedly, I texted, A car, and tossed my phone on the workbench in the garage, not waiting for a response.

A little weird to be texting the father of a girl I presently had a hard-on for.

"Sam, go get the car gassed up while I shower, would you?" I asked my friend after we'd finished tuning up the Boss.

It was Friday night, and I had a race in an hour. I couldn't wait to get on the track. My nerves were shot.

I hadn't been laid in more than a month, and the only girl I wanted wasn't giving me the time of day.

And the worst part?

I'd had more fucking hard-ons lately than in my entire life.

I desperately needed to burn off some steam, and as childish as it sounded, I was hoping some fucking asshole got in my face tonight.

I wanted to be bloody, and I wanted to go deaf.

"All right." Sam took the keys. "I'll be back in twenty."

He backed out of the garage, while I headed upstairs to clean up.

Tate was home. I saw her pull in a couple of hours ago, and I'd thought about asking her to go with me, but I'd shaken off the idea. She would only push questions I didn't want to answer and leave me in fucking knots.

"Jesus Christ," I growled as the cold water hit my body like a fire. The hair on my arms and legs stood on end, and chills erupted across my skin.

Tatum Fucking Brandt.

Wrapping a black towel around my waist, I grabbed another and walked to my bedroom, drying my hair.

I switched on a lamp and walked to my window, looking out through the tree to her bedroom. Her light was on, but she was nowhere in sight. I did a sweep of what I could see of the front and back yards to make sure everything looked safe.

I really hated the idea of her being alone. While I was itching to get out to the Loop tonight, I wanted her where I could see her.

I should just ask her to come.

She'd enjoy it.

Even though Tate was keeping me at a distance, she loved the races. That much I could tell. When we were kids, we'd talked about racing there when we had our own cars.

And if I spent time with her—showed her that I could be trusted—then maybe she'd back off. Maybe she'd forget about the past.

"Jared?"

A soft, low voice ripped through me, and I whipped around, my heart thundering in my chest.

What the hell?

"Tate?" The vision standing in the dark corner of my room startled, confused, and excited me all at the same time.

She's here? In my room?

She stood there, her chin down and her eyes trained on me. She didn't move a muscle as she waited. She looked like she'd been caught doing something she shouldn't.

"What the hell are you doing in my room?" I asked calmly, more confused than angry.

Our last conversation left me no doubt that she wouldn't be the one pursuing me, so what the hell was she up to?

She quietly stepped forward, inching toward me. "Well, I thought about what you said about trying to be friends, and I wanted to start by wishing you a happy birthday."

Huh?

"So you broke into my room to tell me 'happy birthday' a week after my birthday?" An ounce of pleasure shot through my chest that she remembered, but she was lying. That wasn't why she was here.

"I climbed through the tree, just like we used to do," she offered.

"And your birthday's tomorrow. Can I climb over to your bedroom?" I countered sarcastically. "What are you really doing in here?"

I pinned her with hard eyes and came up to her so close that a fire sprang to life in my stomach.

Dammit. I was going to need another shower. Did I have the same effect on her body?

"I . . . um . . ." she stammered, and I had to hold back a smile.

She wanted to play games? She had no idea.

Her gaze struggled to meet mine. She couldn't look away for long, but she couldn't hold my stare, either.

Finally, she took a deep breath and broke into a shaky half smile and pushed some hair behind her ear.

"I have something for you, actually." She leaned in close to my face. "Consider it your present to me, as well," she whispered.

What the . . . ?

Her lips melted into mine, and it was like warm sugar.

Jesus Christ. What is she doing?

Her tight body pressed into mine, and I closed my eyes, a tingling spreading through my hands. The urge to sink my fingers into every curve of her skin was uncontrollable.

Her lips teased and captivated me. She moved her hips into mine in slow, small movements, and her tongue flicked under my top lip, playing with me.

I was in a whole lot of trouble and a world of pain if she stopped.

She wrapped her arms around my neck, and my eyebrows lifted. *Holy shit.* She wasn't ending this. She was grabbing on.

Thank God.

Snaking my arms around her back, I took control and dove into her mouth like I was never going to get this chance again.

I forgot everything. Why she was here. Why she was the one initiating this shit. What she was going to do when we got close to the point of no return.

Who fucking cared?

"Jesus, Tate," I breathed out, light-headed when she dipped her head into my neck. The pleasure of her lips, tongue, and teeth was a dream come true.

This was Tate, but it wasn't.

She was wild, kissing and biting me like the night on the kitchen counter. I could feel the way she moved her hips into mine, pressing herself into me.

She was everywhere, and I couldn't even remember my own name.

I tensed for a moment when her fingers ran over the scars on my back. She knew that they were there, but I hoped she wouldn't notice them. I'd be ready to throw down with the devil himself if she stopped this to ask more fucking questions.

Her mouth was hot, and the sweetness of her breath had me in a daze. I nearly growled every time her tongue shot out to taste my skin as she kissed my neck.

Whispering in my ear, she had my body screaming *Get her on the bed!*

"I'm not stopping," she taunted.

Hell, yes.

Lifting her up, I carried her to the bed. She wrapped her legs around me. It was a great feeling. Having Tate hold fast to me. Wanting me.

I didn't know why she was really in here, and I wondered at her change of heart all of a sudden, but she wasn't faking this.

And I wasn't going to fuck it up.

I laid her down and hovered over her, taking in the sight of Tate underneath me. I inched her tank top up to her bra slowly, loving the feel of her in my hands. Her stomach was smooth and taut, curving in at the sides and looking soft but tight. Tate would be showing me this body a lot, I hoped.

"You're so beautiful." I held her eyes for a moment before dipping my head to her stomach and tasting her hot skin.

Her lips always tasted sweet, like fruit. Her body, on the other hand, tasted wild and raw, and I had a vision of rain falling across her naked chest while I made love to her on the hood of my car.

"Jared," she gasped out, her body arching into my lips.

Not yet.

I kissed and lightly bit her skin all the way down to the top of her jeans.

My brain was in overdrive. I wanted to rush this, because the itch in my head told me we were on borrowed time. The logical Tate— the normal Tate—was going to stop me any second.

But I still didn't rush.

Using the tip of my tongue, I grazed her hot skin before taking a little between my teeth. Her eyes were closed, and she was squirming just enough to drive me insane. I don't even think she noticed me peeling off her jeans or that her underwear was now sliding down her legs.

Jesus.

My heart pounded in the back of my throat, and my stomach dropped like I was on a roller coaster.

Tate was beautiful. Everywhere.

With as much time as we'd spent together in our past and the fact that her window was in perfect view of mine, I'd seen her scantily clad before, but this was new.

I didn't wait. I dove back to her body and left a trail of kisses across her stomach, on her hip bones and thighs.

"Jared," she begged, her raspy voice breaking with her breaths.

I looked down at her looking up at me, and my cock was about ready to explode.

She is going to stop this.

But she didn't. She paused for only a moment before she pulled her shirt over her head, finishing the job of getting undressed.

Hell. And I closed my eyes in relief.

Not waiting, I yanked her bra straps down off her shoulders, and stared in awe at her amazing body—Tate's body—lying bare and open for me.

I couldn't get over the fact that she was here. Naked in my bed.

I'd loved her like a kid before, but we damn well weren't kids anymore.

Kissing my way down her stomach, her hips, and her thighs, I dove for what I'd been dying to taste for weeks.

Hell, for longer than that.

With the tip of my tongue, I slowly licked the sweet length of the soft, wet heat between her legs.

Goddamn.

She gasped and jerked slightly. "Oh!"

I looked up, calm and amused, to see her wide-eyed, surprised look.

And I knew.

No one had touched her like that.

"What are you doing?" she asked, confused.

I almost laughed.

Happiness spread like tingles across my cheeks, and it was a struggle to keep a straight face. "You're a virgin," I stated, almost to myself.

She didn't say anything, only looked a little nervous but excited as I dipped my head again and returned my attention to kissing her inner thighs.

"You have no idea how happy that makes me," I murmured, and moved my mouth back on her.

The wild taste of her center. The sweet smell of her heat. The smoothness of her on my lips and tongue. Everything had me starving for more.

Every squirm and every whimper she let out was because of what I was doing to her.

It was me she came undone for.

I sucked on the hard nub of her clit, taking it gently between my teeth and then releasing it, only to claim it and suck it hard again. I gripped her hip with one hand and pushed her leg up with the other.

I sucked her long and slow, taking hold of her skin again and again, dragging it out until she was gasping for release. I came back down, over and over, tasting and sucking her hard.

When I knew she was hot enough that there was no fucking way she'd ever tell me to stop, I licked.

Hot and wet.

I slid my tongue just a little inside of her and ran it up the length to her clit. Over and over again. In and up. Just the tip of my tongue. In and up. In and up. And then I swirled my tongue around her nub with the wetness of her body and the heat of my mouth.

My dick was charged and rock fucking hard. I couldn't think of anything else but the need to drive it inside of her.

But I didn't. I was loving this part more than I wanted to admit.

She was in my hands, in my mouth, and I wanted her to know that I wasn't thinking about myself right now. I wanted her to see that she had me on my fucking knees.

Looking up, I reveled in the sight of her panting with her eyebrows pinched together. Her lips were moist, and she looked like she was in the best kind of pain. Her nipples were erect, and I reached up to knead a breast. The firmness complemented her skin's softness, and it was just one more thing I wanted in my mouth, too.

"Jesus Christ," I whispered against her sex, "if you could see yourself from my view. Fucking beautiful."

I worked her harder, sucking, licking, and then I plunged inside of her with my tongue. She jerked up off the bed, begging for more, and—shit—my body ached for release. I almost came right there.

Her body moved like we were fucking, her hips like small waves in an ocean against my mouth.

Her chest suddenly stilled like she wasn't taking in air. She was completely silent for a few seconds, and then she moaned my name as her breasts started to rise and fall again with hard, shallow breaths.

She's coming.

Elation spread through me like a windstorm, and I really hoped she knew that we weren't done.

"Damn, Tate." I ran my hand up and down her body from her breast to her hip. "Your beauty is nothing compared to how you look when you come."

"That was . . ." She trailed off, hopefully feeling delightfully lost, like me.

I lay my lower half on top of her and leaned over, looking down into her eyes. "I've wanted you for so long."

She pushed up off the bed and crushed her lips to mine, wrapping an arm around my neck. Reaching over to my bedside drawer for a condom that I didn't want to fucking use with her, I immediately halted when I felt a lightning storm spread between my legs and branch across my thighs.

My hand crashed back down to the bed, because I almost fucking fell on top of her in shock.

Holy shit!

Tate had grabbed hold of me and was slowly moving her hand up and down my cock.

Jesus. I squeezed my eyes shut.

This was not good.

Tate deserved slow. She deserved sweet.

But I knew there was about as much chance of that happening

tonight as me getting into West Point, like her father wanted. She wasn't getting slow and sweet.

I was going to fuck her crazy.

After I peeled her bra completely off, I pushed her back down onto the bed and went for her full breasts, taking each one in my mouth and rocking my hips into her until we were both beyond ready.

"Jared, you ready yet?"

Huh?

A knock on the door and a male's voice registered, making us both jerk our heads behind me.

Sam.

Sweat seeped out of my pores, and a sharp ache settled inside my dick.

Hell. No. This is not happening.

"I'm going to kill him," I bit out. Then I yelled to the door, "Go downstairs!"

"We're already late, man," he pressed. "The car's gassed up. Let's go!"

How in the hell did I forget that he was going to be back? I should've locked the front door.

Damn it!

"I said wait downstairs, Sam!"

"All right!" His shadow under the door disappeared.

Jesus Christ, my fucking heart was racing, I was so pissed. Tate held her arms over her chest, her eyes now embarrassed and alert.

I got off the bed and held my hands up to stop her.

"No, don't get dressed," I ordered. "I'm going to go get rid of him, and we're finishing this."

"You're racing tonight?" she asked quietly, sitting up.

I slipped on some jeans. "Not anymore."

Screw the race. I didn't have the money to pay my father tomorrow, but right now I felt like nothing could tear me apart or take me down.

Everything but her faded away.

"Jared, go. It's fine," she whispered as she stood and slipped back into her clothes, looking so different than she did a few moments ago. I wanted to know what was going on in her head, because it looked like she was thinking again.

I didn't give her a chance to ruin this, though. Lifting her up, I plopped her back down on my dresser top where we could be eye to eye.

"Races aren't important, Tate," I growled softly, leaning into her lips. "There's nowhere else I want to be than with you."

Her eyes, a little happy and a little hesitant, shifted sideways before coming back to meet mine.

"Take me with you, then," she suggested, a smile teasing her lips.

"Take you with me?" I tossed it around in my head. I could earn the money I needed, and she'd be coming home with me afterward. "All right. Go put something warmer on, and I'll come get you when we're ready." I patted her thigh and walked toward the door. "And after the race," I turned to look at her, "we'll come back here and finish this."

It wasn't a request.

Her eyes, sparkling and warm, played me as she tried to hide a grin.

I sent Sam to the track ahead of us and squeezed in another shower before I picked up Tate.

Another cold one.

CHAPTER 28

"You look good there." My voice carried over Volbeat's "Heaven Nor Hell" as I glanced at Tate sitting in the passenger's seat. She was at my side, in my ride. It felt right.

"I look better in your seat," she countered, and the memory of her racing my car came flooding back.

Yeah, I couldn't argue with her on that.

And I damn well wasn't forgetting how she'd tasted a half hour ago, either.

I couldn't wait to get her back to my house, but then I saw all of the lights ahead, the cars and spectators, and in an instant, my house was exactly where I wanted to steer us.

Every fucking person in town was here, from the looks of it. I chewed the side of my mouth, worrying about who we'd run into and what Tate would expect.

I'd always showed up to these things alone.

You'll always be alone, because you know that's better.

Girls liked public displays—hand-holding, hugs, cutesy shit I didn't do—and while I would happily get territorial in private, I didn't like giving the impression that I cared about anything in front of other people.

The crowd of cars, the eyes on us as we drove into the Loop, everything felt like a divider in the car between Tate and me.

The Volbeat song ended and another came on as my Boss crawled up the track, and I just let out a breath and decided to do what I always do.

Nothing.

Tate and I were still up in the air, and I hoped to clear that up later, but for now . . . things would remain simple.

After I put the car in neutral and pulled up the e-brake, Tate popped her seat belt and reached for the door.

"Hey." I grabbed her hand, and she turned to look at me. "I like to keep my head in the game here. If I don't act very friendly, it has nothing to do with you, okay?"

Her eyes dropped for a split second, and I immediately wanted to take it back.

She looked back up and shrugged her shoulders. "You don't have to hold my hand."

I'd done it again.

Pushed her away. Hurt her.

And now her wall was up, just like it had been for the past three years.

Shit.

With my father, I had to be guarded. I had to stand alone, strong. It became too hard after that horrible summer to act one way with people I didn't trust and another way with people I held close, so I stayed distant as a rule.

And then, after a while, I didn't have a one goddamn clue how to be any other way.

I watched her climb out of the car, turning her back and keeping whatever she wanted to say inside.

We were more alike than she thought.

Turning down the radio, I hopped out of the car and walked around to the front to talk to my opponent, Bran Davidson, and Zack.

Tate had walked off, and I shifted my eyes, scanning the crowd to see where she stood.

Son of a bitch.

Ben stood off to the side, and she went straight for him.

Something bitter swirled in my stomach, and I didn't even feel the chill in the night air.

I shook my head, pissed off, and looked back to the two men who were talking to me.

"The odds are in my favor, man," Bran teased, and knocked me on the arm.

I tried not to let my decaying mood seep out in my tone. Bran was a good guy, and we were friends.

"Yeah, great," I mumbled. "That means my win will pay off big."

"I have a Camaro," he pointed out, like I was too stupid to realize what he was driving.

"A nearly thirty-year-old Camaro," I specified, stealing glances at Tate and Ben.

They hadn't gotten physically close. They weren't even facing each other.

But she was smiling.

He was making her laugh, and my eyes narrowed on her like she needed a big, fat reminder of whose mouth had been on her less than an hour ago.

Tate and I were both wearing black hoodies, but while she had her hands stuffed into her front pocket to keep warm, I was sweating and ready to tear mine off.

Just calm down.

Maybe I was overreacting. Maybe they were just talking, or maybe they weren't.

What the fuck did I care?

I wasn't losing sleep over what might or might not be going through her head.

To hell with it.

"Clear the track!" Zack shouted, and I headed to my car without looking at anyone.

Tuning my iPod to Godsmack's "I Stand Alone"—poetic, I thought—I revved my engine and let the noise of everyone around me drown out the ache in my chest.

My head back, I closed my eyes and let the music take control of my brain.

The lyrics made me feel strong again.

The rhythm took away my father's voice.

Everything disappeared.

Until I opened my eyes and immediately let out a groan.

Shit.

Piper.

She stood in front of my car, twisting ever so slightly, showing off her body in her short skirt and a thin, dark blue tank top.

The crowd cheered, and it hit me that she was the starter, sending us on our way.

Piper wasn't a chore to look at, and she knew it.

She also knew that we were done, but that didn't stop her from cutting into my line of sight every chance she got.

She smiled and headed to my side of the car, while I tried to hide my annoyed look.

Leaning just inside my open window, she *tsk*ed like I had something to learn. "When you finish with that blonde, you know where to find me."

My bemused gaze stayed forward, off Piper. "*If* I finish with her, that is."

"You will." Her voice was playful and cocky. "Good girls taste like shit after a while."

I grinned, actually amused. If she only knew . . .

I couldn't imagine ever getting tired of Tate.

Looking softly into her light brown eyes, I tipped her chin up with my finger. "Don't hold your breath, Piper." And I dropped my hand, turning my eyes back to the track ahead. "Now get off my car and send us."

"Ahh!" she screamed, her growl scraping my eardrums as I jerked my head to the side.

Piper's body flailed backwards, and that's when I noticed Tate yanking Piper by her long hair away from the car.

What. The. Hell?

"Tate," I warned, climbing out of the car.

She shoved Piper ahead of her, and I watched, wide-eyed, as Tate just stood there, staring Piper down and clenching her fists.

Her breaths were long and deep. Not nervous.

Just really, really pissed off, and I brought my hand up to my lips to cover my smile.

I shouldn't be this proud of her for picking a fight.

But she was jealous, and that was turning me on.

She was also reacting, too.

Big-time.

And I immediately looked to the crowd, foolishly thinking that they might not be watching every second of this.

I liked a low profile, and Tate was broadcasting loud and clear that I was hers.

That I was *hers*.

"You bitch!" Piper snarled. "What the fuck is your problem?"

And my heart skipped a beat when Piper charged Tate. About to reach out to grab one of them or both of them, I stopped short.

Tate swept Piper's foot out from under her, and my eyes widened as Piper fell flat on her ass on the dry dirt track.

Yeah, Tate doesn't need help. I shook my head in shock.

The crowd was going crazy, chanting for a fight and celebrating with whistles and cheers. I didn't think they knew who they were cheering for. They just wanted a fight.

Tate bent down, clapping twice in Piper's stunned face, and spoke loudly. "Now that I have your attention, I just want you to know: He's not interested in you."

I folded my lips between my teeth.

Such a handful.

Turning to me, she let out a deep breath and her eyes calmed down. She walked up and was the only thing I saw. Piper was forgotten.

"I'm not wallpaper," she said quietly, and I knew I'd hurt her feelings in the car before.

Tate wasn't casual.

If she was in, she was in. If she was out, she was out. And I needed to man up.

She took out the fossil necklace and pooled it in my hand. "Don't hide from me, and don't ask me to hide," she said for only me to hear.

I tightened my fist around the necklace.

She was in.

Tipping her chin up, I kissed her lightly and nearly choked on the urge to take her in my arms right here and now.

"Good luck," she whispered, and her warm eyes leveled me as she walked back toward the crowd.

"Tate?" I called out before I even climbed back into my car.

She turned around, raising her eyebrows as she stuck her hands into her hoodie pocket.

"You're with me, baby," I told her. "Get in."

Not waiting to even see the look on her face, I slid into my seat and leaned over to open the passenger's-side door.

After my win, I blew off the traditional bonfire after the race and dragged Tate out of there, never before in such a hurry to get back home.

Not many people were going to be clueless as to what we were going to go do, either. Immediately after crossing the finish line, I'd taken all of two fucking seconds to snatch off Tate's and my seat belts and drag her into my lap for a kiss.

The race had kicked up my blood pressure. Feeling the energy of excitement as she sat next to me got my muscles and nerves pumping with adrenaline.

Racing had always been enjoyable, but with my father bleeding me for every bit of cash I had, the thrill of it had long since worn off. Now I raced as a way to make money, and Tate had changed that tonight.

As I raced, I had a hard time keeping my eyes on the track. Her delicious little gasps as we rounded turns were addicting.

My blood finally ran hot for this again, and I never wanted to go back to the Loop without Tate.

"Jared?" she piped up from the passenger's seat as we made our way back to my house. "Where do you go on the weekends?"

The weekends.

I narrowed my eyes. A jumble of thoughts swirled in my head, but I couldn't grab onto just one. My stomach hollowed out, and with every breath I wanted to bolt from the car.

My father in prison. I couldn't tell her about that.

Jax in a foster home, and his mother some barely legal teenager that our father had preyed upon. My mother, too, for that matter. What would she think?

The beatings. The basement. My betrayal, leaving Jax behind.

The bile crept up my throat, and I could barely swallow it down, much less tell her the whole disgusting story.

"Just out of town." I kept my reply short and simple.

"But where?"

"What does it matter?" My bite wasn't a cover. She needed to shut up.

The past was embarrassing and dirty, and no one except Jax knew what had gone down that summer. If I could erase it from his memory, I would.

Yanking the steering wheel to the right, I bottomed out as I hit the dip turning into the driveway. Tate grabbed hold of the handle on the roof to steady herself as I sped up my driveway.

"Why can Piper know and I can't?" she pressed, her tone more urgent and defensive.

How does she know Piper knows?

"Fuck, Tate," I gritted out, and hopped out of the car, briefly registering that my mom's car was in the open garage. "I don't want to talk about it." And that was the truth. Not today, not ever. I wouldn't even know where to start. If she really wanted to move on with me, then she'd let it go.

"You don't want to talk about anything!" She followed me out and yelled over the hood. "What do you think's going to happen?"

Happen? She might see me for who I really was. That's what could happen.

"What I do with my free time is my business. Trust me or not."

"Trust?" She scrunched up her eyes and looked at me with disdain. "You lost mine a long time ago. But if you try trusting me, then maybe we can be friends again."

Friends? We would never be just friends again.

Push her down or push her away, I told myself.

"I think we've moved beyond friends, Tate," I sneered with a sour smile, "but if you want to play that game, then fine. We can have a sleepover, but there will be fucking involved."

She inhaled a sharp breath, and her shoulders straightened. Her eyes stared at me with hurt and shock, and I'd fucking done it again.

Why did I keep doing this shit? I could've just let her down easily and walked away.

But no. In the moment, I power on with anger and fight.

But either way, I still saw the same look in her sad, tear-filled blue eyes, and I wanted to grab her and kiss her eyes, her nose, and her lips like it would erase every horrible thing I've ever said and done.

"Tate . . ." I started rounding the car, but she stomped up to me and shoved something into my stomach.

I latched onto it and watched helplessly as she ran across our yards and into her house.

No.

As I stared after her—at the now-darkened porch and closed front door—it was a minute or two before I felt the paper in my hand.

As I looked down, my mouth went dry, and my heart started pounding painfully in my chest.

It was a picture.

Of me.

When I was fourteen.

I was bruised and bloodied from the visit with my father, and Tate had found it at the bottom of a box underneath my bed.

She hadn't come to wish me a happy birthday tonight.

I'd caught her snooping.

And I'd just pushed her away for not telling her what she already knew.

CHAPTER 29

barreled out of the driveway and drove hard. Down the street and to the edge of town, where the lights didn't reach.

Driving helped clear my head, and it was now a mess again because of Tate. I wasn't running. I was detaching.

She wouldn't understand, and she would sure as shit see me differently. Why didn't she see that it wasn't important?

I could've been gentler about it, I guess, but she kept prying into things that weren't her business.

I strangled the crap out of the steering wheel, willing myself to stay on the gas and not turn around.

I couldn't go back. She'd want to know it all, and the shame I felt for what I'd done to my brother outweighed the shame I felt for what I'd done to her.

Didn't she see that some things were better left buried?

"Go. Help your brother," my father tells me, too gently.

My hands are shaking, and I look back at him.

What's going on? *I ask myself.*

"Don't act like you have a choice." He gestures me on with the bottle in his hand.

The wooden stairs creak with each step I take, and the small light below offers me no comfort.

It's like the creepy light coming from an old furnace, but I can feel the air getting chillier the more I descend.

Where's Jax?

I look back at my father, where he stands in the kitchen at the top of the stairs, and feel more and more like I'm being sucked into a black hole.

I'd never be seen again.

But he motions with his hand for me to keep going.

I don't want to go. My bare feet are freezing, and splinters of wood from the stairs poke them.

But then I stop, and my heart jumps into my throat.

I see Jax.

I see them.

And then I see the blood.

I parked my car in the lot near the back entrance to the park. Eagle Point had two ways in: a drive-in front entrance and a rear one for walkers and bikers. But the back entrance offered a parking lot to leave your car and walk through. It was this gate I chose.

The one closest to the pond.

How I got here escaped me, but when I drove, I zoned out. Sooner or later, I always ended up where I wanted to be.

Sometimes I wound up at Fairfax's Garage to fiddle with my car. Other times I ended up at Madoc's house to party. And a few times I'd found myself at some girl's house.

But tonight? The park? The fishpond?

The hairs on my arms shot up, and I felt acid burning a line up my throat. I wanted to be here about as much as I wanted to see my father tomorrow.

But I walked in anyway. Through the gate in the middle of the night. And down over the rocks to the pond I hadn't seen in years.

The pond was man-made, and the area was accented with sandstone rocks, which made up the footing around the pond, the cliffs surrounding it, and the steps leading down to it. A path made of the same stone led away from the pond and into the woods, where you could walk to a lookout over the river.

It was private, quaint, and special to Tate and me. We'd come here for picnics, a neighbor's wedding, and just for hanging out on late nights when we'd snuck out of our houses.

The last time I was here was the last time I cried.

"Tate? Come here, honey," Mr. Brandt calls her, and my heart jackhammers in my chest. I can't wait to see her. To hold her.

And tell her what I should've told her before. That I love her.

My stomach shifts and growls with hunger, and I look down at my hands, grime in the creases. I wish I'd cleaned up before I came to look for her, but I know Tate won't care.

Moving down the stone steps, I see her plop down on the blanket, leaning back on her hands with her ankles crossed.

She's so beautiful. And she's smiling.

Jax flashes through my mind, and I feel my muscles tense with urgency. I have to tell someone.

But first I need Tate.

I start to walk to her, but then I see my mother, and I duck behind the boulder.

Anger and disgust grips me.

Why is she here? I don't want to see her.

I'd called over the summer. I'd tried to get her help, but she'd left me there.

Why is my mother here with them?

I try to get my breathing under control, but I feel my throat tighten like I want to cry.

Tate is my family. My real family. My drunk of a mother has no right to be here, having fun with them.

"I can't wait for Jared to get back." I hear Tate's smile in her voice, and I cover my mouth to choke back the cry creeping up my chest.

I want to go to her, but I can't make a move with everyone around. I don't want to see my mother, and I don't want Mr. Brandt to see me like this. Dirty and bruised.

I just want to grab Tate's hand and run.

"You can show him the moves you and Will learned at karate this summer," Mr. Brandt says, and I stop breathing. The sob held hostage in my throat turns into a fire in my belly.

Will? Geary?

My eyes shift left to right, like I'm searching for an explanation but I can't find one.

She was still seeing him?

"Well, it's nice that you had someone to spend time with while Jared was gone." My mother pops the top on a Coke. "And I think the distance is a good thing. You two were getting pretty close."

My mom smiles at Tate and nudges her leg. Tate looks away, embarrassment in her eyes.

"Gross. We're just friends." She scrunches up her nose, and my breath catches.

I duck completely behind the boulder, leaning back and dropping my head.

Not now. Don't do this to me now!

I shake my head from side to side, the filth on my hands grinding with the sweat on my palms as I clench my fists.

"You're a good girl, Tate," I hear my mom say. "I'm not good with boys, I guess."

"Girls are tough, too, Katherine," Tate's dad chimes in, and I hear him unpacking their picnicking supplies. *"Jared's a good kid. You two will figure it out."*

"I should've had a girl," she responds, and I clamp my hands over my ears.

Too many voices. My head feels like it's in a vise grip and I can't shake free.

My eyes burn, and I want to scream.

I blinked and looked around at the pristine, shining water. I haven't stepped foot in this park in more than three years. When I was fourteen, I was sure this would be the place where I kissed Tate for the first time.

But then it just became a reminder of what I'd lost. Or what I thought I'd lost.

On the last day I came here, I had reached a point where I couldn't be disappointed anymore. I couldn't listen to anyone else not want me.

So I shut down. Completely and immediately.

That's the thing about change.

It can be gradual. Slow and almost unnoticeable.

Or it can be sudden, and you don't even know how you could've been any other way.

Becoming hard at heart isn't an intersection in your brain where you have a choice to turn left or right. It's coming to a dead end, and you just keep going, over the cliff, unable to stop the inevitable, because the truth is you just don't want to.

There is freedom in the fall.

"Jared," a hesitant voice sounded behind me.

My shoulders straightened, and I turned around.

Oh, what the hell?

"What are you doing here?" I asked my mother.

And then I remembered that her car had been in the garage when

I got home from the race. I'd thought she'd been gone for the weekend, as usual.

She was hugging herself against the evening chill, dressed in her jeans and long-sleeved cardigan. Her chocolate brown hair—same shade as mine—hung loose to her shoulders, and she wore brown boots up to her knees.

Since getting sober, my mom was beautiful all of the time, and as much as she pissed me off, I was glad I was the spitting image of her. I didn't think I could stare at my father's eyes in the mirror every day.

Lucky Jax.

"The front door was open." She inched closer, her eyes searching mine for a way in. "I heard what happened with Tate."

Not going to happen.

"How in the hell did you know I'd be here?"

Her small smile confused me. "I have my ways," she mumbled.

I wondered what it was, too, because my mother wasn't that clever.

She sat down next to me, our legs dangling off the small cliff with a five-foot drop to the pond.

"You haven't been here in years." She acted like she knew me.

"How would you know?"

"I know a lot more than you think," she said, looking down to the pond. "I know you're in trouble right now."

"Oh, come on. Don't start acting like a mother now."

I pushed off the ground and stood up.

"Jared, no." My mother stood up and faced me. "If I ever ask anything of you, it's that you listen to me now. Please." Her tone threw me off. It was shaky and unusually serious.

I sucked in my cheeks and stuck my fists in the pocket of my hoodie.

"Last year, after your arrest," she started, "and after I got back from the Haywood Center, I asked you to choose one thing—one idea—that you could focus on day to day. Something you loved or something that kept you centered. You never told me what it was, but then you snuck off around that time and got another tattoo." She jerked her chin at me. "The lantern. On your bicep. Why did you get that?"

"I don't know," I lied.

"Yes, you do. Why?" she pushed.

"I liked how it looked," I yelled, exasperated. "Come on—what is this?"

Jesus. What the hell?

Tate. A lantern. I associated the two, and when she was gone, I needed her.

Why a lantern? I don't know.

"On your eleventh birthday, I got drunk." Her words came out calm and slow. "Do you remember? I forgot about the dinner we were supposed to have at the Brandts', because I was out with my friends."

There weren't many birthdays that sat well with me, so no, I didn't remember.

"I forgot it was your birthday," she continued as tears filled her eyes. "I didn't even have a cake for you."

Big fucking surprise there.

But I didn't speak. Just listened, more to see where she was going with this.

"Anyway, I came home at about ten, and you were sitting on the couch, waiting for me. You had stayed in all night. You wouldn't go to the dinner without me."

Me. In the dark. Alone. Angry. Hungry.

"Mom, stop. I don't want to—"

"I have to," she interrupted, crying. "Please. You were sad at first, I remember, but then you copped an attitude. Told me I was embarrassing and that other kids had better moms and dads. I yelled at you and sent you to your room."

Madman whining at my door. Rain against the windows.

"I don't remember."

"I wish that was true, Jared. But, unfortunately, that tattoo proves that you remember." She'd stopped crying, but the tears were still on her cheeks. "About ten minutes later, I went to your room. I didn't want to face you, but I knew you were right, and I had to apologize. I opened your door, and you were leaning out your open window, laughing."

She paused, lost in thought as she stared at nothing. "Tate," she finally said, "was at her open French doors. Her room was dark, except for a Japanese lantern lamp that you and her father had made for her as an early birthday present." My mom let out a small smile. "She had the Beastie Boys' 'Fight for Your Right' song blasting, and she was dancing all crazy . . . crazy just for you. She glowed, like a little star bouncing around her room in her nightgown." Mom raised her eyes and looked at me. "She was trying to cheer you up."

As soon as I'd seen Tate at her doors that night, I didn't feel shitty anymore. Mom was forgotten. My birthday was forgotten. Tate became more of a home to me than my own blood.

And I never wanted to be where she wasn't.

"Jared, I'm a bad mother." She swallowed hard, obviously trying to hold back more tears.

I looked off to the side, unable to meet her eyes. "I made it through, Mom."

"You did . . . somewhat. I'm proud of you. You're strong, and you're not a follower. I know I'll send you into the world a survivor." Her light voice turned firm and serious. "I wouldn't want any other son. But, Jared, you're not happy."

The air around me got tight, pushing me from all sides, and I didn't know where to turn to get out. "Who's happy? Are you?" I barked.

"Jared, I was seventeen when I got pregnant with you." She folded her arms and hugged herself, more like hiding from something than warming herself. "I'm only thirty-six now. People I graduated with—some of them—are just starting their families. I was so young. I had no support. I didn't get a chance to live before I had my world turned upside down—"

"Yeah, I get it, all right," I cut her off. "I'll be out of your hair by June."

"That's not what I meant." She moved closer, holding out her hand as if to stop my thoughts. Her voice was raspy. "You were the gift, Jared. The light. Your father was the hell. I thought I loved him. He was strong, confident, and cocky. I idolized him . . ." She trailed off, and I swear I could hear her heart breaking as her eyes fell to the ground.

I didn't want to hear about that asshole, but I knew she needed to talk. And for some reason I wanted to let her.

"I idolized him for about a month," she continued. "Long enough to get pregnant and get stuck with him." And then she looked at me again. "But I was young and immature. I thought I knew everything. Drinking was my escape, and I abandoned you. You never deserved that. When I saw Tate trying to make you happy that night, I let her. The next morning you weren't in your room. When I looked out your window, I could see you both passed out in her bed, just sleeping. So I let it be. For years, I knew you were sneaking over there to sleep, and I let it go, because she made you happy when I failed."

The purest, truest, most perfect thing in my world, and I'd dumped pile upon pile of shit on top of her for years.

A knot of realization worked its way into my head, and I felt like punching my fist through a fucking wall.

"Jesus Christ." I combed my hands through my hair, my eyes squeezing shut as I whispered to myself. "I've been so horrible to her."

My mother, like Mr. Brandt, probably knew nothing of what I'd put Tate through, but she did know that we weren't friends anymore.

"Honey," she spoke up, "you've been horrible to everyone. Some of us deserved it; some of us not. But Tate loves you. She's your best friend. She'll forgive you."

Will she?

"I love her." It was the most honest thing I'd confided in my mother about in a long time.

My father could kiss his own ass, and my mother and I would survive, for better or worse. But Tate?

I needed her.

"I know you love her. And I love you," she said as she reached out and touched my cheek. "You're not letting your father or me take anything else from you, do you understand?"

Tears burned my eyes, and I couldn't hold them back.

"How do I know I'm not going to be like him?" I whispered.

My mother was quiet as she studied me, and then her eyes narrowed.

"Tell her the truth," she instructed. "Trust her with everything, especially your heart. Do that, and you're already not like your father."

CHAPTER 30

Yesterday lasts forever.
    Tomorrow comes never.

I looked down at the blank piece of printer paper, the words of my tattoo staring back at me.

Now I knew what they meant.

I was a huge fucking idiot. That was for sure.

Not only had I let myself get tied up by the bullshit my father doled out, but I'd willingly let my hate control me, wrongfully thinking that it made me stronger.

Leaning down, I placed the paper on my thigh and scribbled another line.

Until you.

Feeling the weight lift off my shoulders, I nailed it to the tree between Tate's and my houses and grabbed the rest of the stuff off the ground.

Backing up, I looked at the huge maple, not only bright with the red and gold leaves that had not yet fallen, but with the hundreds of white lights and several lanterns I'd hung.

It was her birthday today, and all I could think about was how she'd brightened my day when I was eleven. I wanted to return the favor and show her that I remembered.

Assuming she was out with K.C., I hung out in her bedroom, leaning on the rails outside her open French doors, and just stared at the folder I'd placed on her bed.

The folder with all of the proof of what my father had done to me.

She already seen it, of course, when she snooped in my room.

But she hadn't heard it from me yet.

A door closed downstairs, and my back straightened.

I breathed deliberately—slow and calm—but my body heated up and my heart raced.

Jesus.

I was fucking nervous.

Will what I tell her be good enough? Will she understand?

Tate walked slowly into her room, and I immediately gripped the rails behind me to stop myself from rushing her.

Her eyebrows were slightly drawn together as she looked at me with a mixture of curiosity and concern.

Her hair hung loose, and she wore dark, faded jeans and a short-sleeved black blouse. Too many clothes, but I liked that about Tate. She never revealed too much, and she reminded me of a present that I couldn't wait to unwrap. She looked sexy as hell, and I had a hard time taking my mind off the bed in the room.

I gestured to the folder on the bed. "Is that what you were looking for in my room last night?"

She kept her head level but her eyes shot down, and a shade of pink covered her cheeks.

Come on, Tate. Don't be a wuss.

It actually pleased me that she'd gone snooping. She cared.

"Go ahead." I nodded toward the folder. "Take a look."

She probably hadn't gotten much time to see them the other night.

Her gaze shifted up to mine for a second, and she looked like she was considering if she should indulge her curiosity.

But she took the offer.

Slowly, she opened the folder and splayed out the photos. Her hands shook as she picked one up and stared at it, almost not breathing.

"Jared," she groaned, lifting her hand to her mouth. "What is this? What happened to you?"

I dropped my eyes to the floor and ran a hand through my hair.

This was harder than I'd thought it would be.

Trust her with everything, especially your heart.

"My father." I let out a long, quiet breath. "He did that to me. And to my brother."

Her eyes widened in surprise, and her mouth opened a little.

Tate didn't know I had a brother. Unless her father had told her, and he never said anything that wasn't necessary.

"The summer before freshman year, I was hyped up to spend my whole summer hanging out with you, but, as you remember, my dad called out of the blue and wanted to see me. So I went. I hadn't seen him in more than ten years, and I wanted to know him."

She sat down on the bed, listening.

"When I got there," I continued, "I found out that my dad had another son. A kid from another relationship. His name is Jaxon, and he's only about a year younger than me."

Jax flashed in my mind, twelve years old and scrawny. He'd had dirt on his face, and his dark hair was short then.

"Go on," she whispered, and I let out the breath I'd been holding.

And I told her the whole damn story.

About how my father used us to make money for him—selling drugs, breaking into houses, delivering shit.

Of how he hurt Jax and then started hurting me when I refused to do his dirty work.

Of how we were victimized by the lowlifes hanging round the house. And I let her see the scars on my back that my father had given me with a belt buckle.

I also told her of how my father hated us and my mother abandoned us, and then of how I abandoned Jax and left him with my father when he refused to leave with me.

Tate's eyes got red and pooled with tears that she tried to hold back.

I released all of the sickness in my head and the crud that had blackened my heart, and I wanted to wipe away the tears that she cried for me.

She'd always cared. She'd always loved me.

I'd treated her worse than a dog for three years, and she still cried for *me*.

I felt the ache in my throat as I looked at her, her face twisted up in sadness, and I knew she had every right not to forgive me.

But I knew she would.

Maybe that's the thing I'd been missing about love.

You don't withhold it or portion it out when it's deserved.

You can't control it like that.

After I told her the ugly story, I sat there next to her, waiting for her to say something.

I didn't know what she was thinking, but she let me speak and she listened.

"Have you seen your dad since?" she finally asked.

Your dad. The words were so foreign. I referred to him as my father only to identify the twenty-two-year-old man who preyed on a seventeen-year-old girl, and I was the result.

"I saw him today," I told her. "I see him every weekend."

Which was true. Even though I technically didn't get my last visit.

"What?" Her blue eyes went wide. "Why?"

"Because life's a bitch—that's why." I exhaled a bitter laugh.

After the punch I threw last week, the judge decided I'd fulfilled my commitment and let me off the hook today. I saw my father from a distance this morning, but I hadn't seen the last of him. I knew that.

Tate looked at me and drank in everything I said. I told her about the trouble after she left for France—how I missed her, how Jax got hit by his foster dad, and how the judge cut me a deal.

I got up and walked back over to the French doors, leaving her on the bed to absorb everything.

"So, that's where you go," she finally said. "To Stateville Prison in Crest Hill."

Crest Hill?

She must've seen other stuff in my room when she was snooping last night. My mother had asked me to save receipts for the motels and gas for tax time. Shit was scattered all over my room.

"Yeah, every Saturday," I said with a nod. "Today was my last visit, though."

"Where is your brother now?"

Safe.

"He's in Weston. Safe and sound with a good family. I've been seeing him on Sundays. But my mom and I are trying to get the state to agree to let him live with us. She's been sober for a while. He's almost seventeen, so it's not like he's a kid."

I wanted him to meet her, and if my mother was successful with the lawyer, then he'd be living with us sooner rather than later.

She got off the bed and walked over to me by the French doors. "Why didn't you tell me all of this years ago?" she asked. "I could've been there for you."

I wish I'd let you.

That was still something I was going to have a hard time with. Tate holding me up—or trying to—made this room feel ten times too small. *Small steps, baby.*

I combed my hand through my hair and leaned back on the railing. "When I finally got home that summer, you were my first thought. Well, other than doing what I could to help Jax," I added. "I had to see you. My mom could go to hell. All I wanted was you. I loved you," I whispered the last part, my stomach knotted with regret.

I tightened my fists, thinking back to that day when I'd changed everything. "I went to your house, but your grandma said you were out. She tried to get me to stay. I think she saw that I didn't look right. But I ran off to find you, anyway. After a while, I found myself at the fishpond in the park." I finally looked at her. "And there you were . . . with your dad and my mom, playing the little family."

I understood the confusion in her eyes. Even now I knew it was a sad series of small events that I took too much to heart. I was wrong.

"Jared—" she started, but I stopped her.

"Tate, you didn't do anything wrong. I know that now. You just have to understand my mind-set. I had been through hell. I was weak and hurting from the abuse. I was hungry. I'd been betrayed by the people I was supposed to be able to count on: my mom, who didn't help when I needed her; my dad, who hurt me and my helpless brother." I took a deep breath. "And then I saw you with *our* parents, looking like the happy, sweet family. While Jaxon and I were in pain and struggling to make it through every day in one piece, you got to see the mother I never had. Your dad took you on picnics and for ice cream while mine was whipping me. I felt like no one wanted me and that life moved on without me. No one cared."

That day and the weeks preceding were too much, too fast, and all of a sudden I was a different kid.

"You became a target, Tate. I hated my parents, I was worried about my brother, and I sure as hell couldn't rely on anyone but myself. When I hated you, it made me feel better. A lot better."

I saw her jaw harden, and I knew that this wasn't easy for her to take in.

But I kept going.

"Even after I realized that nothing was your fault, I still couldn't stop trying to hate you. It felt good, because I couldn't hurt who I wanted to hurt."

Silent tears fell down her face again, and—goddammit—I didn't want Tate crying over me anymore.

We'd had a hell of a lot of good growing up, and I wanted it back.

"I'm sorry," I whispered, taking her face in my hands, hoping like hell she didn't punch me. "I know I can make this up to you. Don't hate me."

She shook her head. "I don't *hate* you. I mean"—she shot me a little scowl—"I'm pissed, but mostly I just hate the wasted time."

Yes.

I grabbed her, wrapping my arms around her waist and pulling her into me.

She is fucking mine. I wanted to scream and smile at the same time. I molded my forehead to hers, my lips hungry to taste her as I breathed her in.

"You said you loved me," she whispered. "I hate that we lost that." Nothing was lost.

I lifted her up, guided her legs around me, and walked us to the bed, feeling the heat of her center on my stomach.

"We never lost that." My hand was on her cheek, and I brought her eyes up to meet mine. "As much as I tried, I could never erase you from my heart. That's why I was such an asshole and kept guys away from you. You were always mine."

"Are *you* mine?" she asked, wiping her tears with her thumb.

Her shaky breath caressed my face, and I couldn't hold back anymore. Lightly kissing the corner of her mouth, I whispered against her lips, "Always have been."

She wrapped her arms around me, and I just held her close and tight.

"Are you okay?" she asked.

"Are you?" I shot back, not deluding myself for a second that the past three years hadn't been hell for her, too.

"I will be."

If we had each other, we were going to be okay.

"I love you, Tate."

And I fell back on the bed, bringing her with me, hopefully forever.

———————————————————————

CHAPTER 31

"*Jared, you're poking me.*" *Tate's sleepy whimper stirs me awake, and it takes me a few moments to open my eyes.*

Poking you? I check my hands, which aren't even touching her, and then I feel the fire and tightness in my pants.

Shit.

I roll over onto my back, so I'm not spooning her anymore, and run my hands over my face.

My dick is hard again, and I'm shivering with discomfort and embarrassment.

This happens a lot lately. Tate's back is still to me as she sleeps, and I start to sit up.

"No," *she groans and rolls over,* "don't leave." *She puts an arm over my waist, and I stiffen right there, afraid to move.*

Damn, damn, damn! I'm about to explode, and I need to leave. Every morning this happens, and I'm so frustrated.

Don't touch me, Tate.

Please.

But I let her anyway. She guides me back down as she nestles her head in my neck and falls back asleep.

My eyes snapped open, blinking, as I felt the same familiar blood rushing south and the burning deep below my stomach.

I sat up and rubbed the sleep from my eyes, shook the dream from my head.

Or the memory.

Tate.

I sit up, scanning the dark room.

Where is she?

I was in her bed. We'd fallen asleep after my confession, and that dream was of the last time I'd lain in here with her. The morning I'd left for my father's for the summer.

But she wasn't here now.

And there was no light coming from her bathroom, either.

"Tate," I called out, but got no answer. The only sound was the pitter-patter of rain on the roof.

Getting up, I stretched my arms over my head, walked out of her bedroom and down the darkened stairs.

Light was scarce, but it didn't matter. I could navigate this house in the dark.

Even if it weren't for the fact that I'd spent so much time here in the past, the Brandts' house always seemed alive. The ticking of the grandfather clock in the foyer, the creak of the stairs, the soft, muffled humming that came from the vents—they all gave each room its own personality and made this place a home.

I was comfortable here.

The living room and dining room were empty as I strolled past each, so I went into the kitchen and instantly saw the open back door.

Walking over, I peered out into the garden, and immediately broke out in a smile at the sight of Tate, drenched and standing in the downpour with her head tilted up to the sky.

My shoulders relaxed, and I closed my eyes all at the same time.

I should've known.

I stepped out quietly and leaned against the back of the house, under the awning.

Tate always loved the rain. She came alive in it, and I hadn't been able to enjoy seeing her like this in years. Part of me always wondered what magic she saw in thunderstorms, and part of me didn't need to know.

Just watching her was like hearing music in my head.

Her long blond hair was dripping wet and her clothes clung to her body, just like the night of our first kiss, when I'd felt her curves and dips perfectly.

She stood there, legs slightly parted and arms at her sides, as she slowly swayed from side to side, almost like dancing.

Her black blouse, shiny with rain, was pasted to her back like a second skin, and I knew when I touched her that I would feel every muscle.

My chest heated up and my hands hummed.

"Jared!" she yelled, and I blinked, realizing that she'd noticed me.

"You scared me." She smiled. "I thought you were asleep."

She held her hand to her chest and waited for me to say something, but I couldn't.

I didn't want to talk anymore. I just wanted her.

Pushing off the wall, I walked over, never taking my eyes off her as I placed my hands on her hips. I locked her to me, sinking my fingers into her, and gazed down into her face, wild and lovely.

Tate never played games. There was never a flirty sparkle in her eye or a play of her lips to get me to notice her. She looked at me right now just like she used to.

Like I was Christmas.

She inched up on her tiptoes, and my breath caught as she touched her lips to mine. I tasted the sweet rain on her mouth, and my pulse rippled through my body, craving more and more.

Damn. So good.

Wrapping one arm around her waist, I held her face with my other hand and guided her lips as I took control.

I moved into her, tasting her tongue and breath until every single little squeeze, nibble, and lick was like lightning through my body.

The storm fell around us, but I barely noticed it.

My hands tingled, and everywhere that I touched her got me hotter and harder.

She shivered, and I held her tighter, not knowing if it was the rain or us. But I didn't let up.

Faster and faster I devoured Tate, diving into her lips again and again, until I was breathing so hard that I was aching to come.

I drew her bottom lip between my teeth, and she grinded her hips into mine, and we were lost.

Maybe it was her soft whimpers or her hands gripping my hips, but I knew she wasn't stopping this.

And I needed to be inside of her right here. Right now.

"You're cold," I said as she continued to come in for kiss after kiss.

Her breath was hot, and her urgent arms caressed up my chest and around my neck. "Warm me up," she pleaded.

Fuuuuuck.

I reached down and grabbed her ass, pulling her into me.

Now.

I wanted her here and now, but she started doing shit to my neck with her lips and tongue, and I couldn't get my head straight.

"I love you, Jared," she said breathlessly in my ear, and I closed my eyes.

My heart filled up so much that it hurt.

"We can wait," I choked out, never in a million fucking years wanting to stop this.

She shook her head slowly, a little smile playing on her lips. Lifting the hem of my black T-shirt over my head, she ran the tips of her fingers down my chest, around my hips, and up my back.

I shivered as she fingered the scars on my back, hoping she wasn't thinking about my story. That's not what I wanted in her head right now.

But she kept her eyes on mine, and I relaxed and let out a breath.

Her hands were going to be on every part of my body sooner or later. I may as well get used to it now.

I clenched my teeth and dug my fingers into her ass as she lifted her flimsy black blouse over her head and stripped off her bra.

Jesus, I mouthed silently.

We stood there, face-to-face, naked chest to naked chest, wet and hot on a chilly October night, and I never before wanted to love someone so much that I worried I would never be able to stop.

I reached out slowly and ran the back of my hand down her left breast. Her nipple, already hard from the night air, was the one part of her, other than her lips, that was going in my mouth first.

Pushing her wet hair behind her shoulders, I looked her up and down, trying to memorize every inch. Tate was athletic—toned and not too skinny. Her shoulders and arms had some muscle to them, but it was subtle, while her skin glowed smoothly, like a piece of porcelain.

She watched me drink her in, letting me look.

Bold girl.

She liked it and never tried to cover up or look away.

Pulling her into me again, I dove into her mouth, sucking and biting on her bottom lip, forcing myself to go slower.

I pushed into her body, my chest on fire with her breasts rubbing against me.

I briefly registered her hands leaving my body, but I didn't flinch until her mouth left me, too.

And then I noticed her peeling off her jeans.

Goddamn. Part of me wanted to undress her myself, but fuck it.

I didn't want to miss a thing, so I kept my hands off her until she stood almost naked in front of me.

Tate. In only her panties. Rain soaked.

Never in my life had anything been hotter.

Lifting her by the backs of her thighs, I wrapped my arm around her slender, smooth back and carried her to the chaise across the patio. It had a canopy, I remembered. There was no way in hell we were going inside now.

In the rain—in Tate's beloved thunderstorm—is where we would make love for the first time.

Laying her down, I glanced at her pink lace underwear.

Thank God they're not black. I smiled to myself.

I preferred black, but I liked that Tate surprised me.

My good girl in pink.

A good girl that was bad only for me.

Leaning down, I took her breast in my mouth and shivered with the pleasure of tasting her soft, supple skin. I reached down and used my hand to explore as much of her as I could reach. Up her smooth thighs and over her hips and stomach, getting more fucking swelled in my pants every time she arched and squirmed under me.

"Jared . . ." she begged. "Jared, please."

Oh, Jesus.

"Be patient," I growled softly as I continued to kiss down her stomach. "If you keep begging like that, I'm going to lose it right now."

I needed to get my body in check. Take some deep breaths and calm the hell down. I wanted everything out of this. More than I needed to come, I needed to feel her body shake underneath mine. I needed to see her face lost when she came with me inside of her.

Peeling off her panties and dropping them to the ground, I stood up and soaked in my girl, who was looking at me with fire in her eyes.

I fished in my wallet for a condom, yanked off the rest of my clothes, flinched when my aching hard-on sprang free, and came down slowly between her legs.

Chills spread across my skin at feeling her heat on my cock.

She wrapped her hands around the back of my neck and I stared down at her, hoping she was ready. Hoping she wouldn't regret this.

I knew I didn't want you. My father's voice echoed from a distant island in my head, and I hesitated.

But Tate looked at me and ran a hand down my face, making me melt into her touch.

I closed my eyes.

Happiness, heaven, euphoria—I had no idea what state I was in, but it was new and it was true.

Fuck you, Dad.

Ripping the condom from its wrapper, I slid it on and shoved my motherfucking father a million miles away from me.

"I love you," I whispered, and, lifting her knee up, I slid inside her.

"*Ahhh* . . ." Her body shook and she gasped, hard and fast. I stilled, feeling a rush of warmth spread over my body.

Tate.

She really was a virgin.

My head spun at the idea of causing her pain, but fuck if it didn't turn me on, too.

She was mine now.

I didn't budge any further, but I pushed myself up on my hands to look down at her.

Her palms were braced on my chest, and raindrops glistened on her breasts as I watched her breathing slow down.

Her eyes squinted a little as she took in the pain, but she didn't cry out.

I was throbbing so hard. I needed to get inside of her, but I damn well gave a fuck about Tate, and I wasn't just going to take her. I wanted her coming back for seconds, thirds, and forever.

"Are you okay?" I asked quietly, hoping like hell she wasn't reconsidering and thinking of pulling away from me.

"I'm good." She breathed out and nodded. "Don't stop, but go slow."

And I didn't need to be told twice.

Slowly, with my nerves heating up at every inch I took, I sank into her beautiful body until I was buried.

Fucking heaven. I let out a breath, dying and coming alive again in her tight, wet heat.

She quivered and her breathing turned shallow for a few seconds, but I knew when the pain was gone.

"Damn." My muscles tensed and I shut my eyes, feeling her soft and hot from the inside. "You feel so good. Perfect."

I stayed, hovering over her, pulling out and then sinking back in time and again. My body screamed, ached, and moaned for more.

After a minute or two, she grabbed my waist and started guiding her body into a rhythm with mine. Her hips moved in little circles, and I couldn't take my eyes off her. She was dancing. Lying down and moving like a sweet dream, her body arching and flowing against mine.

She reached up and took my face in her hands, pulling me down to her lips.

Jesus Christ.

The taste of her—the fucking taste of her—was everywhere. The rain and sweat on her lips, her heat on my cock . . . everywhere. Tate nibbled my lips as she grinded against me like she couldn't get close enough.

I squeezed my eyes shut and attacked her mouth like it was a fucking feast.

Hell, yes.

Pulling back, she panted against my lips. "I feel you everywhere," she taunted, and I groaned.

"Don't talk like that, baby. I'll be done too soon."

Forehead to forehead, I looked down at her wet, hot body fucking me as I fucked her, and I couldn't even remember the sound of my father's voice anymore.

I took her sweet breast in my mouth, sucking the nipple hard, and felt her body quake underneath mine as our hips came together again and again. I sank into her, and she moaned.

Faster. Harder. More. And again.

Her breathing hitched and then stopped altogether.

I looked up and saw her eyebrows pinched together and her mouth not taking in air. Her storm-filled orbs were the sweetest blend of pleasure and pain, caught in the most perfect, raw moment I'd ever seen in my life.

She was coming.

After a second or two, she let out a long, sweet moan and closed her eyes completely. I felt her body clench and unclench, leaving me ready to let go, too.

I kissed her gently, but she didn't return it. Her eyes were still squeezed shut, and she quivered. She was still coming.

After a few more thrusts, I exploded inside her with shivers of pleasure rocking between my legs and spreading through my thighs and stomach.

I gasped out, my head light and my chest surging with heat.

Jesus Christ.

I sucked in breath after breath, jerking into her a couple more times.

More.

I just wanted to rip off the condom, slip on another, and go again.

Damn. I couldn't help the smile that broke out as I kissed her and thought of the irony.

I used to keep her up late watching scary movies, and after all this time, nothing had really changed.

Her ass still wasn't getting any sleep tonight.

CHAPTER 32

I dropped off our wet clothes in the kitchen and came back with two gray towels from her bathroom. I wrapped one around my waist and draped the other over her as I lay back down on the chaise.

"Aren't we going inside?" She clutched the towel to her chest, making sure the important parts were covered.

"Are you cold?" I asked mischievously as I dipped my head into her neck and rested my hand between her legs. "All part of my plan to warm you up again."

She wrapped her fingers around my hand, but she wasn't really trying to pull me away. "Stop," she begged pathetically.

"Are you trying to tell me no?" I teased and slipped a finger inside her.

She gasped, and her body jerked ever so slightly. Instead of her hands trying to stop me now, they instantly reached down, pushing my hand harder into her.

Her lips grazed my chest. "I always wanted you, Jared. Even at twelve, I wanted you to kiss me."

It damn well should've been me who gave her her first kiss. And her only kisses.

"Thank you for what you gave me tonight." I groaned at how wet she was, and I felt myself swell and get heavy.

"I wish I'd been your first. You've had a lot of girls, haven't you?" Her voice held a hint of sadness, and I averted my eyes.

Yeah, I definitely didn't want to talk about this.

"More than I should've." I stuck to the easy answer.

Their names? Gone.

Their faces? Forgotten.

I loved Tate, and nothing was better than making love to someone I actually loved.

I dipped down to kiss her, but she pulled away and looked at me hard.

"I need to know, Jared," she urged gently.

"Need to know what?" I shrugged it off, but dread crept into my chest, anyway.

What is she doing?

Sitting up, she pulled the towel tighter around her body. "I'm assuming most of your past girlfriends go to our school, right? I want to know who they are." She nodded at me, wide-eyed, like I was supposed to expect this or something.

"Tate." I rubbed her leg. "They weren't my girlfriends. I don't have girlfriends."

Her face contorted in a mixture of surprise, confusion, and a whole hell of a lot of pissed-off-ness, and I clenched my teeth and closed my eyes.

Idiot.

"What?" she yelled, and I cringed. "Then what am I?"

Yep. I'm a big bucket of stupid idiot.

But before I could do damage control, Tate sprang off the lounge, stomped across the patio and through the back door, fixing the towel around her as she went.

"Tate!" *Damn it!*

I chased after her and barged through the open door.

"Baby, that's not what I meant," I quickly shot out when I saw her standing across the kitchen with her arms crossed over her chest.

"Don't call me 'baby.' If I'm not your girlfriend, I'm definitely not baby."

I ran my hand down my face. "'Girlfriend' isn't enough to describe you, Tate. That term is disposable. You're not my girlfriend, my girl, or my woman. You're. Just. Mine," I bit out every syllable, so she would fucking understand. "And I'm yours," I added, a little calmer.

She took a breath, calming down. "Jared, you have to tell me which ones."

I let out a bitter, ragged laugh. "Why? So you can get upset every time you see one of them?"

"I'm more mature than that," she snarled. "Give me a little credit. This isn't even about them. It's about you owning up."

What the fuck?

"I told you about my whole fucking past!" I threw my hands up in the air. "What more do you want?"

"I want to know everything! I don't want to walk down the halls at school and unknowingly make eye contact with five different girls you've screwed!" she yelled, her eyes hot and fierce.

"None of it matters!" I tightened the towel around my waist and looked at her over the center island that stood between us. "I just made love to you. *To you.* And it will only ever be you again!"

I mean, what the hell did she want, anyway? I couldn't go back and change anything I'd done, and it made no sense to relive any of that shit. She was my future, and I didn't want her knowing all of that ugliness.

Would I be obsessed over guys that touched her? Yes, goddamn it! Which was why I didn't ask.

"I don't like being in the dark, Jared." She crossed her arms over her chest, pushing her breasts farther over the top of the towel. "It's a lot to ask of me, knowing I share a school with these girls. I want to know who, where, and what you've done. You got off easy. You know it's only been you for me. They don't need to look at me with smug grins, knowing they've had what's mine. And I want to know about K.C., too," she added.

That's what this was about.

And, fuck me, I couldn't help but smile. "You're jealous."

Did she think I even noticed K.C. like that? Or even saw those other girls the way I see her? It was always her face. Since I was ten years old, I only ever saw her.

She lifted her chin, looking resolute, like she was about to send me to my room for misbehaving. "Leave. And don't come back until you can man up," she said calmly.

And she spun around, her wet hair clinging to her back, and walked down the hall toward the stairs.

Leave?

There were at least ten different things I still wanted to do to her tonight, and she wanted me gone?

Fury burned in my stomach, making my blood boil, and I was ready to pick a serious fucking fight. I'd already spilled my guts about my brother, my father, and my whole stupid sob story. I'd talked about shit I didn't want to, because I loved her and wanted her to know that she could trust me.

But I was done being pushed around for one night.

Catching her by the arm, I pulled her up against me, lifted her off her feet, and carried her back into the kitchen.

She tried to wriggle free. "Let go of me."

Putting her down in front of me, I backed her up against the kitchen table and hovered over her. "I've been playing games with you for three years, Tatum. You don't get to run away anymore."

Her eyes sharpened, and she sucked in an angry breath. "Tatum?" she asked, getting in my face.

She knew I called her Tatum only when I was trying to be condescending. Like parents calling you by your full name when they're mad.

But I wasn't mad or trying to be condescending. I was kind of getting off on her anger, actually.

And whether I liked it or not, my cock kept getting harder the more we faced off. It was like electricity shooting to my groin, seeing Tate turn fierce.

Goddamn. She was beautiful.

Her eyes were sharp, and she breathed hard through her mouth. She looked furious and hot, and I had no idea if she was going to hit me or screw me. I knew only that both would be violent.

Leaning in close enough to kiss her, I raised my right hand and ran my fingertips down her face. Her breath shook against my lips as I whispered to her.

"You want to know everything? Then let me show you. Turn around and bend over."

Her eyes went as big as planets. "Wha-what?" she stammered breathlessly.

I met her stare, feeling the intensity and urgency to understand.

"You're not scared, are you?" And the corners of my mouth lifted when she scowled. "Come on, Tate. Trust me. You want to know everything, don't you?"

Her face was pinched tight and her eyes darted from side to side.

She turned around slowly, and relief flooded me. Her back was to me, and she stood there waiting for what she probably thought was going to be some twisted violation of her body.

But I knew she loved me.

She didn't know me anymore. Not really. For all she knew, I could have a kid somewhere, and I might be selling drugs on the weekends instead of visiting my father and brother. She was taking a leap of faith because she cared.

Reaching around in front of her, I slid the towel—her only clothing—off of her gorgeous body and let it fall to the floor. I stepped back a little to look at her. Not part of the plan, but I couldn't help it.

Brave as always, Tate stood there, not trying to cover herself, ready to take whatever bullshit she was probably sure I had up my sleeve. But I could still tell that she was nervous. Her breath was shallow and her body was stiff.

Stepping back up to her with my chest rubbing against her back, I wrapped my fingers around her wrists and brought her arms up across her breasts. My arms crossed her chest, too, and I held her frame—small compared to mine—loving how easily she fit.

She always fit.

"Can you trust me?" I asked again.

"Yes." Her voice was so small. She wasn't sure anymore.

Still holding her, I spread her arms away from her body and whispered into her ear. "Lean down on the table, then."

Her breathing hitched, and it almost sounded like she let out a little laugh. She might be anxious or scared, but she was also going with it.

Her belly, followed by her breasts and then her head, lay facedown on her dark hardwood kitchen table, and I guided her arms to stay splayed out to the sides.

Heat rushed to my groin, and I was twitching with the full-on need to be inside her. Now. And not so slowly, either.

I had fucking problems.

Slow the hell down, man.

This was about Tate.

I leaned in, pressing myself into her ass as my hands glided up her smooth back and across her shoulders.

I lightly caressed the back of her neck and kneaded the sides of her torso, feeling her shiver and relax under my touch.

Bending down, I took the supple skin at her waist in my mouth and trailed kisses up her rib cage.

She arched her back, moaning, as I ran my tongue up her spine and then sank my teeth gently into her shoulder.

Her body felt amazing, and I loved being able to touch her. I'd do it for hours if the blood rushing to my dick wasn't making it ache so badly.

Gliding one hand up and down her back, I slipped my other hand down between her legs to her heat.

She immediately bucked with a gasp and then a moan.

I ran my fingers the length of her, swirling and caressing, but I didn't go right for the endgame yet. I wasn't trying to make her come. Not yet.

With gentle fingers, I rubbed inside her folds and around her clit, feeling her tense but then relax. The nub was hard, and she was already so goddamn wet.

It's not that I wanted to get flashes of Tate as a kid right now, but I still couldn't believe that we were here. This was the girl that used to ride on my handlebars in the rain. The girl that used to let me practice my shots by tossing popcorn into her mouth on a boring winter's day. The only girl I ever hugged.

I was going to fuck her on the kitchen table where we ate birthday cake when we were thirteen.

And my dick got harder just thinking about finally having her beneath me, wanting me, moaning my name.

She started moving into me, and I almost thanked God, because I was ready for a taste.

"Lay your knee on the table, baby." And I helped her bring her leg up to lay her inner thigh flat on the kitchen table while her other foot stayed pinned to the floor.

Fire spread below my stomach and a swirl of lightning shot down between my legs.

God, she was spread for me, her opening right at the end of the fucking table, and I was dying for her.

So I wasted no time and knelt down, burying my mouth in her hot center.

My lips found her clit and sucked.

"Jared," she gasped and squirmed, and I pulled back to lick her length.

"You taste so good," I breathed against her, and then sucked her in again between my teeth.

Her breath got faster, and her body moved like she was in the best kind of pain. I sucked and licked, feeling her need growing. Feeling her body come apart in my mouth.

And then I finally plunged my tongue inside her.

"Jared, please," she cried, throwing her head back.

And, fuck, I was ready, too.

Standing up, I pressed my cock into her and kneaded her hips. "Tell me what you want, Tate. Please. What do you want from me?"

"I . . . Jared . . ." She fought for words; her breath was gone and her need was off the charts. Just like mine.

"Jesus, you're so beautiful." I leaned down to whisper in her ear. "Tell me: What do you want from me?"

Sweat glistened in the dip of her spine, and the room felt on fire. Our soaked skin, the taste of her on my lips—everything created this new world that I never wanted to leave.

She'd be lucky if I let her out of bed long enough to go to school.

"What do you want from me?" I growled, jerking her back into my groin again.

"Hard," she cried out. "Do it hard."

And my heart jumped into my throat.

Grazing her skin, I slipped my finger back inside of her to make sure she was still wet. She'd be sore after her first time, and I wanted to make sure she could take what she was asking me for.

So wet. *Hell, yes.*

Letting out a ragged breath, I yanked off my towel and fished in my wet jeans for my last condom, and tore the wrapper open with my teeth. Smoothing it on, I grabbed her at the hips and plunged inside her.

Hard.

"Holy shit," I groaned under my breath.

So tight.

"Jared," she whispered. "Yes."

My heart was racing a mile a minute, and it took me a few seconds to calm down. I'd never felt anything so good as having her like this.

I dived into her wet, hot sex, but the heat spread over my entire body.

The heel of her foot hanging off the table wrapped around the back of my thigh, pressing me into her, and I couldn't wait anymore.

She wanted it hard, but it was only the second time in her life she'd had sex, and I didn't want to hurt her.

"Hard?" I wanted to make sure.

Her whimper begged. "Yes."

So I rocked into her, slow at first and then faster. Before long I was grasping her hips, pushing inside her until I couldn't go any farther.

But she wasn't content to just lie there and get taken, either.

Not Tate.

She pushed up on her hands, and I almost fucking came right there.

Fuck.

Her palms were flat on the table, holding her torso upright, and her back was arched. I stared in awe at her posture in front of me as she took more control and backed into me as I slammed inside of her.

Tate. Hell, yes.

Every second, the pace and pressure increased, and goddamn, she was wet. I held her hips, wishing like hell I could put my hands everywhere, but I needed to hold on. She was pushing harder and harder into me.

As always, Tate found a way to fuck me back.

Such a handful.

I leaned down into her back, keeping my pace steady, and cupped one of her breasts, wanting one in my mouth.

Kissing her neck, I pressed my tongue to her, tasting her salty skin. My other hand glided over her stomach and then dived between her legs, where my fingers circled her clit again. God, it was so hard now. I wanted to wrap my arms around her and feel every shake and spasm as she came apart in my arms. I wanted to be inside her head and body, knowing what it felt like when I made her fucking crumble.

"Jared. It feels so good," she whimpered unsteadily as our bodies slammed together time and again.

"Yeah, it does," I breathed in her ear. "Because it's yours and mine, and no one takes this from us."

Not even me.

She was mine, and this perfect thing between us was never going to be ruined again.

"Jared!" She threw her head back and screamed. "Oh, God . . ."

"I love you, Tate." I pounded into her harder. "Come for me."

And she stopped breathing and crumbled, coming like the thunder outside the house as she cried out, tightening around me and sending me over the goddamn edge, too.

Jesus Christ!

Fire and pleasure poured through my body and I came right after her, collapsing on her back as we both fell back down to the table . . . and Earth.

We lay there panting, too spent to even move. At least I was.

"I really hate you." Her voice was weak but had an edge that told me she was joking.

"Why?"

"The massage, the oral, the kissing, the talk . . . I don't think I needed to know that you did that with other girls, after all."

"I didn't," I said right away.

"What?"

"I never did any of that with any other girl." I lifted my head up and looked down at her.

She tried popping up, too, arguing. "But . . . but I told you to tell me—"

"You wanted to know what other girls got of me. Well, that's what they didn't get." My voice was firm but soft. I needed her to hear me. "I never touched their bodies like that or held them. I never cared about them enjoying it. They didn't get any part of me worth having, Tate. Especially K.C. I never touched her like this." I stroked her hair. "You own me body and soul, and everyone is going to know it. Sometimes I'm going to go slow with you, and sometimes I'm going to fuck you. But it will always be love, Tate."

Always has been. And always will.

CHAPTER 33

didn't know if she believed me, so I just waited, worried like hell that she didn't feel how much I ached for her.

Holding herself up by her hands, she arched back up to meet me and sniffled.

Shit. I swallowed.

She was crying.

"I love you," she whispered, and turned around.

Her face was falling apart. She was holding back more tears than she was letting out.

Grabbing onto both sides of her face, I pulled her into me. "I don't deserve it, but I will. I promise."

Her small, sweet smile and hooded eyes were so exhausted that I was afraid to let go of her as I pulled out.

"Ow," she whispered, sucking in her breath through her teeth.

"Yeah." I placed my hands on her hips, supporting her. "Ease down. You're going to be sore."

"I already am."

"Stay here," I told her, and handed her a towel. I wrapped the other one around my waist. "I'll go run the shower and come back down to get you."

"I can make it upstairs." She laughed.

"Stay." And I walked off.

After running the water and checking the temperature, I ran down and picked Tate up in my arms.

"So I guess the birthday spankings are out," I joked as I carried her upstairs.

She rolled her eyes. "What is it with guys? Madoc already offered at school yesterday."

"He did what?" I halted at the top of the stairs.

She wound her arms tighter around my neck and leaned in, taking my earlobe between her teeth.

I let out a hard breath, and Madoc was forgotten.

"The water should be good." I pulled back the curtain and set her down in the tub.

"Turn on the shower part," she said sleepily, sitting down on the floor and hugging her knees. "It sounds like rain."

I pulled out the knob, watching the water spray down on her legs, and then I yanked off my towel to climb in behind her.

Sitting down, I wrapped my arms around her and pulled her back against my chest.

"You know," I spoke in her ear. "I stayed in your room for a month while you were away."

"What?" She twisted her head toward me, and I hugged her close.

I didn't know what it was, but all of a sudden I wanted her to know everything.

"When I got into trouble and my mom left to get sober, your dad took me in. Set me straight again. Well, straighter, anyway. I slept on your floor."

I tried to keep my voice light, but I was choking on the words. "I hated that you were gone, Tate. I picked fights with everyone. I skipped classes. Even the love I have for my brother couldn't pull me out of it. When I controlled you, I had one fucking thing in my life that made sense. That made my blood rush. I looked forward to tomorrow when you were around. If I could zone in on you, then I wasn't thinking about everything else that hurt."

Tate laid her head back on my shoulder and peered up at me, wide awake now.

"Why wouldn't you sleep in my bed?" she asked softly.

I touched my lips to hers, soft and warm. "Because you wouldn't have wanted me there."

I was a sick man.

I could humiliate her, isolate her, and hurt her, but sleeping in her bed while she was away was too invasive? Yeah, I couldn't explain it, either.

She leaned in, trailing kisses along my jawline. Shivers spread out across my arms when she whispered against my neck. "I definitely want you in my bed. And I love you."

I closed my eyes and a big fat smile spread across my face. If only Madoc could see me now.

Or maybe not . . .

"Say it again."

"I love you," she said louder, with a laugh in her voice.

"More," I taunted.

"I love you." She kissed my cheek. "I love you." Another kiss. "I love you." And she kept teasing me with her soft, wet kisses until I caught her lips and kissed her hard.

We're never leaving this shower.

"How are you feeling?" I asked when I'd let her go.

"Good." She nodded and wiggled her eyebrows. "Maybe we should see what it's like in water."

Heat and every other fucking source of energy inside of me shot downward, but the crushing disappointment hit me like a brick.

"Can't," I mumbled. "I don't have any more condoms."

Maybe Tate had some.

Wait . . . She'd fucking better not.

"Jared, I want a picture!" my loudmouthed and unusually invasive mother shouted as I raced up the stairs.

Picture?

I shook off my annoyance as I looked for my car keys on my dresser. Tate and I were headed to Homecoming.

Scratch that. Tate, *Madoc,* and I were headed to Homecoming. They were both waiting outside when all I really wanted to do was punch him in the gut, send him home, and skip town with Tate for the weekend.

But . . . the asshole did have a hand in making me jealous and forcing me to act, and he was a good friend.

Most of all, though, Tate wanted to go. I owed her that.

"No pictures. Jesus," I cursed, shaking my head as I snatched my keys and rushed downstairs.

But my mother was waiting at the bottom. "Oh, no, you don't." She grabbed my arm to stop me as I tried to walk past her.

I turned, trying to appear annoyed, but I was a little amused at how naturally she wore the mother role.

Ever since our heart-to-heart at the fishpond, we'd found some common ground. We still weren't all hugs and kisses, but we spoke more gently to each other and showed more patience.

"What?" I couldn't hide the smile that peeked out. "I don't do pictures . . . Mom."

Her eyes widened with a sparkle, and she cleared her throat before straightening my black tie.

"All right, but I do have something to say, and you're not going to like it." She kept her eyes trained on her task of fixing my tie and steadied her voice with a firm tone. "Honey, I couldn't be happier that you and Tate found your way back to each other—"

Oh, Christ.

I started to turn away.

"But," she said loudly, pulling me back around to face her, "baby mamas don't usually marry baby daddies."

Every word was bit out, like I was too stupid to understand.

I cocked my head to the side and looked down at her, indulging her need to make a point I already understood.

Don't get Tate pregnant. Yeah, thanks. I got it!

Her eyes peered up at mine, threatening. "You've been over there almost every night—well, every night, actually—and if you make me a thirty-five-year old grandmother, I'm going to kill you."

She was joking.

I think.

Anyway, my mother had nothing to worry about. Tate and I were careful, and she'd been keeping me off of her all week, anyway. She didn't want to get distracted from classes, and I hadn't been pushing it.

Tonight, though? Yeah, she's in for it.

Letting out a sigh, I gave my mother a quick peck on the cheek and slid out the front door.

Tate was standing on her front porch, looking gorgeous as hell, talking to Madoc like they were friends.

I shook my head, not believing the turn of events. She'd broken his nose, kicked him in the junk, and traded words more than once with him.

But she was like her dad. Solve the problem and move on.

And Madoc was more than ready to move on. He had been excited for the dance and was dressed to impress. We looked almost exactly the same, but whereas I wore all black, he changed up his suit up with a purple tie.

Tate still looked the same—beautiful and glowing—but a little more dangerous. I half expected to get in a fight over someone flirting with her tonight. She was wearing a tight, nude-colored, strapless dress that fell to midthigh. I could see so much of her skin that it was pretty clear what she looked like naked.

Walking up to Tate, I kissed the soft spot under her ear. "Sorry that took so long. My mom was giving me a talk."

"About?" she pressed, as Madoc came over and took her other arm.

"About not getting you pregnant," I whispered out of the corner of my mouth, but kept my eyes forward.

Even though I wasn't looking at her, I could see her stiffen and I heard her clear her throat.

And I shouldn't have told her that.

I really needed to put a halt to my honesty streak, but there was still something I needed to tell her, and I'd been on too much of a high the past week to face it.

Later, I told myself.

"Are we ready?" Madoc asked from her other side.

Her clutch on my arm relaxed, and I felt her exhale a breath.

"Totally." She nodded at Madoc. "This is the start of a great friendship."

"It could be the start of a great porno, too," Madoc shot back, and I clenched my fists.

"Son of a bitch!" I yelled, half-annoyed and half-joking. "You're going to get it tonight," I warned, but they both just laughed.

CHAPTER 34

The Homecoming dance was exactly what I thought it would be: pictures, punch, and poor-ass music. The gym had been decorated in a New York theme, which Tate loved, and I was extremely fucking delighted that Madoc had joined us, after all.

He filled in where I failed.

Dancing in public? Check.

Cutesy pictures with loving poses? Check.

Polite, futile, nonsensical chatter? Check.

I played along, but situations like this were like eating a mouthful of lemons. Madoc made it more fun for Tate, at least.

And her?

She read me like a book.

She was light on the public displays of affection and heavy on eye fucking.

I couldn't wait to get her home.

But we had another appearance to put in first.

"Are you sure you want to go?" I asked her as we walked hand-in-hand up the Beckmans' driveway.

Tori and Bryan Beckman, twins and our classmates, were having an after party, and Madoc insisted that we get our thumbs out of our asses and get crazy.

"I'm fine," she whispered. "Not tired at all."

I raised my eyebrows and shook my head. I wasn't worried about her being tired, but I didn't want to bring up last year's incident, either. That's what I was really worried about.

A year ago, before Tate had left for France, I'd let Madoc dump her car keys in the pool here and watched as she dived in to fish them out.

She'd been humiliated, and I figured this was the last place she'd want to be.

In fact, I wasn't sure if I wanted to be here myself.

Not only did I have our own "after party" planned, but the longer I waited to come clean about the rest of the story, the more it was the only thing I thought about. I'd been sitting on it all week, and it was time to bite the fucking bullet.

I needed to tell her about Jax.

Walking through the ceramic-tiled foyer, we followed Madoc down the carpeted stairs into the huge sunken living room.

The big room already bustled with at least sixty or seventy of our classmates, and the music pounded so hard, I could feel it through my shoes.

My arm stretched behind me and I looked back, noticing that Tate had come to a complete halt.

I let out a sigh. *Shit.*

Her chest rose and fell quickly and she swallowed, clearly nervous. Like a deer in headlights.

My stomach tightened, and I just wanted to take her out of here now. This was a bad idea.

"Tate, are you okay?" I kept my voice soft, but I was afraid she'd haul off and break *my* nose this time instead of Madoc's, like she did here a year ago.

She narrowed her eyes as she looked around, and then she just shook her head. "Yeah, I need a drink."

I didn't believe her, but the corners of my mouth turned up anyway. *Tough girl.*

We squeezed through a throng of people coming out of the kitchen as "Adrenalize" by In This Moment blasted throughout the house. Madoc was already making drinks, and I watched as Tate took the one he offered.

I was the designated driver tonight—well, pretty much any night, since I barely drank in public anymore—and I definitely didn't plan on staying here long, anyway. I just stood there, trying not to laugh as she choked down the dark liquid.

Madoc grinned from ear to ear as she tipped her chin up, swallowed the last of her drink, and threw the cup into the sink.

She coughed into her hand, and all I could do was hold her waist, letting her get comfortable.

She should have fun. I didn't want her nervous or scared that a prank was going to go down.

And that's why she was drinking, so I just let it be.

"Aw, she's as red as a tomato," Madoc joked.

"Piss off." Tate scowled at him, but he just winked at her.

K.C. and Liam sauntered in, looking like yin and yang. She was bright-eyed and smiling, while he looked constipated, with his bored expression and pursed lips.

"Hey, guys," she greeted, pulling Liam behind her.

He pushed the hair out of his eyes and nodded at Madoc and me but said nothing.

I knew it was me making him uncomfortable, and I had to force a straight face.

He probably still thought I'd gotten in his girlfriend's pants, and I couldn't help being impressed with K.C. for not telling him the truth. She was playing with him, making him suffer, no doubt. And why shouldn't she?

She and Tate still weren't back to square one, but they'd get there, and Liam could go fuck himself.

Madoc finished off his drink and immediately started making two more until I shook my head at him. Tate didn't notice it as she talked with K.C., but Madoc got my warning.

I needed her awake for a while.

Leaning in, I whispered in her ear. "Come with me."

I didn't wait for her to even look at me before I grabbed her hand and led her out of the kitchen. We squeezed through the crowd of partygoers, all in little clusters, and tried not to get slammed with drinks in the process.

Once we made it to the stairs, I hurriedly led Tate to the second floor. I had no plans to make use of the rooms here with her, but people saw us go up and would draw their own conclusions when we came back down.

I just needed her alone for a few minutes.

To right a wrong.

Opening the door to the first bedroom, I peeked in and found it empty. Pulling Tate in, I had barely even closed the door before I when her into it and dove for her lips.

She stumbled and latched onto my shoulders to steady herself. The surprised little moan she let loose filled my mouth, and I was so damn hard that I was ready to ride this storm right here and now.

Yeah, this was not what I'd planned, but I'd been good tonight.

I deserved a reward.

She tasted like peaches, and I pulled her barely clothed body into me, close to forgetting why I was up here in the first place.

"God, Tate." I dipped my head to nibble her earlobe. "Your dress should be burned."

"Why?" she breathed out, leaning her neck into me for more.

"Every fucking guy has been looking at you tonight. I'm going to get arrested."

My tone was joking, but my words weren't. I wasn't insecure about Tate. I knew she loved me and I could trust her. I also didn't mind other guys looking at her, wanting her. It kind of turned me on, actually.

No, my crime would lie in the fact that every time some dipshit pointed at her tonight or some asshole did a double take when she walked by, I wanted to put my hands all over her to show them who had claim.

They could look.

They could want.

But she was going home with me, and I felt like rubbing it in.

Couldn't exactly feel her up in public, though.

She pulled away and held my head in her hands, her eyes searching mine. "I'm yours. It's always been you," she assured.

I held her gaze, her fire meeting my ice, and I couldn't deny her one more damn thing that she deserved.

"Come here." I led her to the center of the room and took out my phone. She watched me while I clicked on Seether's "Broken" and placed the phone on the chest of drawers near the balcony doors.

Tate watched me silently with her arms hanging at her sides and a mixture of curiosity and excitement in her eyes.

Taking her hand in mine, I kept my eyes on hers as I guided her arms around my neck and pulled her body into mine.

As we started moving to the music, I barely heard anything. Not the romp of the party downstairs. Not the chatter around the house and outside.

Her eyes were glued to mine, looking beyond everything else.

And suddenly we were fourteen again, back in her bedroom and arguing about Silverchair.

I was Jared. She was Tate. And we were inseparable.

"I'm sorry I didn't dance with you tonight," I told her, regret lacing my voice. "I don't like doing things like that in public. It feels too personal, I guess."

She took a deep breath and leveled me with her hard gaze. "I don't want you to change who you are," she said, shaking her head. "But I might like to dance with you sometime or hold your hand."

I wrapped my hands around her waist, locking her in. "I'll try, Tate. Yesterday is gone. I know that. I want that comfort we used to have back."

"Your tattoo?" She looked up at me, as if realizing something. "'Yesterday lasts forever. Tomorrow comes never.' That's what it says. What does it mean?"

I lightly caressed her hair. "Just that I was living in the past. What happened with my father, what happened with you, I could never get over the anger. Yesterday kept following me. And tomorrow, the new day, never seemed to come."

"And the lantern on your arm?" she pressed further, and I laughed. "Oh, you ask too many questions."

But she just continued to stare at me, mentally tapping her foot. *All right, damn it.*

"The lantern is you, Tate. The light." Her dancing in her light purple nightgown with white stars on it when she was eleven flashed through my mind. "I got it after I got in trouble last year. I needed to clean up my act, and my mom decided to do the same thing with her drinking. We both picked one thought that would get us through the day. A dream or a desire . . ." I'd never asked my mom about her dream or desire.

"Me?" She narrowed her eyes, looking surprised.

"It's always been you." I repeated her same words. "I love you, Tate."

She smiled, bringing her lips to mine. "I love you, too," she whispered, and the tickle across my mouth was like a fire over my body.

Jesus Christ.

My fingers dug into her, but it was her hands that owned me. She ran her hands up my arms before threading one hand through my hair.

She pulled away and then came back in to tease me again and again, flicking her tongue under my top lip and catching my bottom lip between her teeth. The tiny nibbles made tingles electrify my groin, and my stomach damn near growled with hunger.

Fuck. I didn't know whether I wanted to fuck her or eat her.

"Unzip me," she forced out between kisses along my jaw.

Don't do this now, I begged silently.

"Let's just get out of here," I suggested. "I'm in the mood for more than a quickie."

"Well, I've never had a quickie," she taunted. "Unzip me."

I sucked in a breath, throbbing in my pants and too ready for her.

As soon as I'd undone her dress, which fell down and sat at her waist, we were both at the point of no return.

"Where'd my good girl go?" I teased, but I loved it.

Bad only for me.

She was a drug, and I was higher than a kite. In no time at all, my hands were all over her smooth, heavenly back, and my lips were buried in her warm neck.

Her urgent fingers worked my tie and the buttons of my shirt, and I cupped her breasts, eating up every little moan and gasp that came out of her mouth. She was so sensitive on her chest. I circled one arm behind her back and ran the other hand up and down one of her breasts, feeling her nipple get harder every time I trailed across it.

"Jared," she whispered, wrapping an arm around my neck and kissing me. "I really am a good girl, but tonight I want to be really, really bad."

Goddamn. She was killing me, and I swear every time our lips came together, I was about to explode. I couldn't wait until we got home.

Fuck it.

I ripped open my shirt, a few buttons flying off in the process, and watched, half-dazed, as she peeled off the rest of her clothes, leaving only her nude-colored high heels on.

Wow.

My heart raced, my mouth went dry, and my breathing sped up. All of my blood rushed south, and I was harder than a fucking brick. I was definitely in a lot more pain than I'd ever been before.

I needed to get inside her.

"Fuck, Tate." I caressed as much of her as I could reach and kissed her hard. Tightening every muscle in my body, I had to force myself not to throw her on the goddamn bed. "I'm sorry. I want to go slow with you. It's just so hard. Do you think in ten years I'll finally get to where I'll actually need foreplay to get hard with you?"

She stood there, brave and bold, knowing she had me under her thumb.

I took a condom out of my pocket, placed it on the nightstand, and peeled off the rest of my clothes, sighing in relief when my dick sprang free.

Picturing what I wanted to do to Tate wasn't nearly as painful as seeing her look at me. She looked down my body, almost like she wanted to take the time to study it or something. I nearly jumped when she reached out her hand and started stroking me.

I exhaled hard in short, heavy breaths.

This was something she hadn't really done yet. Explored my body like this.

Her eyes seemed amazed and curious, and I didn't want to miss this for anything. She watched me respond to her, how I grew and jerked at her soft but strong touch, and I didn't think I could be on fire any more than I was.

Shit, baby. Now, now, now . . .

I couldn't fucking take it anymore. It could've been the heels, her body, or the way she blew my mind just being herself, but I was done for.

Grabbing the condom, I tore open the wrapper and slipped the sucker on, not taking an eye off of her.

Pulling her close, I crushed her body with mine, feeling her hot, naked skin melting into mine.

She broke contact and whispered in my ear. "My turn."

What?

My eyes widened, not sure what she meant until she pushed my back on the bed and came down to straddle me.

My dick was pressed to her warm, wet opening, and I squeezed her hips, almost growling.

"You're perfect. Perfect for me," I said, feeling the soft, sexy skin in my hands.

Goddamn it, I need you. Now.

Her blond hair spilled around her and she was an animal, looking at me like she knew exactly how to kill me.

Lifting up, she slowly came down as I guided my cock inside her. She was so small that we needed help, and I had no problem with that.

Pleasure swept over me like a wave of heat as I lay back and felt her warmth coat me. I put a hand on her breast and another on her hip, touching and guiding.

"Tell me you like it, Tate." I had to know that she loved this. That she was going to come back for more.

That she was my girlfriend.

I never wanted to give anyone that title, because I thought I wouldn't be able to make the commitment.

That wasn't it.

I already had a girlfriend. All along, even though we were enemies, no one could take Tate's place.

Tell me, baby. Say it.

"I . . ." she gasped as she moved her hips in a wild, you-better-do-that-all-damn-night motion that had me breathing hard.

I jerked my hips up, pushing deeper inside her. "Say it."

Her eyebrows pinched together in the good kind of pain as she stumbled over the words. "I love it." She smiled. "I love it with you."

I shot up and wrapped my arms around her back and buried my face in her chest, taking a firm breast in my mouth.

"You taste like candy," I whispered against her skin as I dragged a nipple between my teeth. "You're not getting any fucking sleep tonight, Tatum Brandt. You know that, right?"

"Do you?" she shot back, taking my face in her hands.

Such a handful.

"There's something I didn't tell you last week when . . . when we were in your room."

We lay underneath the covers, naked and happily exhausted, staring up at the ceiling.

I caressed her arm as she rested her head under my chin.

I didn't want to disturb this perfect calm, but it was time.

Telling the truth is like lying; once you do it, it becomes easier.

"What?" Her voice was raspy, and, as if there were a lion ripping at my stomach or a rhino stomping around my chest, I was nervous.

"I left my brother at my dad's house. I ran out of there without him," I confessed.

She arched her neck back to peer up at me. "Jared, I know. You told me that part. That you tried to get him to leave, but he wouldn't."

I nodded. "I didn't tell you everything, though. The day I ran out, my father had forced me into the basement to help my brother. With what, I didn't know, but when I got down there, I saw . . ." The bile started forcing its way up my throat, so I concentrated on my breathing. "I saw my dad's girlfriend and his friend dead on the basement floor."

She popped up and stared down at me. "Dead?"

"Come back here." I pulled her back down, but she propped up her arm in the bed and rested her head on her balled-up fist instead.

I guess she wanted eye contact.

"Yeah, as far as I could tell with the fucking distance I kept. Jax was sitting against the far wall, holding his knees against his chest and staring at nothing. He didn't look scared or angry, just like he was a little confused or something." I narrowed my eyes, trying to imagine what could have been going through his head.

"How do you know they were dead?" she asked softly, and swallowed.

"There was blood. They weren't moving." I shook the images from my head. "Anyway, I couldn't get Jax to wake up, so to speak. He just sat there and would only say that he was fine, and that we had to clean up the mess. It was like he didn't even know it was me in the room."

Tate looked at me, concern in her eyes, and I hoped she understood.

"You feel guilty." She figured me out.

"Yeah," I admitted. "It was unbearable, being in that house. Being in that basement. Why wouldn't he come with me?" I asked more to myself than Tate.

"Have you asked him?"

"Once." I caressed her hair. "He doesn't remember, he says."

"What do you think happened down there?" She asked the question I'd been asking myself for years. My father wasn't arrested for murder. I don't even know if the police found bodies when I got home and reported my brother's abuse.

I thought for a minute, afraid to admit out loud what I knew was ridiculous to suspect.

"I think two lowlifes got exactly what they deserved."

CHAPTER 35

"Are you sore at all?" I whispered into her hair as we walked into school Monday morning.

Her breathing hitched and I could hear the smile in her voice. "A little."

"Good," I mumbled, and hooked my arm around her neck, pulling her in.

I'd taken her back to her house on Saturday night after Homecoming and punished her for keeping me at arm's length all damn week by keeping her up all damn night.

After spending Sunday with my brother and not being able to talk to Tate—because I'd stupidly left my phone at the Beckmans' party, and it was stolen—I'd crept into her room last night and fallen asleep with her in my arms.

But I woke her up early. We were both half-asleep, but it was still hot.

She rolled her eyes at me. "You're such an egomaniac," she complained.

I looked down at her, grinning. "And you love it."

"Do not," she pouted, and I put my lips to her forehead.

Yes, you do.

I sighed. "Then I'll change," I promised.

"Damn right you will."

She stopped at her locker, but I stayed behind her, holding her hips. I was becoming a big pile of whipped, but I couldn't *not* touch her when she was close.

People had been looking at us during the past week. Used to seeing us as enemies and me never with my hands on a girl in public, they seemed pretty confused.

But instead of shying away and putting on my tough-guy face, I gave them all the middle finger.

Well, figuratively.

Looking down the row, I saw Piper and Nate with their heads together, and then they turned to eyeball me.

My stomach rolled, not because I couldn't handle either of them, but I didn't want Tate to even register their presence.

She was going to be happy . . . or else.

Nate looked amused, even with the remnants of the black eye I'd given him weeks ago, while Piper scrunched up her lips like she was disgusted. Her eyes were angry, though, and unease nestled into the back of my brain.

Great.

I was sure I'd be in for a confrontation before the end of the day.

"All right." Tate turned around and hugged her books. "I'm off. Are you walking me?"

"No, I have to get my ass to the counselor's office, actually."

Saying the word "counselor" had me wanting to upchuck, but it was required for all seniors.

"Ah, the what-are-your-future-plans talk," she teased while nodding her head.

I almost let out a laugh with the way my heart jumped. "The only future plans I have are taking you to see a concert over Thanksgiving," I said quietly as I pulled two tickets out of my pocket.

"Oh!" Her eyes widened, and she snatched the tickets out of my hand. "You didn't! Avenged Sevenfold!"

"Belated birthday present," I explained. "I was waiting for them to go on sale." A grin tickled my jaw as I tried to hold it back. "You like Avenged Sevenfold, right?"

As much time as Tate and I had spent apart, I still had to remind myself that there was stuff I may not know about her anymore.

She looked at me like I had three heads. "Like Avenged Sevenfold?" She held out her arms for me to see the black T-shirt—the Avenged Sevenfold T-shirt—she wore under her little black cardigan. "M. Shadows is my everything," she teased.

"Hey." I partially scowled and partially smiled, pulling her into me. She let out a raspy laugh.

"Thank you," she whispered into my lips, pulling me in.

"You can thank me more later."

Pulling back, she playfully shoved my chest away. "Go. Go to your appointment and make plans for a New York college."

I barely had time to roll my eyes before she turned around and walked down the hall.

"So, your grades look good. Not great, but enough to get into a good school." Ms. Varner opened a file folder—my folder—and regurgitated the same conversation she'd no doubt spewed at the other three hundred seniors she'd talked to this month.

I sat there, arms at ease on the armrests, with one ankle resting on the other knee. The air in the room was thick, but I stayed because the principal would harass the students who made these meetings difficult. I sat, I stayed, and I would get out as easily as possible.

"What colleges are you considering?" she asked, looking at me with concern.

"Undecided." I barely unclenched my teeth for my usual one-word answers.

Her eyes narrowed, and she studied me for a moment before pulling a packet out of the folder.

"Are you interested in seeing what the career test said about you?" she asked without even looking at me.

"No."

"It said," she continued, as if I'd said nothing, "that you have strengths in leadership."

What the . . . ?

"Like a coach?" I blurted out.

Me and sports? Me working in a school for the rest of my life, earning shit pay. Yeah, that'd be a whole fucking waste of a life.

She covered her smile with her hand. "No." Her voice cracked with a laugh. "Like the military or politics."

Like West Point, Mr. Brandt's voice came back to haunt me.

No, maybe owning my own shop someday or running races, but not driving tanks or flying jets . . .

Wait . . .

"Yeah, okay." I shook off the images of me in a cockpit. "I'll think about it." I stood up to leave, with no intention of thinking about it.

"Jared," she called, and I stopped. "The test also says you're a protector, a nurturer . . ." She trailed off as my eyes widened.

What the fuck?

"You might want to consider careers in health care or youth guidance." And she looked down, almost embarrassed.

Youth guidance?

My face probably looked like someone just told me I was born from wolves. When I looked at her, I saw a crazy lady.

"Get your test checked," I grumbled, and walked out the door.

A fucking youth guidance pilot?

And she makes money at that job?

My head was all over the place now, and I'd lost the calm from this morning. Usually my brain was like a warehouse. Take one box, open it, deal with it, and put it away before dealing with another box. Now all the goddamn boxes were open at the same time.

Was it so wrong to just want Tate on the back of my motorcycle forever and not want anything else?

I marched through the front office and yanked open the door leading out.

"Jared!" I heard my name yelled—no, bellowed—off to my left and turned to see Madoc stomping toward me.

My shoulders straightened immediately.

He looked pissed. His hair looked like he'd been combing his hands through it, and his lips were tight.

"What the fuck is the matter with you?" he accused, and I braced myself for a punch that I was sure was coming for some reason.

What?

"What are you talking about?" If the counselor's office was hot, I was in a frying pan now. I pulled the collar of my black hoodie away from my sweaty neck.

He held up his phone next to his face. I grabbed it out of his hands and stared in horror as I watched a video of Tate and me having sex Homecoming night.

What?

My heart was jackhammering through my chest, and I couldn't catch my breath.

Jesus.

Hot air poured in and out of my nose.

We were in the Beckmans' bedroom, and she was on top, completely fucking naked.

How the hell?

Madoc had this video.

He saw her like that.

My fists balled up, ready to slam him to the ground.

But . . . why would Madoc have this video?

And then another thought occurred to me.

"Who else has seen this?" I growled, ready to either throw up or thrown down.

"Um, everybody," he spat out sarcastically. "You didn't send this, then?"

"Of course I didn't send this! We didn't record a sex video. Jesus Christ!" I hollered, and vaguely noticed students around us hauling ass outdoors when they should've been in class.

He looked down. "Well, it came from your phone." He spoke softer.

I closed my eyes. *No, no, no . . .*

"Tate might've gotten this video. Shit." I started for the stairs, knowing she was on the third floor for French, but Madoc grabbed me by the inside of my elbow.

"Brother, she's already gone." He shook his head, and my stomach plummeted.

My phone was missing, and someone had sent a video of Tate and me to the whole damn school from my number.

"Jared!"

I turned and saw Sam running down the hall, jerking his thumb to the double doors leading outside.

"Tate's trashing your car, man!" he shouted, breathless.

Madoc and I didn't wait. We charged out the double doors, only to see a crowd gathering around my Boss.

Tate.

I couldn't see much, but I saw her swinging and felt the sharp slash at my chest every time the metal weapon in her hands hit my car.

She was losing it.

How many times could she be humiliated before she crumbled?

How many times could she be hurt before the damage was irreparable?

"Tate, stop it!" I grabbed her from behind before she brought the crowbar back down.

I had no idea what the damage was, but I didn't care.

She twisted away from me and spun around to face me.

And that's when I saw it.

The end.

The death in her eyes. The absence of emotion. The surrender of everything good between us that we'd built this past week.

She believed I'd sent that video to the whole school. She believed I'd wanted her to hurt again.

"Tate . . ." I tried to speak but couldn't.

She didn't look angry or sad.

She'd given up on me.

And I was so paralyzed by that realization, I barely heard her threat.

"Stay away from me, or it'll be more than your car getting busted up next time."

She walked away, and the crowd around me hushed, but I had nothing to say.

I had no fucking clue how I was going to fix this.

Youth guidance counselor?

Yeah, right.

CHAPTER 36

"Give me your phone," I ordered Madoc as I made my way through the crowd of hushed whispers and nosy, fucking invasive eyes.

"Man, just leave her alone for now," he groaned.

All these damn people. Their eyes were on me, and there were even some hanging out the school's windows. Everyone had seen this, and someone had probably shot a video of Tate tearing up my car.

My car. I groaned. I couldn't even look at it.

"Phone. Now." I held out my hand after we'd gotten some space. He plopped it down in my hand.

"I'm going to look for her." I started dialing Tate's number. "You stay here and go talk to the principal. Make sure she doesn't get in trouble for this."

Principal Masters was scared of Madoc's father, and thank God for that. Mr. Caruthers wasn't just a lawyer. He was the guy whose cases were studied in law schools.

His weight kept us out of trouble, and now Tate was going to keep her record clean, too.

I dug in my pocket for my keys.

"They're going to know about the video, Jared. He'll keep her out of trouble, but he'll call her dad."

Shit.

"Fuck!" I growled, shutting up everyone around me.

Girls squealed and others backed away.

That's when I noticed I still had an audience, and for the first time in weeks, I felt the need to hit shit.

"All of you," I bellowed, pointing my finger around me in a circle, "erase that video from your fucking phones! Now! If I see anyone with it, you're dead! Bitches included."

"Oh, Jesus." Madoc ran his hands over his face. "Are you trying to get arrested?"

Fuck 'em all.

"If she shows up, for any reason, get a phone and call me." And I turned around and climbed into my nearly broken car.

I drove around for about an hour before I worked up the courage to call her father. He might hear it from the school, but he needed to hear it from me first. I'd been calling and texting Tate nonstop, but it was time to face the music.

Tate's dad picked up on the first ring.

"Hello?" he asked, confusion filling his voice. I had Madoc's phone, and he didn't know the number.

"Mr. Brandt? It's Jared."

"Jared?" he blurted out. "What's wrong?"

I almost laughed.

Mr. Brandt and I texted. If I was calling, then he knew something was up.

"Tate's fine," I assured him right away, but it felt like a lie. Physically, she was okay. "But something happened." I paused and then spat it out. "It's probably a good idea for you to come home as soon as possible."

That tasted like vinegar, but there was no way around it.

Tate needed her father right now.

"What the hell happened?" he barked, and I jerked the phone away from my ear.

Slowly and timidly, using the most sugar-coated language I possibly could, I let him know that Tate and I were having sex, a video was recorded of us at a Homecoming party, and it appeared to be sent to the whole school from my phone that I'd lost.

Yeah, I was going to be shot.

The heavy silence coming from the other end of the line had me cringing. I kept telling myself to shut up, because at any moment he'd reach through, grab my neck, and squeeze until he killed me.

"Mr. Brandt?" When he didn't respond, I squinted my eyes like I was bracing myself for a beat-down. "Do you have any idea where she might have gone?"

He was silent for a moment and then cleared his throat. "Maybe to the cemetery."

"Yes, sir. I'll try there."

"Jared," he piped up again, calmer than I expected. "Find my child. Get her home safe," he ground out every angry word. "And don't leave her side until I get home."

I nodded, even though he couldn't see it.

"And then," he added, "I may never let you near her again."

My stomach dropped to my feet, and he hung up.

Driving into Concord Hill Cemetery was like stepping into a dream on shaky ground. I'd been here a lot of times before but rarely without Tate.

Her mother was buried here, and it was where I'd realized that she was more than a friend. I'd brought a balloon to her mother's grave here and stolen the fossil necklace that Tate had left her mother.

Even though this place was tied to something painful for Tate, I looked at it with good memories.

My heart started bouncing around my chest like a tennis ball when I saw her dad's Bronco parked along the side of the lane near her mom's grave.

She's safe.

I let out a breath and pulled in behind her truck, cutting the engine.

As I got out of the car, my boots ground the glass that had been shattered from Tate smashing my windows, but I barely noticed.

My eyes were on her, lying on top of her mom's grave, forehead down to the ground.

I tried to put myself in her shoes.

Did I care that people saw me having sex with someone?

Yes.

Did I care that people saw my girlfriend's body? Not just her naked body, but what it was doing to mine?

Hell fucking yes.

It made what we were doing dirty.

My chest ached, and I wanted to rip the town apart to find out who did this.

"Tate." I couldn't do any more than whisper her name as I approached. She tensed but she wouldn't look at me.

Goddamn it.

Tate, we are climbing out of this fucking mess one way or another, because no one ruins us.

"Haven't you won, Jared? Why won't you just leave me alone?"

"Tate, this is all so fucked up. I—"

She cut me off. "No! No more!" she yelled, spinning around and firing her loaded eyes at me. "Do you hear me? My life here is ruined.

No one will let me live this down. You've won. Don't you get it? You. Have. Won! Now leave me alone!"

I lost my words. I lost my breath. My hands went up to my hair, and I tried to figure out how to get control of this. "Just stop for a minute, okay?" I held out my hands and calmed my voice.

"I've listened to your stories. Your excuses."

She got up and started walking back to the road. To her car.

"I know." I talked to her back. "My words aren't good enough. I can't explain any of this. I don't know where that video came from!" I shouted when she wouldn't stop.

"It came from your phone, asshole!" she shot back, twisting her face slightly back to me. "No, never mind. I've stopped talking to you." And she kept charging ahead.

She wasn't staying and talking this out. She was damn pissed and clearly wanted to be away from me.

"I called your dad!"

That stopped her in her tracks.

She mumbled something under her breath, but I couldn't hear it. I probably didn't want to hear it, either.

She was still. She was quiet.

Move, motherfucker!

"Tate, I didn't send that video to anyone." *Hear me, baby.* "I didn't even record a video of us."

This is yours and mine, and no one takes it from us.

She was listening, so I kept going for as long as she let me. "I haven't seen my phone in two days. I left it upstairs at Tori's party, when we were listening to music. When I remembered later, I went back to get it, but it was gone. Don't you remember?"

The chill in the air made the sweat on my brow feel like ice, and I watched the wind blow Tate's long hair around her back.

As long as she's not moving away, it's a good sign.

"You're a liar," she snarled in a low voice.

Well, that's not a good sign.

Taking a chance, I walked up to her.

Only just this morning, she'd been laughing as my fingers tickled her sides, and then she whispered my name as I made love to her.

She had to feel me. Even if I wasn't touching her, she had to feel me.

"I called your dad because he was going to find out anyway. That goddamn fucking video is out there, and I wanted him to hear it from me first. He's coming home."

The tension in her shoulders slackened, but her head dropped. Almost like she'd given up.

"I love you more than myself," I told her, "more than my own family, for Christ's sake. I don't want to take another step in this world without you next to me."

And as much as I hated to admit that, it was true.

I loved my mother and my brother. But if it ever came between the three, I would always pick Tate.

When she didn't turn around or say anything, I dropped my hand to her shoulder. "Tate."

But she whipped around, flinging my hand off her body. Her eyes were guarded.

I was still the enemy.

"You have every right not to trust me, Tate. I know that. My fucking heart is ripping open right now. I can't stand the way you're looking at me. I could never hurt you again. Please . . . let's try to fix this together." My voice was cracking, and the lump in my throat got bigger.

"Fine." She reached into her pocket and took out her phone. "I'll play along."

Play?

"What are you doing?" I asked, narrowing my blurry eyes at her.

"Calling your mom." She started pressing buttons on her screen.

"Why?"

"Because she installed a GPS tracking app on your Android when she bought it. You said you lost your phone? Let's find it."

CHAPTER 37

"School," Tate almost whispered as she slipped her phone back in her pocket. "It's at school."

"Son of a bitch." My mother tracked me? I guess that explained how she found me the night at the fishpond. "She's smarter than I thought," I said more to myself.

So my phone was at school. I left it at the party, so that meant that someone from our school had taken it, and they had it on.

Well, that was dumb.

It still didn't solve the question of how someone had recorded the video. My phone was playing music that night, but it definitely wasn't recording Tate and me.

Shit.

I blinked long and hard.

The balcony.

Could someone have been out there filming us?

Now my gut was twisted with acid, and I was charged.

That was the first time Tate had taken over, tried something new, and gotten on top. She was brave and beautiful, and I was rocked.

To think of someone outside on the balcony the whole time, watching us. Watching her.

Refocusing, I looked at Tate, whose eyebrows were arched in. Scared. *But she's not a runner anymore.*

"I see that look in your eye." I inched closer and spoke quietly. "It's the look you get when you want to bolt. The look you get right before you decide to stay and fight."

"What am I fighting for?" she said, her voice cracking.

Us, damn it!

"We did nothing wrong, Tate."

Her eyes were red from crying, but I knew she wasn't running away. Her breathing evened out, and her lips settled in a resolved line.

"Let's go." She turned and walked to her truck, swinging open the door.

Thank God. I let out a long breath.

Maybe we wouldn't find my phone. Maybe I wouldn't be proven innocent in her eyes. Maybe taking her back to school, with all of those eyes, was a huge-ass mistake.

But she was fighting for us again, and that had me so happy, I'd dance in public anytime she asked.

"Is . . . um . . . is your car safe to drive?" She gestured to the Boss parked behind her truck.

Baby, I don't even care. I shook my head.

"Don't sweat it. It gives me an excuse to do more upgrades."

Her eyes pooled, but she blinked the tears away and took a deep breath.

"Stop at your mom's firm and pick up her phone," she instructed, as we'd need my mom's phone to find mine. "I'll meet you at school."

Once I grabbed my mother's phone and hurried away from her questions, I sped off to school to find Tate in the parking lot waiting for me.

"Are you okay?" I asked, taking her hand, but she immediately yanked it away.

My heart dropped into my stomach.

"Tate."

She wouldn't look at me. Her eyes were turned away, looking at the school.

"Don't ask me if I'm okay." Her voice was raspy, as if she were holding back tears. "I don't think I'm going to have any idea how to answer that for a while."

She ran a hand through her long, blond hair and took a deep breath before walking toward the school.

God, I hope this works.

The more time that passed, the farther away from me she got, and whether or not I was guilty, this might be the straw that broke the camel's back.

Tate had had enough.

She was walking the line between fighting back and shutting down.

Coming up beside her, I stayed close but didn't touch her.

Everyone was still in class, but not for long. The bell would ring soon, and we'd be like animals in a cage at the zoo.

Eyes all around and nowhere to turn.

I followed the tracker on my mom's phone, still amazed that I wasn't pissed off that she tracked me.

After so long feeling like I was on my own, I actually felt comforted to have someone worry about me.

The light flashed, showing my phone's general location, but it wasn't specific.

There had to be a quicker way to do this.

My hands were shaky, and I wanted to get the fuck out of here before the bell rang.

"Is it still flashing?" Tate asked, looking over at the phone in my hand.

"Yeah." I looked around, waiting for someone to see us. "I can't believe my phone is still on after two days. GPSs use a lot of battery."

"Well, the video was sent this morning," she pointed out. "If what you say is true, then whoever used your phone has probably charged it since Saturday night."

So far away.

"If what you say is true. . . ." I repeated her words, hating how quickly shit changes. This morning I was all over her, and now it was like she wanted me far away.

"Look," she spoke up, killing the silence between us. "This tracker's only accurate within fifty meters. So—"

"So start dialing my phone," I interrupted. "Maybe we'll hear it."

Fifty meters covered a lot of area. The phone was here, but we'd need help finding out where exactly.

She dug her phone out of her back pocket and called my cell. We walked the tiled floors in silence, listening for any rings or vibrations from the lockers.

Even though she had the phone to her ear, I could still hear my voice mail pick up. Every time it did, she hung up and redialed as we continued to walk.

"Let's split up," she finally suggested after the fifth call. "I'll keep dialing. Just listen for a sound. I think it's in a locker."

"Why?" I asked, stopping to look at her. "Someone could have it on them, too."

"With me calling every ten seconds? No." She shook her head. "They would've turned off the phone, in which case it would've gone straight to voice mail. It's on, and it's in a locker."

Split up?

I rubbed my jaw, not liking this idea one fucking bit.

But we didn't have long.

"Fine," I bit out. "But if you find it, call my mom's phone immediately. I don't want you in the halls alone, not today."

She stood there, studying me, like she wasn't sure if any of this was worth her time. She was probably thinking that I did send the video, and I was just playing with her now.

Spinning around, she left and darted up the stairs to the next floor.

I continued searching the first floor, my fists clenching and unclenching inside of the front pocket of my hoodie as I listened for any sound of my phone.

I didn't wear a watch—I usually used my phone to tell the time—but I knew we were close.

The bell was going to ring, and we needed to just give this up and get the hell out of here.

This morning I'd felt her kisses, her hands, and her happiness. But now I felt only her doubt. It sat between us like a ten-ton elephant.

The phone in my hand buzzed, and I jerked it up so fast, I almost dropped it.

2nd floor, next to Kuhl's room!! Tate texted.

Shit.

I fucking bolted up the nearest flight of stairs to the next floor and nearly tripped on the steps when the final bell screamed.

Dread slammed my stomach down to my feet, and I hesitated only a moment before I charged ahead through the doors and onto the second floor.

Students flooded the hall, all trying to get to their lockers or downstairs to leave.

Most of them did a double take at seeing me, but I just turned left and pushed through the crowd as fast as I could.

People coming my way slowed down, while others stopped to

whisper to their friends. There's was no telling what was going through their heads, and my fists balled up in aggravation. Not only was I angry about what had happened, but I was completely fucking pissed that I now had to clean up a mess I didn't make.

I finally found Tate next to a set of lockers toward the end of the hall, and she definitely had onlookers.

Her body was rigid, but she stood tall and didn't hide from their stares. She looked at me, and I fucking melted when I saw her guard with me was back down.

"Are you all right?" I asked, taking her face in my hands.

"Yes." Her tone told me everything. She believed me. "The phone is here, in 1622," she said softly, and I tensed. "I don't know whose locker it is, though."

I do.

I looked behind her, my eyes hardening on the locker.

Piper.

My jaw was glued, and oxygen poured in like fuel.

I didn't hit women, but I'd damn well let Tate hit her.

"Back so soon?" a female voice snipped behind me. "Is your porn career a failure already?"

Tate's body shifted under my hands, and I placed a light kiss on her forehead before I turned around to face the bitch.

I tried to keep Tate behind me, but she yanked me back and quickly stepped in front.

Oh, Jesus. I rubbed my forehead and tried not to smile.

Nothing was funny here, but Tate continued to surprise me.

"Actually, we're just waiting for you," she said with mock happiness. "You know that video that came from Jared's phone this morning? The one that everyone saw? He didn't send it. His phone was stolen Saturday night. Would you know where it is?" Tate asked, crossing her arms over her chest.

The hall had gotten quiet, and everyone stood like they were on the outside of a boxing ring, peering in.

"Why would I know where his phone is?" Piper sneered.

Tate held up her cell. "Oh, because. . . ." She hit Redial, and everyone heard my ringtone for Tate—Limp Bizkit's "Behind Blue Eyes"—coming from Piper's locker.

It was the ringer I'd set up after she'd left for France—like she'd ever call—and I never changed it.

Tate flashed her screen to everyone, so they could see that it was my name on the screen of who she was dialing.

"This is your locker, Piper," I pointed out, so everyone would know.

Tate was humiliated. The damage was done.

But it wasn't a choice. Everyone had to know that I wasn't responsible for hurting her like that. Not ever again.

"You know, I just love that song," Tate teased. "Let's hear it again." She redialed, and people stood around, some waiting for a fight, while others whispered or nodded.

Walking up to Piper, I bent down into her face. "Open up your locker and give me my goddamn phone back, or we'll get the dean and he'll open the locker."

Her lips pursed. "It was Nate's idea!" She cracked and started defending herself.

The onlookers started laughing.

"You stupid bitch!" I heard Nate bark from somewhere in the crowd. "It was your idea."

And I straightened my shoulders when he stepped forward.

Some people are born stupid.

I cocked my fist back and punched him across the nose, sending him down like a dead deer. He dropped to the floor, holding his bloody nose, and I hovered, ready for his ass to pop back up again.

Madoc pushed through the crowd, his eyeballs damn near popping out of his head as he surveyed Nate on the floor.

"Are you okay?" he asked, turning his eyes on Tate.

I didn't hear or see her respond, but Madoc shook his head and looked back down to Nate.

"How did you do it?" Tate asked Piper.

She didn't respond.

"Your dad's a cop, right?" Tate asked. "What's his number?" She held up her phone like she was ready to dial. "Oh, yeah. Nine-one-one."

"Ugh, all right!" Piper screeched. "Nate took me to Homecoming and then to Tori's party afterward. When we saw you and Jared head upstairs, Nate took his camera phone and climbed onto the balcony. When he showed me the video later, I saw that Jared had left his phone on the dresser, so I snuck back into the room to take it."

Son of a bitch.

"So the video came from Nate's phone," Tate confirmed but was looking at me. "It was transferred to Jared's before it was texted."

Our eyes were locked, and a mountain of relief descended on my shoulders.

"Get Jared's phone, Piper. Now," Madoc ordered, and I looked down at Nate, who was trying to get up.

Once our eyes met, though, he seemed to reconsider and lay back down.

Piper took a grueling minute to retrieve the phone, and then she threw it at Tate.

"We're done," she said cattily, and waved her hand, dismissing Tate. "You may go."

I had a hundred fucking names I wanted to call her, but it would be a waste of time. I was going to take care of this. Piper and Nate weren't getting away with shit.

Just get Tate out of here.

But, of course, Tate had other plans.

"Piper?" she spoke calmly. "Do yourself a favor and get some help. Jared is not yours, and he never will be. In fact, he won't ever look at you again and see anything good, if he even saw anything good in the first place."

Tate turned to me, but all of a sudden, Piper was yanking her by the hair!

And I stood there like a damn moron, not knowing which one to grab, because they were moving too fucking quickly.

Tate was slammed against the lockers. Piper tried to punch her. Tate ducked and then smacked Piper across the face. Twice.

Shit.

I caught sight of Madoc waving at me. "Porter!" he whisper-yelled, urgency etched on his face, as I hurriedly grabbed my girl and whispered in her ear.

"Shhh." I tried to control her, but she was struggling.

Dr. Porter was working his way through the crowd. "What's going on here?" he growled as he came to the front.

Tate immediately relaxed into my body. I released my hold, and she stood there silently, looking down, while Porter glanced between the whining lump of Piper on the floor and the bleeding heap of Nate next to her.

"Dr. Porter," Madoc spoke up. "Nate and Piper bumped into each other."

Sweat poured down my back, and I didn't know if I wanted to hug Tate, smack Madoc, or . . . smack Madoc.

"Mr. Caruthers, I'm not stupid." Dr. Porter looked to the crowd. "Now, what happened here?"

I tipped my foot up and put pressure on Nate's arm as a warning to keep his mouth shut. He struggled, but I just pressed harder.

I doubted he'd say anything, anyway. He didn't want us going to the cops with this.

I would if Tate wanted to, but I'd rather handle it on my own.

"I didn't see anything, sir," my friend Gunnar offered.

"Me, either, Dr. Porter," said another student, following his example. "Probably just an accident."

Everyone else in the crowd figured out the game plan and followed suit.

Porter didn't get anything from anyone, and no one got in trouble.

Tate was safe, and I would be taking her home without any complications.

Rubbing his beard, Dr. Porter looked to Nate and Piper. "All right, you two. Get up and come to the nurse. Everyone else. Head home!" he barked.

Nate and Piper stomped down the hall after Porter, although Nate was a little wobbly. The rest of the students departed slowly and quietly. No one laughed behind their hands. No one gave Tate a look.

They knew that the video wasn't my doing, and if I wasn't on board with it, they shouldn't be, either.

People being afraid of you can be useful.

Wrapping my arms around Tate's neck, I brought her into me, where she was safe.

Not that she needed saving.

"I'm so sorry about not trusting you." Her muffled voice vibrated against my chest. "And about what I did to your car, too."

I couldn't care less about the fucking car.

"Tate, you're mine, and I'm yours. Every day you're going to realize that more and more. When you believe it without a doubt, then I'll have earned your trust."

I knew I didn't have it yet. Today was the result of the damage I'd done.

"I am yours. I just wasn't sure if you were really mine," she said quietly.

"Then I'll make you sure." I kissed the top of her head, and the image of Piper grabbing her by the hair flashed through my head.

I tried holding in my amusement at how Tate hauled off and brought her down.

"You're laughing right now?" She pulled back and looked at me, half-angry and half-confused.

Yeah, I definitely shouldn't be laughing right now.

"Well, I was kind of worried about my anger issues, but now I'm kind of worried about yours. You like to hit people." I couldn't hold back the huge grin on my face.

She rolled her eyes. "I'm not angry. She got what she deserved, and I was attacked first."

I picked up Tate, guided her legs around my waist, and carried her down the hall, unable to not touch her anymore.

I was so afraid I'd never get to again.

"It's your fault, you know?" she said against my ear.

"What?" I asked.

"You made me mean. And now I pummel poor, defenseless girls . . . and guys," she added, and I wanted to laugh again, thinking of the damage she'd done to Madoc.

"You might say that I turned metal into steel."

She kissed the ridge of my ear, and a shudder rocked through my body.

"Whatever helps you sleep at night, you big bully," she teased.

And I gripped her tighter, hoping I could someday right all the wrongs.

CHAPTER 38

O ver the next week, we worked hard to take down the video or report it to all the host sites it had been uploaded to.

Tate handled it with a straight face until she read the comments on the video on one of the sites. Some were cruel. Some were twisted. All of them were sordid.

She was ready to torch the entire Internet, so I ended up just telling her to leave it and I'd handle the rest of it myself. Actually, I passed the task to Jax. He knew his way around that shit better than I did. And he'd be faster at it.

Piper's parents found out about the video *and* her involvement. They took her out of school for the rest of the year. She'd be home-schooled until she graduated.

Nate was another matter. He'd been MIA since the shit went down in the hallway last week, so I put him on the back burner for now.

But he'd show up eventually, and I wasn't anywhere near over it.

Tate's dad, on the other hand, was the hardest part to deal with. He supported our new relationship, but we had to "slow the hell down."

He and I took Tate to Chicago this past weekend to buy the G8 she'd been eyeing online. He wasn't thrilled with spending that much money on a car for her, but he wanted to see her smile. Keep her busy. Focus on another project.

Some people might consider his therapeutic tactics hiding, but it wasn't. The Nova project he invented for me last year was a way for me to not think constantly. I could get space, distance, and perspective.

It was already working on Tate. I couldn't believe how quickly she was getting over the video.

"What's this?" Her curious eyes smiled at the box I'd just placed in her hands.

I sat on my knees on her bed, leaning back on my feet. "Open it."

Tate had been in bed when I climbed through the tree—and the rain—to sneak in a visit.

I had dragged Jax with me to some outlet mall Madoc told me about. Not normally a shopper, but I'd bit the fucking bullet and asked for ideas.

I wanted to give Tate something special.

She slid the top off the box and picked out the charm bracelet, her eyes sparkling with surprise and a little confusion.

I watched her study the four charms hanging off the bracelet: a key, a coin, a cell phone, and a heart.

I kept my expression flat, still uneasy about anyone knowing how weak I was. How my hopes rested on this girl thinking I was worth a damn.

After a few moments, her eyes widened, and realization hit her. "My lifelines!" she blurted out, smiling, and I exhaled a relieved breath.

I didn't know, until recently, about Tate's survival tactics. They were things she always carried on her when she went to parties or other social gatherings in high school.

Emergency-type objects that she used to escape me if she needed. Money, phone, and car keys.

"Yeah." I ran a hand through my hair, droplets falling to my face. "When you told me on our way to Chicago about how you always wanted your escape plans when dealing with me in the past, I didn't want you to see me that way anymore."

"I don't—" She shook her head.

"I know," I interrupted. "But I want to make sure I never lose your trust again. I want to be one of your lifelines, Tate. I want you to need me. So . . ." I pointed to the bracelet. "The heart is me. One of your lifelines. I took Jax with me today to pick it out."

I should've just gotten her a bracelet with a heart. That's it. A fucking heart. That was all she needed. I was the one to keep her safe. I was the one she'd run to—if Tate ran to anybody at all—for help or comfort.

"How is your brother?" She brought me out of my thoughts.

"He's hanging in there," I offered. "My mom is working with a lawyer to try to get custody. He wants to meet you."

And he did. My brother's words: "I wanna meet the girl that's made you so boring."

Such a little shit.

"I'd love to," she said softly, and my heart swelled as I watched her twirl the bracelet around her fingers, studying it with a twinkle in her eyes.

"Put it on me?" she asked, and I tried to ignore the tear that fell down her cheek. I hoped it was a happy tear, and all of a sudden I couldn't wait for her father to relax on the rules of how much time we were allowed to be together. I damn well needed to touch her.

And soon.

We were eighteen, but we both respected her dad. But in his

head—and probably most fathers' heads—eighteen was still too young for the stuff I wanted to do to her.

For the stuff I'd already done to her.

I worked the clasp, fastening it to her wrist, and then pulled her onto my lap so that she straddled me.

Oh, Christ.

She wrapped her arms around my neck, her center grinding on me, and I closed my eyes for a second.

It'd been too long.

Okay, only a week, but still.

When you've tasted the one thing that fills you up, it's impossible not to want more of it.

A lot more.

She leaned down, melting her soft, sweet lips to mine, and I held her hips tight. I knew I couldn't stay, but I didn't want to stop, either.

"Jared," a deep male voice threatened, and we both jerked our heads to the door.

Shit. Tate's dad.

I sighed, shaking my head.

"You need to go home now," he ordered me through the closed door. "We'll see you for dinner tomorrow night."

Awesome.

My body was screaming, but what could I tell him?

Hey, I need your daughter for about three hours or until she passes out from exhaustion? Or *Would you mind if I slept over, because I never sleep so well as when Tate's lips are buried in my neck?*

Yeah, I snorted, *that'd go over really well.* "Yes, sir," I responded, and I could feel Tate's body shaking with silent laughter.

I looked back to her. "I guess I need to go."

She held my shirt, touching her nose to mine. "I know," she said reluctantly. "Thank you for my bracelet."

I climbed off the bed and kissed the hell out of her before we said good-bye. She damn well wasn't making it easy, either, looking at me like she wanted to eat me.

But I did as I was told—for now—and climbed back through the tree.

Now I was actually thrilled that Mr. Brandt had never cut this thing down.

Wait . . . He might now, though.

I laughed to myself as I crawled back through my window, waved to her, and shut off the lights.

The hard-on in my pants hadn't lessened, and I was half tempted to bring her back to my room.

Another cold-shower night.

Making my way to the bathroom, I felt my phone vibrate against my thigh, and I grabbed it out of my pocket.

Looking at the screen, I had an urge to flush it down the toilet.

K.C.

CHAPTER 39

—————————————————

groaned.

It was late, and she and I weren't chatty. What the hell did she want?

I slid my finger across the screen, then answered, "Yeah?"

"I have something for you," she sang, her voice slow and sultry and way too unnerving.

I straightened my shoulders, tensing. "I'm sure I'm not interested," I said flatly, turning on the shower.

"Oh, you will be." I could hear the smile in her voice. "I'm at Madoc's house. Hurry or we'll start without youuuu."

Jesus. I wasn't one to judge, but K.C. could be a little stupid sometimes. Right now, however, she just seemed drunk.

"Put him on the phone," I ordered, my patience circling the drain.

I heard her giggle before the rustle on the other end.

"Dude, just get over here," Madoc laughed, keeping his voice low. "You'll want a piece of this."

What the fuck? "Of K.C.?"

"What?" Madoc got defensive. "K.C.'s awesome. She got you a present. He's waiting in the hot tub right now. I'll give you a hint. His name is Nate."

My pulse throbbed in my throat, and my face got hot.

"So get your fucking ass over here!" he shouted at me, and hung up.

Oh, man. I breathed in and out, wanting to laugh and kick something at the same time.

Okay, I guess K.C. wasn't stupid after all.

I had no idea how she wound up with Nate—and at Madoc's house—but it was perfect.

I would pound the shit out of him for myself, but I'd kill him for Tate.

When I thought of how she'd cried, having to face her father last week. Or of how I'd escorted her to every class to make sure no one said shit to her.

Every tear down her face, every shake of her chest, and every time she'd closed her eyes in embarrassment was pain that I'd caused. Nate and Piper didn't have a problem with her. They'd retaliated against me.

I walked into the spare bedroom and shook my brother awake. "Wanna go pick a fight?"

After we'd gone into Chicago today for Tate's present, he'd crashed at my house. Even though I hated that he wasn't with us, I was relieved his foster parents were lenient with the visitations. He'd slept over every night this week, driving an hour to school every day.

"Hell, yes," he mumbled groggily, and got out of bed.

He pulled his hair back into a long ponytail, and we both slipped into our Trent trademark black hoodies before walking out the door. My mom was asleep, and I briefly thought of trying to grab Tate and take her along, but it was better that she stayed home. No use taking the chance of getting her into more trouble.

We climbed into my nearly repaired Boss and set out.

Jax yawned at my side as we cruised the slick black streets to the other side of town.

"You don't get in until late, and you're always up early. You need more sleep." I tried to catch glimpses of him out of the corner of my eye.

He shook his head. "You should talk. I wake up to you cussing in the fucking shower at two a.m. every day. You need to go grab that girl and take her for a nice long drive tomorrow. I'm sure she's hurting for it as badly as you."

I narrowed my gaze out the window but couldn't keep the laugh out of my voice. "It wouldn't make any difference. I'd still need a cold shower. When you've got someone you love, you always want more."

"Oh, Jesus," he whined. "Just don't get her name tattooed on your body, please. The only chick's name a guy should ever have tattooed is his daughter's."

I shook my head but couldn't help the vision of a little brown-haired girl with storm-blue eyes riding on my shoulders someday.

Jesus Christ.

I stared out the window, trying not to think about how my ideas of my future were changing.

Jax and I drove the rest of the way in silence to Madoc's house, which was about ten times classier than the neighborhood Tate and I lived in.

Don't get me wrong. We lived in a great area. Lots of well-kept houses, parks, and cozy neighborhood block parties.

But Madoc? He lived in a place too rich for the town's lawyers and doctors. It wasn't a place for just professionals. It was a neighborhood for surgeons and corporate CEOs who kept their families hidden away while they worked in Chicago.

Driving up to the twelve-foot black metal gate, I punched in the code.

During the day, there was security on duty to check visitors in and out, but at night, the staff was spread thin and usually spent their time patrolling the community in their SUVs.

The gate hummed as it swung open, and I slowly descended the perfectly paved street leading into the Seven Hills Valley.

After a few houses, we turned into Madoc's driveway and curved around the loop in front of his door. Hopping out, I slammed the door shut and clenched my hands, trying to get psyched up. I still wasn't sure what my plan here was, but, as usual, I dove headfirst and acted like I knew what I was doing.

When in doubt, stick to what you know.

I heard Jax fall in behind me, and we both walked into Madoc's house and charged through the foyer toward the back.

Really, it was a mansion, but Madoc corrected me on that term years ago. It was a house . . . or else.

He never bragged about his position in life or his money. If he did, we wouldn't be friends.

"Hey, dude. 'Bout fuckin' time." He jogged up to meet us in the hallway. He wore ridiculous black-and-gray plaid board shorts, and his blond hair, slicked back, looked like he'd just been swimming. But the rest of him was dry.

Halloween was in two days and it was freezing, but Madoc's Jacuzzi would make the weather tolerable.

I stopped in front of him. "So, he actually came into your house?" I asked.

Nate knew Madoc was my best friend. After the video, I didn't think Nate was so stupid that he would trust breathing the same air as Madoc.

He smiled. "That's the awesome part. He thinks this is K.C.'s house." His eyes gleamed like he was so proud he fooled Nate. "K.C. was out tonight and ran into him. She cooked up a scheme and texted me. I told her to bring him here. He hasn't even seen me yet."

He shrugged and waited for me to respond.

I held back, not sure about how far I wanted to take this. I had shit to lose now, and for the first time in a long time, I cared about where my life went.

Jax cleared his throat at my side. "Leash a little tight, Jared?"

Leash?

Fucking little shit.

I cocked my head to the side and shot him a look, but he just smiled and looked away.

Jax knew everything that had gone down with Nate—he was helping with the video, after all—and while he gave me a hard time about my attachment to Tate, he was on our side. He wanted to see that asshole pay as much as we did.

As I stalked down the hall through the kitchen, Madoc and Jax trailed behind me.

I spied K.C. and Nate through the glass doors, carousing in the hot tub, before I walked out and interrupted his relaxed little world.

"K.C., out of the hot tub." I jerked my head to the side.

"Wha—" Nate started.

"Don't talk." I cut him off.

K.C., dressed in only her black bra and underwear, sloshed water out of the tub as she climbed out.

"Get his clothes," I ordered whoever, without taking my eyes off Nate. In a second, it was Madoc who came up and grabbed Nate's shit from the side of the tub.

I wasn't sure if Nate was wearing anything, but knowing him, he was all guts.

He didn't talk as his blue eyes darted between me, Madoc, and Jax. I wasn't sure where K.C. had gone, but I hadn't heard the door to the house open, so I assumed she was still here on the patio.

"Jax, give me your knife." I held my hand out to my side, my eyes still focused on Nate's shocked expression. A moment later, a switch-blade was placed in my palm.

I slid the switch and the partially serrated blade shot out, vibrating in my hand.

Nate's eyes got wider, and his gaze shifted around like he was looking for an escape route.

Yeah, don't even try.

"You know why I'm pissed." I stood on the opposite side of the tub, facing him. "And you should've known I wasn't going to forget."

"Jared—" he started.

"Shut up," I shot out.

His short black hair was sweaty and clung to his forehead, while his lips trembled slightly.

"We could've gone to the police," I told him, "but I settle my own scores." I rotated my wrist, emphasizing the blade. "And it's really going to hurt."

"Please." His voice was raspy as he tried getting up. "I can explain."

"Explain?" I barked, and he sat back down. "Which part? The time you tried to force yourself on my girlfriend in the woods, or when you videotaped us naked and put it out for the whole world to see?"

I circled the hot tub, getting in his space. "You see, I can understand that you're too stupid to understand a simple direction." I dropped my voice to hell and let the knife do some talking. "But you will understand this. You're going to have a very uncomfortable night."

I inched closer, leaning in.

"I'm sorry," he gasped out, his blue eyes dancing between my face

PENELOPE DOUGLAS

and the shiny black blade in my right hand. "I shouldn't have touched her. I won't even look at her again. Please, don't."

"You're what?" I stopped and asked, quirking an eyebrow.

"I'm sorry," he said louder.

"Sorry for what?"

"I'm sorry for messing with your girlfriend," he rushed out.

"No." I shook my head like I was speaking to a toddler. "You're sorry for messing with *Tate*," I prompted.

Whether or not she's my girlfriend, he doesn't mess with her again. Ever.

"Tate." He corrected himself, breathing hard. "I'm sorry for messing with Tate. It'll never happen again. I was stupid. I was drunk. I'll apologize to her."

"No." My voice had gone from slightly amused to death threat. "If you ever speak to her again, look at her, talk about her . . . if you even smile at her, I'm going to add your blood to this knife's collection." My jaw ached with tightness, and I could sense Madoc and Jax shifting off to the side. "Now go home," I ordered Nate.

"What?" I heard Madoc's bellow, but my eyes stayed on Nate scurrying out of the hot tub, completely fucking naked.

"He leaves." I turned to look at my friend and brother, both looking like their eyes were about to pop out of their heads. "This time."

I knew they wanted to see this dickhead get his ass kicked. Hell, I wanted it, too.

But something had changed. I didn't want to always feel like Tate deserved better than me.

Doing what my gut wanted to do to Nate tonight would serve no end. He was a loser. I had my girl. She loved me. I'd won.

"My clothes." Nate looked around, fidgeting and shivering. "My keys are in my jeans."

332

"Then I guess you've got problems." I hoped my smile looked sinister. "Have a nice walk."

He hesitated for a moment, probably wondering how he was going to get home ten miles away and with no clothes in the October chill.

But he didn't argue.

Everyone was quiet as he left the patio.

I noticed K.C. standing a huge distance away, covered with a towel. She had sounded drunk on the phone, but her face was sober now.

"I'll make sure he gets out." Madoc laughed. "Don't want him trying to grab clothes from my house."

Sliding the switch to tuck the blade back in, I tossed it to my brother and started walking toward the house.

"Jared, what the hell? Not even a punch?" His voice was soft. Not really disappointed so much as confused.

"There are other things worth fighting for, Jax."

Walking up to Tate's best friend, I was surprised that I actually felt glad to have K.C. around. I doubt Madoc or Jax could've gotten Nate here tonight. She and I had both been stupid for our own selfish reasons, but I knew she had Tate's back tonight, and I hoped K.C. would come clean about everything. Tate needed an explanation from her.

"Thanks." I nodded to K.C.

"Sure."

Her eyes quickly reverted to Jax, and she pinched her eyebrows together.

Looking over at him, I saw that he was scanning her up and down, violating her in every way a man can violate a woman without touching her.

"What are you looking at?" she snapped.

The corner of his mouth turned up. "Do you need a ride home?"

"I don't know you." Her sneer was condescending.

"You will," he shot back matter-of-factly. "May as well get acquainted now."

Oh, Jesus.

Her face fell, but she returned the favor and gave him the once-over he'd given her. "How old are you, anyway?"

"Old enough to unravel you."

K.C. looked between the two of us, scowling and clearly aggravated.

"You're both the same." She shook her head and turned around to walk away. "Madoc, I need a ride home!" she yelled as she entered the house.

I heard Jax exhale a laugh, and I just rolled my eyes.

We both steered clear of commitment, but we went about it differently. He didn't get caught up in the long line of short, disconnected relationships the way I did. He didn't mind letting people in, because he knew they'd never make it into the end zone with him.

I was afraid that I would care too much.

Jax knew he wouldn't care enough.

"Who was that?" he asked as we walked back through Madoc's house and to my car.

"Tate's best friend, K.C."

We opened our car doors and climbed in.

"What does the K.C. stand for?" He slicked back stray hairs that had fallen out of his ponytail.

"No idea," I sighed. "She's been K.C. for as long as I've known her." I looked over at him before turning the ignition. "And don't," I ordered.

"Don't what?"

"I'm trying to get level with Tate. Shit needs to calm down. Don't create more drama. K.C.'s not a one-night-stand kind of girl, and she's definitely too emotional for friends with benefits. Just leave her alone."

"Too late, brother. My people are hunters."

My people. I laughed to myself, although it was sad. I doubted Jax even remembered what his mother looked like, let alone her tribe's name. And he was only a quarter Native American, anyway, but to him, he was all Indian.

"She's not your type," I pointed out. "Uptight and whiny."

Pulling around the driveway, I laid on the gas, speeding down the road toward the gate.

"Exactly my type." He spoke low. "You can't fall for someone like that."

CHAPTER 40

"Son of a bitch," I grunted, sitting up in bed.

Bending my leg, I rested my forehead in my hand with my elbow propped up on my knee.

I'm so fucked.

My dick was throbbing so hard it hurt.

I was waking up with constant hard-ons, and it was like I was thirteen all over again.

I was actually waking up in pain with the pressure between my legs, and the only thing I wanted was under lock and key next door.

It was going to be a long fucking year. That was for sure.

I still didn't have any plans about college, but one thing was for certain: Wherever I ended up, I looked forward to visiting Tate and screwing her brains out in privacy, without parents around.

A creak interrupted my thoughts, and my head shot up out of my hand to see Tate stepping into my room.

My chest caved, and I blinked a few times to make sure I wasn't dreaming.

She shut the door and leaned back against it.

"Please tell me you're thinking about me." Her lips were soft and playful as she purred her words.

She was fucking me.

With her look, fierce and urgent. With her mouth, moist and open. With her voice, smooth and taunting, and I was ready to thank my lucky stars that she was here.

"Are you kidding?" I raised my eyebrows and whipped off the blanket, gesturing to the very hard bulge poking through the jeans I'd fallen asleep in. "Look at this shit. I can't think straight."

And I jumped out of bed and rushed her. Our lips came together, and the sweetness of how her body molded to mine made me regret every other girl I'd touched.

Tate always tasted good, like hot apples and angry skies, and her tongue was simply candy.

She knew how to move with me. When I leaned in, she arched back. When I pulled my head back, she read my mind and opened her neck to me.

"Wait," she gasped. "Your front door was open. I didn't see your mom when I walked in, but she's got to be up."

I shook my head, scolding her. "You started this. And this isn't your house. There are no rules here." I smiled and leaned over to my iPod dock and switched on Rachel Rabin's "Raise the Dead" to drown out our noise.

"Come here," I whispered, pulling her by the hips into my body.

But she pushed me away.

Disappointment—no, pain and confusion—racked through me.

"Wha—" I started to ask, but sucked in my breath when she began peeling off her clothes.

Fuuuuck.

Her little white tank top?

Gone.

Her pajama shorts and panties?

Off in a single movement.

And when she came to me, I was light-headed and fucking hard.

I glided my fingers up her sides and then down over her beautiful breasts. Her skin was silky and firm, like rain.

Perfect.

I didn't even have time to reach for my nightstand drawer before she pushed me down on the bed and straddled me.

"Tate, a condom," I gasped out.

Holy shit.

My whole body shook with the contact, her wet heat rubbing against me and the blood pumping through my cock.

"Pants," she whispered, and when she leaned over to grab a condom, I knew what she meant.

After about three seconds, the rubber was on, and I thrust up and inside of her.

We stilled for a minute, both shuddering and catching our breath as we soaked in the feeling.

God, Tate. So tight.

Her lips crashed down on mine and I dived into her mouth, moving my tongue against hers as we gasped and came back for more.

"Jared," she whispered between kisses. "Something's wrong with me. I always want more of you."

Her hips started moving back and forth, up and down my cock, making a sweet tightness race down my arms and legs.

Her heavenly skin felt like cream, and I grabbed her ass in my hands, jerking her down on me as the room filled with wet heat and sweat.

God . . . she loved me. I still couldn't believe it, but she did.

"What do you want, Tate?" I breathed against her lips, desperate and fucking lost in my need for her skin, her smell, her fire . . .

"I want you." She closed her eyes and dropped her head back as her body rocked into mine. "Every morning and every night."

Her head came back down, and her fingers fisted in my hair. "I want to feel you all day, Jared."

Yeah, it was going to be a long fucking year.

Wrapping my arm around her waist, I whipped us around so that she lay on the bottom, and I fucked the love of my life hard enough so that she would feel me.

All. Damn. Day.

"Ahhh," she moaned, her desperate eyes meeting mine.

"I love you, Tatum Brandt." I put my hand over her mouth and pushed inside of her harder. "Now come."

I fucking hated rushing. But I knew my mom was already up, and our talking and moaning would draw attention. Even with the music.

"Jesus Christ, baby, you feel good." I dropped my mouth to her breast and sucked her nipple into my mouth.

I knew my back was drenched with sweat already, and I smiled when I tasted her salty skin. She felt this as much as I did.

Her thighs tensed around me, her nails dug into my back, and I felt her pulsate from the inside as she held her breath.

She was coming, and I looked up to see her eyes flutter closed. After a few moments she let out a little whimper and exhaled against my hand.

I always knew when Tate came. She had a thing about holding her breath.

I leaned up on one hand and grasped her thigh with the other, moving my hips between her legs faster and faster. More and more. Harder and harder.

My eyes closed, the pressure inside me at its breaking point.

Fuck.

I looked down into her blissful face and dived into her a few more times before letting it all go.

Cool fire spread through my veins, and all of the air left my body as I collapsed on top of her, breathing like a marathon runner.

"Jared, I need a clean shir— Oh."

My head snapped up. Seeing Jax, Tate squealed and pulled my body down to cover hers.

"What the fuck?" I was naked as hell, and Jax just stood there, wide-eyed, with his lips formed in a circle. "Get the hell out!" I yelled.

After a pause, he broke out in a grin and snorted. "Hey, you must be Tate. I'm Jaxon." And the fucker held out his hand for her to shake.

Thankfully, Tate was shielded by me, but I wasn't covered. The dickhead had left the door open, too.

Tate peeked out and offered her hand bashfully. "Um . . . hi, Jaxon. Nice to meet you."

They shook, and the stupid prick stood there smiling.

"Get the fuck out," I barked again, my eyes burning with murder.

"Jared, why are you yelling?" My mother poked her head in, and Tate shrank up into a ball underneath me again.

Oh, what the fuck?

"Jared!" My mother's shocked gasp when she noticed the extra arms and legs caused me to clench my teeth.

Jax descended into a fit of laughter, and his face was turning red.

"Everyone get out!" I shouted, and Jax cleared out, still smiling and obviously trying to hold back more laughter.

My mother, her face pinched up in anger and looking like she wanted to say something, grabbed the knob of the door and slammed it shut. "Oh, my God!" Tate cried into my chest. "That did not just happen."

"Yeah, I'm afraid it did. But who cares?" I shook it off. I was pissed, because Tate was embarrassed, but my mom and Jax were no threat.

She looked up at me, her sexy hair falling over her eyes. "Your mom will talk to my dad."

"My mom is scared of your dad. We all kind of are. She won't say anything." I kissed her forehead.

"I'm so misbehaved." She sat up, covering herself, looking a little sick. "I just couldn't help it. Or . . . I didn't want to, maybe. I woke up and I wanted you so badly. I didn't think."

"Look at me," I interrupted, holding her face in my hands. "You're not misbehaved. You're a good girl. No one takes this from us, Tate." My voice hardened and my eyes got sharp. I nudged her chin so she'd meet my eyes. "We're eighteen. We're in my home. You're in a safe place. Quit acting like we should be apologizing for being in love. I understand showing your dad respect under his roof, but what's done is done. We're not going backwards." I wrapped my arms around her and kissed her warm neck.

"I know," she sighed, wrapping her arms around my neck and hugging me close. "I love you, and . . . and I trust this."

But I felt the doubt sitting in my gut, anyway.

Is she sure? Too much drama lately, or too much trouble, but she was still afraid of being hurt.

I cleared my throat and shook it off, changing the subject.

"Go get ready for school." I pulled back and looked at her. "I'll be over in thirty to pick you up. And you may as well leave through the front door. They know you're here now," I added as I stood up.

The corner of her mouth turned up, and she laughed when I threw one of my clean T-shirts in her face.

"Wear that." It was another Nine Inch Nails T-shirt. They were one of my favorite bands, so I had a few of them. "To replace the one you burned last year," I added.

"Cool." She smiled and slipped on her underwear and the shirt.

"I always liked wearing your clothes," she whispered sexily and spun around once, modeling the outfit.

Annnnd . . . I was fucking hard again.

"Dude, I take it all back," Jax rushed to say when I entered the kitchen. "You should definitely get *her* name tattooed on your body. Hell, I'll get her name tattooed on my body." He started laughing again, the fucking prick.

"Jaxon, that behavior is not tolerated." My mother walked in, briefcase in hand. "Don't think you're going to get away with it when you live here."

"Yes, Mom." He mocked, but honestly, he had a better relationship with my mother than I did.

"Jared. Be home after school. We're talking." She pointed her finger at me.

"Yes, Mom," I mumbled, echoing Jax.

"Jax, honey." My mother looked to my brother. "Are you done with my laptop?"

"Yeah, I put it back in the case. Thank you." And he spooned in another mouthful of cereal as he leaned against the sink.

My mother walked over to me as soon as she'd swung her laptop case over her shoulder. I let her put her hand to my cheek, but I still couldn't manage to maintain eye contact.

"I love you," she whispered gently. "And be home after school."

I nodded, and she walked out, the sound of her heels fading away down the hall.

Looking over to Jax, who stood there trying to keep his smile at bay, I was suddenly confused.

"You have a phone. What did you need the laptop for?" I asked, grabbing an apple off the counter and taking a bite.

He just shrugged and stuffed his mouth with more Cap'n Crunch.

"Are you sure you feel comfortable in that outfit?" I asked as we walked into school, hand in hand.

She didn't look at me, but her smile reeked of sarcasm. "Is it my comfort you're worried about or your own?"

She didn't look even remotely trampy. On the contrary, she was a fucking magazine cover. But the flimsy black dress was short. Tate usually dressed like a tomboy, but it was like she was on a mission to fuck with my sex drive 24/7.

I was on overdrive.

"My concern has nothing to do with me." I pulled her into my side and hooked an arm around her neck. "I think only of you."

We strolled through the halls, barely noticed, finally, as the school had pretty much moved on to newer drama. Jax was a genius. I did a Web search after I got home last night, and I couldn't find the video anywhere.

Everyone was moving on.

"Let's go for a ride after school today," I suggested. "Just get on the motorcycle and go."

Looking up, she raised her eyebrows and grinned, but then her eyes shifted to the lockers at our side and her bubble immediately popped.

Following her gaze, I saw two girls eyeing Tate and me and whispering. They were being very obvious.

One of the girls I didn't know. The other one I definitely knew.

Shit.

"Tate, just ignore them."

"It's easy for you, Jared." Her voice was low and calm, but there was a bite to it. "You could've been filmed with ten porn stars and you'd be the man. I'm the one that's paying for that video. Not you."

She was right. While I cringed every time I saw that thing, I wasn't in her shoes.

And there was little I could do to protect her.

I wanted to get her out of here. Get on the bike right now and get lost, but she wouldn't go for that. Instead I just grabbed her hand. "Let's get to class."

We started walking through the throngs of people, but she hesitated.

Glancing down at her, I saw her take out her phone, which was buzzing. My eyes shot up when I heard several other phones ringing and vibrating.

Fear hollowed my stomach as déjà vu struck. Everyone was getting a message at the same time, just like Tate told me they did when the video exploded.

My own phone vibrated against my ass, and, with a cringe, I reached in my pocket to grab it.

Madoc.

Glancing around, I noticed almost everyone had their noses in their devices as well.

Sliding to unlock the screen, I opened the message.

Really?!

With piss and fury burning my stomach, I watched a recording of Nate, blubbering last night in the hot tub. I was in the video, too, but I was blurred out, and I couldn't hear what I was saying. All that was visible and audible was Nate Dietrich, pleading for his safety and apologizing.

Fuck!

Heat rushed over my back and a cool sweat broke out across my forehead as I looked to Tate. She was seeing it, too, no doubt. Others started hooting and laughing in the halls, while some whispered and showed their phones around to others who hadn't gotten the message.

The video was not flattering. It clearly protected me and threw him to the sharks as a spineless joke.

Well, good. I was okay with that, but Tate?

Her eyes narrowed as she looked at her phone, and then her serious and very unhappy expression zoned in on me.

"Jared? This is you, isn't it? You're the one he's talking to."

Her breathing was fast and her face was tense.

Son of a bitch. Just when I was hoping things would calm down. Fucking Madoc and fucking Jax. Madoc obviously sent it to the whole school, but it had to have been Jax that filmed it when my back was turned last night. I was sure of it. Madoc didn't know shit about how to edit videos. Jax was the smart one.

And that's why he'd borrowed my mom's laptop this morning.

"Tate, it's—"

"Was this last night?" she interrupted.

"It was spontaneous." I held up my hands and shook my head, inching up to her. "Nate was at Madoc's house, and Jax and I went over to confront him."

"You threatened him? What were you thinking?" she accused. "I mean, don't get me wrong," she continued, "I appreciate the gesture, but it's not worth it. Now everyone's talking about us again, Jared. They all know what this is about."

I looked around and, yes, people were eyeing us again. Talking and laughing, not to mention whispering. The grins weren't snide or spiteful, but it was still talk.

And Tate was sick of it.

"Why didn't you take me with you?" she asked.

I lifted my shoulders a bit and exhaled a bitter laugh. "It seemed like a bad idea to put you back in that mess. You've been through too much. I didn't want you to get emotional—"

"Emotional?" Her voice erupted like an air horn in the otherwise hushed hallway.

Glancing around, I inched closer, feeling my nerves heat up with her obvious anger. "That's not what I meant—"

"Why didn't you tell me about this this morning?" Her wall was up, and I stood there in fucking awe of how close I'd been to her a moment ago. "Another video, Jared!" she burst out. "I should've known about this."

"I didn't know it was being recorded!"

What the hell? Why was she mad? If anything, she should've been happy that I defended her honor! Of course, Nate walked away without a scratch, but the video cut off as my blade went in his face. People would assume the worst until Nate showed up to verify that he was fine.

Tate was overreacting, because she didn't know what had happened.

"That's the same excuse you used last time!" she retorted.

"Excuse?" Was she really implying that I knew about the sex video? "You're blowing up about nothing. Again! Just like with my fucking car!"

I ran my hand through my hair and blew out a breath.

"Look." My teeth were bared, and my voice was low. "K.C. brought Nate over to Madoc's house last night—"

"K.C. was in on this?" she interrupted. "And not me? Why didn't you tell me?"

Oh, for fuck's sake.

"I didn't have a chance," I gritted out, waving my hand. "You crept into my room and jumped on my cock so fast this morning—"

"Ugh!" she growled and slammed her knee right between my legs.

I hunched forward and fell to one knee.

Shit, shit, shit . . . I moaned as a white-hot pain shot through my groin.

Jesus Christ, Tate!

My eyes squeezed shut, and I breathed in and out quickly, trying to keep my legs from collapsing underneath me.

My fucking dick was on fire, and nausea rolled through my stomach in waves. *Holy mother* . . .

I sucked in breath after breath, trying not to vomit . . . or cry.

Tate was gone. I didn't see her leave, but I felt her absence.

And there I was. Alone and stupid in a hallway full of people I couldn't see, because I was blurry-eyed and shaking.

Tatum fucking Brandt.

She was going to kill me.

CHAPTER 41

Weight hit my shoulder, and I sank forward a little farther.

"She does that well, doesn't she?"

Madoc.

He helped me up, and I leaned against the lockers, trying to stay upright. The initial shock had passed, but I was still in bad shape.

That sucked, and I never wanted to feel that again.

"The video?" I grunted, wanting to sound tough, but my voice cracked like I was almost in tears.

"Your brother." He nodded. "I saw him catch the show on his phone last night when you weren't paying attention, but I had no idea what he was doing with it." He raised his eyebrows. "Until this morning when he e-mailed it to me."

"Goddamn, you two," I cursed. "And you thought it would be a good idea to send that to everyone?"

"Yeah." He nodded resolutely, his eyes lighting up. "I thought it was a perfect idea to send it to everyone. Let them see that piece of shit whimpering. Give him a taste of his own medicine."

"Well, Tate's blaming me now."

"Well . . ." He started laughing. "I didn't know she'd react like that, but you knew you had that coming, right?"

He was laughing? Yeah, this was real fuckin' funny.

"She overreacted." I stood up straight, trying to nonchalantly massage my dick back to life in a hallway full of people. "I took the high road last night. Besides, after what that dickhead did, did she really think I was going to do nothing? And why did it bother her, anyway?"

The questions just kept coming. Tate shouldn't have been that angry.

Sweat covered my neck and back, and I felt like chasing her down and throwing her over my shoulder.

"Tate's got baggage, thanks to us. Trust issues," Madoc continued, and walked around in front of me. "Look." He lowered his eyes and shook his head. "Normally, I couldn't care less about who you screwed or what kind of trouble you got yourself into. I've sat back and let you self-destruct. But Tate? She's our shortie. Now go fix your shit."

I watched him walk away, more and more baffled by how my friend continued to surprise me.

Is he right?

Yeah.

Tate needed to trust me. We were *still* working on that, and I could've gotten into trouble last night. She would've been worried and pissed if anything had happened to me or I'd done something stupid.

I'm sure she was also still insecure about anything that she imagined went down between K.C. and me. My being in the same place as her friend, without her, would piss her off.

I barreled down the hallway, ready to yank her out of calculus, but I slowed when I got caught by the masses in the school all headed the same direction.

The crowd was a mess of people walking, yelling, and whispering. I saw some still looking at their phones—the video, no doubt—and some people were calling my name, but I ignored them.

Where the fuck was everyone going?

And that's when I remembered.

The auditorium.

We were having that assembly this morning.

On bullying.

I ran my fingers through my hair, hard enough to massage my scalp, and let out a long, tired breath.

Great. I think I'd enjoy cutting off my arm and rubbing salt in it more.

Damn it.

I charged and weaved as quickly as I could through the long line of students trying to make their way through the two sets of double doors to the auditorium.

"Jared," someone called out, but I waved them off without looking.

Tate was in here somewhere, so I scanned the rows as I walked down the aisles. We boasted about two thousand students at our school, but the freshmen were at a separate assembly in the gym, so this crowd wasn't as thick as it usually was.

Looking for blond hair was a nightmare. I'd really never noticed how many blondes we had until now.

But I knew Tate.

And I'd know her when I saw her, so I surveyed quickly before we were ordered to sit down.

Walking down the center aisle and back up, I felt my heart race when I saw her purple Chuck poking into the center aisle. Her legs were crossed, and one foot darted out of the row.

Quickly, I walked up the violet-colored carpet path, placed my hands on her armrest, and leaned down.

"We need to talk." I spoke low. "Now."

Her blue eyes narrowed on me, and my mouth went dry.

My voice had sounded like a warning, and I was just digging myself in deeper here.

Calm down, man. My stomach tightened, and I didn't know if I liked the drama or if I was just so used to it. But it was something I did well, so I engaged her.

This wasn't the time or place, but fuck it.

"Now you want to talk," she taunted, and I noticed Jess Cullen, her cross-country captain, sitting next to her, completely still as she watched us.

Tate stared ahead, refusing to look at me. "You get to react and behave without any by-your-leave from anyone else, but I'm supposed to drop my shit when you want my attention."

It wasn't a question. It was an assessment.

"Tatum—"

"Now I'm Tatum," she sneered, and looked at Jess. "Funny how that works, isn't it?" she asked.

"What are you mad about? Last night wasn't to hurt you."

I gripped the armrest tighter. I loved her anger. Always had.

Our first kiss on the sink ledge, and I was hers.

But right now she wasn't angry so much as she was distant. Her chin was tipped down, and she still hadn't looked at me.

That I didn't like.

"You don't involve me," she spoke, barely unclenching her teeth. "You don't share anything with me until you run the risk of losing me. Everything is on your terms, on your schedule. I'm always on the outside and I have to push my way in."

Her face was as hard as stone as she gazed out in front of her. "I'll talk to you, Jared. Just not now. And not for a while. I need some time to think."

"To come to your own conclusions," I accused.

"No choice when I'm the only one in the relationship. You humiliated me in the hallway before. Again! You throw me under the bus for your own amusement. When have you ever sacrificed yourself for me?" her calm voice spit back at me.

Air poured in and out of my lungs, thick and painful.

I'd barely gotten her back.

She doubted me. Doubted my commitment to her.

And how could I blame her?

Why should she trust me? I'd told her I loved her. I'd tried to show her. But I'd never shown her that I would put her first.

She'd seen me with my hands all over a ton of girls that weren't her.

She'd felt the pain, time and again, as I'd thrown her to the wolves and made her a joke in front of everyone.

She'd seen me delight in her tears and isolation.

At that moment, the full consequences of my actions descended on my body like a pile of garbage, and I was buried.

Son of a bitch.

How had she ever forgiven me at all?

"Everyone get seated," a male voice, probably the principal, shouted over the mic, and I finally blinked.

I'm always on the outside and I have to push my way in.

I kept telling myself that she was mine.

And I'd told her that I had always been hers.

But she didn't feel it.

With my heart jackhammering through my chest and a fog in my head, convincing me not to think about what I was going to do, I walked down the aisle and climbed the stairs up to the stage.

Principal Masters twisted his head toward me, away from the audience.

His graying brownish hair was slicked back, and his gray suit was already wrinkled. This guy didn't like me, but he'd cut me a lot of breaks over the years, thanks to Madoc and his father.

"You're not going to ruin my day, are you, Mr. Trent?" he asked, almost whiny, as if he was resigned that I was indeed going to pull some bullshit.

I gestured to the mic in his hand. "Can I have a couple of minutes? On the mic?" My throat was like a desert, and I was nervous as hell.

I fucking owned this school, but there was only one person in it I cared about right now.

Would she stay or walk out?

Masters looked at me like I was two years old and I'd just colored all over the wall.

"I'll behave," I assured him. "It's important. Please?"

I think it was the "please" that got him, because he raised his eyebrows in surprise.

"Don't make me regret this. You have three minutes." And he handed me the mic.

Whistles and remarks floated around the room as the whole place came to a hush. I didn't even have to say anything to get their attention.

Everyone here knew that I was low-key. I spoke only when it suited me, and I never sought attention.

Which was why this was going to be fucking hard.

The amount of blood pumping through my heart may have been what was making me a little light-headed, but I lifted my chin and slowed my breathing.

I found Tate—the only person in the room—and I let her in.

"I murdered a teddy bear when I was eight," I said matter-of-factly. Guys hollered their approval, while girls erupted with "aw." "I know, I know." I started slowly pacing the stage. "I was a dick even then, right?"

People laughed.

"I cut the poor thing to pieces and tossed it in the trash. When my mother found out what I'd done, she was horrified. Like I'd turn to animal cruelty next or something. If she only knew . . ."

"The thing is"—I spoke to Tate, but I said it to everyone—"the teddy bear was something I loved. More than anything at that time. He was tan with brown ears and paws. His name was Henry. I slept with him until I was way too old."

I shook my head, embarrassed, while the guys snorted and laughed and the girls mooned. "One day, these kids down my street caught me carrying the bear around, and they started making fun of me. Calling me a pussy, a baby; looking at me like I was a freak. So I threw the bear in the trash. But that night, I went back out and got it again. The next day, I tried burying it in a box in the attic."

I looked to Tate again. Her eyes were on me, and she was listening, so I kept going.

"Maybe if I knew it was near but not gone, then I'd be able to live without it. But that didn't work, either. So after a few days of failing to sleep on my own, to be strong without the stupid animal, I decided to massacre it. If it was beyond repair, then it would be useless to me. I'd have to get by. There wouldn't be any choice."

Tate.

"So I took some garden shears and chopped it to pieces. Cut off the legs. Memories gone. Snip off the arms. Attachment gone. Throw it in the trash. Weakness . . . gone."

I looked down, and my voice cracked, remembering how I'd felt like someone had died when I did that.

"I cried the whole first night," I added, taking a deep breath and clearing the ache in my throat. "It wasn't until two years later that I found something that I loved more than Henry. I met a girl who became my best friend. So much so that I even wanted *her* by me at night. I'd sneak into her room, and we'd fall asleep together. I didn't need her so much as she just became a part of me. I was wanted, loved, and accepted."

My eyes were only on Tate now. She was planted in her seat, completely still.

"She'd look at me, and I'd stop dead in my tracks, never wanting to leave that moment. Do you know what that's like?" I scanned the audience. "Day in and day out, you're thrilled to be alive and experience a million moments of love and happiness that constantly compete with each other. Every day is better than the last."

Shit got blurry and I realized I was tearing up, but I didn't care.

"But just like with Henry"—my voice got strong again—"I concluded that my attachment to her made me weak. I thought I wasn't strong enough if I needed anything or anyone, so I let her go." I shook my head. "No, I pushed her, actually. Away. Out. Over the edge."

"I abused her. Cut her to pieces, so our friendship would be beyond repair." Just like the bear. "I called her names, spread rumors to get people to hate her, kicked her out and isolated her. I hurt her, not because I hated her, but because I hated that I wasn't strong enough to not love her."

The whole room was as silent as a graveyard. People who had laughed weren't laughing anymore. People who hadn't been paying attention were now.

"Now, I could go on about how Mommy didn't love me and Daddy hit me, but who doesn't have a story, right?" I asked. "There are times when we can blame a situation on others, but we *own* our reactions to them. There comes a point where we are the ones responsible for our choices and excuses don't carry weight anymore."

I'd just aired my business to the whole school. They knew I was a bully. A jerk. But the only good opinion I needed was hers.

Descending the stairs, mic in hand, I walked up the aisle toward my girl.

And I spoke only to her.

"I can't change the past, Tate. I wish I could, because I'd go back and relive every day that I existed without you, and I'd make sure that you smiled." My eyes burned with regret, and I saw the pools in her beautiful blues, too. "Every minute of my future belongs to you."

I crouched down next to her chair, thankful to see my world back in her eyes, and placed one knee on the floor.

"I'll do anything to be good for you, Tate."

Leaning into me, she buried her face in my neck, shaking with the release of her tears. I breathed her in and wrapped my arms around her.

This was it.

Home.

"Anything, baby," I promised.

She leaned back and wiped her eyes with her thumb, sobbing and smiling at the same time.

"Anything?" she laughed out, her eyes bright with happiness and love.

I nodded.

Her forehead pressed into mine as she held my face in her hands and asked, "Have you ever considered a nipple piercing?"

Oh, for Christ's sake.

I choked out a laugh and kissed her hard, much to the pleasure of the roaring crowd around us.

Such a handful.

Read on for a special preview of a stand-alone contemporary
romance from bestselling author Penelope Douglas.

Misconduct

**Available from New American Library
wherever books and e-books are sold!**

M r. Shaw gave us an apologetic smile and rose from his desk. "Please excuse me for a moment."

I let out a quiet breath, frustrated, but thankfully no one noticed. Shaw walked around his desk and across the room, leaving me alone with Marek.

Wonderful.

The door clicked shut behind me, and I couldn't ignore the feeling of Marek's large frame next to me—his stiffness and silence telling me he was just as annoyed as I was. I hoped he wouldn't talk, but the sound of the air-conditioning circulating throughout the room only accentuated the deafening silence.

And if he did say anything that rubbed me the wrong way, I couldn't predict how I would react. I had little control of my mouth with my superior in the room, let alone with him gone.

I held my hands in my lap. Marek stayed motionless.

I looked off, out the window. He inhaled a long breath through his nose.

I checked the cleanliness of my nails, feigning boredom, while heat spread over my face and down my neck as I tried to convince myself that it wasn't his eyes raking down my body.

"You do realize," he shot out, startling me out of my thoughts, "that you don't have a union to protect you, right?"

I clenched the binder in my lap and stared ahead, his thinly veiled threat and tensed voice not getting by me.

Yes, I was aware. Most private school teachers were hired and fired at will, and administrators liked to have that freedom. Hence, no benefit of unions to protect us like the public school teachers enjoyed.

"And even so, you still can't stop yourself from mouthing off," he commented.

Mouthing off?

"Is that what this is about?" I turned, struggling to keep my voice even. "You're playing a game with me?"

He narrowed his eyes, his black eyebrows pinching together.

"This is about my son," he clarified.

"And this is my job," I threw back. "I know what I'm doing, and I care very much about your son." And then I quickly added, "About all of my students, of course."

What was his problem anyway? My class curriculum didn't carry unreasonable expectations. All of these students had phones. Hell, I'd seen their five-year-old siblings with phones in the parking lot.

I'd thoroughly reviewed my intentions with the administrators and the parents, and any naysayers had quickly come around. Not only was Marek ignorant, but he was late to the game.

He'd been well informed, but this was the first time I'd seen hide or hair of him since the open house.

"You're incredible," I mumbled.

I saw his face turn toward me out of the corner of my eye. "I would watch my step if I were you," he threatened.

I twisted my head away, closing my eyes and taking a deep breath.

In his head, we weren't equals. He'd put on a good front last Mardi Gras when he'd thought I was nothing more than a good time, but now I was useless to him. His inferior.

He was arrogant and ignorant and not even the slightest bit interested in treating me with the respect I'd earned, given my education and hard work.

I liked control, and I loved being in charge, but had I told my doctor how to do his job when he'd ordered me off my ankle for six weeks when I was seventeen? No. I'd deferred to those who knew what they were talking about, and if I had any questions, I'd asked.

Politely.

I gnawed at my lips, trying to keep my big mouth shut. This had always been a problem for me. It had caused me trouble in my tennis career, because I couldn't maintain perspective and distance myself from criticism when I thought I'd been wronged.

Kill 'em with kindness, my father had encouraged. *Do I not destroy my enemies when I make them my friends?* Abraham Lincoln had said.

But even though I understood the wisdom of those words, I'd never been able to rein it in. If I had something to say, I lost all control and gave in to a rant.

My chest rose and fell quickly, and I gritted my teeth.

"Oh, for Christ's sake." He laughed. "Spit it out, then. Go ahead. I know you want to."

I shot up, out of my chair, and glared down at him. "You went over my head," I growled, not hesitating. "You're not interested in communicating with me as Christian's teacher. If you were, I would've heard from you by now. You wanted to humiliate me in front of my superior."

He cocked his head, watching me as his jaw flexed.

"If you had a concern," I went on, "then you should've come to me, and if that failed, then gone to Shaw. You didn't sign any of the documents I sent home, and you haven't accepted any invitations into the social media groups, proving that you have no interest in Christian's education. This is a farce and a waste of my time."

"And have you contacted me?" he retorted as he rose from his seat, standing within an inch of me and looking down. "When I didn't sign the papers or join the groups, or when he failed the last unit test"—he bared his teeth—"did you e-mail or call me to discuss my son's education?"

"It's not my responsibility to chase you down!"

"Yeah, it kind of is," he retorted. "Parent communication is part of your job, so let's talk about why you're communicating regularly with Christian's friends' parents but not with me."

"Are you serious?" I nearly laughed, dropping the binder on the chair. "We're not playing some childish 'who's going to call first?' game. This isn't high school!"

"Then stop acting like a brat," he ordered, his minty breath falling across my face. "You know nothing about my interest in my son."

"Interest in your son?" This time my lips spread wide in a smile as I looked up at him. "Don't make me laugh. Does he even know your name?"

His eyes flared and then turned dark.

My throat tightened, and I couldn't swallow. *Shit*. I'd gone too far.

I was close enough to hear the heavy breaths from his nose, and I wasn't sure what he would do if I tried to back away. Not that I felt threatened—physically anyway—but I suddenly felt like I needed space.

His body was flush with mine, and his scent made my eyelids flutter.

His eyes narrowed on me and then fell to my mouth. *Oh, God*.

"Okay, sorry about that." Shaw burst into the office, and Marek and I pulled apart, turning away from each other while the principal twisted around to close the door.

Shit.

I smoothed my hand down my blouse and leaned over, picking up the binder of lesson plans.

We hadn't done anything, but it felt like we had.

Shaw walked around us, and I glanced at Marek to see him glaring ahead, his arms crossed over his chest.

"While Mrs. Vincent practically runs this school," Shaw went on, amusement in his voice, "some things require my signature. So, where were we?"

"Edward," Marek interrupted, buttoning his Armani jacket and offering a tight smile, "unfortunately I have a meeting to get to. Ms. Bradbury and I have talked, and she's agreed to adjust her lesson plans to make accommodations for Christian."

Excuse me?

I started to twist my head to shoot him a look, but I stopped, correcting myself. Instead, I clamped my teeth together and lifted my chin, refusing to look at him.

I would *not* be adjusting my lesson plans.

"Oh, wonderful." Shaw smiled, looking relieved. "Thank you, Ms. Bradbury, for compromising. I love it when things work out so easily."

I decided it was best to let the issue lie. What Shaw didn't know wouldn't hurt him, and Marek would most likely zone out of his parenting responsibilities for another few weeks before I would have to deal with him again.

"Ms. Bradbury." Marek turned, holding out a hand for me to shake.

I met his eyes, noticing how one was not quite as wide as the other, giving his expression a sinister look as it pierced me.

Two things could be assumed about Marek: He expected to get everything he wanted, and he thought he just had.

Idiot.

Keep reading for a preview of Madoc's story.

**Available from New American Library
wherever books and e-books are sold!**

MADOC

"Fuck." I breathed out. "Could she move any slower?" I asked Jared as I sat in the backseat of Tate's G8 with my hands locked on top of my head.

She twisted around from the driver's seat, her eyes sharp, like she wanted to drive a knife right through my skull. "I'm heading around a sharp turn at nearly fifty miles an hour on an unstable dirt road!" she yelled at me. "This isn't even a real race. I. Told. You. That. Before!" Every muscle in her face was as stiff as steel as she chewed me out.

I dropped my head back and let out a sigh. Jared sat in front of me with his elbow on the door and his head in his hand.

It was Saturday afternoon, the day of Tate's first real race, and we'd been on Route 5 for the past three hours. Every time the little twerp downshifted too soon or didn't hit the gas fast enough, Jared kept quiet, but not me.

He turned his head, but not enough to meet my eyes. "Get out," he ordered.

"What?" I blurted, my eyes widening. "But . . . but . . ." I stuttered, catching sight of Tate's triumphant smile in the rearview mirror.

"But nothing," Jared barked. "Go get your car. She can race you."

The zing of adrenaline heated up my arms at the prospect of some real excitement. Tate could definitely race a chick that had no idea what she was doing, but she still had a lot to learn and some balls to grow.

Enter Madoc. I wanted to smile, but I didn't.

Instead, I just rolled my eyes. "Well, that'll be boring."

"Oh, you're so funny," she mocked, gripping the steering wheel. "You make a great twelve-year-old girl when you whine."

I opened the back door. "Speaking of whining, want to make a bet on who'll be crying by the end of the day?"

"You will," she answered.

"Not."

She grabbed a package of travel tissues and threw them at me. "Here. Just in case."

"Oh, I see you keep a ready stock." I smiled. "Because you cry so much, right?"

She jerked around. "*Tais-toi! Je vous détes—*"

"What?" I interrupted. "What was that? I'm hot and you love me? Jared, did you know she had feelings—"

"Stop it!" he bellowed, shutting both of us up. "Goddamn it, you two." And he threw his hands up in the air and looked between us.

Tate and I were both silent for a moment. Then she snorted, and I couldn't help but let out a laugh, too.

"Madoc?" Jared's teeth were glued together. I could hear it. "Out."

I grabbed my cell off the seat and did as I was told, only because I knew my friend had had enough.

I'd been trying to bait Tate all day, make jokes, and distract Jared. She was racing a new guy on the scene tonight, Michael Woodburn, and no one knew anything about him. You would think that most guys would have a problem racing a girl, but Zack said this guy took the race with no argument.

It was too convenient, and Jared was uneasy. We didn't know Woodburn, his car, or his driving, but Tate insisted that she could handle it.

And what Tate wants, Tate gets. Jared was whipped worse than cream.

I walked back down the track to the driveway leading in. My silver GTO sat along the side of the road, and I dug in my jeans for my keys with one hand while I ran the back of my hand across my forehead with the other.

It was early June, and everything was already so miserable. The heat wasn't bad, but the damn humidity made it worse. My mom had wanted me to go to New Orleans to visit her for the summer, and I gave her a big, fat "Hell-to-the-no."

Yeah, I love sweating my balls off while her new husband tries to teach me shrimping in the Gulf.

Nope.

I loved my mom, but the idea of having my house to myself all summer, while my dad stayed at his apartment in Chicago, no doubt, was a much better prospect.

My hand tingled with a vibration, and I looked down at my phone. *Speak of the devil.*

"Hey, what's up?" I asked my dad as I came up on the side of my car.

"Madoc. Glad you answered. Are you home?" He sounded unusually concerned.

"No, I was about to head there soon, though. Why?"

My dad was hardly ever around. He kept an apartment in Chicago, since his big cases kept him working long hours. I liked him. Didn't love him, though.

My stepmom had been AWOL for a year. Traveling, visiting friends. I hated her.

The only person I loved at home was Addie, our housekeeper. She made sure I ate my vegetables and she signed my permission slips for school. She was my family.

"Addie called this morning. Fallon showed up today," he explained, and my breath caught as I nearly dropped my phone.

What?

She's here?

I put my palm down on the hood of my car and tried to unclench my teeth.

"So?" I finally bit out. "What does that have to do with me?"

"Addie packed you a bag," he explained. "I talked to Jared's mom, and you're going to stay with them for a few weeks."

"What?" I yelled into the phone, breathing hard. "Why can't I stay at my own house?"

Since when does that bitch get the run of things? So she's home. Big deal! Send her on her way, then. Why do I have to be sent away?

"You know why," my dad answered, his threatening tone deep. "Don't go home."

Copyright © Penelope Douglas

PENELOPE DOUGLAS is the author of the *New York Times* bestsellers *Bully* and *Until You*. Born in Dubuque, Iowa, she earned a bachelor's degree in public administration and then a master's of education at Loyola University in New Orleans before becoming a teacher. She now writes full-time and lives in Las Vegas with her husband and their daughter.

CONNECT ONLINE

penelopedouglasauthor.com
facebook.com/penelopedouglasauthor
twitter.com/pendouglas